WADING HOME

A Novel of New Orleans

WADING HOME

A Novel of New Orleans

Rosalyn Story

A BOLDEN BOOK

AGATE

CHICAGO

Cover: The original artwork "High Water Blues" was created especially for *Wading Home* in 2010 by Jean Lacy of Dallas, Texas.

Printed in the United States of America.

Library of Congress Cataloging-in-Publication Data

Story, Rosalyn M.
Wading home / Rosalyn Story.
p. cm.
Summary: "A multigenerational family saga set against the backdrop of post-Katrina New Orleans and Louisiana"--Provided by publisher.
ISBN-13: 978-1-932841-55-8 (pbk.)
ISBN-10: 1-932841-55-5 (pbk.)
1. African Americans--Louisiana--Fiction. 2. African American families--Louisiana--Fiction. 3. Hurricane Katrina, 2005--Social aspects--Fiction. 4. New Orleans (La.)--Fiction. 5. Louisiana--Fiction. I. Title.
PS3619.T694W33 2010
813'.6--dc22
2010013014

10 9 8 7 6 5 4 3 2 1

Bolden is an imprint of Agate Publishing. Agate books are available in bulk at discount prices. For more information, go to agatepublishing.com.

To my families on both sides, the Story/Williams and the Boswells,
for love, and for history

Storm Warning

Louisiana, 2005

Years before the night the storm made history, it had already earned its name. Those who'd witnessed the worst of them argued that when The Big One finally appeared, it would signal the end of everything in its path. There would be nothing left except the memory of its perfect inception—how it reared its monstrous head over the tropics, then barreled through warm gulf waters that whipped its winds into frenzy before it roared across the thin barrier islands off the mainland toward the coast.

So when the big storm finally trounced in like an unwelcomed though not unexpected visitor, birds flew to cover and a whole city crouched in fear. It pounded the sandy gulf shores, then arced east as the surging waters battered shoddy levees to rage through the city like no other flood before it. Afterwards, 200-year old trees lay uprooted. Hand-built houses passed down through five generations floated away and fell apart. And the lives that survived were forever changed.

Upriver, though, where the winds were calmer, another storm formed under clear skies and bright sun and in the sleep-quiet darkness of night. It shaped in the clouded minds of men, gathered force with ambition, surged with greed and lust. But the uprooting of lives would be as heartbreaking as any hurricane.

A perfect spread of earth one hundred or so miles up from New Orleans, Silver Creek Plantation had begun in 1855 on a whim, a gamble, a bluff made with tongue in cheek. A Frenchman—preacher, planter, and dabbler in games of chance—sat down to a card table with a pair of deuces and got up with 200 acres of God's garden. A place where tall pines and cypresses and sweetgum shaded the fertile earth, egrets and herons swam through thick air sweetened with honeysuckle and jasmine, and in the creek shallows that necklaced the land like a strand of gurgling silver, crawfish grew nearly as plump as the preacher/gambler's fists.

Under the sweating brows of the Frenchman's thirteen new slaves, new life sprang from the freshly tilled soil. Year after year, the rich earth bore crops so magnificent that the Frenchman could scarcely believe his eyes—there was corn as tall as young pines, sugar stalks with the reach of cypress trees, and a cotton crop that stirred the envy of the whole parish.

But if Silver Creek was the preacher's passion, his true love was the young Ashanti woman with soft, almond eyes and a face shaped like a heart. Anyone who saw the two of them together might wonder who was master and who was slave. And either way they guessed, they would have been right. For as much as the papers the Frenchman owned bound her to him, he was as much bound to her by the grip she held on his heart.

Like the land itself, the Frenchman and the African woman bore generations of hearty fruit, beginning with a son who grew tall, steel-eyed, and strong, and as much in love with the land as the master who sired him. For generations to come it was passed down from father to son, bouncing between legend and fact, that the pear-shaped piece of land was a paradise to which no harm could come. Nothing could stunt its bounty or its beauty, and nothing could pry it from the hands of the Fortiers.

And nothing did, until the season of the big storm.

That year, when the old home folks sat on their porches, they shook their heads and sucked their teeth at the bulldozers that pulled up next to the shotgun cabins, and watched meadows of wildflowers and forests of pine fall to the cold sprawl of golf courses and strip mall parking lots. Some chalked it up to the simple business of men in suits, said the old times were done, and the precious land was too rich anyway for the widowed man who'd chef'd in the kitchens of New Orleans. That the drumbeat and forward march of progress was just the way of things. But others thought there was more to it: that a mysterious death by the roadside was really no accident, but one man's heartless plan.

Storm nights. A deep, eerie light. The air heavy, thick, and hot. The swaying branch-dance of live oaks, the scramble of birds and squirrels and dogs to safe havens clear of harm's way. When he was a boy growing up on the land far upriver before he moved to the Crescent City, the chef's young eyes had opened wide at his father's tales of the storms down near where the river met the gulf. The ones that ripped trees from their beds and slammed houses into each other, or picked up trucks and tossed them like toys. Or stirred the waters to rise and swallow everything in sight.

But on this eve of the hurricane, his aging eyes are calm, his mind crowded with other thoughts: a piece of paradise in peril miles away, a father he loved in death, and a son he loves more than life. A son who can scarcely find the land that is his birthright on a map.

The old chef looks out the kitchen window at the still-quiet sky over the city and thinks of the places he calls home, the one up where the creek winds through and the one here at the river's mouth, wondering how long either will survive. He tends his stove—a pot of red beans and rice will surely get him through whatever the days ahead might bring—and waits for the storm.

1

New Orleans, August 2005

Across the whole city stillness lurks like a shadowy intruder: no noise of cars, trucks, buses or streetcars, and instead an unseemly quiet, except for the rustle of the cypress leaves. On the river near its crescent, a moored barge floats, a silent steamboat hugs the dock. And nearby, the *Vieux Carre* stands oddly muted, its rowdiest bars quiet as an empty church.

Up and down the blocks of old Treme, amid the rows of century-old wood-framed houses where neighbors' music usually seeps from open doors and windows (the oldest Carmier boy's sousaphone hoots, or Cordelia Lautrec's little daughter's piano scales) an eerie music holds, all the random noises of the neighborhood yielding to the stealthy overtures of a storm.

In Simon's kitchen, a streak of late summer sun angles through backdoor blinds and sends a blade of gold across his stove. The old man stirs a huge iron pot of beans (only Camellia brand will do) for his domino-night supper of red beans and rice. Leaning a bristly chin over the pot, tasting a spoonful of the liquor, he sprinkles a dash of salt with artful, experienced hands as the steam fogs his glasses and his cataract-weakened eyes squint into the pungent whiff of garlic and thyme. He dips the spoon in for another taste, then glances out the thin pane of the backdoor window at the still-light sky, and sucks his tongue. The sun, usually in slow retreat on August evenings, will surely fade quickly tonight.

With no neighbors' music to entertain his dinner preparation—most have left town for higher ground, and only the cash-strapped or fearless have hunkered down to brave out the night—Simon hums an old Pops Armstrong standard in a warbled, gritty baritone: *Give meee... a-kiss, to-build, a-dream-onnn....* He keeps stirring the beans as the starch breaks down and thickens the soup, wielding the splintered oak spoon Auntie Maree gave him some sixty years ago. With a clean white hanky from his back pocket, he blots the sweat beading on his forehead and turns down the flame.

A loud *thwack* from the backyard breaks the quiet.

"Aw. No," Simon groans, knowing what's happened.

It's surely what he's feared for years. Simon wipes greasy fingers on a dish towel, slaps it down onto the counter, and opens the back door to assess the damage.

Sure enough. The giant live oak—planted by his daddy on the day Simon was born seventy-six years ago—now stands an unbalanced amputee, its long bottom limb lying on the ground.

"Ummph, ummph, ummph." Simon shakes his head, rests a hand on his hip. *That branch was rotten for sure; too many storm seasons, too many nights like tonight.* But he pushes back a thought: *Could be an omen—something about to break apart tonight, something about to change.*

Stooping down to the ground slowly and favoring the weak place in his back, he drags the branch to the side of the house, opens the storage shed door, and hauls it inside, lungs winded and legs stiff. He dusts his dry hands on the legs of his khaki trousers. With a wild storm on its way, that big branch could easily take flight and slam somebody's window, like what happened with the one they called Betsy. Maybe even *his* window. That wouldn't do.

Maybe he should board up his windows like the DuBois's up the street. Or maybe he *should* have, before. Too late now. Simon pulls his cotton shirt collar around his neck against the wind whipping through the tall pecans that separate his yard from the Moutons'. The air is heavy, thick and warmish, with clouds curling in quick choreography, the breeze carrying the faintest scent of salt water drifting in from the gulf, the sky changing fast. Looking up in awe, Simon smiles; despite their frightening intent, the shape-shifting clouds are beautiful, plump tufts of gun-metal gray, silver-rimmed, reluctant light still glazing through.

On the west side of the house, next to a pile of chopped wood along the chain link fence, Simon's herb garden shivers, looking a little wind-whipped. Maybe he should cover it in burlap? He grows everything himself for his cooking, always has, like Auntie Maree taught him. More than thirty years as head chef at a top drawer French Quarter restaurant hadn't dulled his taste for the freshest basil and thyme he could get, and even now, six years after his last shift at Parmenter's, he still demanded the best ingredients for his own table, even though he mostly dined alone.

He stoops and snaps off a leaf of the lavender, crushes it in his fingertips, inhales the sweet scent as a slender face blossoms in his mind. Lavender in the garden had been Ladeena's idea, and on her final birthday he had surprised her with a sachet of homemade potpourri for her sickbed pillow—dried lavender leaves, orange and lemon rind, store-bought cloves. If he'd known the smile his wife surrendered up at that moment would be her last, he'd have framed it in his memory. The other herbs—the oregano, the mint, the basil (now tall as the fence)—bow under the hand he runs across their heads. He will have a lot to repair tomorrow.

Simon glances at his watch; the beans have been on almost an hour now. Sylvia, mad as she was at him, had already said she wasn't coming, not even to say goodbye. And if none of the men are going to stop by for a bowl or two of the best red beans and rice in town, just as they had done for the last seven years, well then, tough luck for them. This andouille sausage was the best he'd ever made.

He and his buddies in The Elegant Gents were among the oldest members of the neighborhood's Social Aid and Pleasure Clubs, and didn't limit their gatherings to the occasional parades through the neighborhood, when they'd strut like black kings in their hand-stitched shirts of blue paisley and matching hats, white suspenders, and Johnston and Murphy shoes, the hot brass band riffs licking the wind. No, unlike some of the other S&P's, the Gents were like brothers—friends, old and true. And true friends, at least *his*, made a point of laughing and lying and signifying over cooking pots and dominoes once a week, come hell or high water.

But not hurricane.

A couple of the men, Eddie Lee Daumier and Pierre "Champagne" Simpson, had called, but most hadn't bothered, just assuming that this time even Simon had the good sense to run for higher ground. Never mind those others, they said, this storm was The One. Hadn't the mayor and the governor been on the TV all weekend? True, he hadn't seen that in a while. He'd heard the men in the white shirts and loosened ties talking from the hurricane center, their up-all-night eyes reddened, their voices scratchy with fatigue, and felt for a moment a slight chill. This time there was something fearful in their tone. If he wasn't mistaken, the governor sure did look a little pale. And the mayor too, bald head shining, his slick, pressed look betraying the scary news, was sounding his own alarm. *Get out. Get out of the city now.*

Simon had flicked away that chill, gave it no more thought. News folk and politicians had a way of exaggerating these things. But the fact that so many around him were leaving this time did make him swallow hard, scratch the back of his head. He'd never seen such a rush of cars lined up to the corner, crowded to the rooflines with boxes and bags. But like he told Raymond LeDoux down at the Field's Grocery, he hadn't left for Betsy and he wasn't leaving now. The vandals and looters would have to move on to another house for their business. Besides, he was a Fortier, and a Fortier did not leave his home to the whims of storms and thieves.

A car horn toots, the rattling complaint of a well-used Toyota Camry announcing Sylvia's arrival. She must have changed her mind. Simon's face breaks into a wide grin. Maybe there'd be company for this storm night after all.

Simon calls out as Sylvia parks along his front fence, "Just in time. Red beans'll be ready in about twenty minutes."

My, my. Looking good today, but didn't she always? Sylvia McConnell, wearing her sixty-eight years gently, stylishly, steps out in green Capri pants and a yellow cotton top, leans her backside against the doors, slender arms folded across her chest and ankles crossed. A scarf of light blue silk tied under her chin stands between her freshly curled and dyed hair and the capricious winds of Louisiana summer. Even now, Simon notes, even in retreat from a hurricane, she found time to keep her standing appointment at Miss Lou's.

"My sister and them called from Shreveport. The brother-in-law is bringing his mama, but they still got extra room if I need to bring somebody else."

A divorced English teacher from Wheatley High and old acquaintance of Simon's and Ladeena's from Blessed Redeemer Congregational, Sylvia reveled in the freedom of retirement, spending most of her days playing bridge, singing high soprano in the gospel choir, occasionally watching Simon cook, and listening to his animated diatribes on his life's loves—cooking, his talented and smart-as-a-whip son, Julian, and a perfect piece of land called Silver Creek.

A year after Ladeena died, when the shine of his grief had dulled, Simon's padlocked world had unlatched to invite Sylvia in. Time had tamed the rough edges of mourning and Simon needed a new comfort—the living, breathing kind.

On a Wednesday morning, when his car battery failed and he had no way to prayer meeting, he remembered last Sunday, the high soprano floating above all the others in "Lead Me, Guide Me." Sister McConnell gave him a ride and, in time, a reason to dream again. She was funny, spirited like Ladeena, with a twist of sass. She could cook up a mean etouffee (though not as good as his) and whenever his spirits darkened, there was that laugh that could soften a man's heart and make his blues disappear like swamp mist beneath a full sun.

In the years since they began keeping company, time, friendship and a mutual understanding had distilled their conversations into shorthand: glances replaced whole paragraphs, sentences rolled out unspoken in a raised hand, a turned head.

He recognizes Sylvia's look now—raised eyebrows, mouth twisted—and shoots up a hand to ward off the argument brewing in those eyes.

"Now don't even start. I already told you what I'm doin'."

Shaking her head, she turns to look up at the sky as a heavy gust sweeps through the trees.

"Don't be a fool, Simon. You need to get out of this place."

And for the next three minutes straight, she rails on about his foolishness. *The storm will be the worst ever! Everybody with four wheels and half a brain is leavin!* And so on.

When she sees his eyes shut down, the thick-bunched veins in his temple twitch, and his mouth clamp tight, she recognizes her cue to stop. For a moment, they look at each other in unyielding silence. Sylvia's glance falls to Simon's khaki pants, where the tree branch has left a swath of dirt.

"What happened to you?"

Looking down, Simon scrapes his thumbnail at the L-shaped mark. "Aw, damn oak. Lost a branch."

Sylvia sighs. "Ummm hmmm, see there. Already." She sucks her teeth. "Somebody trying to tell you something."

Ignoring the fact that he'd had the same thought only a few minutes ago, he turns to walk into the house. "Drive careful. They already talking about traffic backed up. You'd better get on your way if you going."

For all his testiness, it might have been her bossy strain, her spitfire nature that had kept him interested; it was as if Ladeena had left a little bit of herself in this woman to watch after him, remind him when he was being careless. He'd liked that—being looked after, being cared for. Even when he didn't listen, even when he stiffened his shoulders against the headwind of her complaints.

At the steps he turns back to her, his tone kinder. "I'll save you some of my andouille. You not going to believe how good these beans are. Best pot I ever made."

A feathery breeze ruffles her scarf as she pulls it closer. "Does that pot float? You best put those beans in some Tupperware. Eat well, baby, cause you'll need your strength in case you have to swim."

He ignores that, too. "Sure you don't want to stay? I'll make it worth your while." He winks.

Laughing, she shakes her head again. "Simon Fortier. I'll be praying for your sorry butt in my sister's dry house." She gets in the car and leans an elbow out the window.

"By the way, you might as well know, I stopped by because Julian called me, asked me to check on you. He said you all had some words. Did he call back?"

Simon's skin prickles. Two weeks since their blowup over Parmenter and still their words stumbled broken and bruised into the growing gulf between them. And yesterday, when his son had called from New York, told him to stop acting like "a crazy old fool" (even offered him a plane ticket), a slow dirge of hurt still played in Simon's head. He'd quietly hung up the phone in the middle of Julian's rant. Sometimes, Simon swore, all that fame business had gotten to that boy's head, made him forget who the daddy was in this deal.

He, Simon, never would have treated his own daddy that way, lest the back of a hand land upside his head. Nor would his father have treated *his* father like that. The Fortier men were of the no-nonsense breed. Simon's daddy had built this house with his two rock-hard hands seventy-eight years ago and would have thought nothing of using one of them to take down a too-grown son with a runaway mouth.

World-famous trumpet player or not. Julian ought to show more respect.

"No. Julian ain't called." Simon puts his hands in his pockets, and looks up at the ruffled sky. "Not since yesterday."

Sylvia starts the engine. "Well, you know the boy had a point."

Simon doesn't know whether she's talking about Julian's anger at him for not leaving before the storm or for that business with Matthew Parmenter, the latest item on a list of painful issues that divided father and son like prickly thorns, and which was really none of Julian's business anyway.

Either way, he's heard enough.

"I got to check on my pot." Simon says.

"Did you get your blood pressure prescription filled?"

Simon laughs. "Woman, leave me be! If I die, just carry me on up to Silver Creek! Dump me under that magnolia tree next to Ladeena."

"Right." Sylvia rolls her eyes. "You and Silver Creek. Why don't you just go on back there to live? Then you can be *her* problem for the rest of eternity."

She has often asked him that about Silver Creek. And he blows it off with a laugh, and changes the subject. He's never fallen out of love with his boyhood home. But leave the city where he's spent most of his life? Abandon the house built with his father's own sweat and muscle, the place where he's spent forty years with Ladeena, to return to the piece of land he grew up on? It's complicated.

"Been thinkin' about it." Simon strokes his chin, narrows his eyes into a sly squint. "But then who'd be here to meddle you?"

She laughs a little, furrows her perfectly arched brows. "Stay well, Simon. Be careful."

He walks over to her car, leans in to her window to plant a kiss on her cheek. She places her hand softly on the back of his neck.

"I worry about you, silly man."

He smiles through twinkling eyes. "Don't. I'ma be fine."

She pulls away and waves and he lets out a little chuckle as the front wheel tips slightly over the curb. He watches the Toyota sputter away and reminds himself that when she returns, he needs to get her muffler fixed.

"Take care, sweet lady," he says after her, in a voice she couldn't possibly hear.

With the air closing in, the deep silver clouds hardened to a steely dome and the wind began to swirl with the oncoming rain. *It's beginning.* Simon closed the window blinds in the kitchen and turned his thoughts to supper. He could tell by the aroma that the red beans were done. He filled his plate with rice, ladled the beans on top, and sat down at the glass table in the dining room. He pushed his chair back a little from the table and spread a napkin in his lap, and took a bite of the sausage. He was right. This was as good as anything Auntie Maree had ever made, rest her soul; the andouille sausages spiced and tender, the rice all flaky perfection, the garlic and fresh herbs blended flawlessly. Nothing took his mind off a storm like a plate of his own good cooking.

When Ladeena was alive, they'd had a ritual on these nights of big storms. Filling the kitchen air with aromas—pots or pans of etouffee, gumbo, crawfish bisque—a sure-fire distraction from the hollering winds. Reading parts of the New Testament out loud, and later, as the Gulf churned, the river rose, and watery wind gusted through the eaves, huddling between the freshly ironed sheets holding each other so tight no woman-named storm could pry them apart. Making love as if it were their last night on earth, as well it could have been.

It was during the storm nights that he most missed Ladeena. With her gone and Julian having left town years ago to, as Simon put it, "go off and get famous," Simon's life had changed. It didn't seem so long ago that he'd been a busy family man with a wife, a young son, and a job as head chef at the place his best friend and employer, Matthew Parmenter, had billed the "Finest in French Quarter Dining." Now, his starched, monogrammed uniforms and pleated white toques gathered dust in the closet where he'd stored them ages ago. Each long day resembled the one before, and while he could have been a lonely man, Simon figured he had a choice in the matter. He chose not to be.

Each morning whenever the sun blazed through his kitchen blinds, after a breakfast of chicory coffee, eggs, and toast, he walked the neighborhood, up and down the street with his prized possession, the African cane of hand-carved ebony Julian had brought back from a concert tour in West Africa. Along the five-block circle to Field's Grocery and around the school yard and the Mount Zion Baptist Church, neighbors leaned across porch banisters to wave, or slowed their cars to crawling to shout a greeting—*How you feeling, Mr. For—tee—aay!* and Simon nodded, gently touching the brim of his straw gardener's hat, and shouted back, *Woke up this mornin', so I ain't complainin'.*"

Friends chided him for daring to walk in a neighborhood that, though once safe, now had been all but taken over by young boys with a loathsome skulk in their walk and hooded, futureless eyes. Boys that had "the devil all up in them," as the church folks said, with their drugs and guns. And that wasn't the only way the neighborhood had changed; the tight-knit black community, so rich in history, had been broken in two by the wrecking ball. It had been almost forty years, but he still longed for the old days when the neighborhood was whole, before they'd built the awful freeway that sliced through his beloved Treme like a surgeon's amputating knife. Before the shade of the majestic live oaks, perfect for parade watching, gave way to the shadows of a concrete overpass.

Simon walked anyway, head high, defiant, never mind the freeway shadows and the glaze-eyed boys. He used the cane to steady his feet, but if need be, he could swing it like a cutlass. This was *his* neighborhood. He reclaimed it with each stubborn tap of his cane, and nobody—not street thugs nor the thieving city planners—was going to take it away.

After his daily walk, Simon sat with a tray of lunch watching *The Young and the Restless,* then puttered in his garden, fussing over his bougainvillea, hibiscus, and herbs. As early as Tuesday he'd begin plans for the following Monday—red beans and dominoes night. Some Sundays after church, if the sun was shining and he had the urge for conversation, he would put on his red tie and brown straw hat and take the St. Claude bus along Rampart Street to Canal, and then board the streetcar that would take him to St. Charles Avenue.

While the car rattled along past the old mansions and lavish lawns of juniper grass, he would sit near the window that held the best view of the live oaks and cypress trees, and watch the lean young bodies jog past Audubon Park. If he rode long enough, there would always be a tourist or two with an appetite for local flavor, and Simon would oblige with a must-do list that would rival the Chamber of Commerce's glossiest brochure. *What kind of music you like? Jazz? Zydeco? Rhythm and blues? You like barbecued shrimp? OK. Here's where you go...*

If the tourists were a young romantic couple, he'd suggest a place where the lights were dim enough to hide an affectionate fondle—didn't matter so much about the food. But if they were older, more particular, he'd recite his A-list, varying it according to the tourists' station and style. A well-heeled couple—a woman with facelift skin and a Louis Vuitton bag, her hand draped on the arm of a silver fox shod in Italian loafers—could handle Commander's Palace or Galatoire's and not blink at the bill. A pair of twentysomethings in faded jeans and backpacks...well, he'd send them over to Willie Mae's or Dunbar's for "some juicy fried chicken that would make you wanna slap your mama."

He would warn them, of course, that none of the places were as good as ol' Parmenter's, where he'd been head chef for more than forty years. *I was famous for my red beans and rice, don't cha know. Couldn't nobody touch me. I tell you something, when that place closed, New Orleans cooking lost a step!* And as Simon waxed on—about a neighborhood so old it had seen African slaves in Congo Square, dancing *bamboula* rhythms and stomping out the blueprint for jazz; about the Mardi Gras Indians with their wildly feathered and beaded "suits;" about the music, and of course, the famous food—the wide-eyed young or aging couple hung on the master chef's every word. When they stepped off the streetcar into the sunlight and looked back at him with their phone cameras poised, he knew he'd given them what they wanted: a souvenir, an elbow-brush with authenticity. Long ago, he'd not only accepted his role as tourist memento, he'd come to relish it. He, Simon

Fortier, was better than any postcard they could mail home to their friends. He offered up the soul of the city itself.

When Simon got up from his table with his dishes, a cracking noise shook the house. Distant thunder, then a boom and crash like big steel spoons pounding metal sheets. "All right, now, just hold your horses," he said, looking out the kitchen window at falling dark and rain, wonder sketched on his lean face.

The main event was on. In minutes, the wind bellowed, rising now and then into a thin, shrill song like a distressed cat's. Simon's father had built the house well, but it would still be a long night. Simon stacked his dishes in the sink, opened the pantry door, and fumbled through a pile of old clothes, boots, checker sets, and domino boxes until he found the box as big as a hamper. He pulled it out and dragged it to the middle of the floor.

The "hurricane box." Ladeena had always been one to prepare for the worst. After her passing he'd still dragged it out year after year, out of loyalty, or reflex, and now he pulled the items out one by one: an oil lamp, a flashlight, a first-aid kit, a box of wooden matches and an unopened box of tapers, a hand-crank radio, and three bags of dried soups he'd picked up in an Army surplus store in Baton Rouge. He put the dried soups back in, but set the oil lamp and the radio (still bearing its price tag) on the floor next to the box. And from a deep corner, he pulled the Bible Jacob Fortier had given him on his sixteenth birthday, a week before he died.

Simon ran his fingers along the brittle edges of the dry leather. He pulled out a chair from the dining table, sat, and opened the Bible. He turned to the first page, the name page, and at the end of the list of Fortier births, he traced his hand over his father's wiggly script:

Simon Fortier, born July 8, 1929.

And then, his fingers traced the words written in his own hand:

Julian Fortier, born Aug 13, 1969.

Seeing his father's hand always brought mist to his eyes, but tonight, it was the sight of Julian's name that moved him. A frail and sickly newborn delivered with a tiny hole in his heart, the boy had been given a less-than-even chance for survival. On Julian's birth night, during the surgery, Simon found himself sitting in the cold fluorescent glare of the fathers' waiting room, head bowed between both hands, bargaining with God. When the child was finally given a good bill of health, Simon found a pay phone and called his closest relations, his Auntie Maree and cousin Genevieve at Silver Creek.

"How is he?" Genevieve's voice was cautious.

Simon had to push the words out through a clog of tears. "Scrawny, no color. Doc says he'll be OK, though. Prob'ly good as new."

"Lord Jesus," Genevieve cried, and called to her mother.

"I'ma send you some of my herbs for him," Auntie Maree had told him in her usual too-loud telephone voice, her false teeth clicking. "Pack'em tight over his chest at night, and he'll be fine. I done already seen it." When he and Ladeena had brought him home from the hospital, he was so tiny and fragile he seemed breakable, caramel skin turned radish red, bawling a high-pitched wail from lungs that seemed anything but weak. In the sparsely furnished bedroom of the double shotgun, Simon sat on the bed and held his son in the crook of his arm, his face locked into an uncontrollable smile. He pressed his thumb against the baby's palm and felt the tiny fist close around it.

He looked at Ladeena, eyes glassy. "I'd throw myself in front of a train for this boy."

She smiled softly, a mischievous flicker in her eyes. "I know, darlin'. I'd throw you in front of a train for him, too."

He chuckled. That woman's slicing humor had always caught him off guard. He closed the Bible, laid it down next to the box.

Precious, that's what he was, and might still have been so even if Ladeena's frail womb could have accommodated another birth. They had tried not to spoil him, but to each of them the boy had been a reason to get up each morning, to work, to smile, to live.

Cayenne pepper in honey-lemon tea, someone said, would keep colds away. So Simon plied the boy with hot drinks throughout the damp New Orleans winters. Trumpet lessons, somebody else said, might strengthen his lungs, so Simon pawned his wedding ring and bought a silver-plated Conn. And from Julian's first blast of cracking, pitchless air, there would be no turning back. He became a trumpet player first, everything else second.

When Ladeena died and it was just the two of them, Simon and eighteen-year-old Julian found shelter from their grief in a brotherly bond, and stayed close even after Julian left for New York. But an accident, one slick, rainy night a year ago on Julian's thirty-sixth birthday, had done more than throw his brilliant career into a quandary—it had pushed father and son apart. Julian grew cool and testy, found acrimony in everything, humor in nothing. Simon reminded him to be patient; hadn't the doctor said the surgery went well? With time, he'd be playing the trumpet better than ever. But Julian scoffed—a condescending silence that insinuated Simon didn't know what he was talking about, and bruised his father's tender ego. Afterwards, Julian's fragile jaw tightened at the mere mention of his career, the trumpet, or the night when his future had changed.

If it had been only that, maybe things between them would have improved. But the argument over Simon's employer and best friend had further shaken their bond. The horrible business deal with his best friend and boss, Parmenter, had been a mistake, maybe; Simon had never been that good with money. But it was old news. Yet when Julian found out about it recently, he acted as if it had happened yesterday. Money, Simon argued, was not worth breaking up a friendship, but he wondered if the matter would stand between him and his son forever.

And then, there was the matter of Silver Creek.

He grabbed his rib as a small pain shot up his back. He'd forgotten to take that arthritis medicine. Seemed it always happened when he thought about Julian and Silver Creek, and the storm didn't help. Since the end of slavery, the land in Pointe Louree

Parish, with its wild, arboreal splendor, fertile earth and teeming creek, had been his family's blessing—everything that could grow there did so in abundance and untamed beauty. Ever since Simon's great-grandfather, the Frenchman, had bequeathed it to his black son Moses, it had been passed down from son to son with care, like a genetic trait passing through blood.

It was Simon's biggest failing, he believed, that while his son had inherited his thick hair, long-lashed eyes, and taste for music and well-seasoned food, he hadn't gotten the love for family land. It was nowhere to be found in Julian's trove of things that mattered, and it broke Simon's heart.

Money, that's what his son cared about. Cash. Coin. Like every other young man Simon knew. Nowadays it was hard to fill a young man's head with his own history when his heart gave it no play.

Somewhere in the commotion of water thrashing the house and the locomotive howl of wind, the phone rang. Simon's heart raced—the phone still worked? *About time that boy called to apologize.* He shifted his mood to one of forgiveness; Julian was calling, that was all that mattered.

"Hello?"

"Simon, you still there?"

His cousin Genevieve's voice broke up in the weak connection from Silver Creek. He tried not to let his disappointment show.

"Genevieve."

"Simon, Lord, I got to talk to you—"

Though he could barely hear her, it wasn't hard to make out the panic in her voice.

"I know, I know," he said. "I'm still here. But I'ma be all right. I'll be calling you when this storm blows over."

But she wasn't talking about the storm. With the rain pummeling his house and the line growing more staticky, he could hear every other word. Something about the Parettes in Pointe Louree, he thought he heard, the family whose property bordered their land to the east.

Genevieve had told him weeks ago about the rumors: the developers sniffing around in their massive SUVs, shaded gazes lingering over the best properties in Pointe Louree, stroking their chins at green fields and imagining condos and parking lots. The Parette property had been in their family as long as Silver Creek had been in Fortier hands—longer. The Parettes would no sooner sell their land than the Fortiers, and the Fortiers would never sell.

"They found his car, he must of got run off the road..."

Genevieve's speech wasn't the best since she'd lost most of her bottom teeth. But he thought he heard something about an accident. An accident with their neighbor, Nicholas Parette.

"Veevy?" Simon shouted into the phone. "What did you say?"

More static. "Dead. He's dead."

Simon felt heat in his chest. "What?"

But the phone line had been silenced by the storm.

Simon went to the window and peered out, the sky black now, the wind spanking the trees in rhythmic frenzy, the pounding rain all but horizontal. The wind bellowed and cawed like something with bared teeth and scratching claws.

His pulse quickened. Parette? Simon couldn't believe what Genevieve said was true. He'd known the Parettes since he was a boy at Silver Creek, skipping stones with the oldest boy, J.D., catching crawfish, learning to craft a perfect roux or season gumbo at Auntie Maree's knee. Parette must have been ninety-five if he was a day. Lived alone after his wife died. Always drove that Chevy truck to town even with his bad eyesight, sometimes veering slightly off Dutch River Road toward the ditch. Everybody for miles around knew him, and everybody knew to look after him.

An accident, surely, but the combination of Genevieve's tone and a roiling in Simon's gut nagged with other possibilities. Before the storm had knocked out the phone line, something seemed off-kilter. He would call her tomorrow, or whenever the phone was working again.

A coincidence, surely. Nothing to be read into what Genevieve had mentioned to him those few weeks ago.

Simon went to the kitchen to pour himself a drink; the bourbon left over from last year's July Fourth block party might calm his racing mind. He found it on the top shelf of the refrigerator and half-filled a Pilsner glass, then sat in his recliner and leaned back to listen to the banshee screams of the worst winds he'd ever heard.

His heart pounded with the steady drumbeat of thunder and wind and sudden fear. Something unnerved him, and he wished for all the world that he had talked to Julian tonight. There was always a comfort, a reassurance in hearing his son's voice, no matter how far away he was, no matter what they were going through.

He turned up the whole glass, then leaned way back in the recliner and frowned as the slow burn of the liquor took hold in his gut. He closed his eyes and let the drink numb his muddled thoughts. Before long he was in that half-world between sleep and wakefulness, remembering the chafe of wind through the old trees that sang with the memory of a thousand storms before.

He slept the entire night in the chair. The next morning he rubbed sleep from his eyes. "I'm still here," he said to himself, a sardonic smile crossing his face.

He puttered about the kitchen before looking out at the yard, the street. Cooler, darker now, with rain still slashing. The sky gray with the trees bending in the wind. But the drama seemed to have ended. *Thank the Lord*, he breathed a relieved sigh. The worst of the storm had passed the city by.

For the whole day, grayness and spitting rain consumed the sky. That night he slept soundly. And when he woke the next morning, it was to the sound of water crashing through his door, and quickly gathering around his bed.

2

Tokyo, August 2005

He should have been having the time of his life. He'd missed the scene for so long—the cavern-dark room pierced by the spotlights' amber glow, the rhythm section kicking a tight groove, the people digging his music and ready to unleash their adulation. It could have been any stage, almost anywhere, and this was the scene that got his juices going. So the moment he'd stepped onto the Blue Note Tokyo's stage twenty-five minutes ago, it had felt like coming home.

But now, the pain burrowed so deep it made him dizzy. The sound was still coming out of his trumpet, but it was as if he was standing outside himself, watching his own fingers move, almost admiring their ability to go on while everything else in him wanted to seize up or shut down. With the lightning-quick tempo the drummer had set, he struggled to keep up as the wall of sound—piano, bass, drums, tenor—roared like a train on a downhill track, full speed ahead, with him or without him.

Another pain buzzed through his jaw, and his embouchure froze. He stopped playing and shook his head while the piano covered him, took up the slack. The room grew hot, airless, as sweat beaded above his lip and his neck tightened. While the pain burned on, the spotlights glared like headlights. Suddenly he felt like some four-legged creature who'd staggered out onto a highway in front of a truck, blinded by the lights and frozen with fear.

He couldn't do it. Could not go on. So even though they hadn't even reached the bridge of the tune, he leaned over to his pianist.

He whispered hoarsely in his ear. "*Slow.* Anything slow. Then we quit."

He barely got through the ballad, even though he'd written it himself, and he was the first one off the stage, ducking into the small backstage room reserved for the band.

Sitting on the sofa, chest pumping hard as he crossed his legs against the cool black leather, Julian Fortier filled his winded lungs with air and exhaled a ragged sigh, then uncrossed his legs, leaned back, and stared up at the pale gray walls.

One by one the others in the quintet came in, each more deliberately quiet than the next. The pianist gave him a flickering, questioning look, then turned away, and having nothing better to do, pulled out his cell phone and tapped on the keypad. The bass player coughed nervously as he zipped the canvas cover around the rented instrument. The tenor player and drummer, not knowing what else to do after putting horn and drumsticks away, looked at each other, then headed to the table laden with bottles of Perrier and food that the management of the club had graciously supplied.

No one spoke. The tension in the room was as thick as the fog that had rolled in that morning across Tokyo Bay before settling over the downtown of the city. All the men averted their eyes from each other, waiting for their bandleader to explain.

But for the moment, the trumpeter sat smoothing the crease in his pinstriped gray silk pantsleg, his horn beside him, trying to make sense out of what went down in front of all those people, imagining the reviews in the Tokyo press. "Celebrated Jazz Trumpeter Bombs in Premature Comeback." Something like that. Or worse.

He grabbed his trumpet off the cushion next to him and rapidly fingered the valves. It wasn't supposed to have happened this way. He'd been OK at the rehearsals. He should have breezed through the set like the pro he was, his jaw sufficiently healed after the accident, his tone rolling sweetly and effortlessly out of his horn, notes flying unconsciously and his mind zooming in a zone where he could do no wrong. Applause should have thundered from the tables, since the Japanese, among the most appreciative of his fans, were the first to hear him after an eleven-month absence from studio and stage. He should have been the hero of the night.

Instead, the applause had been weak—polite, yet confused. He felt like tucking his tail and running, and that's exactly what he'd done.

He cleared his throat and glanced at his bandsmen across the room, who were now piling their plates. His gaze fell on the wall nearest him, where hung a framed oil painting of a tiny boat on a choppy sea of blues and greens, and wished he could be on that boat, sailing off into…anywhere but here.

He'd have to tell the guys the worst possible news—the gig was over. On top of that, they'd have to take a whopping cut in pay for an incomplete date, and hope the club would let him reschedule when he'd fully recovered—if he ever did. The hottest jazz club in Japan would have to go dark for the rest of the week while he hunted down the nearest orthopedist.

He reached around the sofa for his trumpet case, removed the mouthpiece and put the trumpet in. What would he say to Matsumoto? It was every club manager's nightmare to have his star tank the first night of a weeklong run. A tall, slender, elegant Japanese around his own age, Matsumoto was an all-around good guy whose angular and slightly pock-marked face belied his gentle speech and natural kindness. The guy had played the trumpet himself for a time; maybe he would understand.

"Hey, don't sweat this man. You'll be back."

Antoine, the short and athletically stocky pianist—a hell of a player at just twenty-five, and a loyal friend—stood over him, his large eyes calm, a sushi roll in one hand, the other extended out to him. The trumpeter grabbed it and clasped it. Then put his hand back on his jaw.

"Feels like it's on fire. Damn."

"That sucks, man."

Julian rolled his eyes, leaned against the sofa, stretching out his long legs. Then he raised himself forward and got up.

"Guess I better talk to everybody. Tell 'em what's going on."

He walked over to the refreshment table where the rest of the guys were still loading plates; he remembered from their earliest gigs here how some had balked at the unfamiliar Japanese fare—squid and octopus, soba noodles, the crisp, green vegetables no one seemed to be able to name doused in a fragrant light sauce of ginger—but in time they had all learned to love it.

He rubbed his hands together, not sure what he would say, but began anyway.

"OK, everybody, uh…listen up. I got something to…."

But as he spoke, Jeffrey, the drummer, held up a quieting finger, his head angled up like the other men, their eyes locked on a flat-panel TV screen placed high on the wall in a corner near the door. Across the bottom of the screen broadcasting CNN live, the crawl read: LEVEES BREACHED. EIGHTY PERCENT OF NEW ORLEANS UNDERWATER.

Julian felt a small gasp leave his body and something flip over in his stomach. The band of heat around his neck tightened even more, and crept up to the pained spot on his jaw.

He and the men, each one except him born in the neighborhoods where he now lived in Brooklyn, watched in silence as footage of the flood flashed across the screen and captions told the story of the drowning city. Helicopters like giant steel dragonflies hovered over what looked more like rivers than streets, and boats and makeshift rafts cruised through neighborhoods he recognized as well as his own reflection. And as the camera panned back to a wide shot, all the men, as if on cue, either let out a rush of breath or shook their heads. Most of the city, even its freeways, appeared submerged in inky, shiny blackness.

The thumping he'd felt in his chest as he left the stage now returned. Nothing else mattered now, not the horrible set he'd just played, the guys in the band, Matsumoto, the disappointed audience, or his aching jaw. All that mattered was what was happening to the place where he was born. The place where his father lived.

The camera closed in to show a familiar site. C.W. Peters Elementary, where he'd had his first fight with a squinty-eyed, stuttering kid who had tried to take his turkey and cheese sandwich, and where he'd fallen in love with the sound of the trumpet, was standing in dull brown water up to its windows, the playground swings bobbing like beach toys in the surf.

His mind could barely grasp what was happening; everything he'd known of the city seemed to be sinking as fast as cameras could show it. It was like seeing the face of someone you loved twisted strangely by a sudden and horrible stroke.

Oh, God. What the....? He rubbed the back of his head as the TV screen showed the Circle Food Store on St. Bernard, the black water skirting high up on its arches, their reflection shimmying in the deep, dark pool. Only a short walk from where he'd grown up, that place had been his father's favorite market for years. His earliest memory had been of holding his hand as they walked the distance to the neighborhood store, then peering up while his father studied the fresh redfish and shrimp for his Friday night fish fry, or waiting impatiently in the produce area while Simon, ever particular, scrutinized every pepper in search of the plumpest for his red beans.

The Circle Food Store sat in the middle of the "bowl" of the city near the I-10 overpass, a spot rarely known to flood. *If Circle is flooded, then the whole damn city is done.*

Two days ago (or was it three? He had trouble keeping the days straight after they'd crossed the International Date Line), he'd called his father and the conversation had not gone well. After a half hour of trying to get Simon Fortier to see his point of view—that staying in town through a hurricane the size of this one was beyond foolhardy—he threw up his hands.

"Daddy," he'd said, his voice pitched high with exasperation. "Hell. I'm not listening to this."

Across miles of land and ocean, through the small, static-filled cell phone, the resentment in his father's heavy breaths came through.

"Say what you want. I'm staying. I stayed for the last one, and I'm staying now."

His hands shook. His father was the kind of man who lived by his gut, who prided himself on the wisdom of the still, small voice in his head. But this time, Julian believed, the small voice had lied. He'd never been so disrespectful before; despite his acquired ease with the ways of big-city folks, his finely honed manners were southern-bred. In New York his "yes, sirs" and "no, ma'ams" had drawn smiles of condescension more than once; he'd learned to stow those phrases away and unpack them only during visits home. But with his career in doubt, worrying about his father was something he hadn't figured on, and didn't need. The stress had sharpened his tone to a cutting edge he had never intended for the man who had been his best friend—his ally, his confidant—since his mother died. Even the thing with Parmenter had brought out a side of himself he barely recognized. So when Simon stubbornly refused to leave the city, Julian opened his mouth and out rolled a fiery litany of admonitions that, later, would make him feel more shame and regret than he'd felt since he was a boy, catching it for having a mouth that sometimes trounced ahead of his brain.

At first he thought the line had gone dead, but then realized that wasn't the case. His father had simply had enough. It was the first time they'd argued like that since he was grown, the first time either had ever hung up on the other.

At some point, with everyone's eyes still fixed on the TV screen, Matsumoto entered the room. Julian glanced over to see disappointment darkening his brown eyes.

It had been a sold-out house after all, and the whole set, scheduled to run a full hour, had lasted less than thirty minutes. No doubt, people had complained.

It was all he could do to take his mind off the TV images. His friend Matsumoto had hired him after he'd sworn he was back in good form. He'd always known about the Japanese custom of bowing in apology, and when one felt deep shame, the bow was accordingly deep and long. He hadn't been ready, clearly. But he'd been desperate to play, and the money was good. A Japanese in his position would now be staring at the floor.

"Mat, I'm so sorry, man."

Matsumoto nodded solemnly, said nothing. He would have to take the flack for this, explain to the owners. Leaving a week of audiences hanging at a place like the Blue Note Tokyo was no small thing.

Someone pointed to the television screen again; a helicopter shot showed a group of weary, sweating people trudging through water up to their waists. Others hung on for their lives where the water had chased them—the top balconies of apartment houses and rooftops. Then the camera swept over to other parts of the city. The Ninth Ward. New Orleans East. Pontchartrain Park. St. Bernard Parish. All disappearing in a still, reflective ocean.

Bile gathered in his throat.

He wasn't looking for a convenient out. But even if his chops hadn't failed him, he would have had to bail anyway, leave the country this minute if he could. He looked again at Matsumoto, then at the men in the band.

"I gotta go," he said, his voice breaking. "I gotta get home."

He took the first flight out the next day. By the time he arrived at JFK, sleep deprived, eyes puffy and red-veined, he wasn't even sure what day it was. He was walking down the concourse of the domestic terminal toward the gate for a flight to Baton Rouge when his cell phone rang.

"Hello?"

The static was interrupting, but he recognized Sylvia's voice.

"Wait a minute, I can't hear you too well. Say that again?"

His eyes filled with tears.

"Right. I'll be there as soon as I can."

3

He'd not been away all that long, but long enough. Like a sharp flavor fading on the tongue, the memory of the thick, damp heat—the kind that wrapped around you like a vine, weighed you down and slowed your steps to a sluggish stroll—had all but dissolved in the time he'd been gone. But today the recollection came rushing back. The air here was nothing like Japan, where the days had been humid but the winds brought the rains and the rains brought relief; it was not even like Brooklyn, where the sidewalks stored the August midday sun and threw it back at you late at night while you waited for a cool breeze that wouldn't come until September. And it was not at all like that sunny little part of Spain he liked near the coast, where the nights carried the sweet balm of southerly breezes and the *chicas* on the beach smiled at you when they brought you the umbrella drinks, and you forget all about how damned hot it was. He'd been all over the world, but there was nothing like this crazy Louisiana heat.

As if he didn't already have enough troubling him, the flat tire on his rented Neon threatened to tip his teetering nerves over the edge. His head throbbed. He peeled off his clingy shirt—something he would never have done in New York. But he was a homeboy, and he was down home; humidity like this meant baring your skin. Sweat dripped from his forehead, his shoulders, his back as he squatted on the loose gravel of the breakdown lane, the only breeze stirred by the eighteen-wheelers that roared by.

Having loosened the lug nuts, he rolled the small spare from the trunk to the front of the car. With his slim, muscled back to the September sun, he knelt and managed to jack up the car and get the tire off without screaming profanity. Once he'd secured the spare, he put his damp T-shirt back on and drove to find the nearest service station. Even in a city not ravaged by flood and strewn with post-storm debris, the tiny donut spare would be too treacherous to drive on. Some of the streets in town had been bad enough even *before* the storm.

He spotted a Shell station not far down the road with a single bay for car repair, and pulled up to it as the attendant, a short, brownskin man in his mid-thirties with tightly braided hair and wearing overalls without a shirt, took a drag from his cigarette and flicked it on the ground.

"Help you?"

"Just need to have my flat fixed."

Barely looking at the man, Julian tossed him his keys and went inside the air-conditioned store. An oasis of soft drink coolers consumed one wall, and he opened the door wide and let the clouds of iced air wash over his face. He pulled a bottled lemonade from the shelf and headed toward the front.

An older man, frail-looking with slicked-back silver hair and stooped shoulders, took up the bills Julian placed on the counter.

"Need any cookies or chips with that?" he said.

"Naw. Thanks." Julian opened the bottle and took a long drink. On a high shelf above the counter a boom-box radio blared a news report about the state of the battered city thirty miles east, weeks after the hurricane.

They say it's kinda bad over there in New Orleans." The man put Julian's change on the counter. "National Guard everywhere. I hear they're not even letting folks back in yet."

Julian nodded. *Kinda bad?* The understatement was almost comical.

"They just started," he said. Truth was, he'd sneaked around checkpoints weeks ago to get to his father's house.

He thought about his father, and wondered how long he would have to shoulder the burden of regret over that last phone conversation. *Do you even understand what mandatory evacuation means?* The minute the words were out, he'd felt the blood leave his face. The silence and hangup afterwards had stung Julian worse than the hickory switch spankings that welted his legs during his father's rare moments of childhood disciplining.

He stepped back outside the air-conditioned store, and the choking heat and humidity enveloped him again. The Neon was now stripped of the spare and the attendant was rolling the damaged tire against the cement.

"Nail, right there," he said, looking up at Julian and pointing to the bent metal jutting out of the tread. "I'll patch it up. It'll be a few minutes."

Julian nodded, and walked across the grassy lawn between the off-ramp strip of businesses (a Food Mart, a cell phone store, a laundromat) and the highway, as a rare breeze floated through the fronds of a nearby stand of palmettos. He took a long swig from the iced lemonade. The sky was a brilliant, electric blue and the late morning sun was burning into the concrete. The traffic along the I-10 corridor was still clotting now and then as convoys of cars and trucks, semis, and even government jeeps paraded east, a steady stream toward New Orleans.

He rubbed the slick bottle against his forehead, and breathed rough, deep breaths. The days since the storm had been mind-numbing, and his nerves still jittered just beneath his skin. He'd arrived in Baton Rouge a month ago—after a blur of airport concourses and security checkpoints, rental car counters and baggage claim belts—as quickly as he could, but not quickly enough. Over the phone, his father's friend Sylvia McConnell, her voice wobbly with grief, had spoken in frantic and teary bursts. Like the banging of sharp, dissonant chords, her words exploded in his head. Simon missing. Maybe dead. After that, it was as if those words had damaged his nerves and left him deaf—he heard nothing more as they spun around his brain.

Later, when he could take in the details, he braced for each one. The city was uninhabitable, flooding from the broken levees having left most of it sitting in water that would take weeks to drain. Tens of thousands who hadn't evacuated had been ordered to leave, rescue efforts were slow and chaotic, hundreds had drowned and many more were missing. And while his old neighborhood of Treme had not been wiped out like others near the broken flood walls (in fact, most of Treme suffered only a little flooding), the house where he'd grown up sat in four, maybe even five feet of water. And there was no sign, or word, of his father.

With Sylvia's house bone dry on the high ground of Uptown just off Magazine Street (the little bit of water stopped at the second porch step), she and Julian fixed their minds on the search for Simon, taking back streets into town past phalanxes of Guardsmen to meet at Simon's house. They had opened the door, looked as far as they could for signs of Simon, then backed out, silent.

Nothing was recognizable. It was as if the whole house had been dropped to the bottom of the river, then lifted up a year later. The stench, like nothing they'd ever experienced, was as violent and jarring as a body punch. Viney branches of mold shot up the walls like ivy up a high fence. A blanket of brown sludge draped everything. Furniture lay strewn about like dice after a powerful shake and roll. It was not the place Julian knew, not the place where he'd grown up. That place was gone.

But the house didn't matter; what mattered was Simon. They exhausted every possibility—the Red Cross lists, the Superdome. The Convention Center, where hot, angry masses huddled in the days during and after the storm. The churches. The endless lists of buses that had taken survivors to shelters as far away as California, Utah, Missouri. They posted fliers with Simon's picture on every telephone pole left standing in the neighborhood, an ironic task, since no one was there to see them. They located one of the men in Simon's Social Aid and Pleasure Club, The Elegant Gents, but he knew nothing—he hadn't seen Simon since a week before the storm. They walked the streets looking for anyone who might have seen him, but came up with nothing.

At the end of each day, Julian went back to his Best Western room in Baton Rouge, turned up a minibar bottle of Jack Daniels, and dialed up the A/C. Then he flopped on his squeaking bed and let the liquor slide him into sleep.

Every day for the next few weeks he and Sylvia inhaled bland Food Mart lunches at highway gas stations and downed quarts of black coffee while mapping new strategies. Riding a caffeine buzz, Sylvia's mind raced with ideas—they should get a list of all the hospitals in the state, the clinics, the A.M.E. and C.M.E. and Baptist churches in the bordering states, and maybe even hire someone to help locate him.

They logged so many hours on the phone that their arms became numb. They refused to discuss the obvious possibility—just let it float like a balloon, unacknowledged, in the fragile air between them. If they ever were to consider the worst possible fate, it was still a ways off.

They weren't heading in that direction until there was nowhere else to go.

"Got it ready for you, man." The attendant was handing him an invoice. "That'll be eight dollars."

Julian pulled four folded bills from his jeans pocket, and on second thought, took another two and folded it inside the others.

"Thanks, man." The attendant handed him his keys and Julian headed toward the car.

From behind him he heard another car pulling off the ramp and into the lot of the station. A vintage Camaro, painted a dull and rusting blood-red, heaved and sputtered, then died a few feet from Julian.

Its owner got out, a tall, slender man in worn jeans and a sweat-soaked white T-shirt, his shoulders sagging, a sickle-shaped scar across his cheek, his blue baseball cap cocked down against his brows.

Julian gave the man a nod. "Sounds like you could use an alternator maybe."

The man gave him a long hard look, then his face opened into a smile.

"Fortier? You don't recognize me, man?"

Julian stared at the man, mining his memory for some recollection of those features. The deep brown eyes, what he could see of them beneath the cap, were familiar. And the scar. And the drooping shoulders and the angle of that cap. And suddenly, from Julian's forgotten past emerged the sound of a sizzling trumpet.

"Casey?" he said. "Grady Casey?"

The man's smile flared into a wide grin that made the scar look like an extension of it. He stuck out his hand and Julian grabbed it, pulling him in for a chest-bump hug.

"Been too long, man." Still grinning, Casey dug his hands in both pockets and rocked his weight from foot to foot. "Guess I dropped a few pounds since I seen you last."

"Whoa. I guess you sure did." Julian nodded, smiling, looking him up and down. "I almost didn't recognize you. Good to see you, man. You playing much?"

Casey hunched both shoulders. "Well, you know...," he started, and glanced over his shoulder in the direction of the highway marker: *New Orleans, 30 miles.*

"I *was.*"

Julian's mind hurled back to the seventh grade, Mr. Martrel's band class. Grady had been a pudgy kid with protruding ears and a girl's high-pitched voice, alternately Julian's best friend and worst enemy as the two clashed over bragging rights, each claiming musical dominance over the other. In a town where trumpet players ruled, they had both followed in the city's great tradition, but since their late teenage years, their lives had evolved into opposing sides of a coin. Julian: hardworking, serious, with a passion for music that bordered on obsessive. Casey: careless, unfocused, but with a talent that dazzled, seeming to draw from some limitless source.

As a musician, Grady Casey was, as the close-knit community of horn players in town acknowledged, *fierce.*

Their rivalry, mostly friendly but sometimes strained, had carried underpinnings of one-upmanship. Their cutting sessions, intense battles where riffs shot back and forth between the bells of their horns like topspinning tennis balls, usually resulted in a draw, but while Julian would pull out every stop, lips numbed and forehead lathered in sweat, Casey, at the end, always appeared cool and unchallenged.

But it had been Julian who had left for New York in search of a spot on the big stage while Casey manned the home turf: he married a local jazz singer, a white woman twelve years his senior, Julian had heard, and taught at a local music school by day and gigged at night. While neon marquees back east heralded Julian Fortier as the jazz world's emerging star (a Grammy followed a top spot on the *Downbeat* readers' poll, while club dates and tours crowded his calendar), his brilliant rival was barely known outside the limits of New Orleans, and had no ambitions there.

Hey, seen you on TV a few weeks back, man," Casey said, nodding.

Julian didn't know what the nod meant—a compliment maybe, but not necessarily. He shrugged, not inclined to mention that the *Tonight Show* airing was a repeat from two years ago, back when he could still *play.* Before Japan, he hadn't played a gig in almost a year. The run-in with a wayward Yellow Cab in downtown Manhattan that totaled his two-seater, broke his chin, and spoiled his dream-like career, had humbled Julian in a way that still felt unfamiliar, unnatural, and uncovered a sensation that was totally new—embarrassment.

Julian saw no need to go into all of this with Casey; it was hard enough to admit it to himself.

Casey squinted from the sun, shading his eyes with his hand. "Your daddy and them do all right?"

Julian looked away from Casey toward the bend where the highway disappeared into a grove of cypresses, then turned back to meet his old rival's eyes. "He stayed through it, man. We haven't found him yet."

"Aw, man." Casey pulled a pair of black plastic sunglasses from his sweaty shirt pocket and put them on. "I got three cousins still missing. I think they went to Atlanta, at least I hope. Everybody else, just, you know, trying to deal."

Casey shook his head, his brow furrowed, his eyes glassy. He looked toward the highway. "Man I cain't even believe this mess. It's like...judgment day or something, you know what I'm saying? You been there? Whole city is wasted, man. You seen your daddy's house?"

Julian nodded, turned up the last of his drink, and tossed the can into a nearby trash barrel.

"The house is a bust, man. I just want to find my father."

"I know, man. I know."

An awkward silence passed between them. Finally, Julian said, "What's the deal with your car?"

Relieved to turn the conversation to mundane car troubles, Casey smiled and tapped the hood with his fist. "This piece of crap? This ain't mine, man, it's my brother's. Mine's six feet under water."

Casey told Julian about his adventure in the storm. His wife had fled to Dallas while he'd stayed in their apartment in the Seventh Ward, got trapped on the second floor, and after a day and a half on a balcony, was airlifted to safety by a National Guard helicopter.

"Got my horns out, though, man!" Casey smiled. "I left everything else there, just grabbed my two B-flats and my cornet and my flugelhorn."

Julian smiled. "I heard that."

The two men talked a while longer until the station attendant came out to Casey's car, a filterless cigarette clenched between his teeth.

"Let's have a look." Casey raised the hood and the attendant leaned under it. After a moment, he left to find a battery tester. Just then, another car drove up. An elderly couple, their steps slow and their backs slumped in fatigue, walked toward the store. The woman's arms flailed as she ranted about her ruined refrigerator, while the man mumbled something about the government as he opened the door for her.

Casey turned to Julian. "You know what, man?"

"What?"

"You were smart to leave."

His head hanging and eyes downcast, Julian felt less like a smart man and more like a traitor. When he'd left for New York, Casey had all but called him that, since Julian was so willing to ditch the brass band they had recently formed together in favor of a possible solo recording date and a slim shot at a big-time career.

"Record? We can do that *here*, man," Casey had pleaded. But even before he'd packed, said goodbye to his father, and boarded the last night flight out of Louis Armstrong, Julian was already gone.

A lifetime ago, or so it seemed. Now, the reminder of his betrayal piled on top of everything else he was feeling: anger, regret, confusion, helplessness. He was mad at the city, mad at his father, mad at himself, mad at the world. And now Casey's eyes, aged beyond their years, threw Julian's frustrations back at him like twin mirrors. It was the same look he'd seen in the eyes of everyone as they returned to the battered neighborhoods, the drowned streets of the failing city, a look of utter disorientation, as if the world you once knew had suddenly and sharply tilted, and you were holding on to whatever you could to walk upright.

They found a shady pecan tree at the edge of the lot to stand under while they talked, Julian throwing back another iced drink, Grady taking long drags on a cigarette, and in minutes they were laughing. Casey brought up the time Julian had stepped in a steaming horse pile when they paraded down Canal with the brass band one Mardi Gras Day and never lost a beat, scraping the soiled shoe against the pavement in a footdragging, pimp-limp rhythm. *I was cool, though, wasn't I?* And there was the time they had dropped beer-filled balloons from a French Quarter balcony onto a group of white college boys during Sugar Bowl weekend, then ran like hell when the students spotted them later. They'd hid in an alley off Dumaine, and when the coast was clear, doubled over in laughter. Good times in a city made for little rusty-butt boys with an itch to be free. They talked and laughed on and on, as the misadventures of two cocky kids growing up together poured out in a cathartic litany.

They exchanged cell phone numbers, promising to keep in touch.

"You tell your lady I said 'hey,'" Julian said.

"Will do." Casey nodded. "You married yet?"

"Naw, man."

Casey grinned. "Aw, that's right. You had that one close call, but you got away."

Julian blinked twice, embarrassed as a surge of blood warmed his face. He imagined round eyes set in nut-brown skin, soft, curly spirals of natural hair, and that unmistakable low-pitched, blues-song voice. Vel was the reason, he believed, he was where he was, was *who* he was. Long after it was over, every now and then at night, some old memory intruded, kept him awake, disturbed his peace. And even on his best days before the accident, it would crimp his good mood into a throbbing knot of frustration and remind him of how he had been, when there was more to his life than playing the trumpet.

But that was history, *she* was history. He had moved on, long ago.

He let out a resigned sigh, shrugged.

"Yeah." Julian's composure slipped back intact. "No big deal."

Casey put the card with Julian's number in his shirt pocket. "Look here, bruh. Cindy and me got us a gig at the Embassy Suites in Baton Rouge over by the river. Ain't much, but it pays the bills, you know what I'm saying? You know you got to come on by and check us out."

"You working this week?"

"Got to, man. Life don't stop just because of no storm."

Julian looked away at a sapling tree bowing in the breeze, and a baby cardinal taking flight from the lowest branch. It didn't? No, of course not. Life did not stop. No matter how much you wanted it to. No matter what happened to you, no matter how much you lost and how much you hurt about what you'd lost, you still had to get up in the morning, go out there, and do it again.

No, life did not stop. *Except when it did.*

He tried to banish Simon's face to the edge of his mind.

"Every night through the weekend, in the lounge." Casey looked over at his car and the attendant, busy under the hood, then back at Julian as he opened the door to the Neon.

"And bring your horn."

Julian's eyes glazed over. He hadn't played any place as small-timey as The Embassy Suites lounge since he had left Louisiana. But he would have given anything to be able to do it now. Even if he'd wanted to, there was just no way.

Julian reached up a hand to touch his jaw, a reflex now whenever he thought of playing the horn, then placed it on the steering wheel. Maybe he should just tell him.

The station attendant yelled something across the distance, signaling Casey to come and look at the meter.

"Think about it, man." Casey took off his shades. "And I'm sorry about your daddy. Hope you find him."

Julian looked at Casey's eyes. As boys, their lives together had been one long spitting contest, competition lighting the spark that gave them life, oxygen to the fire of two blazing young egos. But somewhere over the growing-up years, his rival's eyes had become soulful, generous even. Or maybe it had only happened since the storm. They were all in this madness together.

Julian looked away. *Not now, later maybe.*

He reached out the car window and shook his old friend's hand.

"Thanks, man," he nodded, started his car, and drove toward the high sun and New Orleans.

4

On St. Charles Avenue in the Garden District, the grand houses still shone in the metallic wash of the sun like prim, white-haired matrons, as if nothing had happened. Sweeping turfs of green fronted the century-old, wrought-iron-gated mansions, their spines erect, their clapboard unstained, the giant bathtub ring that roped most of the low-lying city having faded with the rising, higher ground. But the St. Charles trees remembered. The nightmare music of the killing winds had stunned them, and the panicked trunks of the cypresses and live oaks still leaned against the memory, the way children flinch away from the hand of pain.

Julian steered the Neon down the avenue, cutting a slalom path around severed limbs and trash. Along the neutral ground of the town's wealthiest street, where the untraveled streetcar tracks lay rusting in the shadows of overgrow grass, the signs of chaos were few; a spotted hound loped along the rails in search of food, and from further down the street an electric saw hacked away at the broken limbs of a battered oak. Spanish-speaking workmen tossed damaged shingles from rooftops while a utilities truck fitted with a cherry picker crawled alongside the loosened telephone lines.

Like the French Quarter and Uptown, the Garden District's flooding had been measured in inches, not feet: no weeks of waiting for head-high water to drain and muddied rooms to dry. Not like his father's neighborhood, where two centuries of history marinated for weeks in four or five feet of brackish muck, or the Ninth Ward, where all life not washed away completely was suspended indefinitely. *Wasn't it always this way?* he thought. *The peasants struggling down in the valley, the rich safe on higher ground.*

He parked across from the Catholic church, dug into his gym bag for a clean T-shirt, and put it on. Getting out of the car, he swabbed at his forehead with an overused handkerchief and stared at the brass numbers 1924, the clean white columns of Matthew Parmenter's Victorian-style house, the gate that fenced in a yard of only slightly overgrown juniper grass. The house looked even more impressive than he remembered. He turned up his bottled water for a last swig, tossed the empty onto the car seat, and tried to brush back a nagging thought: *If things had worked the way they should have, Daddy could have lived on this street. Daddy would be safe.*

Simon's double shotgun was comfortable enough, a sturdy, hand-made house of cedar, maple, and cypress erected by a grandfather Julian never knew. But Julian opened the latch of the massive gate of 1924—a hand-forged system of wrought iron posts in an elaborate crisscross pattern, built by the father of one of Simon's oldest friends in his Social Aid and Pleasure Club—and remembered years ago watching his father's best friend's enormous house being renovated as he rode by on the streetcar. Steps of marble, a huge wrap-around porch, French doors leading to eighteen rooms. Even then he wondered—his father and Parmenter, best friends, business partners. Equals. Except somehow, they weren't.

He climbed the steps to the gallery, glancing into the darkened windows of leaded, beveled glass. Austere and private, the St. Charles houses had never offered visible clues of life inside even *before* the storm, but Julian guessed the old man was inside. Older than his father and many years retired, the former restaurateur rarely left the house. Like two stubborn and embattled sea captains, neither man would have jumped ship for a mere storm.

This would not be easy; his father's horrible business deal—all that lost money—still smarted like a glancing wound. But he pulled the mold-stained note from his pocket and read it again, then tucked it back. *Matthew Parmenter is Daddy's friend.* For Simon's sake, he rang the bell, sighed deeply, and waited.

An hour earlier, he had met with Sylvia at Ondine's Oysters, a little dive at the edge of the French Quarter not far from the French Market—a bar, really, with a cardboard sign outside that had boasted, throughout the entire storm and evacuation, WE NEVER CLOSED! A narrow, red brick-fronted place at the end of a shady courtyard, it sat wedged between a touristy T-shirt shop and a used bookstore, both vacant. In the mostly dark, windowless room, a long, brass-railed bar skirted the west wall and generator-powered pendant lamps swagged from the tin ceiling, lighting the square, laminate tables.

He took a seat in the back and ordered a coffee, then another as he waited. The dark interior seemed normal; the only sign of post-catastrophe afterlife was the clump of National Guardsmen gathered around the bar in severe haircuts and khaki fatigues, some sitting on backless swivel stools turning up glasses of warmish beer and mugs of tepid coffee.

He stood and waved when Sylvia entered, the opened door allowing a momentary flush of rectangular sunlight into the room.

"Morning." He held out her chair as she sat. With no makeup, her hair tied in a scarf, she looked, for the first time since he'd seen her that first Sunday afternoon in town after the storm, close to her age. Her eyes were puffy, red-rimmed by worry and insomnia.

"Morning, baby," she said wearily, untying her scarf and patting her curl-less, gray-rooted hair. "You drinking coffee? Shoot. I need me something stronger than *that*."

Julian smiled. When his father had introduced him to Sylvia, one sunny Labor Day after he and his buddies in The Elegant Gents had second-lined through Treme, a seldom-seen sparkle had seemed to backlight Simon's eyes. Clearly, it had been Sylvia who, after Ladeena had died, lifted Simon out of his quicksand of grief and got him interested, once again, in living. There was a natural kindness about her, Julian had noticed, and from then on, her bluesy, motherly warmth and nurturing nature had spilled over onto him, helping to fill the gap in Julian's life that his mother's passing had left.

"Stronger? I'm sure they can help you with that." He nodded toward the bar. "If you're hungry, somebody brought a whole box of muffalettas for the National Guard and the cops and the volunteers. They're telling everybody to help themselves."

Sylvia glanced toward the bar where the guardsmen and volunteers stood, a big cardboard box on the counter between them.

"They deserve a lot more than that for trying to clean up this mess of a city," she said, pinching the bridge of her nose. "Lord, have mercy. I tell you I haven't had a decent night's sleep since all this happened. I'll split a sandwich with you. But, baby, I got something to show you."

Julian went to the bar and returned with a Bloody Mary for Sylvia, a plastic cup of water for himself, and a ridiculously large muffaletta sandwich sliced in half on a paper plate.

Sylvia ignored the sandwich and the drink and reached into her purse. The folded paper she handed Julian was wrinkled and stained the color of tea.

She exhaled a huff of air. "Well, I went back to Simon's," she said, leaning forward with her eyebrows arched up and her eyes bright and brimming with something he hoped was hope. "I just felt like we missed something. So I took my nephew with me, Rashad. You know him."

Julian remembered the gangly six-foot-six kid, a star forward at one of the high schools in the city. He unfolded the paper. The handwriting was unmistakable—the dramatic, forward-leaning slant, the longish serifs. It was Simon's.

Julian's heart jumped. He looked up, his eyes wide. "Where'd you…?"

"Rashad climbed up to the attic through a little door in the ceiling of the bedroom closet. Simon must have been up there for hours. Days, maybe."

"This note was wedged in between the beams in the attic ceiling." Sylvia reached for his arm and squeezed it. "This is it, baby. Simon got out! He's safe somewhere."

Julian flinched at the thought of his seventy-six year old father having to climb up into a hole in the ceiling. He read the note slowly, his eyes brimming.

Julian,

I don't know where I'm going but I got to get out of here. I don't know if I will make it because there is so much water out there. Find me if you can or what's left of me. If something bad happens then take me back home to Silver Creek and lay me down besides your mama.

I love you son no matter what.

Your dad.

Julian looked up from the letter, his eyes glazed, his throat tight. The last two lines sank and burned like a sharp knife pressed to his chest, and would have hurt even if he hadn't wasted his last conversation with his father being disrespectful.

Julian rubbed his temple and looked down at the letter again. This didn't necessarily mean his father was alive. "He could be anywhere. He could have…anything could have happened after he wrote this."

"But this tells us that he tried to get out. He *tried*, baby."

Julian cleared his throat, took a long drink of the coffee, and stared at the sandwich, the spicy olive salad over sliced salami on the huge, thick roll. He tapped his knuckles on the table. Suddenly, he wasn't hungry. As a child, and then more proficiently as a young man, he'd learned to freeze his mind—block out every thought—to steel himself against erupting emotions that might trigger tears. He did that now.

Sylvia went on, telling Julian about the hole Rashad had found in the roof, probably made with a pickax. Simon must have gotten out onto the roof and waited for help from one of the helicopters or good Samaritans in makeshift boats, who'd trolled the murky waters looking for people in distress.

"Did your father ever talk to you about Silver Creek?" Sylvia took a long sip from her Bloody Mary, then put it down.

He almost laughed. When had Simon missed a chance to burn Julian's ears about Silver Creek? "There was five feet of water in the street." Julian said. "Silver Creek's farther than Baton Rouge. No way he could have gotten there without his car. And his car is still at the house. Rusting away."

"He could have gotten a ride there."

"You know I tried to call Cousin Genevieve at Silver Creek. Bunch of times. Nobody there, Sylvia."

He'd also continued his daily check of the Red Cross list of the missing online at the hotel, and gotten a list of twenty-eight more hospitals in every parish between New Orleans and Silver Creek. Nothing.

Sylvia pondered this, took a small bite out of her sandwich, then another sip of the Bloody Mary. She stirred the drink with the stalk of limp, brown-edged celery the bartender had placed in it.

Finally she reached into her purse, pulled out a thick fold of papers, each one with hand-written names and phone numbers. She waved them in the air. "I don't know what else to do. Between the two of us, we must have made four hundred calls all over the state. I think we need some help now if we're ever going to find out what happened to your father."

In her next breath came the words, *Matthew Parmenter.* The man had wealth, and therefore, power. Like a lot of restaurant owners in the Quarter, he'd been friendly with the police for years.

"Remember, the man's got connections, and he's your father's best friend." She leveled her gaze at him. "No matter *what* you think about him."

How did she know? Simon must have told her. Or had he given away his feelings at the mere mention of the man's name? Julian had often wondered whether if he saw Matthew Parmenter lying on his back in the street, how much time would pass between spotting him there and reaching out a helping hand? Well, he'd been raised right, so not that long. But he probably wouldn't lift a hand until the scolding fire in his father's eyes filled up the back of his mind.

It was nearly noon, and the door continued to open and close intermittently, sending flashes of light against the dark interior like a slow-motion strobe. Someone had brought in a CD player, and from the front of the bar upbeat music streamed. The cheap speakers blasted the bassy beat of Koko Taylor's "Wang Dang Doodle," lightening the mood. Three of the guardsmen lifted their glasses for a drink, and whoops of laughter went up after one of the men yelled out a loud punchline to a joke, "And he wasn't even wearing any!"

There was so little laughter in town these days that even those beyond earshot of the joke laughed along—its sound bubbling like a tonic, a much-needed bromide everybody in town seemed to crave. The door opened again. More volunteers, Red Cross employees, government workers—three young college-age women in baseball caps, two young men in faded cutoff jeans, and a man with silver hair and shorts poured into the room, along with another long shaft of hard, white light.

The intruding sun glowed on Sylvia's face, outlining her sharply angled bones, the deep hard crease between her brows.

"Will you go see him?"

A heavy sigh forced from Julian's chest. "I'll do it today."

"Good." She took another drink and her face tightened into a serious frown again as she leaned over to pat Julian's arm.

"You know, your daddy was so proud of you, baby," she said. "He told me about your accident, your not being able to play and everything."

Julian blinked, turned up his plastic cup of water, and swallowed long and slow.

"Sometimes when things aren't going so well, it can make you, you know, a little uptight. Your dad wasn't mad at you, baby. Just a little…" she shrugged. "He knew you were going through a hard time. He understood."

Julian looked toward the door, counted people huddled around the bar. There were eleven now.

"Yeah. I know."

"I know you had some words..."

Julian shifted in his seat, held up a hand. "You know. I really don't want to talk about this."

A quick wave of disappointment shadowed Sylvia's face as she sat back.

"I...I'm sorry." His shoulders arched up apologetically; he hadn't thought about the fight with Simon, the accident, or the sad condition of his chops for almost a whole day. But now, something made of iron twisted inside him. Now he was treating Sylvia as rudely as he had his father.

"Look," he said, his voice fainter. "I didn't mean...I just can't think about all that right now, Sylvia."

Sylvia sighed, placed a firm hand on Julian's and looked toward him, her eyes softening in the lamplight.

"Julian, I don't know if your daddy told you, he proposed to me. Six months ago."

Now it was Julian's turn to be stunned. "No, I don't think he..."

Sylvia rolled her eyes up toward the ceiling, exhaled heavily, then looked back into Julian's eyes. "Well, I said no. I didn't see any reason to change things. I thought we were doing just fine like we were. But your daddy, he's the marrying kind. He seemed all right about it after a while. But I felt guilty."

"Why?"

Sylvia considered the chipped glaze of Cherries Jubilee polish on her fingernails. Resignation and regret clouded her eyes. "Well, I guess this city girl just couldn't see herself ending up one day at Silver Creek. You know how much your daddy loves that place."

Fleeting sadness turned down the edges of her smile. "The way things turned out, I think it wouldn't have been such a bad idea."

A wave of relief, unbidden, swept over Julian. Regret, like misery, loves company. He patted the top of her hand.

She looked up again toward the slow-whirling ceiling fan.

"You know, me and your daddy, we always had so much fun.

He has to be the youngest seventy-six year old man I've ever seen. Did he ever tell you about when he started the conga line at Jazz Fest? The Preservation Hall band was playing and decided to go salsa on us. Now you know your daddy—that man loves to dance! So he jumps up, grabs my hand, and off we go! Everybody in the tent joined in." Sylvia shimmied her shoulders, counting out the syncopated beat—one, two, three-*four!* "Child, that tent was *shaking!* After a few minutes my feet were cryin', 'cause baby you know I was tryin' to be cute in my little high-heeled sandals and whatnot. I wanted to sit down so bad, but we kept going for a good twenty minutes! There had to be a hundred people following your daddy and me."

Julian smiled at the image of Simon leading a conga line. That was his daddy, for sure. He remembered his mother insisting that her husband learn to ballroom dance, and his father insisting later, after demonstrating precocious smoothness on the dance floor, that the whole thing had been his idea.

And as if Sylvia had read his mind, she said, "You know, he used to talk about your mama all the time. Ladeena. His eyes lit all up when he said her name. Lots of women wouldn't have that, their man always talking about his deceased wife. But I didn't mind. I liked it that he thought so much of her. It told me what kind of man he was. Sometimes he'd just go on about her, respectful, like he was so proud of her, you know, and I'd just say to myself, Sylvia, this is a *good* man."

She paused, her eyes wet. "Julian, I don't know what I'd do without him."

He leaned forward, patting her arm again. "We're going to find him. They're finding people every day. We'll find him and we'll bring him home."

They half-finished their half-sandwiches and stood up to leave. The back door of the dark bar swung open onto a blinding shock of noon sunlight on Esplanade Avenue, where banana trees, bright red hibiscus blooms, and palmettos—once resplendent with tropical beauty—now looked battered and beaten, their heads drooping in the sun. The streets were empty, absent the normal traffic sounds, but now and then a single car or utility vehicle or construction truck motored by.

They were both getting into their cars, parked illegally at the curb, when Sylvia raised her finger to Julian.

"Oh! I almost forgot. There's something else I got for you."

She reached inside her car through the window and picked up an object lying on the seat.

"Rashad and I found this. I couldn't believe it was in such good condition. I thought you'd like to have it."

It was a cardboard sleeve, the kind that housed 78 rpm recordings. The cover was faded and water-rippled, but when Julian reached inside, a pristine vinyl disc slid out. It was a 1955 pressing of Louis Armstrong's "West End Blues." Simon had bought it at a little shop off Pirate's Alley.

Somebody told me you might like this. The man gave me a good deal...

He had just turned sixteen, and music was the elixir he lived and breathed. Louis Armstrong, his father's favorite, had become Julian's idol too. His father was so excited his wide eyes blazed above a smile that erased years from his weathered face. It was as if he was presenting his son with the keys to a castle.

He'd never taken the record to New York with him, choosing to listen to it on visits home. His turntable didn't work anyway, and he'd believed that the valuable recording would be safer at his father's house.

The things that survive. If he'd wished for anything from the ruined house, it would have been this.

"Wow," he said, blinking back tears. His voice cracked, tamped down to a whisper. "Thank you, Sylvia."

"I don't know how it made it. None of the other records did. Your daddy's jazz collection, your mama's opera records, all messed up."

There was a wistful look on her face as Sylvia fished in her purse for her keys. "Oh, listen," she said, "why don't you come by my house tonight, 'round six? I figure people coming back to town to see all this mess need something decent to eat. Just a few folks from church; I'm celebrating my electricity coming back on."

A feeling of clarity, like a cooling breeze, swept his skin. He knew he was home, now. When people here were happy, they cooked, and when they wanted to celebrate something, they cooked.

And when they were frustrated and angry, and their lives were uncertain, and their hearts were torn with worry and grief, they cooked.

"OK."

"Nothing fancy, you know. Just a big pot of red beans. And don't be expecting them to be as good as your daddy's."

He sighed and blew a slow stream of air through his lips, scratched at the itchy bristle of his unshaved cheek. Sometimes he wondered what in hell was keeping him going. Days went by in a haze of lists: Get up. Shave (or not). Eat. Meet Sylvia. Call hospitals, churches, insurance agents. Listen to the news. Eat. Make more calls. By evening, his mind was a swamp where thoughts trudged along in hip boots, each step heavier than the one before until his brain stopped, bogged down in muck. Misery lolled alongside the notion that the next few days or even weeks could not be anything but hard, or even heart-breaking, if he did (or did not) find Simon.

All this—not to mention his career, his band, the draining of his cash, and figuring out when, if ever, he could play again.

But here was Sylvia, a hand stretched out from the fog. Seeing Sylvia was like coming home. Simon was the spine that joined them, him and Sylvia, front and back covers of the same book, and if he needed to, he could reach around that spine to cling to the other side.

She reached up to give him a hug, and he almost resisted, thinking about the way he must smell. But she pulled his shoulders down into hers, her hand on the back of his head.

"We're in this together, baby, you and me," she said. "You're not alone."

From outside on the gallery, Julian could hear the shuffle of slippers against hardwood.

The French door opened with a groan, and from the room floated the smell of Ben-Gay ointment and Old Spice. Matthew Parmenter, in powder-blue pajamas and a burgundy robe, stood a little shorter than the last time he'd seen him. He used a cane now, his big frame marked with an arthritic stoop.

Parmenter had always looked to him like a cross between a tall Santa Claus and an avuncular Confederate general. A thick mop of unruly snow-white hair flopped in his faded blue eyes, and his skin, ghostly pale, seemed as if it repelled sun. At eighty-five he stood about six-three, a good two inches taller than Julian, and probably fifty pounds heavier. The pale eyes glistened with a kindness Julian hadn't remembered.

"Oh, my God! Julian?" Parmenter's face opened into an exultant smile.

"You're here! Is your father all right? Have you seen him?" His thick New Orleans accent rolled out in fat, longish vowels. "Sorry, my boy, come in. Come in. Suffering through the apocalypse is no excuse for bad manners."

Julian stepped inside, and Parmenter reached for him and grabbed him into a hug so tight Julian could feel the heat of his sluggish breath.

Parmenter stepped back and pulled his robe close. "Ah, excuse my appearance. No reason to get dressed these days, what with…. Sit down, son. My God, I haven't seen you since…how long has it been? Come on this way, it's cooler in here. And please tell me you have good news."

5

Matthew Parmenter led the way into the high ceilinged foyer of red-striped embossed wallpaper, cherry wood paneling and gilt-framed paintings. In the living room, two wing-backed chairs slipcovered in linen flanked the enormous red-brick fireplace. Matthew sat in one, and gestured to the other. Julian sat and leaned forward in his chair, his hands clasped together, elbows on his knees.

There was no sense in beating around the bush. "Sir," he said, "my father is missing." A pall shadowed Matthew's face. He bowed his head, mired for a moment in thought, then lifted it.

"I was afraid…I tried to get him to come and stay here. But he wouldn't…"

He shook his head and sighed heavily.

"There was a lot of water in the house, five feet maybe, but I think…there's a good chance he got out safely," Julian said, rubbing his hands together. "And he left a note. We just have to find where he went."

Parmenter massaged the space between his eyes and frowned, then, as if he'd come to some indisputable conclusion, gave a quick, resolute nod.

"You'll find him. I know you will." From a nearby window, an arrow of sunlight pierced the room, and Parmenter stared at the dust motes dancing in it. "I've been listening to the radio. It's so sad, what's happened in this city. So much heartbreak…"

His voice trailed off. He looked up at Julian. "Simon is a strong man, resourceful. We have to believe that he's all right."

"Yes, sir." Parmenter slapped a hand on the arm of his chair. "Well. May I offer you a drink? Cognac? A glass of lemonade?"

"Anything cold would be fine."

"Thank God for generators. Have you eaten yet? I'm afraid my cook is in exile in Bogalusa, but I've been known to put together a sandwich that more than one person has survived." He pushed back a lock of too-long white hair from his eyes. As an afterthought he added, "Though, mind you, it won't be as good as your father's."

"I already ate. Thanks."

"Just make yourself at home."

Matthew got up and went to the kitchen, his house shoes scuffing and cane tapping along on the high-glossed red oak floors. Julian stood up and stretched his arms. He hadn't realized how tired he was until now, as heaviness draped his body like a curtain of lead.

Julian's gaze fell on a long wall leading to a hallway, where hung a huge, gold-trimmed oil painting. Dressed in a white gown that swirled at her feet, a woman smiled cryptically from the canvas, her long white arm extended, her gloved hand resting on a wooden banister at the bottom of a large staircase.

Parmenter's wife, Clarisse, Julian thought. A real New Orleans socialite. Probably done before one of the Mardi Gras balls.

He remembered vaguely the last time he'd seen her. *I heard your mama was feeling poorly.* A thin white woman in thin white linen standing at the screen door. Straight-backed, defiant against the codes of her station, the woman had boarded a streetcar and then a bus that took her across town to a place she'd never been—a handmade world of shotgun houses, lazy remnants of jazz, whiffs of barbecue, and angel's trumpet trees. All just to bring an ailing black woman a tuna-salad-on-lettuce-leaf lunch and a pot of clove and sassafras tea. She'd put the picnic basket on the kitchen table while Julian told his bedridden mother, "You got some company."

The woman had smiled and followed him into the sickroom, where white curtains ruffled from a breeze through the open window. She turned to him. *Would you mind putting water on for tea?* Bands of sun through kitchen blinds laying golden stripes across the walls, the water's slow boil, the scent of gardenias hanging over the porch steps where she had been. A "fine lady," his mother's frail voice had uttered later. But only now, years later, Julian wondered. Could she have known what her husband had done?

It was a thought that did not ride in alone—it was saddled with a twinge of guilt. No reason to suspect the kind woman's visit was in any way an apology for a husband whose business affairs were as unknowable to her as the mountains of the moon. Just a charitable gesture, the way southerners do. The woman's visit, the tea and lunch, seemed to lift his mother's spirits that week, which would be her last. When a stroke claimed Clarisse's own life less than a year later, the image of the delicate southern lady, head high, dressed in crisp white linen, stuck in Julian's mind.

Another frame held an enlarged black and white photograph, grainy and slightly faded—Simon Fortier and Matthew Parmenter, right hands clasped in handshake in front of a green awning and a sign announcing PARMENTER'S CREOLE KITCHEN. Opening day. Both men nattily dressed in starched and pressed white shirts, heads full of thick, longish hair, faces full of cocky grins. Two bright young men on a tear in the world, owner and head chef, employer and employee, friend and friend.

But the next frame dulled his eyes, drained blood from his face. Parmenter again, smiling, shaking hands in front of the awning of the restaurant. But his father's image was replaced with another familiar one—the president of the United States

"I hope you like iced tea. It's all I have." Parmenter was standing behind him holding a tray with two full glasses. Seeing Julian's stunned eyes and dropped jaw, he said, "Oh, haven't you seen that before?" He ambled to the living room and set the tray of glasses on a small table near Julian's chair.

Julian no longer had a taste for tea, but sat and sipped anyway. He well remembered Simon coming home excited that night. It was more than a dozen years ago, just before his father retired. *Simon, I want you to meet someone*, Matthew had yelled above the cackle of boiling pots on the six-burner range, while his head chef wiped greasy fingers on a towel. *The man was in my kitchen!* Simon said, his voice pitched high, ringing with giddy joy. *The man was actually in my kitchen!* The president's strong paw engulfed Simon's hand, and his eyes seemed fixed on his as he praised Simon's shrimp etouffee, his bourbon-laced bread pudding, and of course, his red beans and rice. Then, he truly *listened* while Simon told about his Auntie Maree, his teacher and the true chef in the family, from the old home place at Silver Creek.

But a picture with the president? Apparently an honor reserved only for owners, not the lowly genius chef whose artistry had put the restaurant on the culinary world map, and more money in Parnenter's pockets than he could spend in a lifetime.

"The president was a big fan of your father's cooking. He came whenever he was in the state, right up until the week we closed."

Right, Julian thought. *Maybe the president would have been a decent business partner.* He stared down into the tea, then took a long, thoughtful drink.

Parmenter put down his cup, his whitish brows furrowed. "I want you to know, Julian, I will do whatever I can to help you find your father. I count him among my dearest friends. You know that."

Julian paused a moment, then spoke quietly.

"Yes, sir."

"I know a few people at the police department. They are stretched horribly thin, but there's at least one or two men I can count on for help."

"I'd appreciate whatever you could do, sir."

"By the way, where are you staying?"

"At the Best Western in Baton Rouge."

"Oh? Why don't you stay here? I have so much room. My chef, I'm sure, will be back soon, my housekeeper too. You'll be so much more comfortable..."

Julian bit his bottom lip. *Stay here?* He didn't even want to be here now.

"Thanks. I'm good where I am."

For the next few minutes, Julian listened while Parmenter went on about the night of the storm, the sounds of deafening thunder and rain, the crashing of tree limbs. The feral braying and cawing of the wind and the eerie calm when it finally ended. How it was so different from anything he'd been through before, even Betsy.

"It was terrible, I must say, a little frightening. But I suppose here in the Garden District we fared better than most."

You got that right. Julian finished his tea and got up to leave. Parmenter hobbled up with his cane. "Well, all right. I'll make some calls today. You checked the whole neighborhood? No one has seen him?"

"Sir, there's nobody *in* the neighborhood. Daddy's part of the Treme took on about four or five feet of water in most of the houses and the streets. But there was a whole lot more than that in some of the other parts of town."

Julian told him about the Lower Ninth, where houses had floated from their slabs, and New Orleans East and even further away in St. Bernard Parish, where the waters rose to the eaves and even covered some rooftops until the whole city was drained.

Parmenter bowed his head, frowning, his face pale. "I haven't been too well lately. I haven't been out of my house since...I listened to my radio for a while yesterday until the battery died. I guess I didn't realize..."

For a brief moment, Julian felt a twinge of sympathy. If Parmenter had had children, grandchildren, they would have rushed in to look after him, occupying rooms in the enormous house, fluttering and fussing around him. And maybe he would have had a clue about the devastation in the rest of the city.

Parmenter opened the door and the two stepped out onto the gallery. The afternoon sun was full, the twisted branches and leaves of trees spindled out like disheveled hair after a night of restless sleep, and the air was thick and muggy.

"By the way," he said, "how is the young lady, your friend? I remember meeting her once years ago. What was her name? Very beautiful."

Where did that come from? He had not thought about her in months, and now, twice in one day, the thought of Vel had been forced on him by people who barely knew her.

Even Sylvia hadn't brought up her name (out of kindness, he was sure), a fact that had made him more grateful than ever to his father's girlfriend.

"Velmyra," he said. "Hartley. And I haven't seen her in a while."

Parmenter's face flushed. "Oh, my. I'm sorry. I thought you two were, you know. I remember your father seemed quite fond of her."

True. Simon had loved her as much as he had, or so it seemed, and appeared crestfallen when it had ended. He felt something bob in his stomach, again.

Like this was all he needed, like he didn't have enough on his mind. If he was put out with Parmenter before, he was pissed at him now.

"Yeah, well," Julian looked at his watch. "Sorry, I have to be someplace. Daddy's friend Sylvia is having some folks over and I'd told her I'd come by."

She'd said around six. And even though it was not yet three, Julian couldn't see staying at Parmenter's another minute. The man had offered his help; he'd done what he came to do.

Parmenter followed him to the edge of the porch as Julian descended the steps.

"One minute, Julian."

Julian turned to see the frail-looking man, narrow shoulders hunched, clasping his robe close around his neck as a breeze ruffled it. In the outdoor light, his skin seemed more tawny and ravaged with time, his eyes two shallow pools of fading light.

"There's something I need to tell you," he said, squinting as the afternoon sun blanched his face. "I…I am not well."

"Sir?"

"What I am saying to you, Julian, is that I am dying. I don't have much longer to live."

Julian felt his breath catch for a moment.

Parmenter looked out over the street at the magnolias beyond the neutral ground, at the sway of cypress leaves on the trees that hovered over the streetcar tracks. "As you know, I have no family here. After I lost Clarisse, your father was like a brother to me. And you. You were like the son I never had. Oh, I know we have not been close. I wasn't even sure that you liked me. But Simon told me so much about your life, your success, I felt as if you were mine. I never watched television, but I bought one the day you were to be on that late night show…what's the one?"

"*The Tonight Show.*"

He smiled. "Yes, that's it. I was as proud of you as your father. I have to believe Simon is safe somewhere. That being the case, it is imperative that I see him right away. I…ah, I have some unfinished business with him."

Julian nodded, centering his gaze on Parmenter's weakened eyes. He wondered if the "unfinished business" had anything to do with a small fortune that should have been his father's.

"I'll contact my friends with the police department today. And when your father is found, please bring him to me as soon as possible. Your father owes me something, and it is important that we settle it before I, uh, expire."

Julian's eyes bulged—he couldn't help it. Owes *him* something?

"When you find him, would you bring him to me? I am asking as a favor."

What else could he say?

"Yes, sir."

He had three hours until dinner at Sylvia's. So he drove through the streets of the city he barely recognized.

He steered the Neon through blighted neighborhoods of ruined houses, streets piled with debris, missing street signs, and blue-tarped roofs. Stray dogs nibbling at garbage piles. Homeless men, dazed, wandering the streets. And occasionally, a rental car parked in front of a water-ruined house while family members, faces distorted with shock or disbelief, empty their homes of drowned possessions, the flotsam of upended lives.

It crossed his mind to take the bridge over to the Lower Ninth, where some of his old friends lived, but the thought of it made his heart cringe. He'd seen the TV coverage—it was like a war zone, the TV anchors had said. Some houses twisted, buckled, smashed, crumbled, reduced to piles of rotting wood, and some missing altogether. Worse than any catastrophe the country had ever seen, but he would have to save it for another day, when he had the stomach for it.

As he turned the corner to Lavalle Street in the Treme where his father lived, Matthew Parmenter was still on his mind. What in the world could his father owe *him?* As for the man's startling pronouncement about his health, it had softened Julian's heart—some. How old was Matthew? Eighty-five? He lived his last decades in wealth and leisure. Simon was seventy-six, and as Matthew's life was ending, Simon's was in doubt. But today the hope in Sylvia's eyes shined like a lighthouse beam piercing thick fog. It helped him cling to a slippery notion—*Daddy is all right, Daddy is alive.*

And if he's alive, Julian thought, he'll want that book.

The idea came to him after Sylvia had given him the Louis Armstrong record. If its retrieval could mean so much to Julian, the recovery of the old family Bible, no matter its condition, would mean everything to Simon. Little things. Little things mattered in big times. Julian pulled up to the house, parked near the rusting chain-link fence, took the paper filter from his pocket, and strapped it over his mouth and nose.

The Bible had been in the family for more than a century, his father had said. And while the names of the ancestors had meant little to him when he was a boy, Julian's young eyes had grown to incandescent globes when his father pointed to Julian's name, telling him the story of the night he was born.

How he'd slid out of his mother's belly that night barely breathing, with a tiny hole in his heart. How the doctors shook their heads—they just didn't know about his chances. How, even though the rain was blinding, Simon took the streetcar home during the surgery just to get that Bible and record his son's name and birth date—etching a new life into being with a firm hand and India ink. How he'd prayed with that book in his hands, imploring God and every ancestor he could think of to hold fast for his son.

And finally, how Julian, tiny, runt-like, sucking life through a tube, had pulled through against all the odds, his lungs and heart gathering breath and strength with each year, and in time, as sturdy as any child's. And how years later he'd been given his greatest joy—a trumpet to breathe life into—to keep it that way.

The front door was even more swollen than before, and finally gave way with a few minutes of fist-pounding and a couple of body slams. Inside, the mighty stench had not subsided; its sharpness hit him full in the face, and seemed to have ripened with the recent days of dampness and heat.

He stepped over sludge-covered furniture and moldy objects tossed about and strewn across the floor—a coffee table of glass and chrome, a rolltop desk, two brass floor lamps, Simon's record collection buckled and blackened over with slime, framed photographs and books, and Simon's recliner chair—to get to the kitchen pantry, where the "hurricane box," as his mother liked to call it, was kept.

The box of corrugated cardboard, where his father had kept the Bible since the last big storm, had completely fallen apart and had floated into the living room with nothing in it. The contents—the oil lamp, the radio, the flashlight, the dried rations—were covered in mud next to it.

But no Bible.

He checked the entire house—living room, kitchen, bedroom, bath, and even climbed into the attic. He wondered if it had simply disintegrated in all the water, but the leather covers would have survived. It was not here.

Which meant that Simon had taken it with him. And it dawned on him as clearly as the sun was inching downward in the western sky. He knew where his father was.

6

He got back in the car, started the engine, and drove toward Sylvia's, feeling real relief for the first time in weeks. Resting his shoulders back against the car seat, he tapped his fingers on the steering wheel in time to a country and western song he didn't recognize on AM radio, and whistled. Of course, Simon would be upset about the house, but Julian would explain how the insurance company had been giving him grief. It would take months. And even if Simon's house could be restored, the neighborhood had no services—electricity, gas, even streetlights—and wouldn't for a long time. The whole place was uninhabitable—his father would surely see that—and Simon would have no choice but to come home with him.

He turned the corner by the used-to-be wine and cheese shop to head to Sylvia's neighborhood, and thought about how Simon had called New York, "not my cup of tea," even though he'd never seen it. And though Julian had begged him to come up for a Christmas week or Thanksgiving weekend—*Let me show you* my *city*—he would hunch up his shoulders and hug his elbows, his skin bristling at the prospect. He was a country man. Tall buildings made him feel "as hemmed in as a pig in a closet." Big crowds made him "nervous as a Betsy bug." Julian argued—wasn't Simon's favorite spot to watch the Zulu floats on Mardi Gras Day the corner of Orleans and Claiborne, where a shoulder-to-shoulder throng always gathered, yelling, cheering, throbbing, and bobbing to the high school marching bands? "That's different," he'd said. "At Mardi Gras, everybody's smiling."

By the time he reached Sylvia's sky-blue Creole cottage just off Magazine Street in Uptown, a plan had unfurled; he would leave the first thing in the morning, go get Simon, and take him to New York for a few weeks, or months, or as long as he would stay. He hoped his father had been eating well, and had remembered to grab his blood pressure medicine before he left. Whatever, Julian would deal with it, take care of it. He'd take care of it all.

A fallen tree in the yard, and a branch that broke a window; that was the extent of the storm damage Sylvia's cottage had suffered. Along her block, paper trash lined the street, torn branches from the trees lined the gutters; otherwise, the house and the neighborhood looked as though nothing had happened.

As soon as he entered the noisy living room, he slipped into the liquid embrace of home and its familiar rhythm—around homefolks, his shoulders, his back, even his feet relaxed. The smothering hugs, the long, lilting vowels that seemed to liquefy in the heat, the uninhibited laughter, the kind eyes that searched others as though they truly cared, all warmed him like a bath. Around the room, as people sat or stood over paper plates buckling under barbecue chicken and beans and rice—some whispering and shaking their heads in corners, others grinning and laughing in doorways—the scene reminded him of a wake where humor and gloom abruptly traded turns; laughter might dissolve into tears, tears might bubble into laughter, all without warning.

The church members from Blessed Redeemer had known Julian from a child, and because they loved his father, loved him. Now, they'd all become a family of survivors; everyone here, he was sure, knew someone who knew someone who'd lost a house, a loved one, a life. Eyes strained with fatigue or stress, knotted foreheads and wringing hands bespoke their recent trials, but today was the day for the healing salves of food and mood—at least *they* had all made it through.

"Julian Fortier!" A sixtyish woman in orange striped jeans and a white T-shirt that read, "It Wasn't the Hurricane, It Was the Levees" spotted Julian from the kitchen and squealed with delight. "Come and get you some of this food, baby!"

He smiled and held up a hand in the direction of the voice. The scent of barbecue was a welcome change from the acrid stench in the dead neighborhoods. He was hungry now; knowing Simon was safe had given him an appetite again.

It took minutes to get to the kitchen, as arms reaching out to hug him slowed his progress. Elaine Stout, a cherub-faced woman who lived up to her name (and who, his father once told him, had worn something red every day since 1997, when she won a $5,000 scratch-off lottery wearing a red dress) caught Julian in a doorway and pulled him into a lilac-scented bosom of scarlet polyester.

"How you doing, Miz Stout?"

She shook her head. "Oh, baby. It's rough. Child, my house is *gone*. My whole *house*. I mean it just slid on down the street in all that water and fell apart! The whole neighborhood…it's just…" Looking away, she took a deep breath and put her hand on her hip, still shaking her head, her voice quieter. "I'm still here, though. I didn't lose nobody. I'm blessed. But baby, it's rough."

Her large brown eyes glazed over a moment as something snapped inside her. "I'm sorry, baby," she said, embarrassed, her hand to her mouth. "I'm so sorry. I heard about your daddy."

She put a hand to Julian's cheek, and he felt a strong desire to reassure her.

"He's OK," he said. "I went to the house so I know he got out. And I know where he went. I'm going to pick him up tomorrow."

Her face brightened. "Well, that's good news! Where is he?"

But before he could answer, a deep baritone voice called him to another corner.

"Julian! Saw you on TV! What's that Jay Leno like?'

And before he could answer that, others yelled out. "I caught your thing on Letterman. You played real good, baby!"

"The boy wasn't on Letterman, it was Leno," somebody else said.

"What you talking about? I got it on tape."

"Then you got Leno on tape."

"Julian, you bring your horn with you?"

For the next few minutes a crowd of four or five gathered around, assaulting him with affection; his back got slapped, shoulders squeezed, cheeks pinched, head rubbed. He was the made-it-big homeboy, back from the world stage, a welcome distraction from the woeful world of storms and floods.

Julian ducked his head and resorted to monosyllabic grunts, embarrassed. No one seemed to know that the Leno rerun was two years old, before everything had changed, and he wasn't about to mention it. He grimaced at the reminder that he was not the player he once was, and might never be again.

On Sylvia's green cotton slip-covered sofa, with paper plates balanced on their knees, sat two other church members he remembered well from his youth. Gideon Deslonde, a thin, retired carpenter with a mane of Afro-thick white hair, enjoyed local celebrity masking as a Mardi Gras Indian during carnival, and sitting next to him, Emma Zerra Pendleton, a willowy six-foot-tall jazz singer with an alto voice that occasionally dipped toward bass, was known to carry a black plastic urn with her—full of her deceased husband's ashes—everywhere she went. Julian looked down at Emma Zerra's purse near her feet, relieved to see no sign of Mr. Pendleton.

Spotting an escape from the adoring group, Julian squatted down near the sofa to talk to Mr. Deslonde, one of his father's oldest friends, whose worn face seemed shaded in sadness.

"How you doing, Mr. Deslonde? You all right?"

Deslonde put the barbecued chicken leg back down on his paper plate. He took off his black baseball cap, scratched the back of his head, then put his hat back on and shrugged.

"No good," he shook his head, sighing. "Lost it all. Lost my suit. Had to start all over again."

Deslonde was not grieving over his house, safely upriver away from the levee breaches, but a loss nearly as heart-wrenching. His half-finished Mardi Gras Indian "suit," an enormous costume festooned with wildly fanned plumage and thousands of colored beads in elaborate patterns, had been stored at a lady friend's house in the Ninth Ward. The friend had survived, but the suit had not. Half of a twelve-month task of eye-straining needle-and-thread work (from the day after one Mardi Gras until the eve of the next), lost to the flood.

"I'm really sorry about that," Julian said, and bowed his head. "I know it was pretty."

"Aw baby." Deslonde's brows furrowed. "Pretty like you ain't never seen." He shrugged, took another bite of his chicken, wiped his mouth with a napkin, then looked up, eyes hopeful, glistening. "Started me a new one last week. Got me a whole five months 'til Mardi Gras. I'ma be ready! But it won't be like it coulda been."

Mardi Gras? Julian's eyebrows flew up. The city was in ruins. Some were doubting whether there was enough of it left to call a city. Yet Deslonde, chief of the Red Feather Night Warriors tribe of the Mardi Gras Indian nation (a decades-old traditional homage to Native Americans who sheltered runaway blacks during slavery), was talking about the next Mardi Gras. But that was the way the city was, had always been—the biggest flood of the century was no match for the rolling tides of tradition. If the city was going to go down, it would go down fighting, with people like Deslonde on the front line of the battle.

"Hey, son. Where your daddy at?" Deslonde took a forkful of the red beans and rice on his plate.

Julian rose up from his squat and dusted his pants legs with his palms, reminded of his purpose. "Not far. I'm gonna pick him up tomorrow. Uh, can you excuse me a minute? I've got to find Sylvia."

He patted Deslonde on the shoulder and went back to the kitchen.

The kitchen was noisy and cramped, as Sylvia and two other women bustled about, preparing food. Sylvia was pouring ice water into tall plastic cups from a large glass pitcher. Two other women from Blessed Redeemer, Vivienne Ponder and Lenessa Bishop, held casserole dishes covered in foil and were unveiling them—deviled eggs in one, Popeye's chicken legs in the other.

Lenessa, a petite woman with her right arm in a sling (she'd sprained it being airlifted into a helicopter from her roof), used her good arm to put the platter of deviled eggs on the counter. "Hey Julian how you doin' baby. Where you want these eggs to go, Sylvia?"

"You can put those in that big Corning Ware dish, and that white platter I set out," Sylvia said, pointing to a counter top. She turned to Julian. "You made it! I'm glad you're here, baby. I got something to tell you."

But Julian didn't hear those words. "Sylvia," he said. "I need to talk to you."

Vivienne and Lenessa took their dishes to the dining room, and Sylvia and Julian sat down at the kitchen dinette table near the back door, the fading window light dimming, while Julian poured out his theory about Simon.

When he was a boy, Julian's fourth grade teacher had spent a whole class period talking about hurricanes, and for homework assigned them to make an emergency plan with their parents. Figure out a place outside the city, she'd said, where they could all meet if they were separated after a storm and couldn't contact each other. Someplace they could all get to that was safely away from the storm.

Simon took two cups from the cupboard and turned off the percolator.

You can find me at Silver Creek.

Julian was nine. Silver Creek may as well have been on the moon.

That's too far. How am I gonna get to Silver Creek?

Figure it out. Cause that's where I'll be. Something happens, I'm going back home. Simon poured coffee from the pot into a white clay cup.

Come on, Daddy.

He put a teaspoonful of sugar in the coffee, tasted it, made a face, then put another teaspoon in. In Julian's cup of hot milk, he poured a tablespoonful of coffee and two teaspoons of sugar.

I'm gonna get my daddy's Bible and I'm gonna go to Silver Creek. Even if I have to walk there.

Julian contemplated his father walking along a stretch of barren road, a Bible tucked under his arm. He took a sip of the coffee-flavored milk, then looked up, confused.

What if I can't find it?

Simon smiled, took a long, slow drink of coffee, and smacked his lips. *When the time comes, you'll know,* he said. He looked down at the big eyes of his young son.

Cause it's your land, too.

Shortly after that, the family had made their annual summer trek to Silver Creek and Simon had pointed out every bend, every turn, every tiny creek along the way. It was the trip Julian best remembered, because he had fought so hard not to go.

Sylvia frowned. "I thought you said you called Genevieve and she didn't answer. And if he's there, why hasn't he called?"

"Daddy never could remember my cell phone number. And I don't know why Cousin G didn't answer. Maybe they got some storm damage up that way too. Whatever, that's where Daddy is, I'm telling you. Daddy walked to Silver Creek. Or hitched, or talked somebody into driving him there, or something."

"What gave you that idea?"

"The Bible. The Bible is missing from the house."

Sylvia's eyes clouded in skepticism, but she conceded, "It's as good a place to look as any. When you going? In the morning?"

"As soon as I figure out how to get there."

"You don't know?"

He shrugged, embarrassed now. How many times had his father explained the route to Silver Creek while he, distracted, barely listened?

"Roads are kinda crazy down there, twisting and turning. When I get up, I'll look it up on the motel computer, or call Triple A. I'll call you as soon as I get there."

He ran a hand along the back of his neck. "So anyway, what did you want to tell me?"

"Tell you?" Sylvia's eyelids fluttered. "Oh, right. Just that someone you know, someone you used to know very well, might be stopping by, and I wanted to tell you in case you—"

The din of chatter rose in the living room; somebody everyone seemed to know had entered the house. The woman at the door greeted the friends gathered in the living room cordially, then walked straight back to the kitchen and stood in the doorway.

The last time he had seen her they had had a fight, a big one, and she had been walking away.

If she was as surprised to see him as he was to see her, she didn't show it. She wore yellow. Her frizzy curl was longer, and she was still small, her compact, athletic body boasting hidden strength. Her eyes still glinted like those of a woman with a secret.

Velmyra Hartley reached a hand to her hair and twirled the ends of it in her fingers.

"Hey," she said.

"Hey."

An awkward silence passed between them.

Finally she said, "You know, I saw you on TV."

7

On any other night, there'd have been lights on the river.

Any other night, at any other time, when the biggest storm of the century had not just swept through the town ravaging buildings and houses and parks and streets; any other time when the government levees had not failed and the flooding waters had not filled up the giant bowl of the sinking city and laid waste to thousands of acres and hundreds of lives; any other night when all that had not happened, there would have been lights on the river.

There would have been bridge girders strung with necklaces of white pearls, platinum jeweled steamboats and ruby-studded ferries and tugboats floating like giant party hats at sea. White gold beads of light from the Riverwalk shops and flickering bulbs from the houses of nearby Algiers. Carnival lights from the French Quarter bars and dives, the casino, the cafes, the taxis, and the red swirling lights of the police cars. And always, there would have been the rhinestone sparkle in the eyes of tourists, especially in the eyes of the children.

But tonight the only light on the river came from a pale, gibbous moon casting oyster-colored shimmers across the rippled surface of the water. Downriver, a lone barge floated without sound.

Julian sat in the unfamiliar dark on a bench near the water and put his trumpet case down near the leg of the bench. There was a small rock near his foot, so he picked it up and hurled it as far across the water as he could, and watched the small splash, the growing circles, the wider and wider spirals of concentric ripples spanning outward until they stilled, and the water near the splash finally restored itself to calm.

After he'd left Sylvia's in a daze of humiliation, he'd driven to the French Quarter, parked the car illegally near the recently re-opened Café Du Monde, grabbed his horn from the trunk, and headed over the levee down to the river. It was something he'd done as a boy; whenever he'd slipped into a deep funk—botched a solo in the marching band, or a girl he'd liked had shined him on—he found himself down near the water with his horn in his hands. The old heads, the musicians who'd been around forever, had told him how the hand-in-hand tourists went crazy for the romantic standards— "After You've Gone" or "Sleepytime Down South"—and between sips of chicory coffee and bites of beignets, would pay good tip money for a ballad or two. They were right. And if anything was bothering him, the feel of his trumpet, the flow of the music, and a pocket full of coin always made it go away.

No music-loving tourists tonight, and just as well. So he leaned forward, elbows on his knees and head between his hands, and tried to figure out what had just happened an hour ago.

Now, of course, he could think of a thousand ways it could have gone, a thousand things he should have said. Clever things, cavalier words to flaunt his impenetrable cool. But with everything else he'd been going through these last weeks, his emotions bound in a knot so tight he could not find one loose thread, he'd been blindsided. He hadn't seen it coming, hadn't known what seeing her again would do to his equilibrium, his balance. It was as if he'd been hit by a car all over again.

She'd started to make conversation, something about seeing him on TV. He'd said nothing, just kept looking at her like an idiot. She'd asked him something else, and he couldn't hear it because his face was too hot, and the bile in his stomach was rising too fast. So what had he done? "Excuse me," he'd said. And disappeared inside the bathroom off the kitchen.

Inside he'd tried to gather himself. *This is old business,* he thought, shocked at his reaction. He looked in the mirror and saw a man trapped in trouble and pain. "Nice going, genius," he said to the sad figure looking back at him. His eyes sagging, his face shiny and chin covered in stubble, his hair too long and untrimmed, his T-shirt sticking to his chest. He'd always been a fairly good looking man, or so he'd been told—he enjoyed reasonable height, a trim and fit body from his daily standing date at the Gold's Gym two blocks from where he lived, the blessing of his father's luminous eyes, thick hair and long lashes. But that was not the man he saw. The man he saw looked like hell.

She, on the other hand, looked exactly the way he remembered, they way she had entered his dreams for the first eight months after their breakup.

She looked, well, perfect.

He'd washed his face with liquid hand soap and cold water. When he finally left the bathroom, she had moved to the other room. And he'd left through Sylvia's back door, got into his car, and headed for the river.

It made sense that Sylvia would invite her. After all, she and Sylvia were tight; in fact, it was Sylvia who had introduced them all those years ago. "There's a young teacher I work with," she'd said, sidling up to him one Sunday afternoon after one of Simon's elaborate Creole meals. "I want you two to meet."

Julian had been interested. He'd split with the accountant/yoga instructor he'd met at the gym and was looking to meet somebody new. He'd been doing little more than teach a couple of classes and a few private students at Tulane, play a gig or two on the weekends, then go home to an empty place. Why not?

The restaurant on Tchoupitoulas Street where he'd taken her had been lit with geranium-scented candles that turned the ends of her hair to deep red. The suspended stereo speakers above their heads dispensed a dreamy, big band version of "Moonglow," and they had talked until the waiter had asked them for the third time, with practiced subtlety, if they "needed anything else?" And then until the chairs were flipped onto the tabletops.

He'd taken her home, where they'd talked outdoors in front of her apartment for another two hours. She spoke thoughtfully, her timbre low and eyes flashing, her hands in constant motion. She was an artist, a painter: mostly figurative stuff, occasional abstracts, some collage. She liked the play of bold colors in neo-Afrocentric themes, and managed to sell at least two paintings a year, each bringing in enough for about two months' rent.

She liked jazz, she told him, the older stuff mostly, Peterson on piano, early Miles. For a living, she taught art to thirteen-year-olds in the school district—her real passion. Teaching delighted her—the silly jokes, the sharp, curious challenges of her smartest kids—and he loved that she loved it. When she talked about them, the air around her seemed to amplify, charged with light. Her brown eyes warmed to amber, and her smile nearly took his breath away.

He'd started to leave sooner, but wanted to memorize her face, trace her profile in his mind so he could call it up that night while he slept—the loose, raw beauty, the strong features gently framed in red oak skin.

Within weeks, they were a thing. They spent long hours talking on the phone, then met for even longer dinners at Dooky Chase's or Parmenter's, where his father sent special hors d'oeuvres from the kitchen, or floated winks and smiles between the stage and the back table while he played the late set at Snug Harbor. They rode their bikes through Audubon Park and jogged along the levee by the river. He washed her car on Saturday afternoons, and she picked up his shirts when he was running late. She fixed him cinnamon coffee while he practiced arpeggios in her studio, and he baked his special lasagna while she painted, her stereo rolling out vintage Miles.

Their engagement ended abruptly. To this day, he couldn't remember what happened between them at the end, just the muddy weight of his heart after it was over. He was in New York when he heard the news of her marriage, a few months later, to a man he thought she barely knew. That sent him reeling. And a year later, news of her divorce left him just as dazed.

One good thing had come out of it all. From her, he learned to play the blues—the deep-down, been-there blues. After their breakup, everything in his playing shifted; he dared to reach deeper inside, walk the tender landscape she had bruised, and turn the journey into liquid sound. Minor thirds, salted with tears, spilled from his downtilted bell, and soulful riffs of heartbreak became his signature. When he arrived in New York, heart scarred and mind numbed, music flooded from his horn, from him, unstoppable.

He could even say it was Velmyra who'd made him famous. It had taken him a while to put the whole business behind him; but when the heat of his hurt had cooled and he could walk upright again, the memory of her, which had been dense and imposing, thinned to vapor. The stamp she'd made on his music, though, was still there. The pain let him tap into something real, something everybody knew, and it had taken his playing from good to great. From that point on, his life hummed. Things came easily, quickly, perfectly. A recording deal with a major label. A great deal on the best apartment on a gentrified street in Brooklyn Heights. Dates at the best clubs in town—the Village Vanguard, The Blue Note, Birdland—and a major network TV appearance that fell into his lap.

He fashioned an image that was cool, clean, and marked by a sartorial elegance he associated with success. Tassled loafers handcrafted in Italy. Hand tailored shirts from London, and gig suits designed by Hugo Boss. His people marketed him a "young lion of jazz"—accessible, with a nouveau-bop edge that straddled a graceful line between the mercurial tastes of the young and the older jazz purists. He made more money than he had time to spend, and women clung to him like lint to coarse black wool. Once he became well known in top music circles—when the word went out that another new hotshot was up from New Orleans—he was the curiosity everyone wanted to hear.

His life was exactly the way he wanted it to be—every day, another dream.

Until the accident.

He stood up from the bench. He could have sworn he heard a sound—like a ship's foghorn—coming from the river. But maybe not, maybe it was just in his head. Whatever, the music of the sound—a low, husky B-flat—was enough to make him unpack his horn.

The metal mouthpiece was a cold shock to his lips, as always when he hadn't played for a while. The valves were stiff; he drummed his fingers, miming a quick scale. His lips and fingertips had grown tender and uncallused since the surgery. He started blowing a flood of hot air through the horn.

A small sharp burn swelled in his jaw, then went away. He touched his hand to the spot and held it there. He waited, then tried again.

A scale stumbled out—his tone cracking horribly, notes splitting like dry wood. But in a moment, through a dull film of pain, clean notes streamed into the thick night air.

The doctor said the soreness would go away and the nerve endings would take a while to heal. Didn't make sense to press his luck. But after a minute, he put the horn back up to his lips and played again.

The moon, arced higher now, its silver reflection casting longer tendrils of light on the surface of the river, bathed everything in deep purple and strands of muted light. A tune surfaced from somewhere beneath his jumble of thoughts, low and lazy like a whisper of sea-fog, a blues drenched in flood water and rising like mist from a childhood summer night. He felt lightheaded. He was a little kid again, playing street tag, double-dog-dare, stickball. And like most of the kids he knew, he felt safe, like nothing bad would ever happen in his life.

No thoughts of his city sinking in on itself, or simply washing away.

Standing by the river in the dark, he realized he'd thought little about the city itself, about what all this meant. This was his *home,* the place where he'd been born and grew up, where his roots stretched so deep into the sandy soil that their beginnings seemed to have no end. Now, it was unfit for human life. He closed his eyes and his tears burned and in the shadow of the song a rhythm section grooved in the breezeless night—wire brushes soup-stirring watercolor patches of blue—while the sodden soil of home grew soft beneath his feet.

Tomorrow he would go to Silver Creek to find his father and bring him...home, whatever that meant now. If he was there.

If he was there.

As he lifted the horn high and played out over the big, silent river, he wondered if anybody out there in the endless dark was listening, if maybe he could play so loud that Simon, wherever he was, could hear him. From nowhere, the legendary musician Buddy Bolden sprang to mind, the golden brass god blowing the city's first song, a sound so big it soared across time to split the air where he stood now.

When he was small and his friends' fathers spooked them with stories of ghosts and dragons, Simon had made up tales to get Julian to practice. He told stories about the mythic cornet player who blew way back when the city was young, when jazz crawled up from cradle-high to paddle upriver to the world. *He was a genius, the best anybody ever heard. A horn player who blew so loud that clouds trembled and birds' wings stuttered in flight. Handsome, too—a ladies' man. Or so the story goes.* In Simon's stories, Buddy Bolden's power was mighty, fierce, and the sound of his horn could level mountains and raise the dead. Julian's young eyes lit up, his mind filled to overflowing, and he could not wait to play.

He wondered if Bolden were here tonight, what notes would blast from his horn. For a moment, he wished his father's fables were true. But even if they were, it would take something more powerful than Bolden's horn to bring this dead city back to life.

After a while, his jaw was still sore, but his breathing felt easy and his head lighter from the lift of his music, so he got back in the car and drove toward his Baton Rouge motel. He didn't turn on the radio—the road hum and darkness beyond the headlights' reach felt right for thinking. He thought of so many things. Simon. Ladeena. A pot of red beans and rice saturating the kitchen air on a Monday afternoon with a smell to make a grown man weep. His daddy, stirring the pot and going on and on about Silver Creek. His mother, reading by the window on a summer Sunday after church. The city he called home, sick at heart and sinking.

All of that, and Velmyra Hartley's smile.

If he hadn't remembered that she rose early, sometimes before dawn, to capture the colors of morning light on her canvas, he would not have gone. But she was one of the few people he knew for whom seven a.m. was not an unreasonable hour to call.

He had called Sylvia at midnight after lying in his Best Western bed, sleepless, for an hour. He could have sworn he heard a small chuckle of glee in Sylvia's voice when he told her what he wanted. Sylvia hadn't hesitated. It was as if she'd been waiting for him to ask.

"She's not too far from you. She's staying at the Day's Inn right there in Baton Rouge, the one closest to the river," Sylvia had said. "Room 212."

Of course. Half the town of New Orleans had picked up and moved to Baton Rouge, at least temporarily. And even though Velmyra's house in Uptown was not damaged by the storm or the flood, she was still without power and her plumbing didn't work.

He had gotten up at five so he could bathe and shave unhurriedly, then called the auto club to get directions to Silver Creek, a place not even MapQuest seemed to know about. He hadn't brought his good clothes with him, mostly just T-shirts and jeans. He found a pair of clean black denims he hadn't yet worn, then reached in the bottom of the suitcase to find one of his newer T-shirts, one emblazoned with the logo of a new New York club where he'd played a year ago, and pressed out the packing folds with the iron he found on the closet shelf.

When he had showered and arranged himself in a reasonable way—face meticulously shaven, hair washed and neatly combed, shirt tucked in—he got into his car and drove from the Best Western toward the Days Inn, which was, to his surprise, at the next light.

The streets were still quiet, shiny after an early mist that beaded his windshield, the silver sky fissured like marble, the red and green of the traffic lights and cars protruding in bold relief from the flat gray of the wet, early morning streets. He pulled into the lot as light misting thickened to light rain.

This was not something he particularly wanted to do. Through his night of fitful sleep, he'd remembered his tears, actually *crying* over this woman. Whatever he felt about her now, however undefined, was clearly uncomfortable. It wasn't that he wanted to be with her—it was *so* over after all this time. He just wanted to clear out whatever lingering webs of hurtful memory still cluttered his mind, and then move on.

And since he'd been raised not to be an ass, running out of Sylvia's house like some loser would nag at him until he did something about it.

He knocked softly three times on her door.

When she answered, he couldn't help but float his gaze down, then upwards again. Her hair, still fluffed out in crinkly curls, was lighter than he remembered from last night. She was dressed in white shorts and a short-sleeved green tank. Her eyes looked rested, bright. Clearly, she'd been up a while.

He had planned to smile, as if everything was cool, say a few appropriate words, then be on his way. But when he saw her, he felt his tongue thicken and the smile didn't come the way he'd planned.

"Sorry, I know it's early and everything," he started. "I just want to say I'm sorry about last night, running off like that. The stress and all, you know, with Daddy missing and everything, I guess…"

"Julian." She opened the door wider, letting the morning light spill onto her face. "Why don't you come inside? You're standing in the rain."

8

He hadn't realized it was raining, even though his face was covered with water. He hadn't particularly wanted to come inside, to be there any longer than necessary, but he didn't know how not to, so he stepped inside the tiny motel room while she closed the door behind him.

"Like I said," he began again. His hands were hot and moist. He stuck them both in the back pockets of his jeans. "I'm sorry about running off last night."

Almost every inch of the room was filled, but there seemed to be a sense of order about it. A pot of coffee, buried behind bottles of toiletries, made gurgling sounds on the bath area counter top. White towels sat neatly folded on racks near the mirror. Two full-size beds filled most of the space—one with stacks of laundry folded on top of the paisley spread, the other with disheveled sheets and pillows thrown about. On a luggage rack near the TV, a full suitcase sat open, and on the table near the window sat boxes of cereal and crackers, bags of nuts, a few apples, and a half-dozen bananas.

It looked remarkably like his motel room, as if someone had taken up permanent residence, except for the large wooden artist's easel near the television with a blank canvas sitting on it.

"You want some coffee?" She looked back toward the gurgling pot. "It's the worst coffee I've ever made."

He smiled a little. "Naw. Thanks."

For another minute they both just stood in the middle of the room, trapped by a silence so awkward Julian coughed just to interrupt it.

"Look, Julian," she said. "I'm really so sorry about Simon. I was so upset when I heard. I just hope he didn't—"

He narrowed his eyes as he cut her off, and started to turn toward the door.

"He's all right. I'll find him."

"I didn't mean…of course, you'll find him. Simon's strong. If anybody can survive all this, he can."

She smiled, leveled an assuring gaze at him. "And knowing you, you won't stop until you find him."

Some people just knew they had a great smile, and Velmyra must have learned this early on. Milk-white sea-washed pearls set perfectly within the strong bones of her face, her smile was something she could measure against the moment, time to best effect: to tease, cajole, gain advantage, defuse an argument. Right now, she had caught his testiness in her perfect teeth and rendered it numb.

"Anyway, he's lucky to have you for a son."

A decent thing to say. Her smile tried to ignite the one buried deep in him that somehow could not surface to his face.

"Well. OK. Thanks," he said.

Light blinked through the parted drapes on the long window facing the parking lot, as if the sun, held captive by a thick cloud, had been set free. Realizing his shoulders had been tight, arched slightly up the whole time he'd been in the room, he let them down, and reached up to massage the side of his neck.

She played with her fingers, interlacing them, in and out. The fact that she seemed no more comfortable than he did pleased him a little.

"Well." She let out a breath heavy with resignation. "What happened with us doesn't matter much now, does it? I mean, everything's so…horrible. You know how I felt about Simon. He was always so kind to me. I hate that he's missing. So, truce?"

He remembered the bond between Simon and Velmyra. During their engagement, when Julian brought her to his father's for Sunday afternoon dinner, Simon seemed to step a little lighter in Velmyra's presence; chairs were held back, doors held open, jokes told in a doting fatherly tease framed by an almost boyish smile. A special spark lit Simon's eyes, his voice pitched to a lighter lilt, and Velmyra obliged with smooth but genuine affection.

That last evening when she'd left him, the words they shot back and forth lit up the space between them like bright shards of glass. One particular shard had nicked his heart—she'd accused him of being selfish, uncaring. Nothing she said had hurt him worse than that. Afterward, the boil of their anger cooled to glacial silence. Remembering, he was angry all over again.

But the anger crowding his mind did little to erase the fact that right now, he really wanted nothing more than to trace the smooth lines of her mouth with the tip of his finger.

Truce. Julian looked away in a manner that told her he was weighing the word.

He gave a quick half-nod, and glanced over at the white canvas sitting on the easel. "What you working on?"

She shrugged her shoulders. "Nothing. As you can see. Haven't been able to paint since everything happened."

He nodded. "Your mama and them OK?"

She sat down on the edge of the bed and rubbed a hand against the back of her neck, telling him, in the language of people who once knew each other well, that she was fraught with worry.

She sighed again. "They're OK. Family's scattered everywhere, though. Cousins in Atlanta. My sister and them in Houston. Momma and Daddy came here to Baton Rouge, just like half of New Orleans. They...lost everything. But they've got insurance. They wanna go back as soon as they can."

Julian knew where her parents lived, and he'd heard about all the water Pontchartrain Park took on when the levee broke. At least Simon's house only had a few feet, for what it was worth. Her folks' house, he figured—the house she grew up in—was probably destroyed.

"I'm sorry."

She nodded. "Well, *my* house in Uptown did OK, you know, it's not too far from Sylvia. We were so lucky."

"That's good." It hadn't occurred to him that she might be suffering, too. The storm and flood were so easy to take personally, everyone buried so deep in their own troubles, but truth was that no one seemed to escape its effect.

No matter how flawless they looked.

She took a sharp breath. "Look, I just want you to know that if I can do anything to help you find your father..."

He felt the smallest smile emerge, softening his face. "Thanks, but I think I know where he is. I'm on my way there now, in fact. So I better be going."

"Well, OK. Like I said, if you need help.... I loved your father. Simon was like another daddy to me."

His smile grew, and he nodded. "Well, Daddy was always crazy about you. In fact, he got really pissed at me when everything happened, like, you know..." He stopped, hoping she hadn't caught the small note of irritation.

"Like it was all your fault? I hope you told him it wasn't."

In fact, he hadn't told Simon much of anything. "It's over," his ragged voice confessed when Simon had asked, "How's our girl doin'?" and the throbbing vein in Julian's temple had warned him not to press. But the breakup seemed as hard for Simon as for Julian. Maybe even harder, as Julian had watched loneliness pale his father's deep caramel eyes in the weeks after. He had brought this lovely young woman into his father's life, not realizing that, after a time, whenever Simon had looked at Velmyra, he'd seen family. He'd already lost a wife; now he had lost a daughter, too.

He told Velmyra where he was going, and she smiled, remembering stories of how he been dragged there as a kid, and how much Simon just loved to talk about it. He'd even bent her ear a couple of times, when Julian wasn't around, about Silver Creek.

"Well, I guess I better go," he said, looking out the window. "Looks like it might be a nice day after all."

When he finally left her room and got into his car, the rain had let up and the sky was brightening into pale blue. The air felt steamy, the day heating up. He rolled down his window and as he pulled out of the lot, he caught a glimpse of her in his sideview mirror. She was running toward his car, waving a hand.

He stopped. She leaned over, looked into his window, her shoulders hunched and arms folded across her chest.

"Hey, this is just an idea. If you don't like it, feel free to say no. I won't mind."

He hadn't expected it, and didn't know how to respond. So he just said, "Sure, get in." She said she'd always been curious about the place, and she wasn't doing anything except sitting around worrying about her folks and her friends. That, and waiting. Waiting for a plumber to call, waiting for her electricity to come back on, waiting for her folks' insurance guy to give a damn. Waiting for the whole nightmare to be over, and everything to be the way it used to be. She said she just wanted to get away, and a drive to Silver Creek sounded like a trip to Shangri-la, someplace away from Baton Rouge and anything that reminded her of New Orleans.

So they pulled out of the lot, onto the slick streets and under a warming sun, and then onto the highway, toward his father's home.

It was when Julian was about eleven that the stories began about the Silver Creek land. Simon had a captive audience in Julian on gumbo night. Julian would pull up a chair to the big round table in the tight kitchen and start his homework while the mixed scents of sausage, shrimp, chicken, and okra swirled in the steam, almost potent enough to taste.

"Pay attention to what I'm saying," Simon would say, stopping in the middle of stirring rice to point an admonishing spoon at Julian. "Someday that land's gonna be all yours."

Simon told Julian how his grandfather Moses, a freed slave turned sharecropper, had inherited the land from his master and mulched it with sweat and blood. It had been left first to Jacob, Simon's father, and Jacob's first cousin, Maree, and then, upon their deaths, to the next generation of Fortiers—Maree's daughter Genevieve and Simon.

Simon bragged as if his name were on the deed of the Taj Mahal. Two hundred and forty acres of sugar-rich bottom land, black and fertile as a young womb. Pines, magnolias, live oaks by the hundreds, and honeysuckle and jasmine that turned the air to perfume. And the creek snaking through it like a thick vein of silver.

Wistfulness played in Simon's eyes when he talked about how nightfall wrapped Silver Creek in darkness so velvety you "could feel it on your skin," and set off a symphony of cicadas and night-birds that "could drown out a brass band." About how Auntie Maree, his father's first cousin, had yoked him to her apron strings until he could craft a perfect roux. And how Jacob had taught Simon the ways of fishermen and hunters, so he'd never know an empty supper table.

"Uh, huh." Julian would flip to the next page in his geometry book. When Simon went on like this, it meant one thing—supper would be late, and he'd have to cut short his practice time. But he always indulged his father the endless paeans to the skyward-reaching oaks and clear-water streams and earth so sweet it could grow damn near anything. The more Simon talked, the more excited he got, the more loose and free his spice-sprinkling fingers, the more delicious the gumbo. But Julian was more interested in mastering a page in the Arban trumpet method book than in any talk about land he couldn't care less to ever own.

The first time Julian remembered seeing Silver Creek, he must have been four. The last time he saw it was just after Ladeena died. The creek that Simon always described as a ribbon of sparkling silver winding through rich earth and shaded by luxuriant trees and thickets, was, to Julian, just a hot, bug ridden swamp. Simon tried to teach him hunting, but the buckshot noise hurt his sensitive ears. He was equally unimpressed with the joys of fishing, lacking the stomach for worms and fish guts. The only good part was when Simon and Genevieve decided to throw down in the kitchen. Then, everything was good.

Crawfish etouffee from fresh-caught mudbugs, red beans and rice with homemade andouille, tomato-ey shrimp Creole, and peppery gumbo with all manner of whatever swam or crawled thrown in, and fresh herbs and spices from Genevieve's garden that made every inhaled breath a joy. Simon invited everybody he knew from the nearby town for supper. As impatient as Julian was with logging in country time, he had to admit, the food made it worth the trip.

But after his twelfth summer, Julian did not return to Silver Creek until he was eighteen, for his mother's burial. And then, never again. He and Simon rarely talked about it any more. Julian had other plans that did not include spending his life holed away in some backwater when there was so much world to get out and see.

At thirty-one, after his engagement to Velmyra ended and he was itching for change, Julian had packed up his trumpet and headed for New York, and any other part of the world where he could lose himself in his own, self-made blues. Simon's steps slowed, his eyes paled, his shoulders fell. He had been to a war in Korea, cooked in foreign kitchens in exotic villages, seen so much of the world—and still longed for home, talking about his land the way some men talked about their first love. That his only son didn't share his southern-boy homing instinct was more than heartbreaking, it was an assault to his history.

But Julian couldn't understand his father's obsession with a stretch of flat, lifeless land called Silver Creek.

"Do you mind if we turn down the air a little?"

"Oh. Sorry."

He reached over to dial down the air conditioner, which had been blasting since they left Baton Rouge. To Julian's mind, the noise helped to quell the awkwardness dividing them.

For a half hour they had been driving westward over the long bridge stretching across the Atchafalaya River, where the giant cypresses and pines, their thick trunks moored deep in the mirroring swamp, filtered flashes of sun as the car made its way over the jigsawing wetlands. As they crossed the broad basin, there was no sound except the air conditioner and the wail of the tenor saxophone from a radio station just outside of Baton Rouge. Grover Washington—Julian recognized the silky tone, the post-seventies groove. He tried to listen to the music, nodding his head to the rhythm, his arm resting lightly on the top of the steering wheel. Feigning nonchalance, when actually there was a constant nerve-jitter in the pit of his stomach.

When he'd first turned on the radio earlier, bad news had blared mercilessly. All about the hurricane, the levees, the current state of the whole town and its nearby parishes. The government failures. The second hurricane that had followed, adding insult to injury, another blow to an area already bludgeoned by the first. The missing people and the ones who were not—the ones who floated face up in the flood waters, bloated, found at last.

But there were a few good stories—the reconnection of loved ones once lost and returned to each other, the rescues of old women or young children on rooftops, who told their tales of hopelessness, heat, exhaustion, and fever dreams of heaven, until the whir of chopper blades sounded like the battering wings of angels. The volunteers who'd rescued starving dogs destined for disease and death. The tearful cries of defiant citizens from their outposts of exile—Houston, Dallas, Denver—determined to return and rebuild.

But after a while they had both had enough. "Do you mind?" she said. And Julian was relieved, too, when she reached a hand across to the radio, inviting Grover to float them away to a mindless refuge of fusion funk.

Soon, Velmyra broke the silence, but not the way he would have preferred. She wanted to talk about his career.

"So, anyway, like I was saying the other night. I saw you on *The Tonight Show*," she began, proud at having taken a good whack at the icy barrier between them. "It was a repeat, I know. But I had missed it the first time, a couple of years ago, so I was glad I got to see it."

This was not cool. Not at all what he wanted to talk about. She went on praising his playing, telling him how happy she had been for his success (despite what they had been through, but that was all past, wasn't it?) and how she'd even taped the show so her mother could watch it.

He said very little, an occasional nodding grunt, and she seemed perfectly fine with a conversation that was decidedly lopsided, her questions exponentially longer than his answers. How did it feel, being famous like that? Did people recognize him on the streets? What about the travel? Did it get old after a while, never sleeping in his own bed? And what was Jay Leno like?

"I mean I know this is what you wanted, but is it, you know, as great as you expected it to be? Does it—"

"Velmyra," he interrupted, gritting his throbbing jaw. "I can't play right now."

There. He had said it. And he realized that, since the accident, it was the first time he'd ever said those words.

"What do you mean?"

"I mean, I can *play*, a little, for a little while. But I had a car accident several months ago. My jaw…I had surgery. The doctor said it should be as good as new, but it's…slow. And I tried to come back too soon. Right now, my embouchure is crap. Nothing feels right."

Out of the corner of his eye, he could see, feel her looking at him, eyebrows raised, eyes stunned, lips parted. She was silent a moment, then turned to stare out the windshield.

"Oh, my God. I didn't know. I'm so sorry."

"It's OK. I'll be able to play after a while. I'm just impatient."

The awkward silence began again. He was testy now. He fidgeted in his seat, lowered the armrest, and put his elbow on it. Adjusted the seat with the knob under it.

"Damn rental cars," he said.

Now he was angry, at what he didn't know. Why did she have to bring that up?

Part of him wanted to ride in silence for the rest of the trip, and part of him wanted to tell her about how he'd cried when he'd come out of surgery and felt the huge bandage on his face. About how it felt to have to cancel a boatload of gigs. About the embarrassing comeback disaster in Japan, at only the hottest club in the whole damn country. Not to mention his band.

The quintet he led—Antoine Johnson on piano, Hector Rubalcaba on bass, Walter Haymaker on tenor, and Jeffrey Mobile on drums, all good friends—had been with him through fat times and lean, but had all taken gigs (temporarily, they said) while he healed. They had to make a living, didn't they? They would be back, for sure, the minute he was ready.

Sure.

And part of him wanted to say something to her that would make her feel what he was feeling now. Regret. Anger at the past. Something like, *Why'd you marry that dude, so quick after we split? How could you have? What was that all about?* Or, *How soon did you realize what a horrible mistake you'd made?*

But he said nothing.

They drove on mostly in silence. Velmyra made an occasional comment about the landscape, about how she wished she had her sketchpad with her, then reached in her huge cloth shoulder bag and realized she did. She made etchings on the paper with a charcoal pencil; cypress trees, egrets, oaks dripping moss. An eagle in flight, a pelican perched on a telephone pole. They stopped for gas and bottled water and clean restrooms, and Velmyra bought potato chips and orange juice. When they got back in the car, Julian looked at his map, then turned off the interstate onto a smaller highway.

In a few minutes they were miles into deep country, and the sun sat higher now above tall pines in variations on a theme of green: the pale greens of saplings, the deep summer greens of the mature trees. Julian stretched his shoulders and looked across the road at row after row of straightback evergreens and wispy clouds pasted against the piercing blue. He felt better now, and thought, *this is not so bad.* The air was cooler among the trees, the sky bluer. It was actually good to get away from the city.

They drove on, and he sensed something had changed with Velmyra. Her silence now had an uneasiness about it; she blinked her eyes the way she used to years ago, when she had something that needed saying on her mind.

"I'm really sorry, Julian." She was shaking her head, her eyes apologetic. "I didn't know anything about your accident. Sylvia didn't tell me. It must have been horrible for you. For your career, and everything."

Sympathy always made him feel a little uncomfortable, softening his defense, breaking him down. But still, he was impressed that she had been thinking about it all this time. He sensed her comment was genuine, and he allowed it to comfort him.

"It's OK. I just need to wait. Work my way back into playing slowly. I'll be all right. Daddy kept telling me not to jump back into it, but I wouldn't listen."

She nodded, smiling slightly. "Speaking of your father, how's his friend, Mr. Parmenter? The one who owned the restaurant? Did he make it through the storm OK? I know your dad and he were close."

Parmenter. She had a good memory. He wanted to tell her that the man who'd shamelessly ripped off his father was just fine for someone who should be in jail.

"Parmenter? He made it through the storm OK but his health's real bad. Told me he wants to see Daddy as soon as I find him. Says Daddy 'owes him something.' Strange, considering how much he owes Daddy."

"What do you mean?"

He hadn't talked to anybody about this. But what the hell. He felt like talking now. He was away from the city, on a country road, sheltered by tall trees. He felt safe. There was something about being here in the country, and being with the woman he once believed he could trust with his life, that made him feel he could tell the truth.

He turned off the narrow road onto one even narrower and full of gravel that spat up like popping corn against the undercarriage of the car. Trees hugged the roadside, their thick branches trellising the road like a dark, shading arch.

"There's a story about that," he began. He slowed the car and leaned back into the seat, his wrist resting on the top of the steering wheel.

"Years ago, when Daddy was young, he was just about the best damn chef in New Orleans."

9

Two Louisiana boys, one a tall and strapping blond, the other as wiry as a willow branch with skin the rich brown of live oak bark, came back from their tours of duty itching to begin the lives spared by an undeclared and nameless war. Matthew Parmenter had been thirty-one and Simon Fortier twenty-two when they met in a MASH in Korea. Country-mannered, with Crescent City grit beneath his nails, Matthew had been a supply sergeant, and young Simon, fresh from a wooded backwater called Silver Creek more than a hundred miles from Parmenter's home, brought the Fortier family recipes to his job as an army cook.

It was the dark, nutty, spicy roux of Simon's gumbo that seasoned their friendship. Sitting in the mess tent at dinner, Parmenter tasted the savory sauce, and a single spoonful brought New Orleans to mind. A second one, and he was walking through its jasmine-scented gardens of New Orleans and palm-laden courtyards, his homesickness kept at bay by French Quarter cooking half a world away. Parmenter lingered over Simon's artfully prepared meals and took a liking to the homeboy chef. Their conversations over coffee and bread pudding ran to boyhood stories, teenage tales, and boredom with Army life. When the war finally ended, they shook hands and parted, each heading back to their respective Louisiana homes.

Home just long enough to shake foreign dirt from his shoes and an odd war from his mind, Matthew wandered the French Quarter one sun-blazed Sunday after church, and stumbled upon a hand-scribbled chalkboard menu outside a tiny café. Hungry and aimless, he stopped in to try his luck with the red beans and rice. One spoonful of the familiar sauce and he smiled, asking to see the cook. When Simon strolled out in a white apron splotched with gumbo roux, Matthew grabbed him into a bear hug.

"You?" Matthew said, a smile lighting his lean, suntanned face. "What are you doing here?"

Simon's grin was electric, his brown eyes sparkling. "Didn't I always tell you I was the best cook in the South? Where'd you think I'd be?"

The two swapped wartime memories and peacetime plans while Matthew downed three bowls of Simon's special. More than a year passed before Matthew's vision, planted that day in the back of his brain, bloomed into something worthy of words. With the blond man's small inheritance from a recently deceased uncle, and Simon's wizardry at a kitchen stove, Matthew conceived an elegant French Quarter restaurant that could play host to the world. Down-home friendly, uptown chic. High toned, yet easy mannered. Dainty white candles set on fine white linen spread across intimate tables, courtyard seating out back beneath blue sky and sun dappling through palmetto leaves. A Creole restaurant with Simon as head chef and Matthew as owner and manager.

Within six months, Parmenter's Creole Kitchen opened its doors in a run-down space oozing rustic charm on Chartres Street next to an Irish bar. And in six more months, Friday and Saturday night reservations at premium tables were booked weeks into the future. If the prime location and the tony yet casual atmosphere brought first-time customers in by the dozens, the menu brought them back again and again.

From soup to nuts, the entire menu was superb. Simon's Original Belle Rive Bread Pudding, sumptuously dressed in dark rum and cherry liqueur, made mouths water, and the crawfish jambalaya with a side of spicy boudin disappeared from plates within minutes after it was served. Even the Blanche Dubois Mint Julep Sundae, hastily concocted by Simon at Matthew's request, was an instant success. But the red beans and rice starred on the small menu, barely altered from Auntie Maree's recipe, and before long famous politicians, actors, athletes, and musicians from all over the world pulled up to the tables and rolled their eyes dreamily between mouthfuls of the delectable Creole fare.

By its fifth year, Parmenter's had been mentioned in no less than four national culinary magazines, and even enjoyed a paragraph of praise in the *New Yorker*. But the restaurant's fate was sealed one afternoon when the president of the United States reserved the restaurant for a night and brought in a party of nine. Each ordered the red beans and rice, and each got another order to go.

Years passed. Hungry people came in droves, then told their friends, who also came and then told their friends. Simon was doing what he loved best in a state-of-the-art kitchen for people who were as grateful as they were hungry and free with their praise. Matthew kept the bottom line steeped in black ink and ran the restaurant with army efficiency. In time both men got married; Simon to Ladeena, his doe-eyed childhood sweetheart from Pointe Louree, and Matthew to Clarisse, a petite blond legal secretary who'd winked at him daily from her cross-legged perch at the restaurant bar. While Matthew remained childless, Simon sired a son.

It was when Julian was in high school that Matthew's new idea took shape; why not package the red beans and rice in a dry mix and sell it at the restaurant? A little bit of New Orleans to take back to Cleveland, Washington, or Kansas City. A souvenir of a sumptuous dining experience near the mouth of the Mississippi.

"It's a natural," Parmenter said. "People will buy it like crazy."

Simon frowned. He used fresh herbs. No way to substitute dry ones and get the same result. "And besides," he said. "My recipe's not for sale."

But the mix wouldn't have to taste exactly like the restaurant dish; it only had to be a reminder. And the family secrets of the recipe would be guarded like gold.

After hours of wrangling, Simon agreed to concoct a special dry-herb version of his family recipe. Wrapped in clear plastic packaging with a colorful label and an artfully tied red ribbon, it was sold in the front of the store near the cash register, along with T-shirts and postcards of the restaurant. Matthew was right. The mix, Parmenter's Creole Kitchen Red Beans and Rice, was an immediate and huge success.

Velmyra turned to Julian, perplexed.

"So what was the problem? It sounds like things worked out OK."

Julian slowed the car to accommodate an S-curve in the road. "Things worked out great," he said, "for Matthew Parmenter."

He breathed a sigh, then went on. "Parmenter offered Daddy a flat fee for the new recipe and the right to reproduce it. Ten thousand dollars. More than he'd ever seen in his life, so he grabbed it. But Parmenter said the mix would be sold in the restaurant—he never said anything about taking it to national grocery chains. That's what he did, though. A year and a half after the deal the stuff was everywhere: the French Market, souvenir shops, grocery stores as far away as New York and California. Even airport shops all over Louisiana and the South. I saw an article about Parmenter a few years ago in *New Orleans Business Weekly* about *his* red beans and rice mix. He'd grossed millions from it."

Velmyra let out a long, low whistle. "You're kidding."

"Daddy took his ten grand and fixed the roof on the house, and helped me pay my tuition at Tulane," Julian said. "Parmenter took his money, bought that fancy mansion in the Garden District, and retired."

Velmyra nodded soberly. "I see."

They were silent for a while, as Julian negotiated the snaking turns through wooded backcountry. When the road straightened again, he turned to look at Velmyra.

"Daddy never complained. When I saw the stuff on a shelf in a deli in Manhattan, I asked Daddy about it. He just laughed it off. Said it wasn't his best business deal."

"Daddy never cared all that much about money. It was never that much of a big deal to him. But Parmenter knew what he was doing; he knew he was cheating Daddy. And Daddy still treated him like his best friend."

"So you believe Parmenter deliberately took advantage of your father."

"What do you think?" Julian snapped toward her. "When I found out about it, Daddy and me, we had it out. I told him the man was getting rich off of his recipe, and he should go to Parmenter and demand a fair share of the profits. Or get a lawyer. Daddy thought I was nuts. He blew me off."

"Like you said, Simon never cared that much about money."

"It wasn't so much about the money. It was about friendship. It was about what's fair. Would you have done that to a friend?"

Velmyra tilted her head thoughtfully toward the window. "I'd like to think not."

"Exactly."

"I get your point. But maybe your father thought it was about friendship, too."

"What do you mean?"

"Maybe he thought keeping his friend was more important than money. Maybe he thought about the money and the friendship, and chose the friendship. And if…ooh, be careful."

Julian swerved to miss a squirrel darting across the road as he made another sharp turn.

"I think this is the right way," he said. "At least I hope it is."

At the right of the turn he spied an old barn with chipped red paint and slouching as if it could be tipped over with a good strong push.

"There. That's the barn. This is the right way. We're almost there."

Velmyra turned to look at the barn and the stand of trees surrounding it. Banks of trees and brush hugged the road. As they drove further, taller trees canopied the road and veiled it in dim gray light, almost completely obscuring the sun. This was the part Julian remembered as a boy, being in the deep country surrounded by so much lushness it was almost scary, caught in the dark huddle of trees, nested in a mystery of green.

"This was what Daddy cared about. Land. Land was always Daddy's fortune."

Velmyra gazed out the window. "Well, it's gorgeous land."

They drove down the path, the Neon kicking up red dust and rocks and bouncing along on the uneven grading. When they reached the end of the lane, Julian pointed to an old cabin nestled between two live oak trees.

Julian looked at Velmyra. "We're here."

"This is it?"

"Yeah."

Genevieve lived here alone now. The front of the cabin, the patchy siding showing more raw wood than paint, the crude, warped cypress floorboards of the porch and sagging eaves, gave nothing away; it looked the way it always had when he was a young boy. Untended, like no one was home.

But the certainty that his father was not here descended from the air around him, worked its way into his throbbing temples, his shoulders, and his back, and settled over his eyes like a cloud, darkening everything in view.

"I don't have to go inside." He looked over at Velmyra. "I know he's not here."

"How do you know?"

"I just do."

Julian got out, leaned against the car door, arms folded across his chest, his head down. Velmyra got out, walked to the porch, and knocked on the door. When she turned the doorknob, the door gave out a squeaking groan.

"It's open."

When Julian joined her on the porch, they went inside. It was a sea of white; white sheets covering most of the furniture, white dust covering everything else. There was a faded yellow and orange plaid sofa and a recliner covered in green velour. A chrome-legged table of yellow Formica and four chrome-trimmed vinyl kitchen chairs sat near a window. A small ash coffee table, a china cabinet of knotted pine, and an old portable Magnovox television atop an older television console took up space in a tiny living room that smelled of damp wood, mildew, and old bacon grease.

"There must be someone close by." Velmyra touched a lace doily on the back of the recliner. "The place was unlocked."

Julian looked at her with a wry half-smile. "It's unlocked because we're in the country. Nobody ever locks anything around here."

Velmyra nodded, smiling. "Right."

Julian walked around the dusty room, absently fingering the backs of chairs and the tops of tables, thinking about his father's house in the city, covered in brown sludge and consumed in mold.

"If you had told me a year ago that this place would look like a palace compared to Daddy's house in New Orleans, I would've thought you were crazy."

The walk through the kitchen against the unenven floors took him slightly uphill, then level, then down, as the settling floorboards squeaked beneath his shoes. A swarm of memories nested in his head: the steaming heat of the damp kitchen on summer evenings, sniffing the Old Bay spice can while Simon and Aunt Genevieve prepared dinner from Auntie Maree's sacred recipes with fresh Creole tomatoes and herbs his mother Ladeena had picked from the garden, and whatever Simon had caught that morning in the creek.

In the deep backwoods of memory, Aunt Genevieve hummed church songs as she rolled out dough for biscuits. *This little light of mine, I'ma gonna let it shine…* She sprinted around the kitchen like a woman half her age, snapping her fingers at him—*Bring me that bucket of crawdads from the porch*—or scolding him for not wiping his feet before he placed them on the pockmarked linoleum.

With closed eyes, he could smell the raw fish laid out on the table waiting for Simon's gutting knife, the rich spices of a tomato-ey Creole sauce bubbling on the stove while his father stirred plump white rice in a cast iron pot. He was still stranded in the sepia fog of a childhood summer day when Velmyra came in the kitchen.

Mist glazed Julian's eyes. "Well. I guess I'm back to square one."

"I'm sorry, Julian."

He took out his handkerchief and wiped his face.

He was silent a moment, then said, "Cousin Genevieve must be staying somewhere else. It looks like she hasn't been here for a while."

He pondered this a moment. He hadn't seen her since the last time he was here, when his mother died.

He took a deep breath, shook away the memory.

"I'm gonna go over and see Mama's grave before we go. If you want to you can stay here and I'll come back for you, or you can go with me and wait in the car…just, you know, whatever you want to do."

"Is it OK if I go with you?"

He smiled at her through the bars of dust-moted sun and nodded.

"Sure. If you don't mind stepping through a lot of high weeds. This is deep country, you know."

The Neon rambled down a rutted path so thick with brush, branches scraped the sides of the car. When they came to a clearing where a brilliant patch of wildflowers trembled in the breeze, he stopped and stared at them.

Reading his intention, Velmyra nodded and smiled. "Great idea."

They trekked through the bramble and brush to get to the clearing, and a meadow full of sunflowers, brown-eyed susans, evening primrose, and passion-flowers stood out in blinding bold yellows and purples while golden monarch butterflies flitted between them. Gnarled live oaks stood over them like sentinels, Spanish moss dripping from them like the long locks of gray-haired women. Even in the deepening sun of late summer, the dew-moistened velvet of the flowers and the blaze of color dazzled Julian enough to suspend his dispirited mood. When they had gathered a clump of thirty or more blooms into a bouquet, Julian stripped enough Spanish moss from one of the oaks to wind it around the stems and tie into a bow.

"Beautiful," Velmyra's smile widened. "In the city, this would have cost a fortune."

He looked across the field and pointed toward the tallest tree. "I think it might be over that way. We can get there quicker if we walk across, instead of driving around."

They trampled across the field in their sneakers, high-stepping over cattails and dandelions and clover and every type of weed until they found the small ruin of a stone church and its yard, where several headstones of white rock, dating back to the 1800s and most with the name FORTIER emblazoned across the front, tilted like tall, drunken chessmen in the deep grass.

Only one of the old headstones stood perfectly erect: the one with MOSES FORTIER, his great-grandfather, chiseled in. The gritty, chipped headstone for Julian's grandparents Jacob and Liza leaned so far toward the ground that Julian couldn't straighten it, and the stone for Auntie Maree leaned as far in the other direction. They came to a stop at a newer, double headstone glinting in a shaft of sidelong light; beneath the FORTIER chiseled across the top was his mother's name, and next to it SIMON, b. 1929, d --. Julian wondered what year would have to be etched into the slick granite. Was this the year? And if it was, would he be able to fulfill his father's last wish? *Put me down beside your mama.*

Julian glanced at Velmyra, who was strolling among the headstones, dusting off the soil on the engravings with her fingers and squatting to read the names and dates of his ancestors. To his surprise, he didn't mind her coming along after all. But he wondered if it would have been better for him if she hadn't; then, he could have let his anger rise and consume him, and boil over into whatever it would be.

If she were not here, he would have been free to do what he'd often done as a child when the world had gone all wrong. He would have found the biggest stick he could and flailed away with all his might against the biggest tree he could find, until he'd chiseled a gash into the bark and chips flew and disappeared into the wind. And then he would have gone down to the creek where as a boy he tried hard not to learn to fish, and sat down on the nearest rock, and cried.

But he was not alone, and when Velmyra gently wiped a clump of dirt from the surface of his grandfather's headstone with a tissue, he felt a quieting in his chest. So he squatted down to prop the flowers up against the base of his mother's headstone. As he did, a yellow butterfly lighted on the top of the stone near the family's name. He wondered for a moment where this butterfly had been, where it was going and how it was possible for something so delicate to survive more than a minute in a world where life seemed so fragile.

"I wish I'd met your mother." Velmyra walked toward him and stood, both hands fisted on her hips, looking down at the headstone. "I remember the pictures you showed me. She was beautiful."

Julian smiled. He never thought of her that way when he was a child, but yes, she was. A stately woman, two inches taller than his father, with high patrician cheekbones like her Seminole ancestors and skin the color of a ripe banana. When he was a boy, she'd always been his ally, taking his side in small father-son wars of spirit and will; when Julian wanted to spend his summers in New Orleans and play brass band gigs with his friends instead of coming to Silver Creek, his mother's words—*Simon, let him stay in town and play his music*—tipped the scale in his favor.

That Julian felt no particular affinity for the land his father cherished was no secret; that his mother took it to heart was testimony to her powers of perception and maternal genius. She allowed her son's disaffection, but told her husband, "Give him time." Now, seeing the high grasses and scrub and wildflowers flecking the luxuriant green with dabs of color, and the open sky's blaze of blue broken with snowy tufts of clouds backlit by an extravagant sun, he found it quite beautiful. His father's eyes drank in this miracle every day, yet Julian had never really seen it before.

They headed back toward the car. Velmyra stumbled on a rock and Julian caught the tip of her elbow, and she grabbed his arm and almost pulled him down. She let out a little squeal of a laugh, which made him laugh. The sound of their conjoined laughter felt oddly pleasurable, and without thinking, he did something he hadn't done the whole day; he walked her to her side of the car, and opened the door for her.

An old reflex, reborn. Something his father, a model of southern gentlemanliness, insisted that he learn to do. The New York women taught him differently; they were out of the car and waiting for him before he'd made it to the other side. The memory rushed back in waves. Him opening her door, her sitting and lifting her legs with a graceful swivel into the car, then gathering in her skirt before leaning over to unlock his door—for more than a year, this had been the step-ball-change, one routine in the detailed choreography of their romance.

He opened his own door and sat, not looking at her, but sensing the awkwardness between them, as if he'd seen a fleeting glimpse of a stranger's nakedness. He started the car and the silence swelled, the past rearing up and hovering in the air between them like water-filled balloons.

"You thirsty? I could use a soda or something." He caught her eye and she looked grateful for the break in the quiet.

"Yeah. It's really hot, isn't it?"

He remembered a place just off the main road before they would get into Local, if it was still there. A general store of sorts, just like in the movies, where they sold tackle and bait and nickel candy and pickles in a jar. They pulled out onto the gravelly road, but before they'd driven more than a few feet, a huge pickup with oversized tires and an extended cab honked its horn. The truck stopped in front of the Neon, blocking their path.

The engine noise stopped and out hopped a young white man with a gangly, Ichabod Crane frame and wispy, shoulder-length, dirty blond hair. His faded jeans ended just below his knees, and his oversized Saints jersey hung loosely on his thin frame. He walked toward them, his shoulders slightly hunched.

"Excuse me. You folks wouldn't know the Fortiers, would you?"

Julian got out of the car.

"Julian. Julian Fortier." Julian extended his hand. "My father's family owns this place."

The young man brushed a clump of hair from his bright blue eyes, smiled broadly with straight white teeth, and shook Julian's hand. "Kevin Larouchette. I'm looking for Simon Fortier."

Julian and Velmyra exchanged looks. "We're looking for him too," Julian said. "My father was in New Orleans during the flood. He stayed through it, and....well, we haven't found him yet."

"Oh, gosh. I am so sorry. I sure hope you find him."

"We thought he might be here." Julian folded both arms across his chest. "But there's no sign of him."

"No, maybe if he'd of been here things wouldn'tna happened the way they did. With the land and everything."

"What do you mean?" Velmyra asked.

"You mean you don't know?"

Julian hunched his shoulders. "Know what?'

The young man looked down at the brown earth at his feet and shook his head. Then looked back up at Julian.

"Sir, I'm sorry to be the one to tell you. This land, your daddy's land, has been sold."

10

They had been sitting around the table for a few minutes when Velmyra looked at her watch. "Julian, why don't we go get something to eat and bring it back here? We haven't really eaten anything all day."

It was true, they hadn't eaten, but with the news about his father's land, food was the last thing on his mind. From his childhood, though, he remembered something his father's first cousin was famous for—a well-stocked pantry and freezer full of good food and an open kitchen where friends, family, and kind acquaintances were welcome to walk in and help themselves.

"Cousin G's a great cook, like Daddy—always keeps enough food to feed an army. She won't mind if we eat whatever we find."

Velmyra smiled and nodded. "OK. I'll check out the kitchen."

Earlier, the three of them had stood outside in the yard talking when, from the East, a clap of thunder halted the conversation. And in less than a minute, low clouds like tufted gray wool had gathered and sharpened the air to autumn-crisp, and the wind had picked up and spun the dirt in small circles. Paintbrush strokes of rain raked down from the distant clouds, promising a good soaking on its way. So when the sky released the first few heavy drops, they headed inside the cabin.

Kevin Larouchette was a local boy who'd recently graduated from LSU law school. He had an earnestness that reminded Julian of the young white boys he'd met down by Silver Creek when he'd been a kid, whose faces were marked with an innocence Julian associated with growing up miles away from a city. His sea-blue eyes were large and bright, and on his left forearm just below his elbow he wore a tattoo of a bright yellow bird in flight. Taller than Julian and leggy, the young stranger couldn't have been more than twenty-five. He was all blond hair and right angles, and Julian believed he'd never seen a skinnier man in his life.

His low-pitched southern drawl reverberated in the small room, and he spoke softly, almost apologetically, as if bad news couched in a sympathetic tone could ease the pain. But to Julian no calm delivery could soften the blow that felt like a cold-cock to his face. The Fortier land—gone. Two hundred and some acres of the most beautiful and fertile land in Louisiana, in his father's family since before the Civil War, handed off to strangers. A small knot tightened in Julian's stomach when he imagined how Simon would feel if he knew.

The land could not have been sold fairly, Julian figured. Simon would never have allowed it.

Velmyra came back to the table with a tray holding three Mason jars of what looked like cola. "You're right about the food. There's plenty of it in the freezer. If you're sure your cousin won't mind, I could heat something up. In the meantime, I thought we could all use a drink."

Kevin took a long swig from the jar Velmyra sat down in front of him.

"That's good. That hits the spot."

Then he rocked back in the chair, balancing it on two legs. "Y'all aren't the first this has happened to, by the way. It's been happening all over these parts."

"What's been happening?" Velmyra sat and took a sip from her own glass.

It had become a common occurrence, Kevin explained. Rich, overweight men in summer-weight suits with slit eyes and crooked mouths, cruising the land, just waiting for people to let their guard down so they could descend on their properties like vultures, picking it clean of all the proud black owners, as well as their family legacies.

Land speculators. They were all over, especially in places like this where black folks, land rich and cash poor, had owned parcels of valuable land for generations, and most of the owners no longer lived on the property.

"I been studying on this awhile," Kevin said. "It happened to the Navarettes down the way, the Beauchamps, Smiths, too. Then there was Mr. Parette. That was the worst one. You folks were the last ones, so I knew it was coming."

He described, in detail, how such a thing could happen. Land in Pointe Louree Parish, especially those acres owned by black families, was most often "heirship" property, sifting down through generations from kin to kin without formality, and more often than not, without wills. Legally, when the owner of a piece of land died without a will, all the heirs—children and other family—automatically owned all the land in common, with no one owning any specific part; each simply having an equal share of the total estate. Then, any one of the partners could sell his or her portion to anyone wishing to buy.

And once the new shareholder became part of the group, he was entitled to the full rights of co-ownership, including the right to go to a judge any time and request that the entire estate be auctioned to the highest bidder.

It was designed, Kevin explained, to settle land disputes among families, but it often worked against them, making it easier for developers to pry the property from the unsuspecting family's hands. Just buy your way in for a song, then force a sale. Before anybody knows anything, the family who had a beautiful spread of land for generations has lost all of it.

"That's what happened to you folks," Kevin said. "Somebody bought a share of your land—weaseled their way in—then requested an auction. Then whoever they were working with bid on the land, and got it."

The money from the sale of the land, he said, got divided up between all the owners, after the legal fees were paid.

"Your daddy should have known about the auction, he should have gotten a notice." Kevin tapped his knuckles against the table. "Your property—I looked it up—went for $118,000. About a third of what its worth. And by the time it's divvied up and the legal fees are taken out, we're not talking about a lot of money. Your daddy and all his kin might have got their checks in the mail by now."

Julian and Velmyra looked at each other. The flood. It had wiped out more than just phone lines for weeks. All mail delivery had stopped, and even now had not yet fully resumed.

Julian leaned forward in his chair. "I still don't get how it could have happened. Daddy would never sell his share of this place, even a piece of it. Cousin G either."

"Well, somebody did." Kevin took another drink, then gave Julian a quizzical look. "These guys are slick. All they have to do is find one person willing to sell. And of course they never tell them about the consequences, that all the other owners could easily end up with no land at all."

"What about your daddy's other relatives? You think any of them might've wanted to sell?"

Simon had always said there were some "kin" in California, descendants of his grandfather Moses's sisters, even talked about going out there someday to visit them. Julian studied a worn place in the wide-plank oak floor and scoured his mind for some helpful information, coming up with nothing. He'd been so uninterested in anything having to do with Silver Creek that he barely knew where it was. His father had stopped talking to him about the land years ago.

"We've got a handful of cousins, I think, living out near L.A., but I don't even know their names."

Kevin stroked his chin thoughtfully, then took another swig, emptying his glass. Velmyra got up and refilled it.

"Hey, this is pretty good. Tastes a little like Royal Crown, 'cept it's got a little kick to it. Something else in it?"

Velmyra shrugged. "I don't know. It was in the fridge in a big plastic bottle."

Julian groaned. "Did it have a red seal on the top?"

Velmyra shrugged again. "Maybe. I just opened it."

Julian remembered the sharp, burning edge of the drink from when he was a kid and had dipped into the big cola bottle by mistake. "Well, it's Pepsi. Except it's been spiked with some of Aunt Genevieve's home brew."

Kevin laughed out loud. "Moonshine! Pure corn liquor. Damn. I knew it was making me feel a little too good."

Julian heaved a sigh, ran his hand along the back of his neck, as a slight buzz eased up his spine. "I wonder how much more I'd have to drink to forget everything that's happened in the last month."

Velmyra got up from the table, looking pale. "Sorry. I'll get us something else to drink."

"No, no. This is fine. Really." Kevin took his glass and took another long drink.

Julian turned up his glass, too. "Vel, just bring out the whole bottle."

A half hour later, they were still talking as the rain poured down, drumming a percussive roll on the tin roof. The big bottle of moonshine-cola was almost empty.

Returning to the issue of food, Velmyra went back to the kitchen in search of something that might make a meal. In minutes a familiar aroma wafted from the kitchen, bringing a smile to Julian's face. In spite of all the bad news. It must have been written in some southern etiquette book that bad news should always be accompanied by good food, as if well-seasoned beans splashed with hot sauce had the power to salve the wounded soul. The bank foreclose on your house? Sit down to these collard greens. Wife walk out on you? Try some of this sweet potato pie. Left you for another man? Then *hot* pie with a scoop of vanilla ice cream. And if someone died, the bereaved family would never go hungry again as small country kitchens became arsenals of succulent, deep-fried chicken.

Cousin Genevieve had kept a covered dish as close as her double-barrel shotgun, ready to assault any ailment, physical or spiritual, so it didn't surprise Julian when Velmyra placed three bowls of what looked like gumbo on the table, silverware by each place.

"Look what I found. Jars of this stuff in the freezer. It looked pretty good, so I microwaved it."

"Smells great." Kevin looked around the spartan dwelling, and nodded toward the rustic kitchen. "There's a microwave in *there*?"

"Daddy bought it for Genevieve last Christmas, but she never used it," Julian said. "Scared of it. Said she could never trust something that cooked food that fast. Had to be something evil about it."

Julian took one whiff of the steaming gumbo and felt a chill, his heart racing. It was Simon's recipe, handed down to him and Genevieve from her mother Auntie Maree, who got it from her mother, who got it from hers. According to Simon, the recipe was as old as the family itself. Large hunks of chicken and sausage and okra in a dark, medium-thick roux, shrimp as big as a thumb. At once sweet and savory, spicy and peppery, with a dash of something he didn't recognize but that made the whole dish complete. Julian felt emotion swelling in his throat. He'd been weaned on this stuff. It was as if his father was back in the kitchen, stirring pots.

"What's this?" Julian pointed a spoon at a platter Velmyra had set down in the middle of the table laden with marinated vegetables.

Velmyra smiled. "There's a million canning jars in there full of good stuff. Pickled okra, pickled green beans, stewed tomatoes, pickled cucumbers..."

He remembered that about Genevieve; she would pickle anything that would stand still long enough.

Julian looked up. "Pickled cucumbers? You mean...pickles?"

Velmyra laughed. "Oh. Right."

For the next few moments there was a silence that Julian remembered well; the Fortier recipes had a way of quieting a room to the sibilant sounds of swallowing and clicking teeth and the clank of forks and spoons against stoneware. The only other sound was the drumbeat of rain against the roof.

"Damn." Kevin broke the silence, leaning back in his chair and licking his lips. "This is the best gumbo I've ever had. Tastes like something you might get in one of them fancy restaurants in New Orleans."

They talked on as hours passed and light descended. After the distraction of moonshine and food, Velmyra leaned back in her chair and turned to Kevin. "Do you mind if I ask you how you got so interested in all this…this land stuff? And how you got to know so much about it?"

Kevin laid down his fork and sat back, his blue eyes luminous in the fading light. He had grown up in Pointe Louree Parish on a ragged remnant of land called Terre Rouge, not far from Silver Creek. In his first year at LSU, he'd studied contracts with a professor named Spencer LeClaire.

"He had to be the most brilliant man I ever met. Black man. His family lost a huge spread this way, up around Jackson Parish, a long time ago. A couple of years ago, he saw stuff happening again, land changing hands quickly, around these parts. So Prof decided he was going to try to help folks, you know, school them on how to protect their property, make wills and stuff. He got a couple of us students to help him, for a little extra credit." Kevin spread his hands across the table and looked at his long fingers, his voice quieting. "Prof died last year. Eighty-three years old. Now it's just me. So anyway, I'm hearing about somebody cruising around this property, somebody who sure as hell don't look like they belong here. Then I'm reading about this auction. Didn't smell right. That's why I was looking for your daddy."

Julian leaned forward, burying his head in his hands. The young law student cleared his throat, lowered his head and spoke quietly. "Sure sorry about what you folks been through, down there in New Orleans. Sure hope you find your daddy."

"Me too," Julian said.

Kevin told Julian he'd be willing to help him get the land back. "There might be a way we could fix this thing. There might be a loophole we could take advantage of."

Julian sat forward, his arms on the table. "You think we got a chance if we fight this?"

"There's a chance. There's always a chance."

They decided to meet the next day and try to find Genevieve. And maybe, Kevin said, Genevieve could lead them to the other relatives of the Fortier clan, one of whom had to have sold their portion of the land.

When Kevin stood up, his long body lurched forward into a stumble that almost landed him on the table. "Whoa. I guess I better get going. It's getting late, and you folks've been awful nice. That gumbo. That was something special."

From his mouth came the sound of a low, drawn out belch. He covered his mouth with three fingers. "Whoops. Sorry 'bout that."

Velmyra stood and touched his shoulder. "You OK to drive?"

"Yeah. I'm good. I'm just down the road."

"Why don't you let us take you there?" Julian's voice was etched with concern.

Kevin straightened up and arched his back. "I'm really OK. It'll take me about ten minutes to get home. I been gone a while and my girlfriend's gonna have a fit if I don't get home pretty soon. She's pregnant. Seven months along."

He looked at his watch. "I'm more worried about you folks. The roads are gonna wash out pretty good with alla this rain. Maybe y'all oughta be staying here tonight. I wouldn't try to go too far in this weather."

Julian and Velmyra looked at each other.

"Maybe he's right." Velmyra shrugged. "That little road wasn't that easy to navigate when it was dry. You think your cousin would mind if we stayed here?"

Julian parted the café curtain covering the small window that looked out on the front yard. Rain came down in thick gray sheets, made opaque by swirling wind.

Julian couldn't help the twinge of guilt. He hadn't been to Silver Creek to see Genevieve in years, even though she'd constantly asked Simon about "my young cousin."

"If she knew I was here, she'd love it, after she'd ride my butt about staying away so long. We should be able to find some sheets or something around here."

"Good." She nodded. "Then we can look for your cousin in the morning, maybe visit her."

Kevin walked toward the door. He took a long step, stumbled as if he were trying to board a passing train, and Julian grabbed his arm. "Easy, friend," he said, and looked at Velmyra. "I think we better take you home, man."

Julian drove Kevin's big Ford truck, following Velmyra and Kevin in the Neon, through wooded, water-sludged paths in a slashing downpour. The truck rambled along the muddy road that rimmed the swollen creek, and when Velmyra and Kevin headed down a pitch-black path under canopying cypresses, Julian wondered if the young lawyer was sober enough to remember his way home. He was relieved to see the glow of a porch light at the end of the road. By the time they returned to Genevieve's cabin, the rain had stopped and the clouds had parted to reveal a bright, full moon.

Four hours after he had found the sheets and pillows for Velmya and had stretched himself across the lumpy divan in the living room, the luminous moon shone through the sheer curtains in the living room, waking Julian from restless sleep. That, the soft rasp of Velmyra's snoring, and the river of thoughts coursing through his brain.

There had been a time when that snore was as familiar as his own breath. The bedroom door was only half-closed, and from the pitch of her snore he knew exactly how she lay—on her side, one hand tucked under her face, mouth slightly open, and eyelids fluttering as the light of her dreams flashed in her sleep.

From time to time, she would arch her back, throw her arm across his torso, a signal for him to slide himself into the S-curve of her body as if she were the mold that defined his form.

That was how it had been with them—natural, easy. He had thought it would be that way forever. He got up from the divan and walked with the sheet draped around him like a bath towel toward the moonlight spilling in from the window.

The air in the cabin was as thick and moist as human breath, and the house seemed to heave and swell as the rainwater soaked deeper into the wood. He leaned his arms on the small sill and looked up at the blue-black sky. He looked over his shoulder at the thin bluish light seeping from the open door, and turned back to the moon. He thought about the last time he had seen her, years ago, before the breakup. How had they gotten to this point? A few feet away and worlds apart, two strangers on opposite sides of a half-closed door.

He hadn't been the only one who needed to recover. When the thing with Vel ended, and Julian fell into moribund silence, he felt a steady beam of curious light from his father's eyes. Tacit questions lay stranded in the air between them, the unease between father and son palpable.

The old man would have loved to play consoling confidant with mother-wit advice; often he had surprised Julian with his country brand of wisdom plumbed from some deep store of life lessons. But Julian, hard-headed, reticent, embarrassed, had put up a wall that even a father's love could not pierce. One night after Simon grew weary of his son's silent moping, he put away the supper dishes and turned to Julian with a frustrated sigh. "Why you ain't out finding you another somebody is beyond me." The words stuck in Julian's throat: he didn't want "another somebody."

Simon shook his head and went back to rolling dough for his crawfish pies, while Julian took out his trumpet and poured his blues into it.

Outside, the leaves of the sprawling oaks and the eaves and gutters of the cabin continued to echo the random dripping rhythms of the just-ended rain. Julian went back to the divan and arranged himself between the lumps in the cushion and pulled the sheet back over himself and thought about the heaped-on hurts in his father's life; Ladeena, the flooded, drowned city he loved, and now, Silver Creek. The Treme house had been in his family for generations, but the Silver Creek land, his great-grandfather Moses' legacy, was Simon's life. Julian's stomach knotted once more at the thought of having to tell his father, if ever he saw him again, that it was gone.

Find me, or find what's left of me. Put me down beside your mama.

Dread stole into his mind as it had so often over the last couple of days; and as he had done each time before, he pushed it back. *Daddy is not gone. Daddy is alive somewhere,* he told himself, as if the words alone had the power of miracles. It wasn't easy; he felt like a small boy floating a flimsy kite on a dying wind. But he had to keep that thought aloft.

Julian closed his eyes and eased himself back inside the refuge of Velmyra's rhythmic snore, pulling it around him like a favorite childhood blanket, its familiar sputters and groans offering the only comfort there was now. Later, when the morning sun arced over the cabin between the branches of the oaks and spread long rods of light across the cypress floors, Julian woke again to the pungent aromas of frying bacon and French-roasted cinnamon coffee.

11

Velmyra handed him a cup of coffee as he stood in the doorway of the kitchen. "Hey."

"Hey, yourself."

"I didn't want to wake you up. Figured you had a hard enough time sleeping on that little couch."

He took a sip from the smooth, strong brew that tasted like heaven, not bothering to ask her how she'd remembered the little touch of cinnamon he liked, and where she had found it. Velmyra was nothing if not resourceful. It was exactly the way he had drank it for the last twelve years, with just enough sugar to round the edges.

"Thanks. This is just what I need."

He rubbed sleep from his eyes. "I must've been unconscious. With these thin walls, I can't believe I didn't hear you in the kitchen."

Standing at the stove, she had an eyes-wide freshness that he envied, her nutmeg skin glowing. The tufts of tight curls rising from the red bandana crown she'd arranged made her look like some kind of fashionable, New Age Jemima. She wore a clean white T-shirt emblazoned with the picture of a black woman blues singer and the words "Mardi Gras '96" in red letters, and crisply pressed red shorts. It was like her to prepare for a situation like this, tucking a change of clothes inside her bag, just in case.

He looked at the gateleg table by the window set with places for two.

"Vel, you didn't have to do all this. We could have gone out somewhere."

Velmyra took the spatula she was holding and pressed bacon into the small iron skillet. Her eyebrows lifted above her smile, her laughing eyes, as she pointed the spatula toward him. "You're kidding, right? From here, we'd have to drive for miles just to arrive at the world's smallest town. By the time we got to...wherever you had in mind, I would have passed out. Blood sugar, you know."

Right. He felt a twinge of embarrassment; she'd remembered how he liked his coffee, but he couldn't remember how her blood sugar dipped now and then, and she would climb the walls until there was food in front of her.

She was bustling around the kitchen as if it were her own, opening drawers, finding silverware and glasses.

"I went outside early this morning." She turned over a slice of bacon. "I took my sketchpad and sat under a tree. This place is a paradise for painters. The light! The sun, when it comes up from the trees, it's amazing."

This was the first day, she explained, that she'd been able to draw—really draw—anything since the storm. She went on about the light, the lush green of the trees, the grasses and wildflowers, and as if she hadn't said it before, the magnificent sun.

Velmyra nodded toward the door in the back of the kitchen leading to the yard, where the morning sun blazed into the house.

'I explored around and went for a little walk. God, the sunrise! The sky is so...I can't even describe it...primordial, you know? The pines in the back go on forever. And the birds, amazing. And her garden! Everything you could imagine. Beets, turnips, snap peas, and three kinds of greens! There's even a blackberry bush still going crazy out there, and there must be a zillion tomatoes, some on the vine, and a whole bunch on the ground. So plump and red and ripe! I got us a couple for breakfast."

Velmyra pulled a pan of grilled tomatoes from the oven's broiler and set them on the top of the stove.

"We can have this bacon and tomatoes and then I found some good crusty bread that looked homemade way back in the freezer. I sliced some and spread some butter on it and put it under the broiler, and then I improvised some hot syrup with the really ripe blackberries and some honey I found. That should hold us for a while."

Her energy, he'd forgotten. When it came to morning habits, the two of them had been a study in opposites. She would eject from bed at first light like timed toast, her mind at full throttle, while he played the snooze button like it was his trumpet. Useless, until that first cup of caffeine.

He rubbed his hands together. "Anything I can do to help?"

"Nope. I've got it together. This bacon is the best—thick cut. Not that skimpy stuff they sell in town. This is the real deal."

"Smells great." He took a seat at the table with his coffee while Velmyra dished bacon and tomatoes on his plate, and poured hot blackberry syrup into a white plastic bowl.

Velmyra sat and poured hot coffee into her cup. "So what's the name of that little town close by?"

Julian broke a piece of bread from the large hunk on the plate, dunked it into the hot blueberries, and drank again from the white porcelain coffee cup with butterflies on the border. He took a bite from the bacon, and smiled to himself. It was the best bacon he'd had since the last time he was here.

The food theory, again, at work. He remembered how Simon would roll up his sleeves and haul out his pots and stuff Julian with everything from jambalaya to bread pudding when he was feeling down. It always worked, even now. He felt better just looking at the food.

Simon. It was the first time this morning that the thought of him entered his head.

"Local," he said, his tone laconic as he gazed out the window. "It's not that far. A few miles away. It's the only town of any size around."

"What do you mean, Local?"

"Local. It's the name of the town."

"Local what? Local Hero? Local Talent? Or maybe Local Flavor?" She smiled at her lame joke, then ate a bite of the bacon and rolled her eyes in appreciation. "Wow. This is amazing. There's nothing like country bacon, don't you think? So, anyway, you think your aunt really…"

She was going on and on. But he could no longer hear her for the swelling pain near his eyes and across his temples. He cut her off and stood up, running a hand along the back of his head. He felt his nerves unravel and for a brief moment wanted to throw something against the wall.

"I've got to find my father. I've got to find Daddy."

There was a bite in his voice; unintended, but the words shattered the air like bricks flung against glass. He sat back down and leaned forward, rocking, elbows on his knees, massaging his temples.

"Sorry," he said.

She put her fork down slowly and sat back in the chair. She nodded, absorbing the sight of his grief, and spoke quietly.

"We'll find him. We'll keep looking until we find him."

"I mean," he sat up, his voice quieter, "if he's alive, or if he's not, whatever." He got up from his chair again and walked to the window. The sun was arcing upward toward the center of the sky. Across the yard, the leaves of the giant magnolias and live oaks shimmied in the soft southward breezes floating up from the creek.

He put both hands in his pockets and turned to Velmyra. "And I can't just let them take Daddy's land. If he's not already dead, it would kill him."

Velmyra was quiet for a moment. "Maybe Kevin really can help with the land."

"Maybe." He took deep breaths, trying to settle himself. He looked at his watch. "Didn't he say he was coming by this morning? Like, right about now?"

"Well, he had quite a bit to drink last night."

"So did we."

"Yeah, but he *really* did."

Velmyra ate another bite of bacon and tomato, and pushed her plate aside. "You know, I think it's cool that he's so interested in all this. But I wonder if there's more going on than he's telling us."

Julian sipped from his cup and gave her a cursory look. "What makes you say that?"

Lifting her face to the stream of sun coming into the window, she closed her eyes against the warming light. "I don't know. It just seems a little unusual."

"Why? Because he's white?"

She shrugged. "Not so much that. He's so young. And does he even practice law? He didn't mention having a job or anything. And his wife—girlfriend, whatever. She's seven months pregnant and he's out trying to save the world from land swindlers?"

"Whatever his reasons, doesn't matter."

When they'd finished, Julian got up and stacked both plates and took them to the kitchen. In the bathroom just off the living room, he took off his shirt and splashed soap and water on his face and under his arms. He looked in the mirror. Matted hair, overnight stubble, and red eyes circled with bags stared back from the glass. "Wow," he murmured aloud, amazed that he could look this bad, rubbing the rough fuzz beneath his chin with the back of his hand. He hadn't thought to bring a comb or a razor. He'd always been particular about how he looked, but he was even more self-conscious now, and knew why. As soon as the thought was out, he banished it. Why should he care about what *she* thinks about how he looks?

OK, she was good company, but there wasn't anything between them anymore, and there wasn't going to be. So it didn't matter, did it? She was not in his life now and would never be again. He put his shirt back on and breathed deeply, relieved. Problem solved.

By the time he came out of the bathroom, Kevin was standing on the porch, knocking on the screen door.

"Sorry I'm late. Raynelle was a little sick at her stomach this morning."

Velmyra opened the door. Kevin stepped in, wearing a red and blue plaid shirt and jeans, his long blond hair wet and stringy, his eyes veiny and red.

"Want some breakfast? There's a little bacon left, and some bread."

Kevin flinched and shook his head. "No, ma'am. No food. Man, my head feels about to burst into pieces. Might take a sip of that white lightning if you've got any left, though. Hair of the dog, you know."

Julian remembered from his boyhood days that Genevieve had always been devoutly loyal to Sunday morning church services, so the three of them piled into the Neon for the twenty minute drive into Local to find her church, or at least the name and location of it. With the Neon rambling along the uneven terrain, Julian navigated the narrowest of country roads past acres and acres of wild, wooded Silver Creek land lush with tall, straight pines, cypress, and oaks that stretched their long arms high above the road and laced their fingers together in a shading arbor. Thick, viney brush and tangles of kudzu and wildflowers crowded the gravelly shoulders, and damp air rushed past the open windows. When they edged along the creek, the sun cast metallic flecks of dancing light on the water, silver-tipping its waves. In the middle of the creek, an egret swooped down, perched on a floating log for a moment, and then flew away.

Velmyra pointed through her open window. "That," she said, "is beautiful."

Julian did not look. Suddenly, he could no longer stomach the feral beauty of this land. If he'd taken an active interest in it, the way Simon wanted, things might be different. If it was all slipping away now, he had himself to blame.

Kevin looked back at Velmyra. "Beautiful. Yeah, y'all are real fortunate. My daddy left me a little bit when he died. A little bit of money, a little bit of land. But nothing like this, nothing this pretty."

He nodded, gazing out the open window. "Let's hope it stays this way."

They rode in silence for a while, the two men up front and Velmyra sitting in the back seat, her knees pressed up to her chin, gazing out at the sun-tinged landscape like a small child on a family vacation trip.

"So." Velmyra leaned forward, resting her arm on the back of Kevin's seat. "You practice law, right? What got you interested in all this land stuff?"

Kevin turned around, smiling impishly, like a small boy not wanting to let go of a secret.

"Like I said before, my teacher, Professor LeClaire. He had a way about him. Made stuff sound real interesting, important."

"No, I mean, this case. How'd you know about the auction?"

He ran his fingers back through his damp hair. "Like I said, I been checking on the auctions for a while. Prof and I always checked the paper. He showed me your land before he died. He had a hunch something would happen with it."

"Ummm." Velmyra nodded, her voice laced with skepticism.

Julian shifted in his seat. Velmyra had a way of pressing sometimes, when she suspected there was something hiding between the lines. He'd often thought she would have made a good lawyer herself. But now he wondered too why a young white kid with a pregnant girlfriend would be out with a couple of black strangers on a country road on a morning when he should have been helping the mother-to-be deal with her pregnancy.

"So, where'd you say you practiced law?" Julian steered the car left along the creek's sharp bend.

"Me? Oh." Kevin scratched at the back of his neck, and turned to look out his window. "Well, truth is, uh, I haven't taken the bar yet. Planning on doing it this fall, though."

He pushed a loose clump of wet hair back from his eyes. "By the way, what do you folks do?"

Velmyra told him she was an artist and art teacher in New Orleans. Julian cringed at the thought of discussing a career that was currently going nowhere.

"Musician," he said, looking away.

And after a little coaxing from Kevin, he admitted that he was a trumpeter from New Orleans now living in New York, that he had "traveled a little" with his own group to a few countries, and that he had a "couple of recordings" that had done "OK."

Kevin, a lover of music since he was a twelve-year-old trying to learn guitar, had cut his teeth on old vinyls of Eddie Van Halen, George Benson, Wes Montgomery, and Stevie Ray Vaughn. After a couple of minutes of lawyerly prodding, it didn't take him long to deduce that he was riding in a car with a world-class, and by many accounts, world-famous jazz musician.

"Aw, man!" he said, eyes wide and grinning, his face lit up at full wattage. And then he lit into a spiel about his fascination with classic jazz, his favorite players who'd come from New Orleans, his interest in all kinds of music, including hip-hop and rap, which he believed to be social commentary of the highest order, and grossly misunderstood.

He went on and on, while Julian listened patiently, nodding occasionally. Velmyra, realizing Julian's pain at this reminder of his predicament, took the lead in responding to the young law school grad with an occasional "really?" and "that's so great."

Kevin admitted, apologetically, that he was not too familiar with "straight ahead" jazz and had never purchased any of Julian's recordings, but promised to correct that as soon as possible. Then pointing ahead at the changing landscape, he said, "I think we're here. That's Ray Simpson's Texaco on the left. Local's just right around the next little turn."

Julian slowed the car to the new speed limit as the little town emerged. A sleepy, small bubble of civility in the raw landscape, Local, Louisiana, population 820, consisted of little more than a couple of stoplights, a gas station, and a square clustered with mature magnolias. The square was surrounded by a courthouse and a few shops: a used appliance store, a tea room, and a shed with broken down furniture outside that announced "Auntie's Antiques" in Gothic lettering on its window.

At the Texaco, Julian got out of the car, ambled inside to the small grocery, and came back out in less than two minutes.

Both Velmyra and Kevin gave him a questioning look.

He closed the door, and popped a piece of the sugarless gum he'd bought into his mouth.

"The church we're looking for, in fact the only black church around here, is back near Silver Creek."

So they drove all the way back down the twisting road to an area less than a mile from where they'd begun. They drove past the church twice, each time missing the clearing tucked back behind a grove of pines. They pulled up into the sandy yard of the weathered white clapboard building with its left-leaning steeple, sitting on twelve-inch cinderblocks. A wooden sign with the words "Elam C.M.E. Bible Church" hung askew just above the door, and a rooster pecked around beneath the crawl space. Even before Julian knocked on the door, it was obvious to all of them that no one was there. But a few yards back behind the church sat a small, steep-roofed house of white siding trimmed in red brick. Next to the house sat an old Buick Park Avenue and a dark blue Ford Mustang, with one door a dull primer-gray, baking in the sun.

The strains of rhythm and blues greeted Julian as he climbed the steps to the porch—it was the thumping bass of a familiar tune, a love song by Al Green.

The door opened and a man about Julian's height with an untrimmed salt-and-pepper Afro and matching beard, about fifty years of age, shaded his eyes from the sun.

"Can I help you all?"

Julian cleared his throat. "Uh, yes, sorry to bother you. I'm trying to find my cousin. Her name is Genevieve Callers. Or she might go by her maiden name, Genevieve Fortier. I understand she goes to the church over there, and I just wondered if you might—"

The name lit a spark of recognition in the man's eyes. "What'd you say your name is?"

"Just tell her Simon's son Julian is here."

"You Simon's son?"

"Yes, sir."

A smile spread the full width of his face. He looked behind Julian at the waiting car where Velmyra and Kevin sat. "Y'all come on."

The man turned down the boom-box volume, quieting Al Green's boisterous rendering of "Love and Happiness" to subtle, bass-backed musings, and disappeared into the back of the house, calling Genevieve's name. Julian waved to Velmyra and Kevin and they both got out of the car. He was a little confused; he didn't remember his Cousin G having a son. But maybe he was a handyman of some sort, or a gardener.

The scents of Pine-Sol, garlic, and the faintest hint of peaches drifted out from the living room. It was dark inside and somewhere an electric fan whirred beneath the gentle roar of a window unit air conditioner. Several faux-oriental area rugs of every color imaginable partially obscured dark, rustic hardwood floors. An exercise bicycle stood in one corner, and a portable television sat atop another television housed in a mahogany console. Oversized furniture crowded the room—bureaus, upholstered chairs, tables—giving it the appearance of a small warehouse.

A slightly sunken blue and green striped sofa sat in front of a curtained window, neatly folded stacks of white laundry covering every inch of it. The three of them stood in the middle of the floor and waited.

"Oh, my sweet Jesus!" a voice cried from the back of the house as Cousin Genevieve came into the room, clapping her hands and smiling.

Grabbing Julian into her neck, she rocked him in a smothering hug. "Julian! Look what the storm blew in!"

She pulled away from him and looked him up and down, her eyes dancing. He hadn't seen her in years, and she didn't look like the woman he remembered, or imagined he would see after all this time. She was his father's age, maybe older, but her eyes held the spark of a woman in her forties, and her deep brown skin was unblemished and barely lined. Thinner than he remembered, she wore a short, reddish-blond wig with bangs that covered her forehead and reached down just over her eyes. Her jogging suit, a deep red, matched her eyeglasses, designed in a flattering, thin-rimmed style.

But she was unmistakably his father's first cousin; she had his high cheekbones, and beneath the youthful veneer, this was a woman of the deep country. It was in her voice, her manners, the tilt of her head, and even in her misting eyes.

She gripped his shoulders, shaking her head—her brows furrowed above still-smiling lips. "Child, child," she said. "I never thought I'd see you again, baby."

Julian smiled, feeling a warmth that seemed both to come from the air in the room and the heat of his cousin's hug. This was what it was like to come back to the people who had prayed for you when you were a sickly infant, had watched you grow from a toddler, had spanked your bottom with one hand when you reached your fingertips to a too-hot stove, and then slipped you a fresh, ripe peach from the backyard tree with the other.

"I'm here looking for Daddy." Julian coughed a little at the smells of disinfectant and mildewed wood. "I haven't been able to find him since the storm."

Genevieve's eyes darkened and she looked away for a moment, then looked back at him.

"I was so afraid for him." She touched her hand to her chest, her voice quieter. "I talked to him that night, so I know he stayed there. I been calling him every day since then, but I just can't get through."

"We thought he might be here. We drove to your house hoping to find him."

Genevieve turned to the sofa and sat down on the edge of a pillow with both hands on her knees, rocking forward.

"Lord, have mercy."

Julian pushed aside a stack of towels, sat next to her, reached an arm around her.

"We think he got out; he left us a note. We think he's safe somewhere. Lots of folks are missing but a lot of 'em have been found, safe and sound."

With those heartening words, Genevieve's eyes lifted, and she looked up at Velmyra and Kevin.

"Y'all know Simon too?"

"Oh, sorry." Julian got up. "These are friends of mine, Velmyra and Kevin. They're helping me look for Daddy."

"Bless you both." Genevieve stood up and hugged each one. "Y'all had breakfast yet?"

Julian glanced at the other two. "We had a little something earlier. I sure hope you don't mind us raiding your fridge."

Genevieve waved her hand dismissively. "Baby, you always know whatever's mine is yours, too. Make yourself at home over there. So, y'all had breakfast already. How about a little peach cobbler?"

They followed Genevieve into a dining room filled with two large china cabinets piled with silver-rimmed dishes and a sideboard piled high with ceramic serving bowls. Wide-striped patterns of rose and gray flowers trailed up the sun-streaked walls. The man who had greeted them at the door, Pastor Jackson (head of Elam C.M.E.'s twenty-four member congregation), brought an enormous pie plate from the kitchen filled with a deep-dish cobbler glazed to a perfect golden brown and still bubbling from the oven.

Between delectable bites of Genevieve's cobbler, the talk centered around New Orleans—the condition of Simon's house, the stories they had heard on the news of government bungling, the horrible reports from the Superdome and the Convention Center and the tens of thousands stranded in the flooded city waiting for help, the good Samaritan doctors saving lives, the insurance shysters, and the dogs reunited with their masters. They talked about whether the city would ever be itself again, and how long that would take. Pastor Jackson sat quietly, sometimes nodding, saying next to nothing. It was when they were halfway through the pie that Julian figured the time was appropriate (if there was an appropriate time) to bring up the Silver Creek land.

"Cousin Genevieve, did you get anything in the mail a month or so ago about Silver Creek?"

She waved her hand dismissively. "No baby. Your daddy took care of all that business with the land. I sent him money but he took care of all the legal stuff, taxes and whatnot."

"Do you know anything about people coming around Silver Creek, trying to buy it?"

Genevieve wiped pie crust crumbs from her mouth and put down her paper napkin next to her plate. Her eyes darkened.

"Child, it's so much stuff going on around here," she said. "I called Simon the night of the storm to tell him about Mr. Parette."

Julian remembered the Parettes, whose land bordered his father's property. His father talked about growing up with the old man's son, James Earl. Both the son and daughter had moved to Chicago years ago, and the father, past ninety, lived on the property alone.

"What about him?"

"Oh, child. You don't know?" Genevieve rested her cheek on her hand, her elbow on the dining table. "Something awful. Just awful."

She told him what she knew, what she'd seen. Strangers in big expensive-looking cars cruising through the area, property "changing hands faster than you can say Jack Robinson." Beautiful spreads of land being cleared for factories, condominiums, golf courses, and time-share communities.

Parette had told her he would not sell, not for any amount of money. Not for any reason. Then suddenly, he was found slumped over the steering wheel of his car, in a ditch just off Dutch River Road.

Could have been an accident. He was half blind, old as sin, and shouldn't have been driving anyway, Genevieve said. But everybody looked out for him. He only drove about twenty miles an hour and he'd never had an accident before on that road.

And two weeks after his funeral, all the property he owned suddenly belonged to the developers who had tried to get him to sell his land.

"Scared the devil out of everybody around here," Genevieve said. "Everybody afraid something bad might happen to them if they don't sell."

"My church friends got so worried for me, they said I ought to get away from my house for a little while. So Pastor Jackson here was kind enough to let me stay with him."

Julian looked down at his hands, then ran a hand along the back of his neck. "Cousin G, I got something to tell you."

At the news about the land, she stared at Julian in disbelief, then bowed her head, her eyes closed. She wrung her hands together, shook her head. "They can't do that. They just can't do that to us. This land has been ours for over a hundred years, way back since before slavery ended." Her chin jutted forward, and there was a streak of fire in her eyes. "We got to do something. They just can't take it away from us like that."

Kevin put his empty pie plate aside and leaned forward across the table.

"I know how you feel ma'am. I'm hoping I can help out, help you keep your place."

Julian explained that Kevin was a law student interested in the land. For the next half hour Kevin explained the "partitioning laws" and how families the law had been designed to protect from disputes had been ill served by them, and how the land often ended up in the hands of greedy developers.

Pastor Jackson brought in a pitcher of lemonade and filled everyone's glasses. Kevin took a sip, then put his glass down, frowning thoughtfully. A streak of late morning sun from the window behind the sofa sent a shaft of angled light into the room.

Kevin rocked back in his chair, tapping his fingers lightly on the tabletop. "Miss Genevieve, do you have any relatives you haven't heard from in a while who might have wanted to sell their portion of Silver Creek?"

Genevieve pondered the question a moment. Besides her and Simon, there were only a handful of cousins, descendants of her grandfather, Moses, who lived in California.

Kevin eyebrows arched up. "Are you in touch with them?"

Not really, she said. A holiday card now and then, and every year, a check to help pay the taxes on the land.

"That's got to be it," Kevin said. "We need to get in touch with them."

Genevieve went to a bureau drawer, pulled out an address book and wrote down the number for one of the relatives, and handed the paper to Kevin.

"You say you a lawyer?" Genevieve asked Kevin.

"Yes, ma'am. Well, almost. Finished law school."

"And how you know about all this stuff going on?"

He told her about Professor LeClaire, and Genevieve pursed her lips, frowning.

"LeClaire. Seem like he called me about a year ago. We kept playing phone tag, just couldn't get connected. I guess he was trying to warn me."

Kevin's gaze fell to his shoes. "I'm so sorry we missed you, Miss Genevieve. That musta been around the time the Prof got sick." He looked up at her. "Professor LeClaire died about this time last year. I'm trying to keep up his work. Trying to find ways to help folks like you keep their land."

Genevieve's eyes narrowed and she leaned forward, shaking her finger. "Well, they gonna half to drag me offa Silver Creek. My whole family is buried here. I'm not giving this place up without a fight, no sir."

As they walked back out to the yard, the rooster still pecked around the front of the house, and a rabbit darted out from beneath the crawl space and disappeared deep into the grove of pecan trees. When they reached Julian's car, Genevieve hugged Kevin and Velmyra before they got inside. Before Julian opened his own door, Genevieve pulled him aside.

"Now, baby," she said in a whisper, "When you find your daddy, don't tell him what you saw here."

He gave her a confused look. "What do you mean, Cousin G?"

She looked back toward the house where Pastor Jackson was sweeping off the porch. "Well, you know, me and Pastor Jackson."

Julian's eyes glazed over, his face a question mark.

She cocked her head to the side, her hands on her hips. There was a slight twinkle in her eyes and a shy smile curling the corners of her mouth. "Child, you know, they used to call it 'living in sin.' But me and Pastor Jackson, we feel we been blessed by the Lord. Oh, I know it's a little unusual with him being twenty-five years younger than me and everything, but that man just brings me more joy…I tell you."

Now he got it. But his confusion was replaced with genuine shock. Cousin G's face opened like a flower as she gazed at the man on the porch. Pastor Jackson looked up from his sweeping and grinned back at her.

"We got together 'bout a few months ago. It just happened. He used to take me home from missionary board meeting after I had my knee surgery and couldn't drive. Well, we got to talking about this and that and one thing led to another. Turns out we both liked to go bowling over by Oak Meadows. And we started playing in the bid whist tournaments at the Y over in Percy around the same time. But that ain't the best part." She lowered her voice to a conspiratorial whisper—"Child, that man is got some stamina, you know what I'm saying? Makes me feel like a young bride, don't cha know"—and elbowed Julian in the side.

Julian felt his face flush.

"Why are you looking so surprised? Old women like me, we got our needs too! And I'll have you know, I used to turn many a head back in my day."

Julian wanted to laugh out loud. This was not the woman he imagined living a quiet life in the Louisiana backwater, Bible in one hand and tumbler of sweet tea in the other, rocking on a porch while the sun dipped into the pines.

"Your daddy, well, he just wouldn't understand. He was always the most Christian of all of us. So just keep it between you and me, OK?"

"OK, Cousin G."

She reached up and gave him a hug. "You stay at my place long as you want," she said. "Come back soon as you know something about Simon, or Silver Creek, and bring your friends with you." She shook her head for a moment, her mood sobered by a thought. Then she looked up again at Julian, her eyes brighter. "That young lady, my she's a pretty thing! And look like she got a little fire in her, too. Like your mama. Don't let her get away."

He wanted to explain, but decided not to bother. If she wanted to believe he was involved with Velmyra, fine. He wasn't about to burst a romantic old woman's bubble.

On the way back to Genevieve's, Kevin and Julian pieced together a plan: locate the other family members in California, find out who sold their portion of the land, then get a copy of the contract.

And then hope the buyers made a mistake somewhere along the way.

But as Kevin talked, Julian thought about his father. What would he have done in a situation like this? Simon was a stubborn, determined man guided by principle, and never surrendered once he decided something was unjust or unfair. If he'd been here, he'd never have let this happen to the land.

When they pulled up to the cabin, the sun had slipped behind linen-thin clouds and a cooling afternoon breeze stirred the leaves of the magnolias. On the ground beneath one of the trees, new tire tracks lay in the rain-softened earth and trailed away from the house toward the west, disappearing on the road toward the highway. Both Julian and Velmyra stared at the fresh tracks, then the door of the cabin.

Something wasn't right. When they pulled even closer, they could see the huge iron padlock hanging from the doorknob.

Julian ran up the porch steps to the door and grabbed the padlock in his hand. "What the..."

Kevin and Velmyra were right behind him. Velmyra looked back toward the road. "Somebody was just waiting for us to leave."

Kevin's face was ashen. He muttered a name under his breath, then said, "No, no you didn't."

Julian's ears got hot. He clinched his mouth, took three steps back, and with a running start, kicked the door in with his foot.

When the door jolted open, he examined the torn hinges.

"I'll find some tools and fix this." He turned to Velmyra and Kevin, who stared at him and the torn door in astonishment. "What are you all waiting for? Come on in."

By the time Julian returned from the hardware store in Local with a hammer, screwdriver, new hinges, and screws, Kevin and Velmyra had finished off the dregs of the moonshine-cola and, on finding a mason jar of clear liquid buried deep in the cupboard, had launched into Cousin Genevieve's supply of white lightning, straight and uncut.

They both sat, dazed, at the table, Kevin slouched in his chair, legs sprawled and head thrown back, as if he'd been dealt a body blow, and Velmyra bowed her head into her folded arms on the table, a half-empty glass of the corn liquor next to her elbow.

Julian fixed the door in a few minutes and joined them at the table. He poured himself three fingers, and drank down one of them. He coughed once, his face contorting with the burn of the drink, then drank another finger and pulled his chair up close to the table to look Kevin in the eye.

"You know, man. I really appreciate all you're doing, trying to help us and everything. But I'm just wondering if there's something you want to tell us."

As if on cue, Velmyra lifted her head from her folded arms, looking first at Julian, then at Kevin.

"Yeah. You said something, somebody's name when we saw the padlock. It was like you weren't surprised, like you expected it. We're just wondering if—"

"If you know something about these people. The folks who bought, well, *stole* Silver Creek from our family."

Kevin ducked his head, took a long slow swallow of the white lightning, and shifted his gaze from one pair of eyes to the other. He drummed his thin knuckles on the tabletop.

He smiled a sardonic half-smile. "Well, it's not something I want to tell you. But I will. Hell, I don't want to tell nobody this."

He took another drink and ran his hand along the back of his neck.

"The man who's doing this to y'all? You could say I know him." He took a deep breath.

"The son of a bitch is my granddaddy."

12

"I shoulda told y'all from the start."

As Kevin talked, his complexion reddened, and water pooled in the corners of his glazed eyes. Julian couldn't tell if it was from the truth that had finally been lifted from his heart or the residual burn from the corn liquor.

"I don't know." Kevin shook his head, looked down at the table top, and made wide circles with the flat of his palms. "Sometimes I think I must be crazy to take him on like this."

Velmyra put a hand on top of his wrist. "Just tell us what's going on."

He nodded, pushed back the mop of blond hair from his eyes, then rubbed his fist in his eyes like a sleepy, innocent child. He leaned back in his chair, his eyes closed, his head tilted toward the ceiling.

His voice wavered. "I'm just so sorry."

All three were silent a moment. Velmyra and Julian looked at each other. Clearly, Kevin was in a state, and needed a minute to gather himself. "You haven't eaten a thing all day. You must be hungry," Velmyra said. "You want me to fix you something?"

Kevin opened his eyes and looked toward her. "Yeah, actually. That'd be fine if it's not too much trouble."

When Velmyra returned from the kitchen with a bowl of leftover gumbo, Kevin stirred his spoon in it, then ate a mouthful. He didn't stop until the bowl was empty.

He pushed the plate aside. "Thank you, ma'am," he said quietly. Then looking at each of them, said, "I don't know where to start, so I'll just start at the beginning. First, I want y'all to know, he's my grandfather, but that's it. He ain't nothing to me, and I ain't nothing like him."

Kevin explained that it was his grandfather, Nathan Larouchette, who had been responsible for Professor LeClaire's family losing their land years ago. He learned about it when he was a first-year law student. One day in contracts class, the professor invited any student who was interested to travel with him around the parish as he went from one farm to another, schooling landowners on ways to protect their property from unscrupulous land grabbers. "Learn how to make the law work for real people," he'd said, smiling, tugging at his trademark bright red suspenders. Kevin, enamored of the brilliant man he held in rock-star esteem, volunteered along with two other students.

With the professor's rusted white van piled high with briefcases, greasy lunch bags of homemade shrimp sandwiches, a cooler of ice and soft drinks, and three eager would-be lawyers, the professor set out on sun-filled Saturday mornings for the gravelly roads and deep-wooded winding paths of Pointe Louree. The country folk of the mostly rural parish were friendly, so unannounced drop-bys and cold-call chats were greeted with hospitable smiles and iced sweet tea. In many cases, the families were living on land that had been passed down so many years they not only didn't have wills, but had to be convinced there was even a need for them.

One rainy March morning the professor arrived late to class, one hand holding a steaming coffee cup, the other brandishing a copy of *The Advocate*, Baton's Rouge's daily, folded open to the real estate section. The students leaned forward in their seats, straining to see the photo of the balding, bespectacled, and bearded white man, looking to be in his late seventies, who filled up a corner of the page.

Prof put his coffee on his desk, thumped the picture with the back of his hand. "See here? This here is the man we're up against.

This is the man who took my family's land, and who's still taking prime land from good hard-working folks."

Kevin's fair skin turned apoplexy pale. *This was the man? His own grandfather?* Nathan Larouchette, his daddy's daddy, had disappeared from his life long ago, just after Kevin's own father died. He'd only seen him a few times, and what little he knew about the man he had gleaned from his father's silent stares and the hard burn in his eyes when anyone in his family mentioned the name Nathan Larouchette.

At the end of class, Kevin went up to the professor. "I was shaking, tears in my eyes. Prof was quiet a minute after I told him. But then he said, 'Son, if you want to back out of this, I'll understand.'"

Kevin hadn't hesitated. "I told him, hell, no. I was in. Truth is, I wouldn'tna cared if the old bastard went to prison for the rest of his life."

Looking from Julian to Vel, Kevin scraped his feet against the wood floor and sat back. "He just didn't give a damn about people, you know?"

Kevin looked Julian in the eye, then lowered his gaze, nervously fidgeting with the sleeve of his shirt.

Julian rubbed his temples. "So the accident. Mr. Parette. You think it was your grandfather."

"Oh, I know it was him. He killed that old man. Oh, I don't think he meant it to turn out how it did. Probably just was trying to scare him, but..." He looked toward the window as his words trailed off.

Julian's brows furrowed. "Kevin, really, man, why are you doing this? Why're you putting yourself in jeopardy?"

Velmyra crossed her arms across her chest and leaned back in her chair. "Yeah, Kevin. Why would you do this if you don't have to?"

Kevin arched his shoulders up, then let them down again as if the weight of soul-baring was something he needed to shrug off. "Prof was my idol, like a daddy to me or something, especially after my old man passed. One thing he taught me was that once you know what's right and what's not right, you stand up and say so. No question, you just do it. Now if you don't know any better, then you can slide. But once you know, you can't pretend like you don't. You got to stand up."

"When Prof got real sick last year, I went to see him. He had that look, like he was about done. He looked at me, didn't say anything. Too weak. But it was like his eyes were talking to me, and I could almost hear him. So I said, 'Yeah, Prof, I know. I'm hearing you. You don't have to worry. I'll keep it going.'"

"That was the last time I saw him."

Kevin's eyes shifted from Julian to Vel, and back. "And I'm not gonna lie and say it ain't a little bit personal. Folks like Nathan need to be brought down. Blood or no blood."

The light in the room dimmed as the sun shifted to the western sky. From outdoors came the sound of chirping birds, and the dim rustle of a breeze through the live oak branches. They talked on for more than an hour, Kevin transforming before Julian and Vel's eyes from simple stranger to complex, vulnerable friend.

When Vel's cell phone broke the quiet, they all jerked, as if jolted out of a reverie.

"Hello?"

It was Sylvia. Julian could tell by Vel's expression, starting with a lift of her eyebrows, then blossoming into a full smile, that there was good news. His heart raced.

"Really? Oh, that's great!" she said, her face breaking into a smile.

Lucille Tuffins, an elderly neighbor of Velmyra's who'd had open heart surgery after being evacuated to Houston, had pulled through in good shape. It was good news, but not the news Julian wanted to hear.

"Thank you so much, Sylvia. Thanks for calling and telling me. Julian? Oh, sure. He's right here."

She handed the phone to Julian.

"Hi, baby." Sylvia's soft, low voice and motherly tone always set him at ease.

"Sylvia. How you doing?"

"Oh, you know. One day at a time. Every day is different. I guess there's no news about Simon or you would have called."

"We're at Silver Creek. He's not here. I was hoping you had some news."

Sylvia told him she had talked to Parmenter. He'd made good on his promise to help; he called an NOPD sergeant, an old friend. The department was stretched thin, but the sergeant made inquiries anyway, with no luck.

Simon was an old man, the officer said, living alone. More than a month had passed, and his chances of being found alive decreased with each passing day. They had so many cases of older folks trapped in neighborhoods or trying to make it through the water. Unless he was rescued, the officer said, Simon's chances were slim to none.

Julian fell silent.

Sylvia went on. "Julian, there is something I do want to talk to you about."

"What's that?"

Julian's head went light when she told him. She allowed that he was the son, the next of kin to Simon, and it was all up to him. But since so much time had passed without a word, without a sign, maybe it was time start thinking about doing something. Not a funeral, but some kind of memorial, maybe. It might do them both good. Free them from what they could not control, set the rest of their lives in some sort of forward motion.

He knew what she was really saying. Her nerves were shattered. She wanted to put an end to the frustration of searching and hoping, and move on.

Julian felt his sore jaw tighten, and for a moment couldn't speak. "Sylvia, I just can't—"

"Baby, I know, it's really up to you..."

"I appreciate what you're saying, but I'm just not ready to give up on him yet."

Silence. "I understand. It's just that...it's so hard."

"I know. But I have some other ideas. We could still find him. It's not impossible."

His words felt hollow, even to him—he had no other ideas. He thought of telling her about the land, but decided this was no time to dish out more bad news. The sigh she breathed was thick with fatigue and ragged at its edges, and for the first time, he considered what she must have been going through. Day in and day out, she had been closer to Simon than anyone, including him.

Sylvia's tone lightened, her voice lifting half an octave. "Maybe you're right. They're still finding people, you know. Remember old Mr. Davidson, used to be the janitor at Tubman High?"

"I remember. What happened?"

"Child, they found him! He got on one of those buses and ended up in Salt Lake City! Up there with all those Mormons!"

"Wow."

"Can you imagine what those folks must have thought the first time he went out looking for the nearest casino?"

"Not to mention his taste for, you know—"

"Right! Can't be too many ladies of pleasure up there in Salt Lake!"

They both laughed—the giddy, nervous laughter meant to loosen the grip of grief—and when their conversation ended, Julian tried to savor the tickle of the laughter on his skin, to wrap his mind in it. Mr. Davidson. Crazy old Mr. Davidson, up in Salt Lake City. A salty tongue that could shame Miles Davis. He tried to imagine the old rascal walking the streets in the citadel of Mormon faith, as out of place as a whore in the Sistine Chapel. Funny.

But he could only think of Simon.

By the time Kevin left, evening light had paled the sky to lavender, the slanting sun elongating the shadows of the oaks. The three of them would meet again the next day. Julian and Velmyra both stood on the porch, waving goodbye to Kevin as he tooled his truck toward the road, the oversized tires spinning up spirals of brown dust in its wake. When they went back inside, Julian sat on the plaid sofa, his elbows on his knees and his head between his hands.

He'd been sitting only a minute or so when it happened. From deep in the pit of his gut, a storm churned and spiraled up to his neck. He tried to gather a breath, but his throat tightened and his windpipes felt choked and nothing came. His chest burned. He heaved and panted and gasped, and finally got up and staggered to the bathroom, where he leaned over the toilet and retched.

Hearing him in the bathroom, Velmyra rushed in and found him kneeling on the floor, his head near the toilet bowl.

"I'm OK, I'm OK," he said. But when he tried to get up, the room whirled before his eyes like an off-kilter merry-go-round, and the taste of bile bubbled again in his throat.

"It's all right." Velmyra knelt beside him, her voice calm. "Just stay here, stay quiet a minute." With one hand on his arm, she smoothed his back with wide circles as he gave over to violent spasms of nausea.

"I'm OK now." He got up and made his way past her to the living room and sat again on the sofa. The room tilted again, moved in circles, and felt close, airless. He felt a chill. Sweat beads sprouted on his forehead as tiny quakes exploded beneath his skin. Velmyra sat next to him and put her hand on his shoulder.

She spoke quietly. "Julian, it's all right. It's all right if you want to just let it out."

He looked at her as tears filled his eyes. Then he leaned forward and looked straight ahead, holding himself, rocking.

"I think…" he said in a whisper. "I think he's really gone."

He felt himself go limp in her arms as the flood of tears came, first quietly, then in shuddering sobs. As grief breached his wall of strength, she put both arms around him and held his head to her chest. And they sat like that, quietly, as Julian rocked and cried, until night darkened the room.

Neither would remember how the next thing happened, or even whose idea it had been. Whether he'd led her or she'd led him to the small, cramped feather bed framed by rusted brass where

Velmyra had slept that first night, and where now they both lay knotted into each other, a welter of angles and curves beneath the raw, floursack cotton backing of Genevieve's handmade quilt.

It had been years, but their bodies remembered the details of the dance. There had been no words—only the smooth step and glide of old partners, the entwining and uncoiling, the shifting from one side, quietly, gently, to the other, his arm just beneath her neck, her head buried in the crook of his shoulder. His tongue dipping into the small well at the base of her throat, her back arching as his arm circled the slim world of her waist. Remembering, rediscovering, as forgotten passageways opened and memory guided them through.

They moved carefully, delicately, because the fragile balance of air and light between them could be so easily tipped with a misplaced word, a gesture. As she offered herself without restraint, he folded her into the space where his pain dwelt, and breathed softly as she filled it up. *Easy now,* he told himself, and felt, for the first time in a long time, at home.

Before the morning light, she'd awakened to find him gone. Walking out onto the porch in her T-shirt, she heard the sound coming from the direction of the creek and followed the muted, high-pitched wail.

Standing in the pale glow of the early morning moon, he was shirtless, shoeless, his unbelted jeans sagging slightly below his waist, the trumpet pressed to his lips and its bell lifted out over the bank of the creek. The thin brassy moan thickened in the damp air, floating between the rustle of leaves and grasses, and the shrill whir of cicadas and crickets.

He was playing something familiar, no doubt something she'd heard him play years ago. A simple melody, childlike, pure, but with an underpinning of old-time blues. A love song, maybe, for two people adrift in different worlds. She stepped on a branch and the sharp breaking sound startled him.

He looked up. "Sorry, I guess I woke you."

"I reached over and you were gone." She folded her arms against her chest. "Sounds beautiful. You OK?"

"Yeah." He held up his horn, shiny in the moon's light, and touched his jaw. "Feels a little better now and I messed around with my embouchure. I think I'm on the right track."

"Great."

He nodded to her, then looked across the dark creek, its rippling surface dimly illumined by the shine of the moon.

"Daddy used to bring me down here. We used to sit right over there on that bank." He pointed across the water to where an oak branch dripped gray fingers of Spanish moss over the water, and where, when he was five, his father had tossed him into the creek to get him to swim. He had splashed about violently thinking he would surely drown, until his feet touched bottom and he realized the water was only waist high.

He smiled, remembering. *Someday you're gonna appreciate this place, son. I hope it ain't too late when you do.*

Velmyra sat down on a patch of grass at the water's edge and drew her knees to her chest.

"Daddy tried to get me to fish, but all I wanted to do was get back to town. Play my horn." Julian exhaled a slow breath. He removed the mouthpiece and placed it against his lips, buzzed softly through it.

He lifted his chin to the moonlit sky, closed his eyes. Then opened them and looked at her. "I got a feeling he tried to get here, 'cause that's what he would do. But he just didn't make it."

Velmyra looked down at her bare feet. "Maybe you're right."

"You know, even if Daddy had made it, I'd almost hate to see him now. I don't think I could stand to tell him what happened to this place. Crazy, I know."

"I don't blame you. Next to you, this place was the most important thing in his life."

"I feel like it's my fault."

"No. Don't even go there."

Julian opened the spit valve of his trumpet and let the condensation run onto the ground. He lifted the horn again and played a long, slow, loose-lipped note at the bottom of his range, then let the tail of the sound disappear into the trees. He sat down on the wet grass next to Velmyra.

"I didn't love the place like he did—he knew that—but at least I could have been on top of the legal stuff. I could have gotten him to get a lawyer so something like this wouldn't have to happen."

Velmyra put a hand on his shoulder. "Stop it. Stop being so hard on yourself. You couldn't know. Maybe things happen..."

She stopped, but he knew where she was going. *Maybe things happened the way they did for a reason.* If Silver Creek was fated to fall into strangers' hands, maybe it was best that Simon wasn't around to see it.

He reached an arm around her.

"Thank you, for coming with me," he said, and bit back the urge to say, *What happened to us?* Since the night he'd first seen her at Sylvia's, he'd been thinking about the way they'd been before. Sure, there'd been a storm or two in their time together—that was normal—but even their roughest tempests had calmed after heart-to-hearts over red wine, misty-eyed apologies, and nights of make-up passion. He remembered earlier, the heat of her hand on his back as his body convulsed with grief, and thought to himself that only a fool would have let this woman get away. He'd been that fool, for sure. Some way, he had blown it. If only he could remember how.

In the far corner of the sky, he thought he saw a glimmer of the new day, but realized it was just the moon's lingering light. He looked down at his hands, fingered a chromatic scale on the valves. Finally, looking at her profile, he said, "I hate we couldn't make it work. I just don't know what happened."

A quizzical light filled her eyes as she looked at him, then turned away. "There were reasons."

"Like?"

She examined a hangnail on her index finger. "We were...different, you and me. We were headed different places, had different dreams. Sometimes, things just don't work."

In his recollection, the differences between them had best played out one evening in May. They hadn't been together long when he and Velmyra were window shopping at the Riverwalk shops and ran into Mr. Martrel, his old junior high school band teacher. Sporting his favorite red plaid jacket and too-long 60s Afro, Mr. Martrel was a well-known local pianist, on his way to a gig at one of the local courtyard cafés in the French Quarter.

Julian hadn't seen this man who'd most inspired him—one of the main reasons he'd become a musician—since he'd retired years before. Martrel's slumped shoulders and graying hair contrasted sharply with Julian's memory of the youthful teacher sprinting across the field and yelling orders to the marching band. Over the years, the stressful classroom days and jazz club nights that found his arthritic back hunched over an upright piano had clearly taken their toll.

Still, Mr. Martrel wore his usual jovial smile and acted as if life could not be better. His smile stretched even wider when Julian introduced Velmyra. He put an arm around them both. *Come on over to the café, and I'll buy your pretty young lady a drink!* Martrel's youthful eyes gleamed. While Velmyra sat crossed-legged at the bar sipping a potent peach daiquiri, Julian and Martrel cranked out one upbeat standard after another—"Cherokee," "Caravan," "Donna Lee," "Salt Peanuts." With lightning-quick fingers and an equally quick mind that still blazed at full power, Martrel had not lost a step—the ivory keys still dipped beneath his genius touch like magic, flooding cascades of sound from the wooden upright. At the end, the dozen or so customers were on their feet cheering.

Julian and his teacher hugged when they'd finished, and when he and Velmyra walked to the streetcar stop, Velmyra was still clearly under the older musician's spell.

"He's an amazing player." Her eyes sparkled with excitement. "Unbelievable."

"Yeah." Julian grabbed her hand as they crossed the street. "Folks oughta be bustin' down doors to hear him play. What a waste."

Velmyra's eyes narrowed as she pulled her hand back. "A waste? How was it a waste to do what you loved and were good at?" Julian stuttered, backpedaling. He'd planned a quiet dinner for two at his place featuring homemade lasagna and a pricey Valpolicella. This was no way to start the evening.

He had gone on to explain that when Martrel was young he had unwisely forfeited a shot at real success; turning down offers that could have paved a path to wealth, he'd decided to stay in New Orleans. She'd flinched, cut him a look. "But then where would you be?" she threw back at him. They had gone around and around—about the city and its limited opportunities for so many brilliant artists, the merits of nurturing talent and of preserving culture, the selfless passion of the teacher versus the ambition of the performer, and so on, until finally, picking over her Caesar salad, she let drop a revelation that pumped a rush of blood to his face.

How was he supposed to know she'd recently turned down an offer to work in the art department of one of Boston's top advertising firms, so that she could keep her low-paying teacher's job in the New Orleans school district? After that, the romantic wine-and-candles evening that Julian had staged descended into strained, sparse conversation with gaps of silence as wide and dark as the Mississippi. But the message was clear to both of them: as much as Julian loved the city, he was not about to wind up in a café in the French Quarter when he was sixty, playing for scale and tips.

Had that been the beginning of the end? He'd found a way to calm the waters stirred by that unfortunate misstep, cajole his way back into her good graces. But they'd never had that discussion again.

Velmyra looked up from the creek to the starry sky. She turned to him, an uneasiness dimming her eyes.

"Julian, there is something I want to tell you. About why I got married so soon after we broke up."

Now he turned away. "Not important. Old business."

"Well…"

He got up and dusted off his jeans.

"Let's go back." Whatever she had to say about her marriage, he didn't think he could hear it. Not now, and possibly never. He reached for her hand and helped her up, turning his thoughts back to the land, his father, the things presently at hand.

A southward breeze from the creek cooled the air as they walked toward the cabin. For tomorrow, his to-do list seemed endless: call the California Fortiers, meet with the insurance agent about the New Orleans house, check in with his house sitter in New York, pay bills (as many as he could), and meet again with Kevin to discuss the legalities of fighting for the Silver Creek land. He'd promised to call the guys in the band, who he hadn't talked to since Tokyo, to let them know what was going on. And even though he was no longer hopeful about Simon's survival, he had to find out what happened to him. Had he struggled, suffered? Had anyone tried to help him? He needed to know.

But now, the desperate urgency had passed; the tears had calmed him, ushered in resignation, acceptance. Simon was gone. But he had Vel with him, and was suddenly aware of the difference one person—the right person—could make when the rest of your life was as off-course as a storm-tumbled boat at sea.

As they neared the house, Julian stopped, reached for Velmyra and pulled her into his chest. Her face was moist, cool. The tender, soft kiss was as natural as breathing, without awkwardness or effort.

"I'm just now figuring out something." He leaned his cheek against her forehead.

"What's that?"

"How much I missed you all this time."

The quiet of the creek gave way to the faint crowing of a rooster somewhere in the distance. He reached again for her hand, and as soon as they had walked up the steps to the porch, the *pop, pop, pop* of gunshots, each one closer than the one before, fired in the night.

13

The door to 291 on the East Wing was half closed, but the young, Latina nurse heard the groan of the electronic equipment, the rhythm of the heart monitor, and the hum of the oxygen machine before she'd entered. An IV bag hung next to his bed, feeding him through the one bulbous vein in his bony left hand, while his right hand lay across his chest as if he were pledging allegiance to an unseen flag. His thin face was a parched landscape of patchy white stubble. His eyebrows arched upward in a nuanced frown and his dry lips gapped slightly, as if he were organizing his thoughts to begin a speech of major importance.

"Hello, mister, how you doing today?" the young nurse whispered as she leaned toward the old man's ear. She smiled, patted his hand, then looked at the chart at the foot of his bed and checked his numbers. His blood pressure, though still high, was down considerably, and his oxygen saturation oscillated from so-so to fairly good, but from what she could tell, he still hadn't had a moment of true consciousness. Clearly, he wasn't in the best shape, but something about him told her this one was a fighter, unlike so many of the John Does that drift into the emergency room of Mercy.

She'd been there the day they brought him in, took one look at him, and said, "He'll never make it." She'd asked about him and learned he'd been found a mile from the hospital, passed out on a bench near the access road to the highway that led into town. A middle-aged white couple, sixties hippie types, had pulled their van over onto the shoulder. Seeing he was still breathing, they hauled him into the back seat of their van and made tracks to the emergency room.

So many stories like that since the flood—people wandering away from torn lives like nomads in search of terra firma, some dry plot of earth not threatened by broken levees and rising water. When he had been placed in a room on Two East, though he wasn't her patient, she'd still gone in to check on him. His face, weathered and rough from what must have been an extreme ordeal, still possessed an angelic calm, and his chest rose and fell ever so slightly with each faint, steady breath. *Somebody's looking for him,* she'd thought. This man was no vagrant. She'd imagined him in a dining room full of laughter, sitting at the head of a Thanksgiving table, great-grands bouncing on his knee.

No one else was there, so in a moment of impulse, she had squeezed his hand.

His fingers were callused, steel-wool rough and dry. "Squeeze back." She'd whispered. "Tell me you hear me."

She knew it was harder for the ones like this, the ones with no family present, no memory-triggering voices to remind them of blood bonds and guide them through the wilderness of their barren minds.

She'd said it over and over again—*Squeeze my hand, tell me you hear me*—and kept clenching his hand, even through part of her lunch break. After fifteen or twenty minutes, she was about to give up when she felt a tiny, feeble pressing into her palm.

"*Dios mio,*" she had whispered. "Do it again! Do it one more time."

She'd needed to know that it wasn't just her imagination, it had really happened. But the next time she'd gotten nothing. She'd told the nurse supervisor, who'd also tried, and gotten nothing.

"Well, he might be in there somewhere." The nurse supervisor had released his hand and shaken her head. "But if he is, he's still got a long road ahead. He's so thin. And besides his blood pressure getting a little better, he's not showing us much."

That had been weeks ago. The young nurse was barely in her twenties—new to the routine—but had seen enough to know his chances were not good; his age worked against him and her supervisor had been right. His breathing, though steady, was shallow. At first figuring him to be in his late sixties, the young nurse remembered the jokes of her black girlfriends in nursing school whose racial bragging rights included phrases like "black don't crack," referring to the age-defying complexions of African Americans. She had a feeling he could be older than he looked.

Now, she looked up to see a round-figured, chubby-faced black nurse, her thick braids piled atop her head like a swirl of soft-serve ice cream, enter the room. They exchanged silent smiles.

"He a friend of yours?" The black nurse reached up to replace his IV bag.

"No." The young R.N. shook her head. "I just saw him when they brought him in."

"Well, he belongs in ICU, except with the flood and everything there's no beds down there," the black nurse said. "Somebody said they thought this one walked all the way from New Orleans or somewhere down there. In this heat, can you believe it? But I guess you do what you gotta do, you know?"

"Do they still not know who he is?"

"No. Nobody's even called about him. So many folks missing down that way, and a lot of folks don't even know where to look. He didn't have any ID on him. All he had was an old Bible."

"May I see it?"

"I don't know what they did with it. Check the drawer on the night stand over there."

The young R.N. walked to the side of the bed near the large window and opened the drawer to the oak night table. The Gideon Bible? Surely she couldn't have meant that. She placed it aside and kept looking. Housekeeping had apparently washed his clothes; a neatly folded shirt of bright red flannel, a sleeveless undershirt, and a pair of khaki pants lay beneath the Gideon Bible. *Odd that he would have worn a long-sleeve shirt in such heat.* She ran her fingers along the smooth cotton of the red shirt; it was thick, not at all the weight for these humid summer months. Maybe he'd grabbed something to wear that would make him most visible, attract the attention of passers-by. Or perhaps he was thinking of protecting his arms from the blazing sun.

She opened another drawer and there lay a larger book, the words "Holy Bible" embossed in gold, and the corners of the thick skin of black leather frayed to brown.

She opened it. The leather was hardened but it was otherwise intact; corners of the onion-skin pages were water-rippled, stained the color of tea. She found the name page.

Ever since they moved to North America from Cuernavaca, her own family had kept such a Bible, where on the first page the births of each family member had been listed, from her grandparents to her own young children. There was clearly writing on the page, but dirt or stains had blurred the family name.

All she needed was a last name, just something to go by, anything at all would help. With a closer look at the faded ink, she could just make out the first three letters of the last name.

She took the Bible and placed it on the bed next to the old man. She leaned over to whisper in his ear, and took his hand in hers.

"Mr… ah…Foreman?" she tried. "Forrest? Mr. Forrest?"

He didn't respond, of course. But she held on to his hand, squeezing and releasing in a rhythmic pattern…squeeze, release, two, three, four, squeeze, release…

After the fourth squeeze, she felt his hand gently closing around hers.

She sucked in a small sharp breath. She reached for the nurse's call button and soon after she pressed it, the heart monitor droned in a loud, continuous beep. She looked up at the machine, the green numbers changing rapidly. Her own heart raced as she watched his begin to fail.

She rushed to the wall and pressed the alarm button for Code Blue.

In the next few minutes there was a flurry of activity as a team of three tried to revive him. His pressure was dropping, but there was still a pulse, still a chance.

The young nurse's racing heart now stood still. She watched, frozen in a corner while they worked on him. *Please, Mister,* she thought. *Please. You can do it.*

They went on working while she closed her eyes and crossed her heart. "Mother of God," she whispered, then reached into her pocket to take out her rosary beads, and said a small prayer for the man with the angelic face and the rough, dry hands.

In Bobby Petit's Shrimp and Oyster House just off Duck Creek Road, a mango-colored autumn sun glimmered through the windows between the branches of southern pines onto the dingy, boot-scuffed cedar floor. Nine customers, all young or middle-aged men dressed in workshirts, workpants, or jeans, crowded the cigarette-butt charred counter or sat at booths of cracked vinyl while eggs and sausage patties sizzled on the long, grease-blackened griddle.

Near a window covered with yellowed Venetian blinds, Velmyra, Julian, and Kevin sat hunched over plates of sausage and crawfish omelets, their faces clouded with worry. A nearly empty carafe of coffee sat at the edge of the table.

"You mind moving your cup, sir?" The plump young waitress flicked auburn bangs from her eyes. She smiled at Kevin through silver braces.

"Huh? Oh, yeah. Sure."

He moved his coffee cup, and the waitress placed a saucer overrunning with crisp bacon near his plate.

"I'll bring you some more coffee in a minute."

The waitress took the carafe and left, and Kevin put a forkful of omelet in his mouth and chewed thoughtfully.

"I don't know." Kevin put down his fork. "It doesn't sound right. Doesn't sound like Nathan."

Julian looked up from his plate. "So you think we imagined gunshots? Both of us?"

Kevin held up both palms, backing off his words. "I'm just sayin.' There's no point in jumping to conclusions. Folks around here love to shoot guns off. Didn't have to mean somebody was after you, is all I'm sayin'."

Velmyra looked over her shoulder toward the kitchen and the front of the restaurant. "Well, I'm going to find a bathroom," she said. "I'll be back."

Julian watched her leave, giving nothing away in her easy glide, shoulders squared, head high. Like him, she'd been scared to death. So much happened, it seemed, in the seconds between the three shots. The distant first shot had left them as stunned as headlight-blinded deer—what had they actually heard? The snap of a tree branch finally giving way after the pounding of heavy rains? The backfire of a pickup? Or maybe just someone looking to bag a squirrel or rabbit for supper. The second shot, though, closer, ripped apart the innocent notion of morning hunters and snapping trees. Quick as a reflex, he grabbed Velmyra's hand and hurried into the house, his breath racing like a dog's while his bare feet pounded the porch floor. When the third shot fired, insistent, closer still, he flung her to the wood plank floor beside the bed, his back a curled shield over hers. For what seemed like an hour they had crouched like frightened animals, his heart thundering hoofbeats, her breath a rhythmic pulsing as audible as his own.

When their breathing settled into normal rhythms and they finally felt no imminent danger, they got up from the floor, only mildly relieved. The memory of just hours before, when they had stoked the fires of a long-extinguished love, had been riddled by gunshots; there was no thinking about that now. Fear clotted in both their minds; if not fear for their lives, then the strong realization that someone might want them gone badly enough to bring out a gun.

So they dressed nervously, hurried to the car and sped to the sheriff's office in Local.

The sheriff was not in yet. They sat quietly in the Neon, hearts still pounding and hands silently fidgeting, each ruminating over the events of the night-into-morning: Julian's tearful breakdown, the creaking complaint of Genevieve's brass bed beneath their passion, the muted strains of trumpet over the gurgle of moonlit Silver Creek, and the quick reports of a gun that had sent them running into the house. With the pale sun climbing higher, they waited until the sheriff, a slim man with rounded shoulders and a thick, whitish, curly mane, pulled up in his two-tone Chevy truck. He stepped out holding a coffee cup, cell phone pressed to one ear, belly laughing at some joke told from the other end.

In his hot, airless office the sheriff, still smiling at the joke, leaned back into his swivel chair, chewed on a toothpick, and thumped absently at his brass belt buckle while Julian told him about the gunfire. The sheriff shrugged, took a sip from his steaming cup of gas-station brew. A hunter, probably, was his guess—somebody with a brand new piece, time on his hands, and fingers itching for the feel of steel. "This *is* the country, you know," he'd advised, and assured them there was little likelihood of danger. "I'll keep an eye out, though." He'd reached for a nail clipper on his desk, a patronizing grin clearly reserved for city folks stretched beneath narrow, topaz eyes. "Oh, would y'all excuse me?" he said as his phone rang. He held it to his ear, and began laughing again.

They'd left and called Kevin, who also wasn't fazed. Gunshots in the early morning? Didn't they know they were in the Louisiana woods? And, wasn't it already early October? A little too soon for quail, but rabbit and squirrel hunting season had started, let's see, four days ago. Didn't see any reason for alarm, but since he'd been awakened anyway, he was hungry for some of Bobby Petit's strong, hot coffee and one of his big crawfish and sweet red pepper omelets.

Julian took a long, slow drink of ice water and looked toward the restroom door Velmyra had just entered. He glanced over at

Kevin, who was deep into his eggs. Still pondering the morning, his appetite stunted by gunfire, Julian took his fork and absently lined his potatoes in neat rows on the side of his plate.

He was not convinced there was nothing to fear, but for now, he tried to set aside his worries. "I guess I was…we were, a little spooked." He recalled Velmyra twisting the edge of her T-shirt in her fingers for the entire drive to the diner. Julian looked toward the window. "Where I come from, gunshots mean trouble."

Kevin grinned through a mouthful of buttered wheat toast. "You mean up in New York, or down in New Orleans?"

"Both."

Kevin nodded. "Ladies and guns don't go too well together, do they?" He tipped his chin toward the restroom door, and gave Julian an inquisitive glance. "How long y'all been together?"

Julian cleared his throat, looked down at the plate and plucked a loose tomato from his omelet with his fork. "We're not..." he started, then halted, sat back in his chair, remembering the moon through the blinds striping the bed in silver light, her thick hair brushing his cheek as her arm flung across his chest in the early hours before dawn.

"We, uh, had something going a few years ago." He spoke quietly. "Now we…she's just helping me find my father."

He didn't know what else to say.

Kevin blinked, his eyebrows flicking upward. "You mean, y'all don't stay together?"

"I live in New York, like I said before. And she lives in New Orleans."

Kevin shook his head. "You kidding? Damn. Y'all just look like, you know, a couple. She's real pretty, that one."

Julian tore off a piece of toast, looked thoughtfully at it, then put it in his mouth.

"Yeah. True."

That morning, in the moments between lying with Velmyra, first as her lover and later as her shield, Julian had sensed something he hadn't felt in a while—a soul-bonding with someone other than his father. As if after holding his breath without knowing it for years, he'd finally been introduced to the miracle of exhalation. As if returning from a landscape of chaos, he'd found a place of peace.

But the gunshots had rung out like an alarm thumping him out of a dream, bursting a hole in the afterglow. A warning, maybe? *Tread this ground carefully.* Velmyra had reawakened something in him—that was certain. But now he wasn't sure what any of it had meant, and neither, he believed, was she. He thought of disaster movies where doomed lovers clung to each other while ships sank or buildings burned, and wondered if their passion, having bloomed from the muddle of chaos and fear and tasting slightly of desperation, was not to be trusted. Once, in the car, he had looked over at her, glimpsed her twisting her shirt in her fingers, her brows furrowed, her eyes somewhere between concern and fear. There was so much going on now, how could anything seem real?

So they had ridden together in silence to meet Kevin, each in their separate confused worlds, as distant and uncomfortable as they had been when they first left New Orleans.

Kevin was stabbing a lump of sausage on the edge of his plate. "I know that whole thing with old man Parette probably scared the hell out of both of you. I truly think they were just trying to scare him, running him off the road. It just went bad, the way it turned out. But guns? Nathan's mean, but he ain't no killer and that ain't his style. He's too clever for that. Believe me, I been following this a while.

"Truth is, it's a whole lot more likely that those Thomas twins up by Swan River were out popping squirrels than that somebody was out to mess with y'all. But if you're worried, you can stay with me and Raynelle until you head back to New Orleans."

Julian told him thanks, but they were only staying until the evening and had plenty to keep them busy: after going back to Genevieve's and calling the Fortiers in California, Julian would head back to New Orleans, deal with Simon's property, and continue the effort to find out what had happened to him.

Julian looked up to see Velmyra returned from the restroom, sitting back down on the bench next to him, smelling faintly of citrus lotion. She gave Kevin and Julian a quick, uncertain smile.

She leaned her elbows onto the table and reached for the coffee carafe. "So have you got it all figured out? Are the bad guys after us?" She smiled a little broader as she poured coffee into her cup, making light of the tension that had settled between them like a mute visitor.

Kevin repeated his hunting season theory, trying his best to assure her there was no reason to be fearful. Velmyra, however, wasn't convinced. Those shots had been awfully close. *And what about the padlock?* For that, Kevin also had an answer: the padlock and the gunfire didn't have to be related. The "new owners," Nathan or whoever he was working with, probably didn't know anyone was living there, since the little bit of furniture lay under white sheets and Genevieve was never there.

Julian wasn't sure whether Kevin really believed what he was saying, or if he was only trying to massage the battered nerves of his new friends. At any rate, it made some sense. Looking at his watch—had they really been there two and a half hours?—he asked for the check.

When the waitress came, Julian took the bill and reached for his wallet. Kevin complained, digging in his pockets for his own money, but Julian held up a hand. "No way. I owe you. I don't know what I would have done if you hadn't come along when you did."

Before they left, a plan was laid out. Kevin would go back to Genevieve's with them, and after she made initial phone contact with the relatives to determine whether they had sold their portion of Silver Creek, Kevin would introduce himself as the family's lawyer and explain the situation. Once they had all the information they needed, Kevin would proceed with mounting a legal challenge to the sale of the land.

They were in the parking lot about to get into their vehicles when Julian's cell phone rang. It was Genevieve.

"Oh, sure, yeah. We were just talking about coming over to see you again anyway."

He listened a minute, then said, "OK, sure, of course." He folded the phone back into his pocket. Genevieve, he said, was delighted they were coming back over, and would they please stop by her house and bring something from her kitchen pantry?

"Umm, hmm. Don't tell me. Let me guess." Kevin got into his truck, rolled his window down, and leaned an elbow out.

Velmyra slung her purse over her shoulder as she got in the Neon. "Did you guys leave any of that stuff? You were hitting it pretty hard yesterday."

"I sure hope so," Julian said. "If not, we'll have to go down one of these country roads and find the nearest moonshine still."

When they arrived back at Pastor Jackson's place in two vehicles, a full jug of white lightning in hand (Velmyra turned up a stash of three jugs on the pantry floor), they found Genevieve sitting in a white ladderback rocker on the porch, shading her eyes from the sun as they climbed the steps.

"Heard anything about Simon?" she asked.

Julian told her what the police officer had said, but added that they wouldn't stop searching until they learned what happened to him.

Genevieve shook her head. "I been praying every day, every night since I talked to Simon. Praying he's somewhere safe. Had the TV on all day, terrible. Just terrible. They're talking now about those levees. Turns out they weren't even made right. Can you believe it? I knew Simon should of got out."

Julian took a deep breath. There was no point in telling her what he now believed about Simon's fate. There would be a time for that later. "We're doing our best to find him."

"You know, he's been through many a storm, him and Ladeena. You weren't even born when Betsy came through. We thought that was the worst of it. But we never thought we'd ever see anything like this."

Genevieve's eyes glazed over as she seemed lost in thought. Abruptly, she turned to Kevin and Velmyra, still standing. "Lord, y'all forgive me. Come on inside. I just made a pitcher of iced tea."

Julian thought about telling her about the gunshots, but decided against it. No use making her worry unless he was certain there was a reason. They sat around the huge dining table while Genevieve brought out a pitcher of tea from the kitchen and a cordless phone from a bedroom. Four phone calls yielded no answer, but at the fifth one Genevieve connected with a Miriam Longstetter, who was in her nineties, and a cousin of Genevieve's mother, Maree. Yes, Miriam said, she had been contacted by a representative of a real estate development company who offered her $11,000 for her share of the Silver Creek land. She was old, and she had wanted money to leave to the grandniece who took care of her. Kevin took the phone and after introducing himself, explained what had happened to the whole property after she sold her portion. Once the woman understood, she became silent. "Oh, my Lord," she finally said. "I would never have done something like that if I'da known what it meant. I just didn't know."

Kevin talked to the woman for more than a half hour. When he hung up, he folded both hands in his lap.

"We got our work cut out for us," he said. "The woman is old. I could try to prove that she was feeble-minded or something, that she didn't know what she was signing. That they deliberately misled her. But I don't know, she seemed awfully sharp to me."

She said she'd rarely thought about the land in Louisiana after living in California for sixty years and didn't see any reason not to sell off her own small share of it. What harm could it do? And of course, no one explained how the sale of one portion could jeopardize the rest of the family's ownership.

Kevin leaned back, stretched his legs under the table, and crossed his feet at the ankles. "These guys are smart. They love it when people don't know the law. And if they can't read—and some of these old folks can't—even better. They pretty much can have things the way they want them."

"So what do we do now?" Velmyra poured iced tea from the pitcher into her glass and stirred it with her spoon.

Kevin had asked the woman for a FedExed copy of the contract. He'd go over it for loopholes and errors, and study land dispute cases in the Parish to see if there were any grounds for a suit appealing the sale of the land.

Everyone was quiet a moment. "I just can't believe it's gone—the house, the creek, all of it." Genevieve wrung her hands together. "We've always had this land. It's been in our family forever." She looked at Julian. "Baby, we got to get it back."

Then she reached for the jug of white lightning Julian had placed on the sideboard and held it up. "Anybody care to join me?" She poured some of the clear liquid over her iced tea and shook the glass.

Julian, Kevin, and Velmyra looked at each other. "No, ma'am," and "Thank you," they all said.

Julian leaned forward, his elbows on his knees, his hands clasped. His head throbbed, and his eyes were strained and tired. *Enough for today,* he told himself. Fatigue draped his body like a leaden sheet, and he remembered how little sleep he'd had. Even though it was only late afternoon, the day had seemed endless. He looked at his watch. "I guess we better be getting back to Baton Rouge."

As they got up to leave, Genevieve raised a hand.

"Wait, y'all," she said. " What's your hurry? Pastor Jackson's out visiting the sick and shut in—a few of the church members caught some awful bug. He'll be a while, since they all missed communion last week. I could use a little company."

They looked at each other, at their watches, and shrugged.

"Come on out on the porch," she said, as if the decision to stay was never in question. "There's usually a nice breeze coming through this time of day."

Carrying the iced tea pitcher and all the glasses on a tray, Genevieve led them to the porch. Kevin and Velmyra sat in the ladderback rockers while Julian sat on the steps. Her eyes glassy, Genevieve sat in the green painted rocker and took a long drink of the spiked iced tea. She put the glass down on the wooden floor next to her chair, and leaned back with her hands folded across her lap.

"Whew!" she said, exhaling with a tired huff and fanning herself with a cardboard fan decorated with a picture of a blond Jesus, the words Elam C.M.E. written across the front.

"This reminds me of the old times." She smoothed the wrinkles of her warmup pants with her hand, and smiled thoughtfully at Julian.

"Baby, I remember when you were nothing more than a little boy, coming up to Silver Creek in summer. When you were just a little thing, you couldn't wait to get here. Your eyes lit up when you picked blackberries off the bushes and apples and peaches off the trees. You chased lightning bugs with those Beaulieu boys till it got so dark you couldn't hardly see. You'd rip and run all day long in those woods if we'da let you. When the summer ended, you cried when you had to go back home."

Julian looked down, smiled and nodded, then took a sip of tea. There was something resigned in Genevieve's manner as she spoke. Something in her face, her manner told him there was a point to all this, a purpose to wanting him to stay.

Her words grew softer, yet more deliberate. "But I watched you, and I saw a change. Started in your eyes. The way they kinda dulled when you and your daddy and mama would pull up into the yard in that white Ford on the first Sunday in June. Saw it in your shoulders, too, drooping and sloping when we all sat on the porch at sunset, and you sat right where you're sittin' now, looking as bored as you could be. The last time I saw that look in your eyes and that slump in your shoulders, you musta been no more than eleven or twelve."

"Your daddy was so proud of you. You strutted around with that horn of yours like it was the holy grail, and your mama asked you to play for us one evening after supper. You played "Just a Closer Walk with Thee," and had us all in tears. Remember how we made such a fuss over you? That was the only time you smiled the whole time you were here. I said to myself, 'Umm, hmm, it'll be a long time before I see my cousin's young boy down here again.'"

Looking down at the yard dust on his shoes, Julian remembered that day, and how much he hadn't wanted to come even then. The light on the porch grew dim as a cloud passed before the sun, then brightened again as the sun peeked through it. "That land? That creek? It meant everything to your daddy. But after a certain age, you got to be a real city boy." She paused and heaved a slow, silent breath, looking across the yard at the grove of trees.

"I know you want to get the land back," she said. "Cause you know how much your daddy loved it. But it's harder, fighting for something *you* don't love, something that don't move your heart. So before you go trying to get the land back, it needs to mean something to you."

"I'm so happy you came home," she said. "You came home to where you were born, New Orleans, and now you're here. But I need you to know something, and for that you need to go all the way home. Home to where your people came from, to where it all started."

"Stay just a little while longer. I'll fix you some food if you're hungry. Cause I got a little story to tell you."

14

How long had he been here? A day? A year? He stared through closed eyelids toward beaming light. Was it the sun? It couldn't be, for the surface where he lay was soft and cool and the place smelled of something pungent, like alcohol, or antiseptic. He tried to open his eyes to let in the stream of brightness, but as hard as he tried, his eyelids, dream-thick and heavy with sleep, would not part.

He drifted back into the dream, then again into a milky wakefulness, then into sleep again. He had no idea how long he had been in this place, but as he lay against the coolness, he couldn't remember when he had last been anywhere else. His mind, it seemed, was a thing acting of its own will, a ship drifting into strange waters without a steering hand.

He was standing on a rooftop, looking over something resembling a river. Or a creek? He wasn't sure. No, it had been a street. Only there was so much water (and so little street), more than he'd ever seen. Walking with a full sun beating against the back of his neck, throat gritty as sand, leaving heel tracks in roadside dust. Walking, walking. Hungry. Head feeling woozy. The sharp burn of sun and vibration in his feet as trucks screamed by.

Soft hands, softer voices. Women turning him over in bed.

He tried reaching a hand forward, but nothing moved. He tried to turn his head away from the light, but nothing moved.

Slowly, the name of his son gathered in his frail mind and he tried to call it out. But the word seemed trapped somewhere in his throat, fully formed in his mind, but resisting his tongue.

And then he slipped further back. Way back before his son was born, when he was a boy himself, before he'd ever heard of New Orleans. And another name came to mind. Again, he tried it out on his tongue, but it was like pulling a tooth from his mouth. His chest heaved as he tried to force the words from his lips. And finally the words came: *John Michel.*

Or as his father had always called him, *The Frenchman.*

A summer night at Silver Creek, damp jasmine-scented breezes ripple through sloping eaves. Like the ancient evenings buried deep in the memory of the live oaks, back before ropey moss hung from each branch like the beards of ancestors. His father Jacob, and Jacob's sister Maree, seated on the narrow gallery of the cabin, tell the story yet another time.

His ears numbed to the telling of old folks' tales, young Simon sits after supper on the cabin steps, restless; he's heard the story a thousand times on these sultry nights while rocking chairs creak to the rhythm of cricket calls and nightbird songs from the woods. How his grandfather Moses' mother, Claudinette, had found comfort and peace with the man who had given her the name Fortier, for he had loved her as well as any white man could love an Ashanti woman in 1855. Planter, part-time preacher, and master of thirteen slaves (including Claudinette), John Michel Fortier had truly grieved for his wife who'd died and left him with a single boy child, but not long after found salve for his sorrow with the dark-skinned beauty, laying his grief to rest in her heart.

Claudinette had been a cook without peer. The buttery scent of her biscuits and the savory aroma of her pot pies as she brought them into his kitchen didn't hurt her appeal, but it was in Claudinette's heart-shaped face that John Michel had seen treasures—the Louisiana sunrise in her eyes, the wide sweeps of Africa in the broad planes of her face. An abiding love for the woman he owned was something he could never admit (to himself or the world) until his mourning was complete, after his own wife was long buried.

And Claudinette grieved too, for her husband, a man with bull-hard shoulders, powerful hands, and a generous but weak heart, who had left her in his sleep one September night with two bright-eyed toddling daughters.

So when the grief clogging both their hearts had thinned to a fine stream of longing, John Michel came to Claudinette, removing his hat and bowing his head at her cabin door. He scuffed the Louisiana mud from his boots, the small rose in his hand nearly wilted from the August heat.

Peering into John Michel's evening-gray eyes, Claudinette saw advantage and a way to take it. She examined the proposal budding in them and offered one of her own—her whole hand and a piece of her heart, in exchange for freedom for her and her children.

Jean Michel mopped the sweat from his brow with the sleeve of his jacket.

"I'm an old man. When I die, you and your children will be the freest of the Lord's creatures. I swear it on the written word of God."

The sun turned her almond eyes into stones of fire.

"Free my children now," she said.

John Michel looked into her eyes and saw winters warmed by wood flame and her long brown arms. He saw a child with his shoulders and her upturned chin, a future where she would have what pleased her, and he would find his joy in the pleasing.

So John Michel cared for Claudinette as kindly as he had his own wife—keeping her distant enough for the sake of southern propriety, but close enough to bear him unbounded joy, and a second son. And so they lived, John Michel in the modest main cottage, Claudinette in a cabin in the quarters near the creek with her two girls, and John Michel's two sons by the two women (one white and one black but each equally free), scampering back and forth on the packed earth in between.

The two half brothers—John Paul, blond and fair as southern white pine, and Moses, dark as river stones—had grown up close as twins, and not until they were seven and five did they sit laughing beneath the sweetgum tree near the creek comparing the stark difference in the skin of their arms, the texture of their hair. Their curious wonder soon turned to casual indifference. Both boys enjoyed the favor of their father, and Claudinette doted on the smiling blond boy as much as she did her own three children. But after the boys grew to strapping young men, the differences that had seemed inconsequential before loomed larger.

John Paul, who grew into a smallish young man with eyes like his father's and golden hair that curled to his shoulders, was bighearted, foolhardy, and aimless. He loved to wander along Silver Creek, empty-minded and full of drink, and had a predilection for gambling, lying for sport, and slim-waisted women who belonged to other men. Moses, who stood half a head taller than most young men his age, with thick eyebrows set at an angle of worry that nearly met in the center of his forehead, worked hard, smiled infrequently. The laughter he'd shared with John Paul as a boy quieted the more he learned the real differences that separated him and his father's first-born.

But Moses was a hopeful man. By the time he'd reached his full impressive height and learned to carry his shoulders like a man with purpose, slavery had been over a while. Men who looked like him now had their own land. While his brother sat on the creek bank with a bottle of Kentucky rye and played on the bugle his father had given him, or traveled down to New Orleans for a midnight stagger through the Vieux Carré, Moses sharecropped a parcel of his father's land, fancying himself one day a successful planter the way his father had been. Why not? He was a strong, free man. As strong and as free as anybody.

But the more his plow-hands callused and bled, the more he understood that sharecropping was a long, hard road that led to an empty ditch. A sharecropper just picked at the crusted rim of freedom, and could never enjoy its sweet center. No way to earn enough to buy anything of real value, let alone a decent spread of land. No way to see a time of ease and rest in his old age. No way to have something to leave to his own children, should he have them. So when John Paul became twenty-one, and Moses watched as his father gave his older brother two hundred acres of fertile black earth veined with a sparkling creek, the frown between Moses' eyes deepened.

He went to his father, who now walked with a stoop and a cane. Moses still loved his brother, but fair was fair. After all, John Michel was *his* father, too. Wasn't he entitled to land as much as his white brother, who'd done nothing to earn it?

John Michel stroked his yellowing beard. His beloved Claudinette had been dead for years now. In both his son's eyes were the gentle smiles of their mothers. But give Moses his own land? Afraid not.

"But when I reach twenty-one years?"

John Michel had witnessed the heedless pride, the erect walk and upturned head of his son. Black skin, a straight spine, an unbowed head and eyes that looked straight on at white men—all were an open invitation to trouble. Make him a landowner too? John Michel shook his head.

"It is for your own good. You think you can hold on to this land after I am gone? Ha! These folks around here, they will ruin you, take your land, if they do not kill you. Likely, they will do both."

Moses turned away, his resentment brick-hard at the bottom of his heart. Was it really fear for his safety that was his father's concern? He didn't know, and his ire toward both his father and brother grew darker as time passed.

But on a late summer Sunday evening, John Michel knocked on Moses' cabin door, his eyes wide and breath short. John Paul was missing, and Moses was to go and look for him.

Moses shook his head sardonically. Probably playing that bugle, down by the creek. But at the creek he was nowhere to be found, so Moses hitched his horse to the wagon and drove into town. And there was John Paul in his favorite watering hole, drunk out of his mind, a dazed look on his face, staring down the barrel of a gun.

Flickering light from the oil lamps outside the saloon glowed through the dirty windows and glazed the bald head of the man holding the gun. He was the biggest white man Moses had ever seen, even taller than he was and twice as wide, and his hateful smile revealed a large gap between his teeth. From what Moses could tell, he'd caught John Paul with his woman, and was determined to end any possibility for another tryst.

The gap-toothed man stepped toward John Paul and cocked the trigger. Moses raised his hand toward the man and glowered at his brother with narrowed, contemptuous eyes.

"Wait. Let me do it," Moses told the man. "I've got more issue with this man than anybody. If somebody's going to kill him, it ought to be me."

The gap-toothed man looked up at Moses incredulously. To prove his words, Moses lunged toward his brother and landed a heavy blow on the side of his face, then planted another deep in his gut. John Paul cried out, doubled over in pain and fell to his knees, his blue eyes gazing in confusion at the brother who was now betraying him.

The man tossed Moses the gun. "Be my guest," he said, the vision of his enemy being shot by this tall darky gleaming in his mind.

Moses took the gun, aimed it at his brother's heart.

Then he grinned and tossed it back.

"Don't need that," he said. "I'll finish this fool with my own two hands."

The man laughed as Moses dragged his bloodied brother out of the saloon. Outside, he put John Paul into the wagon and headed it back toward Silver Creek.

When he arrived at his father's house, Moses carried his brother over his back past John Michel, sitting in his parlor with his Bible open, up the staircase to John Paul's room. There, he dressed the wound he'd inflicted, and rubbed ointment on the gut he'd bruised with his own fist. Then he undressed his drunken brother and put him to bed.

John Michel understood the heart of his darker son, who had beaten his beloved, feckless brother to save his life. The dusk-gray eyes brimmed with gratitude. Not speaking, Moses walked past him, watered his horse, and went to bed to get up early and tend his fields.

When John Paul recovered, he came to his brother, his head bowed in contrition.

"Thank you," he said, "for my life."

Moses placed a hand solidly on his brother's shoulder and gave him a hard, determined look.

"He'll be looking for you. Always. You'll never be safe here."

John Paul looked down at the ground, kicked the dirt off one boot with the heel of another. Then, hearing a fluttering overhead, looked up as three blackbirds winged north toward the unknown world. It was as if he needed to hear the words to do the sensible thing, the thing that was already flitting around his mind. The next day, at dawn, Moses woke his brother and pressed eight silver dollars into his palm.

"You best go now, before it gets light."

And without saying goodbye to his father, John Paul saddled his horse and rode as far away from Silver Creek and the gap-toothed man as he could get.

Months passed and John Michel listened in vain for his son's hearty laugh, the wail of a brass bugle coming from the creek. Moses measured the bloom of grief in his father's eyes, and as the winter turned to spring, then summer, then winter again, John Paul did not return.

But John Michel never forgot that wherever his son was, he was alive, and for that he had Moses to thank. After John Paul left, John Michel studied his black son—the manly set of his brow, the back muscled by hard work, the large hands toughened by plow handles, the intelligent eyes that seemed to know more of the world than most of the white men he knew.

On Moses' twenty-first birthday, John Michel called him to his bed.

Frail, sick with consumption and the grief-wounds of loss, John Michel reached out a pale, white hand to his black son.

"I placed my trust in the wrong son—you were always the worthy one." His breath came hard and heavy from his sunken chest. "You will never find a better piece of land than Silver Creek. Guard it with your life. Don't let anybody take it from you."

He handed his son the old black Bible from the table by his bed.

"Everything you need, son, you'll find in here."

Moses took the old weathered Bible and pressed it to his chest. And with that, he became the sole steward of the land at Silver Creek.

When the old man died, Moses was left with his half-sisters, Belle and Patrice, the memory of the golden-haired brother whose life he'd saved, and the most beautiful stretch of green, fertile land in Pointe Louree Parish, if not all of Louisiana. With his sisters, their husbands and their children, Moses worked the earth until it bled riches, and turned it into a profitable paradise.

But as time passed, the place his only brother occupied in his heart still felt hollow. He missed the hearty laugh. The foolhardy, fun-loving ways. The music of a bugle wafting up from the creek. Many nights, Moses questioned himself in the depths of his soul and found no answers. For a brief moment, when he'd seen his white brother staring down the barrel of a gun, a notion had pawed across his mind: *If this man shoots my brother, Silver Creek could be mine.* The bitter taste of betrayal still coated his tongue.

Had he betrayed him? No. He had saved his life, he told himself. But he had sent his brother away, breaking his father's heart, and to his surprise, his own? Had he done it for his brother's safety, or to tilt an unbalanced world in *his* favor? It crossed his mind to saddle up and search for John Paul. But search where? North? West? In time he resigned himself to three things: that he would never in life see his brother again, that he had a hand in the heartbreak that hastened his father's death, and that both truths were the price he'd paid for beautiful Silver Creek.

He brooded over this for a while, until he met Clothilde, a sweet-faced woman with eyes like new pennies and a voice that reminded him of morning birds. At the Sunday church supper beneath the stand of oaks, he studied her bowed lips, the long graceful curve of her neck, the slim fingers, and asked her name. And a year after they married, Moses pulled out the old leather Bible his father had given him and turned to the first page. On a rare frostbitten day in February, after his wife's long and painful labor, he wrote the name of his newborn son, Jacob.

And to Jacob, a caramel-skinned child with the lightly textured hair and light eyes of his grandfather John Michel, Moses passed on the word: love the land, take it and make it your own. And Jacob did—but John Michel's prophesied peril, having skipped a generation, came to light in Jacob's time. When he grew to manhood and inherited Silver Creek, jealous white planters and townsmen, looking to increase their fortunes and destroy his, tried every trick they could think of to break his spirit. Cheating him out of payment for his crops. Stealing his plow, his mule. Burning crosses in his yard. Starting small fires in the middle of the night, one that even burned down his barn.

There were times when it seemed the whole world conspired to break him. But like his father had, he wrapped his soul around the land and clenched it like a fist.

The air in the room was cooler now, or at least the sweat on his forehead had seemed to disappear. As he lay remembering Jacob, Simon felt his lips move, and the memory of his words seemed to unfurl like a long litany in his head.

Sundays after church, all of them sitting on the cedar plank gallery in cane-back pine rockers. Jacob's eyes glistening, his preacherly voice tromboning through the trees as he fanned himself with banana leaves and addressed his wife Liza, his son Simon, and his cousin, Maree, her husband James, their daughter Genevieve, and anyone else who would listen.

Nothing is as enduring as land, because it's land, not water, that covers the whole earth. Beneath every pool of water—every stream, creek, marsh, lake, river, ocean—you go deep enough, you'll find land. Water, always in motion, shifts and moves. Rivers dry or change their course, sometimes disappear. But land will always be. They say the world is mostly water, but what's beneath all that water? Land. Earth. Way down deep, maybe, but it's surely there. Land needs water, true, but without land, water knows no bounds. With land, you can make a life for yourself, be lifted up. Love it, tend it, take care of it, and it will take care of you.

Tall and slender like Moses, Jacob would roll his head back against his rocker squinting against the fierce Louisiana sun, a wooden pipe clenched between strong white teeth, his gaze spanning Silver Creek. He spread his long arms wide in an evangelical pose, his sing-song baritone thundering with conviction.

I'm tellin' you, the Lord and the land will provide! You got you some good land, a strong back and two hands, you ain't never got to go hungry, you can work that earth and beat it and tame it til it feeds you, you can eat every day God sends. You can hunt, you can fish, you can plow, you can plant.

You can live.

And Silver Creek provided. Through all the years of hard summer sun, spring floods, and the rare winter frost, the land gave selflessly, generously. Maree, a tiny but sturdy knot of a woman, would shell, clean, skin, or gut whatever the menfolk had netted, hooked, trapped, or shot, and with the treasured recipes learned at the knee of her grandmother Claudinette, turned her daughter Genevieve and her nephew Simon into masters of the kitchen. Through every turn of fortune the whole country endured, the Fortier table was never empty, and savory stews and soups and smoked meats and fruit pies overflowed from the cabin near the creek, and the aromas circling in the evening air mixed with the fragrance of the green, nurtured land.

As Jacob's fortunes increased, he bought more land. And built himself a second house in New Orleans, just because he wanted to, and could. And burned his son Simon's ear with the story of how the richest land in the whole parish became a tall, thick-browed black man's land.

He felt a dryness in his throat, a thirst beyond any thirst before, as he remembered his father's last days, and the promise he, Simon, had made to Jacob. A crying-out sound was trapped in his throat, but his mouth still would not work. He tried to lift his hand, but it would not move. He would just have to wait for the woman with the soft hands and the blues-song whisper. She would bring the water.

So he let his mind go where it chose.

Julian. Julian had not yet found him.

The land. It was all gone now. The house in New Orleans built with Jacob's own hands. Gone, more than likely. That, he could live with; that, he could fix. But Silver Creek? He had tried to make Julian understand, if only for the sake of his unborn children, the grandchildren he would never see. But early on he'd seen a glow in his eyes, the same glow that rose in Jacob's eyes whenever he'd spoken of Silver Creek. But in Julian's eyes, that glow reflected the whole world beyond it.

But did it really matter? The end of the line had come, the end of him, the end of Silver Creek.He turned his head, and surprised at having the strength to do it, he relaxed his lips into a smile. It didn't matter. His son, after all, had his own life to live, his own dreams. God bless him. He, Simon, had had his run, and it had been a good one.

15

When Genevieve finished her story of the Fortiers and Silver Creek, Kevin folded his arms in front of him and bowed his head. Velmyra smiled, her eyes moist.

Julian leaned his elbows on his knees and rested his head between his palms, as if Genevieve's story weighed so heavily in his mind it took both hands to hold it. If this was the story Simon had told him a million times in his kitchen while crawfish pies browned and bubbled in the oven and gumbo cackled on the stove, he hadn't remembered it seeming so real.

Genevieve looked up at Julian, the light raking across her brows. She folded both hands in her lap resolutely and aimed a soft gaze at him.

"So baby, when you go trying to fix all this business with Silver Creek, think about your daddy, his daddy, and his daddy before. What the place meant to them. You got to know exactly what it is you fighting for."

Julian inhaled deeply, then frowned. "Daddy told me some of the stories, but I don't think I knew all of this before."

"Oh, baby. You been told all this before." Genevieve nodded, gave him a wizened look. "Ain't nobody blaming you for forgetting, but you been told before."

Either Genevieve had rendered the ancestors' lives with a fullness he'd never realized before, or it was just that now he was willing to listen, not just hear. John Michel. Claudinette. Moses. What must their lives have been like? He half-remembered that John Michel, a white planter, loved the pretty-eyed, boot-black woman who had been his slave, and from them had come Moses, who had gotten the land intended for his brother. But none of these people had meant any more to him than characters in a book.

Even grandfather Jacob, who'd died when Simon was only sixteen, had been little more than myth to Julian. While he vaguely recalled something about Jacob and his trials with the land, none of the details sounded too familiar; he'd always listened with half an ear and an itinerant mind, wandering to thoughts of whatever he planned to do as soon as the storytelling was done. But in death, his father now resided in the realm of his ancestors—alongside John Michel, Claudinette, Moses and the others—and Julian had listened to the story with both ears and a full heart.

Julian was silent, lost in a memory. Back when he was small, four or five, he'd actually enjoyed those summers skipping across the yard, picking the bushes and trees clean of their sugary fruit, catching crawfish in the creek shallows for Simon and Genevieve to boil for supper. But Genevieve was right; as he grew older, things changed. He remembered being eleven or so and bored to distraction as Genevieve, his Auntie Maree and his father told the family stories, while all he could think of was the city where he lived.

He'd been a young musician in love with the sound of his own horn. New Orleans had been a street party begging him to join in and cut a step, and when its two/four time clicked in with the rhythm of his pulse, he couldn't tell where the city's heartbeat left off and his began. Even at Silver Creek, the music lingering in his head, he would catch his foot tapping to a city groove. He had had no patience for a country backwater where the only night music was the swelling ring of cicadas and the reedy whine of wind through pines.

Julian blinked his eyes. These last couple of days, he'd begun to see how a place like this could crawl under your skin and get into your blood. Velmyra had been right; Silver Creek mornings were miracles, liquid sun spilling gold onto green earth like a primordial dream. Honeyed air sagging with a weight that seemed to settle the rhythms of the heart. Tall pines sheltering the secret and the eternal. A creek as timeless as memory itself. From Jean Michel to Simon, one hundred and fifty years of Fortier men crazy in love with a piece of land. They'd all known something from birth that he was just beginning to see.

Genevieve's ladderback rocker squeaked against the floorboards of the porch as she got up.

"I'm a little hungry. Anybody else want a little something to eat?"

They ended up staying for an early supper. Fresh-made collard greens with smoked hamhocks and butter beans with sweet onions were staples in any kitchen where Genevieve cooked, even if it wasn't her own, and she hummed as she bustled around the stove. In a cast iron skillet she poured a little fat, then batter for hot water cornbread. When the smell of the homemade Creole spice she'd used in the deep fried chicken began to scent the air, Genevieve laid out china on the dining room table, and her guests sat down and gorged themselves.

After supper, Genevieve's first words after table-clearing seemed to come from nowhere. "Let's go for a walk. I got something to show y'all." And as if her voice had levitating powers, they all got up. The sky was still light, the breezes cooling, and nobody could think of a reason not to go. Besides, after a meal like that, it would be ungracious to refuse a hospitable old woman who cooked like a dream.

She grabbed her yellow straw sun hat, a hickory walking stick, and a green plaid shawl from the front closet and draped it around her thin shoulders, and laced on a pair of purple Adidas sneakers. "This way," she said, stepping back out onto the porch and pointing the stick toward the afternoon sun. The west end of Pastor Jackson's sixty acres butted against the northeast corner of the Silver Creek land, and what she wanted to show them was close enough to get there and back long before dark.

They struck out toward the descending sun where the pines near the horizon shielded them from its low slanting glare, and Julian kept his eyes on the leaf-and-twig-strewn path. This was no leisurely stroll through a cleared patch of flat earth; this was the woods, thick and deep. What had Genevieve called Julian? City boy? Well, they'd not walked more than fifteen minutes before his basketball jock knees began to ache, and his second stumble on a break in the earth had Velmyra reaching for his arm. A few weeks away from the gym, and he wasn't sure he could keep pace with a seventy-something-year-old woman.

But these woods were amazing, like nothing he'd seen before, at least not since he was a child. The air ripe with pine, the silence almost sacred, broken only by leaf crackle beneath his feet or the sounds of birds whose names he didn't know. Before long, the deep light of afternoon sun was so hidden by the spindly trees that it seemed the evening dark had already taken hold.

Genevieve and Kevin had taken the lead, Genevieve with a hand on her walking stick and an arm strung through Kevin's, both occasionally laughing as Kevin's tall frame leaned over now and then in her direction to hear her speak. They seemed lost in conversation, and every few minutes Genevieve would stop, turn around, and point, her voice intoning like a tour guide's. "Now those three cypress trees over there—that's where the school house used to be," or "See beyond those pecans? That's where the church used to be where I was christened." And later, when they'd gotten closer to the creek, "Slave cabins. Right down that path."

Vel's gazed lingered in the direction of Genevieve's last announcement. "Really? Are they still there?"

"No, baby. Burned down a long time ago."

Julian had thought of apologizing to Vel for the inconvenience of the long hike—this wasn't part of the deal—but was stopped by her contented smile and easy bouncing gait as she ambled alongside him, wide-eyed, hands dug into her shorts pockets when she wasn't pointing out some sort of interesting bird or patch of wildflowers or tree or berry-laden shrub. She was, it appeared, enjoying herself. In fact, everyone was, he realized, as Genevieve's and Kevin's laughter mixed with the rustle of scraping branches and leaf against leaf in the light swirls of late afternoon breeze. If Genevieve was upset about any of the recent events—Simon's disappearance, the whole land thing—she didn't show it. Or maybe this was how she handled it: walking out her worries in the woods.

As they walked, patches of Genevieve's and Kevin's conversation came through: Genevieve was talking about the creek, which was not within sight, but faintly audible, if you kept real quiet, from this part of the land. The creek, she'd said, fed into a small river with an Indian name she couldn't quite pronounce, which fed into another, which fed into the Mississippi, and on into the Gulf. He'd never thought about that before—how the smallest little thing can move along to become part of something bigger. Like a chain of lives that began long ago, one small life flowing into another, and another, and on and on, until a whole lineage is born.

Nearly a half hour had passed when Genevieve stopped and pointed her stick to a space between four live oak trees where stood a decrepit cabin of old, weathered wood.

The trees hovered over the house so close they seemed as one, their leaves and branches crowning the roof like the elaborate headdress of an African queen. Eaves sagged where birds had nested in them. The roof showed gaping holes, and dry vines splayed out like boney fingers as they trailed up along the clapboard sides. It was much older and smaller than Genevieve's house but in a similar Creole style—the broad roof sloping down over the gallery, the thin wooden columns spaced a few feet apart, and the whole thing raised up on blocks of stone, allowing a foot of crawl space beneath it.

"This was Claudinette's place, the only house still standing from back in those days," Genevieve explained, according to the handed down stories, that Claudinette insisted her lover Jean Michel build her a place where they could meet on equal terms, a place of her own that was neither slave quarters—reminding her of her station—nor plantation house, reminding her of his.

They all stared in awe. The house and its sheltering trees had an organic quality to it, almost spooky, like something alive. It had the slightly withered look of something that should have crumbled into the earth long ago, but apart from its sagging eaves and the holes in the roof, stood stubbornly straight and tall, defiant against the ravages of time.

"What's that?" Velmyra pointed to a wrought iron chair the size of a small loveseat on the west side of the house, rusted and slightly tilted on lopsided earth, but wholly intact. In the middle of the back was a swirl of iron ornately curled into the letter "C."

"He went down to New Orleans, my great grandfather did, found the best colored blacksmith in town, and had that seat made for her to sit and rest her feet under the trees after a long day of standing in his kitchen. Or at least, that's what my grandmother told me." Genevieve looked up at the house. "Not too fancy, but you see it's still here." she added. "Built it himself. This is the house where Moses was born."

She looked at Julian. "And your grandfather Jacob, too."

Julian ran his hand along the side of one of the wooden posts, thinking about the unlikely pairing of his great-great grandfather and grandmother, secreted away in a love nest in the woods. And as much as Simon had talked about the family, Jacob was a man he knew little about. He knew his grandfather had died fairly young, suffering a long sickness, but Simon rarely mentioned his father's last years.

"How did my grandfather die? Daddy never talked about it much."

Genevieve leaned on the hickory stick. A breeze rose up from the floor of the woods, swirling in air cooled by a slipping sun and the shade of pines and oaks. She pulled her shawl around her shoulders.

"Well now, I'll tell you what I know."

After John Michel died, she said, white men had simply seen Moses as a black man stewarding his dead white master's land, and pretty much let him be. Not so with Jacob. He was a black man tending his own land, the best land in the parish, and he was living well. That had been his crime.

"Then that boll weevil came along. Ate up everybody's cotton crop for miles around, but not Jacob's!" Genevieve threw her head back and let out a cackling laugh. The deadly pest tore through the southern states, destroying acres of crop and bringing cotton farmers to their knees. "Yessir, that boll weevil knocked King Cotton on his sorry butt! But it never had a taste for Jacob's crop. Folks couldn't figure it out, how Jake got so lucky. Some said it was God's miracle, some said Jacob had the devil on his side. Then the Depression came. Jacob had food on the table all the time, when everybody else—white farmers, mind you—was going hungry."

Genevieve sucked her teeth. "I tell you, jealousy is one powerful force. I mean, they treated him something terrible. Night riders. Klan. You name it. If it wasn't one thing, it was another."

Genevieve looked toward the distant trees and squinted at the sun. Jacob's wife, Liza, she said, died young, giving birth to her second child, who also didn't live. And it was not long afterward the fires started: first the barn, then the shed. They weren't accidents, she believed, but acts of spite. "That just about did him in; seemed like he didn't have no more fight left."

"He took to his bed for a long time. Just couldn't get up, too weak. Doctors said it was his heart, but we all knew what it was. It was his heart all right—heart*break*. Heart *sick*ness. Worry. Nowadays they woulda called it stress."

"Simon wasn't much more than a boy, but he took over, did most of the work. After my own daddy died, it was just us, my mother Maree, Uncle Jake, me, and Simon. My mother took care of Uncle Jake and looked after Simon too, 'til he got old enough to take care of himself.

"But Uncle Jake still ran everything from his sickbed. Funny thing. Uncle Jake never lost his appetite, loved good food. Loved my mama's red beans and rice 'til the day he died. I always thought Simon let Mama teach him how to cook just so he could have something to give his daddy every day. A sweet biscuit rubbed with butter. A bowl of red beans. Something to bring a smile to his face."

Julian smiled. "That sounds like Daddy."

Genevieve nodded. "Before he died, he made Simon promise to keep the land in the family, whatever it took. Said if the land ever left the family, get this, said he'd come back from the grave *himself* to make things right. From the *grave*. Well, that got Simon's attention. Simon said he would, but he was just a boy, you know, sixteen years old."

Pulling her shawl closer, she turned to look toward the creek. "There's nothing harder to hold on to than a good piece of prime land, or at least that's the way it seems these days. Rich folks always seem to find a way to get it, poor folks always manage to find a way to lose it. Every three or four years, some slick fast-talking somebody tried to get me and Simon to sell. They just wouldn't quit. Now..." She shook her head. "Look like they found a way."

She pointed her hickory stick toward the north end of the woods. "There's a new golf course less than four miles that way with a big ol' concrete parking lot. Right where there used to be a thick forest of pines and pecans and sweetgum. And they put up a strip mall two miles away from that."

She looked at Julian. "Things change, I know. Your daddy saw how things were changing. Plus, he was no farmer, he was a cook to his heart. Farming just wasn't what it used to be anyway—got harder and harder to make a living. Then, you know, he went off to Korea to fight."

Julian raised an eybrow. "You mean, to cook."

Genevieve smiled. "I guess you're right. He mighta used that gun they gave him once or twice—to kill a rabbit for the cooking pot! But he was real proud of how he kept those soldiers going with my mama's recipes. When he came back, he went straight to New Orleans. Jacob had built that Treme house, but after he got sick, he stopped going, so Simon just moved in. He got himself a good job, cooking the best food in town. Met Ladeena down there, even though she was from these parts. Had you. Things were going real well for him down in New Orleans. But his heart was really right here, at Silver Creek. That's why he wanted you to have this place, Julian. He wanted the things he most loved to be together."

Julian nodded, his voice quiet. "Yeah. I get that."

On the walk back to Pastor Jackson's house Velmyra spotted a wild bush of plump blackberries—still thriving six weeks after the normal season—and stopped to pick them, then carried them in the broad, flat leaves Kevin had picked from a banana tree just behind Claudinette's cabin. The air, cooler now, carried a faint breeze from the nearby creek and the cicadas were beginning their evening song.

Exhausted, too tired to hold his mind in one place, Julian let it drift with the prevailing breeze, back to when he was a boy. He half-remembered, half-imagined lightning bugs as golden flecks against the dusk, foot races in these woods, barbecue cookouts and fish fries, and sleeping out on the porch under the night-lights of a million summer stars. Then he imagined his father, years before, doing the same thing, and his father before him, and on back to Moses and John Paul.

What had Simon told him years ago? *A man is really what he leaves behind when he is gone.* His footprint on a piece of land, his smile etched on the face of a child. For years Julian thought Simon was imposing Silver Creek on him, the burden of a gift he didn't really want. But the gift really had been Julian's to give to his father—to steward his father's treasure, to be caretaker of what he would leave behind. His memories, his history, his home. The things that mattered, the things that proved he was here.

By the time they got back to Pastor Jackson's, the flaming sun had descended halfway down the trunks of the slender pines nearer the road, and the sandy yard was awash in a long slant of afternoon light. The Pastor's car sat in the yard, and from the living room floated the stereo bass of rhythm and blues. Genevieve walked up the steps and stood on the porch, her hands on both hips.

"Thank y'all. That walk did me some good," she said. "Simon and I used to walk those woods all the time. I felt close to him out there."

She waved and turned to walk back into the house, then turned back again. "Your daddy's all right, Julian," she said. "He's either being looked after by all the ancestors, or he's one of 'em now. Either way, I'm all right with it. You will be too."

They drove back to Genevieve's cabin to check on it; nothing had changed. The place looked untouched and the gunshot incident had receded so far back in Julian's memory he could hardly believed it had happened. Standing in front of Kevin's truck and viewing the cabin from the distance, Julian saw something he'd never seen before. Crudely etched in one of the stacks of cinderblocks on which the cabin sat, written in the awkward hand of the old or barely literate, were the words "Jacob Fortier, 1925." A hand-made house, built brick by brick and board by board with his grandfather's hands. He'd never met the man, but here was indelible proof of his life.

"I like your cousin Genevieve, she's real sweet." Kevin opened the door to his pickup, then reached out his hand to shake Julian's. "I'll talk to you tomorrow, soon's I know something."

Julian pulled him in to his chest for a quick hug and slap on the back.

"Can't thank you enough, man," he said.

Kevin's face gave way to a blushing, boyish grin. "You can thank me when we get your land back for you."

"Well, even if we don't—"

"We will, man."

So with the afternoon light elongating the shadows of pines, he steered the Neon toward the highway beneath a chalk-blue sky, and Velmyra, chin resting on her cupped hand, stared thoughtfully at the blur of trees and shrub through the window. Flashes of evergreen and thick brush now and then blanked out the dying sun, while the groan of engine noise coated the air.

His head heavy with deferred sleep, Julian remembered something his father would say after a particularly busy shift at Parmenter's restaurant stove—*It's been a long week tonight.* The morning had begun, it seemed, before the previous night was done. The early shock of gunshots puncturing the delicate bubble of romance seemed forever ago, and now faded like the mist-veil of the October moon that had ushered in the morning's sun.

They rode in uneasy silence until Velmyra's cell phone rang.

"I'm fine, Mama, you OK? I know, I know. Yeah, we're on our way. We should be there in another hour or so. Yeah, OK. Me, too," she spoke into the phone.

More silence, before Julian spoke.

"If it's OK with you, I'd like to make one stop before we go."

He pulled the car onto the narrow, rocky footpath alongside the cemetery, with its cattails and dandelions that towered above the leaning headstones, some so old they seemed to rise out of the ground like ancient markers of a past civilization. Julian stared at the field a moment before he turned to Velmyra.

"Just give me a minute, OK? Then we'll get you to your folks."

She smiled. "Take your time."

The bramble and grasses were high and wet as he tramped through them, making his way to the Fortier family markers. The flowers he'd set by his mother's stone were, to his great surprise, still fresh-looking, glistening in the late sun and watered with dew. He walked further until he came to the oldest section with the smallest, crudest-looking stones. He searched until he found the ones he was looking for.

JOHN MICHEL FORTIER b—1810, d—

He couldn't make out the date of death, but walked further until he saw other markers, MILDRED, BELOVED WIFE, gouged into the rough stone in crude script, and MOSES, the simple word carved into a ruggedly cut stone slab eroded by wind and water, and faded by a century of sun. And one simply bore the word CLAUDINETTE.

There were others he didn't even notice when he'd been there before, or if he'd seen them, their meaninglessness at the time had rendered them invisible. Clothilde had been laid next to her husband, and he found Belle, but not Patrice. They'd all lived here together back then, one big close-knit family, wagons circled against the blustery winds of a sometimes unkindly world.

There was one name he knew he wouldn't find, but his eyes searched anyway. The one who drank, caroused, and played his bugle all day while his black half-brother, Moses, rose with the sun to plow the land. The one who escaped a cuckolded husband's bullet by fleeing, never to be seen again, leaving his own Silver Creek acres to languish.

Julian couldn't help but flinch when Genevieve told John Paul's part of the story. A bugler, a musician. It almost seemed too coincidental to be true. Had he, Julian, become that man generations later, turning *his* back on the land that was his birthright?

He searched the stones for the one he really came to find, and he was just about to give up when his foot nearly tripped over it. It was small with rounded corners, almost black with dirt, but the etched name glinted boldly in the sun, as if some cosmic spotlight bathed it in revelatory light.

Jacob Fortier. Long dead before he'd been born. But Julian vaguely remembered something about the promise Simon had made to his father, and his father's rueful reply that hung as heavy and redolent in his memory as overripe fruit on a low branch. What had Genevieve said? *To make things right, he'd come back from the grave.*

Never one to put stock into this whole spirit business for which his hometown was so well known, Julian allowed himself, this one time, a desperate man's indulgence. He looked around to see if anyone was looking. The car was too far away for Velmyra to see him, and there was no one else in sight.

He knelt near Jacob's stone, reached out and dusted the name where soot clogged the etched grooves. He swatted at a mosquito, cleared his throat, then placed his hand firmly on the stone and closed his eyes.

Embarrassed and feeling more than a little foolish, he mumbled words in his head, then decided to speak them out loud.

"Well, sir. You said you would fix this…this thing; you told daddy that you'd—" He cleared his throat again. "Uh, so, I mean, if you could help, somehow, I'd appreciate it. I just want to find daddy, you know, wherever he ended up, and I've got to get…"

He stopped and coughed against the lump that broke his voice. "I've just got to get Daddy's land back. I need help. So if you could, you know—"

Like a twig breaking, something snapped inside him. What the hell was he doing? He looked around to see if anyone had seen him. Only one witness, as far as he could tell—a red-tailed hawk perched on a telephone wire high over his head. With the sharp light overhead, Julian squinted through watery eyes. "Yeah? What you looking at?" As if in response, the hawk fluttered, lifted itself, and flew away.

Damn. This was nuts. Amazing what no sleep and stress will do to you. He got up abruptly and clapped dust from his hands and wiped them on his jeans. He often wondered if, when folks lost their minds, if they could point to an exact moment when it happened. Maybe someday he'd look back and remember this day, begging for help from a dead man's gravestone.

He closed his eyes and crossed his heart, even though he'd never been Catholic, but it couldn't hurt. He looked up at the fading blue of the sky, and blinked tears from eyes too tired to fight them. Then he walked back toward the car.

Velmyra said nothing, just looked at him and smiled as he got back into the car. These last couple of days, she had played cooling showers to his dry desert. She had kept him sane. If ever there had been a time in his life when he needed someone beside him—quiet, assuring, strong—this was the time.

He stole sidelong glances at her now and then as he drove toward the interstate, her head tilted toward the window, sleeping now, her mouth slightly agape, a small track of drool trailing from the corner of her mouth. Even now, her face puffy from lack of sleep, mouth trickling spittle, her hair a wiry mess, he wanted to reach over and stroke the soft hollow beneath her cheekbone with the back of his hand.

Neither of them had spoken about their night together, it had seemed like ages ago, and there had been too much else on their minds. And considering the tumult they were caught up in, the rekindling of an ancient, used-to-be love seemed ridiculously trivial with all that had happened—to them, to their families, their friends.

To Simon.

But there was a burn of desire inside him, even while the world he'd known his whole life stood precariously on end.

When they crossed the bridge into Baton Rouge, the hotel and industrial lights from the river shone like uniformly cut stones against the pink bank of sunset clouds gathering along the horizon.

"We're here already?" Velmyra stretched, frowned and rubbed her eyes. "Wow. Guess I was a little tired. Sorry I wasn't exactly good company."

He said nothing, but smiled in her direction, decreasing his speed as he exited onto the ramp that led off the highway into the city. Suddenly aware that in a few minutes Velmyra would be gone and he would be alone again, he felt the bloom of loneliness around him, and his pulse quickened with the certainty of her absence.

He slowed the car as he pulled into the lot of the Day's Inn, and wheeled around to the back side of the motel where Vel's parents' room overlooked a large cement patio and swimming pool painted robin's egg blue.

"Looks like they're not even here," she said, staring at the empty parking space. She looked at her watch. "She said they might go over to Copeland's for something to eat. Do you want to come inside for a minute?"

"Just give your folks my best when you see them," he said. He got out of the car and held open her door as she stepped out.

He put both hands in his pockets. "Vel, look..."

"I know," she said. "We should talk...about everything."

"When?"

"I don't know. So much is going on. Let's just keep in touch by phone."

"Before you go, I just want to say how much I really appreciate..."

She touched his chin with her finger. "You don't have to thank me. You know that."

He nodded.

"Call me tomorrow?"

"For sure."

She reached up to him and gave him a small hug. He could smell the burn of sun on her hair. And without looking again at him, she turned and went inside her room.

He was just getting back onto the highway when his cell phone rang.

It was Sylvia, her voice urgent.

"You OK?" he said.

"I'm fine, well, you know, OK. Are you heading back this way?"

"I'm in the car now."

"It's Matthew Parmenter. They took him to Baton Rouge General, and they're not giving him much time at all. He's asked to see you right away."

Julian's heart skipped. He pulled the car into the fast lane to pass the traffic.

"I'm on my way."

16

Another city by the river—lights gleaming from ferries and barges cruising by. This one, though, a safe harbor from the other, its streets bulging with the overflow of the dispossessed. The once modest, workaday city of Baton Rouge had swelled into a bustling metropolis overnight, and the influx of evacuees had turned the city into one large, frayed nerve: intersections were choked with cars backed up at stoplights, drive-in bank lines snaked around corners, restaurant and grocery store parking lots bulged at their seams. Throughout the day, irritated drivers honked car horns, their patience worn as thin as the fine mist that settled over the Mississippi.

Located in the Mid-City section of town, Baton Rouge General unfolded like a city within itself; inside, it opened into a vast welter of fluorescent-lit corridors leading to wings in every possible direction. Julian inquired at the information desk, then got onto and off the wrong elevator, found the right one leading to the cardio care unit, and arrived at Matthew Parmenter's private room.

The room was dimly lit except for the red and green glow of computer panels. The entire room chattered like a thicket of electronic chirps, whistles, and hums—a night garden of life-sustaining noises.

Matthew lay sunken into the white sheets, his white hair thick and tussled in vertical clumps, his skin ghostly pale and veiny, his closed eyes centered in dark rings. When Julian stepped across the room and sat in a wooden armchair next to the bed, the pale gray eyes opened.

A small *hnnnn* came from Parmenter's throat, not so much a groan, as Julian first thought, but more a noise of acknowledgement, of recognition. The old man tried to prop himself up with his elbows.

Julian stood and reached behind Parmenter's head to plump the pillows. "Careful. I'll help you."

A faint smile curled Parmenter's thin lips.

"Doctors," he said. "One thinks I'm too old to survive surgery, the other thinks it's the only chance I have. I told them both to leave, and let me be."

He leaned back and let out a labored sigh.

"Thank you, Julian," he said. "I hoped that you would come, that I would see you again before I…"

He strained against the pull of cords and tubes, one carrying a supply of blood into his arm, another feeding him oxygen.

"Hell of a way to go, considering, huh?" he said in a near whisper.

Julian guessed at the intended sarcasm. It was true—it wasn't only hurricanes, broken levees, and floods that moved the hands of fate these days.

Matthew fixed a sharp gaze on Julian, though his voice was paled by exhaustion and a weakened heart. "Have you found him?"

"No sir."

He leaned his head back and sighed again. "Don't give up hope, son. You have to keep looking." He coughed again.

"Don't worry. I will."

Parmenter let out a choked wheeze, then sat back on the bank of pillows, and rolled his eyes upward toward the ceiling.

"I am so sorry that nothing came of my inquiries about your father. The police were…well, you would not believe how they've struggled with all this." He pointed to the television, and told

Julian about a ninety-year-old man who was found recently in a shelter in Denver, Colorado. "So you see, it's still possible."

He pointed to the wooden chair next to the bed, and Julian sat again. "Thank you for coming. Did I say that already?"

"It's OK, sir." Julian didn't know what else to say, so he continued, "I, uh, I got here as soon as I heard. Sylvia called me. Are you feeling all right?"

"I'm feeling lousy," he said. "But I'll get right to the point. I know your father told you about our little business deal a few years ago."

His voice was whispery as words rushed out in a long, labored breath, then another struggling breath and another rush of words. Julian fidgeted in his chair, crossed his right leg over his left.

"And I know you think I cheated your father."

The man's bluntness shocked Julian. He looked away a moment, and folded his hands across his lap. "Well, I…"

"You don't have to worry. You can speak freely to a dying man. You thought I cheated him." His voice was insistent.

"Yes, sir, I did."

He nodded, with a faint smile on his lips. "I appreciate your honesty. But let me tell you, I had no idea your father's recipe would take off the way it did. It was a gamble for both of us. It was entirely possible that the product would not earn even as much as I paid Simon. The fact that it became wildly popular was highly unlikely, but fate is peculiar sometimes. You never know how things will turn out.

"But all that was many years ago. Since then I've learned that some things are more important than business. I saw how your father struggled with money when your mother was ill. I offered to help him. But he refused. My wife, Clarisse…" He coughed again, sitting forward, again straining against the restrictive cords.

"Clarisse never let me forget that we had money while Simon struggled, and why things were that way. She thought of me…well, the way you did. I have tried many times since then to get your father to accept money from me, but he wouldn't hear of it. Your father is a proud, stubborn man.

"So I wanted you to bring your father to me when you found him. As I mentioned before, he owes me something. And I have something for him he'll not be able to refuse."

Julian shrugged. He didn't know what the old man could be talking about. "If....when I find him, and he's...OK, I'll bring him here."

"Good. And I have another favor to ask you."

Parmenter's words dissolved into a sharp fit of coughs. A monitor beeped steadily and a nurse rushed in. Julian stepped aside, and as another nurse entered, began to move toward the door.

And that was when he noticed him. Julian hadn't even heard the stranger enter the room. He was a tall, broad-shouldered black man who looked to be in his late-forties, and dressed in a finely tailored dark blue pinstriped suit that hugged his muscular frame perfectly. His head was shaved; a thick bushy mustache and bristly beard consumed the bottom half of his face, and a diamond stud blinked from his left earlobe. His well-heeled look, given the recent realities in Louisiana, made Julian think he must be an insurance agent (a highly successful one), a lawyer, or a funeral home director.

The man waited silently at the doorway until Julian headed to leave.

"Mr. Fortier. If you have a minute, I'd like to talk to you."

In the coffee lounge/waiting room at the east end of the wing, the man introduced himself as Cedric Cole, Matthew Parmenter's attorney. He and Julian sat together opposite each other on low faux-leather sofas in front of a coffee machine.

When the man placed two Styrofoam cups of coffee on the table between them, Julian thanked him and took a sip from the one nearest him. With his black leather briefcase placed on the floor next to his feet, Cole leaned forward.

"Mr. Fortier, Mr. Parmenter has instructed me to hire you—that is, you and your band, or whatever group of musicians you can organize—to play for his funeral. That is, if you're willing. A traditional New Orleans jazz funeral with parade, second line, the full works."

Julian was speechless. Stunned, first by the presence of Parmenter's slick-looking black attorney who dressed like a million bucks, and second by the request itself. A jazz funeral for Parmenter? Well, that figures—everybody in New Orleans wants a jazz funeral. He blinked twice, then leaned back against the sofa pillow, rubbing his knees with his palms.

"Certain things will have to be arranged slightly differently, the conditions in the city being what they are," Cole continued. "He wants the second-line parade to course through the French Quarter, ending at the location where his restaurant used to be. There are a few other specifics Mr. Parmenter has asked for, certain musical selections, et cetera. And you and your friends will be generously paid, of course."

Still dumbstruck, Julian looked at Cole in bewilderment, and it struck him that his father's oldest friend was actually dying. He hadn't played such an event since he'd lived in New Orleans, and didn't even know where the guys in the band were, if they were in town, or if they even made it through the storm in one piece. Or, if they were alive and well, would be able to take time from rebuilding their lives to play a funeral.

"Mr., uh—"

"Cole. But call me Cedric."

"Right. I…I'm honored that Mr. Parmenter would want me to play. I don't know if I—"

"I know about some of the things you're dealing with," Cole assured him. "Your father missing—Mr. Parmenter told me. I know how highly he regarded him. He's also instructed me to furnish you with as much money as you need to find him. I'm prepared to write you a check today, to hire an investigator, if that's what you need. Or if you'd like me to hire someone for you, I have a few contacts."

He reached in his pocket, pulled out his business card, and handed it to Julian.

"There's very little time, I'm afraid. The doctors say things could change very quickly, given Mr. Parmenter's deteriorating condition. But he's asked me to tell you that if your father is found well and healthy while Mr. Parmenter is still alive, he would very much like to see him, to talk to him. He says he has something very important to say to him."

Julian stroked the back of his neck with his palm, and took a long, tired breath.

Why was the man so insistent about seeing Simon? What could he possibly do or say that would make any difference now? Julian strained his memory, calling up his last conversations with his father for some hint of what Parmenter could possibly want. But Simon and Julian hadn't talked about Matthew in months. It had been such a thorny issue with them, since Julian hadn't exactly tried to hide his resentment for the man. And accordingly, Simon had simply stopped mentioning his name.

Parmenter was dying now, and Julian was sorry about that, but he could only think of his father, who had loved this undeserving man like a brother. Whatever Parmenter had in mind now, it was too little too late. Too late to make the past right, too late for deathbed amends.

And now the guy wants a jazz funeral. What was he supposed to do, put together a band with players he might not be able to find, and who probably wouldn't speak to him?

Six years had passed since the last time he'd seen any of them, and it had been the worst night of his professional career. It was the last weekend of Jazz Fest, a balmy evening in early May, and he and the band were about to perform their last set, a tribute to New Orleans trumpet players—Bunk Johnson, Joe "King" Oliver, Louis Armstrong—in the WWOZ jazz tent. A half hour before they went onstage, Julian had surprised them with an announcement that he was leaving for New York—not in the fall, as he had told them earlier, but in the next few days. He'd lined up a meeting with a recording company executive. And a pianist buddy from Tulane was saving a spot on his couch, and promised him all the freelance jobs he could handle.

Onstage, the music had been cool, stiff, the men unyielding. The silence afterwards still rang in his ears, the cold stares still frozen in his brain. They had a right to be upset, and he'd wanted to explain, tell them that he *had* to leave—now—while his heart was still in one piece. But the words would not come. After the last chord, the other players clustered together backstage, and no one spoke to him as he cased his horn and started the walk back to his car. Eventually, it was his old friend and trumpet-playing rival, Grady Casey, who came around. "Good luck man," he'd said, when he came by Julian's place the next day. "Knock 'em dead, up there."

They went out for a drink that night at Sorrelle's Hibiscus Lounge at the far edge of the French Quarter near the Market, and under a half moon casting silken light on the river Julian had confessed about his troubles with Velmyra and how it had ended. Grady lowered his eyes in sympathy, saying, "That's rough, man, I'm so sorry." And without dropping a beat, added, "So you don't mind if I call her?" After a deadpan moment, they both broke into outrageous laughter. The rest of the evening, they had drank themselves as silly as rookie tourists, starting at one end of the Quarter—plastic go-cups in hand, loaded with high-octane daiquiris—and stumbling all the way to the other.

He put three quarters in the machine. The ice clanked into the cup, then the liquid. Julian could feel Cole's eyes on him as he took a swig of the cold Coke. The coffee was lousy, it was hot in the waiting room, and the memory of the daiquiris put him in mind of something to take the edge off his thirst. He turned up the cup and swallowed, long and slow.

He wondered if the man knew he was stalling.

Finally he said, "I don't know if I can even find them, the guys I played with. I wouldn't know where to even look for them."

Cedric nodded. "I understand. But Mr. Parmenter realizes that your friends might need a little financial help at this time. He's offering a very generous fee for the musicians. Fifteen hundred dollars each. And in addition, he will cover travel expenses from wherever they've evacuated to back to New Orleans, if needed, and lodging."

Fifteen hundred for a funeral? Outrageous cash had a way of smoothing the blunt edges of hard feelings. Nobody in New Orleans made that kind of money for a one-day gig. The guys could use the money, no question. Hell, he'd hardly worked in almost a year; he needed the money himself.

One more thought sealed the deal: if Simon were here, he'd want him to play—no doubt.

Julian nodded. "I'll do it."

Cole's serious face relaxed into the smile of a man who did so rarely, showing two rows of perfect teeth.

"Great. And, ah, there's one more thing I'd like to ask you."

He reached into the pocket of his jacket and pulled out a CD, its cover showing a chest-cropped photo of Julian with trumpet in hand, looking out over the Left Bank of the Seine in Paris, the cathedral of Notre Dame looming in the backdrop. A closed-mouth, confident smile, eyes in a slight squint from the brilliant sun. Titled "Boplicitude," the CD was the last he'd made three years ago after his first European tour, and it had gotten him the Grammy. He looked at his image on the cover, self-assured, happy, even cocky, and barely recognized himself. In his air-brushed face, there was no hint of the uncertainty his life held now.

The man on that cover had no idea what was coming for him.

"I'm a big fan," Cole said. "Maybe you could sign this for me?"

He pulled out a black felt-tip pen. Julian nodded politely, took the pen and the CD, and scrawled his name illegibly across the image of his face on the booklet cover.

"Thanks," Cole said. "By the way, caught your spot on Leno. Nice."

They shook hands, and Julian strode away, wondering if his chops would hold up long enough to get through the gig.

Back in the motel, he flopped on the bed and picked up the remote control. But the TV news was all about what the mayor had called "Look and Leave" and the papers had called "Look and Grieve"—the residents of New Orleans coming back temporarily to their city to find, in so many cases, complete chaos: shattered homes, drowned possessions, remnants of what had been normal lives. The local news stations in Baton Rouge covered the influx of the displaced filling up the hotel rooms, grocery stores, shelters, church basements, and the extra bedrooms of every neighborhood in town. Exhausted, Julian remembered how the day had begun so long ago, and didn't want to hear another word about life gone wrong, about things he couldn't control.

Sitting up in bed, he reached for his cell phone, wondering what Velmyra was doing, and looked at his watch. The thought of not being with her tonight sank his spirits deeper than the news had, but when he thought of calling her, he rejected the idea. There was a serious conversation in their future requiring thought and energy, and he didn't have the capacity for either. The truth was, he had no idea what to say to her. After what had happened between them, and given their history, there should be some kind of plan. But he had none. If she were to fit into the weird puzzle of his life at this point, he wasn't at all sure how it would happen. Or even if it should.

He turned the TV off and tossed the remote onto the nightstand. He needed to talk to someone, and he could use a beer. Within a few minutes, he was back in the car.

The bar and grill in the atrium of the Embassy Suites in Baton Rouge was decorated in a lush, tropical theme, with tall palmettos, yuccas, and elephant ears situated between tiered waterfalls, and sun fed through an enormous skylight six stories high. Julian could hear the sound of the trumpet from the reservations desk, and by the time he entered the bar, sat down on one of the five, leather-topped barstools, and ordered a beer, Grady Casey had caught his eye.

It was just a quartet tonight, apparently; his wife, Cindy, a bluesy, dreamy eyed singer, was not around. A young male pianist sat at a shiny black seven-foot grand, a bushy haired man of sixty or so hugged a deep brown upright bass, and a red-haired drummer, the only white guy in the group, kept time with wire brushes swirled against a snare head to the muted tones of Grady's version of Miles Davis's "Blue in Green."

When Grady nodded toward the bar where Julian sat, he gave a quick salute in the direction of the bandstand. The bartender, a smiling young blonde with frosted brown lipstick and a sunflower tattooed on her bare shoulder, poured a light ale into the huge frosted mug before him. Julian closed his eyes as the icy brew slid down his dry throat, and felt as if he could drink this beer until the end of time. If it wasn't the best beer he'd ever tasted, it was surely the most appreciated one. There were only a few people in the bar; the quiet, relaxed scene was a comfort, almost as if the world were a normal place, as if it hadn't tilted so far from upright that everyone within a sixty-mile radius of New Orleans (or even much further) was not walking uphill, pushing and bowing against a strong wind.

Julian closed his eyes and listened to the trumpet's fat, lazy tones, his head nodding as the misty ballad floated around him. It had been a while since he'd done this—actually listen to somebody else play. He'd never really been jealous of Casey before, but after seeing Cole with a copy of his CD, and hearing Grady's sweet tone filling the air in the bar, he was reminded of his stalled career and a cool sadness enveloped him. The guy sounded better than ever, his tone crisp and clean, as pure a sound as he had ever heard. His head bobbing on the beat, fingers dancing on the valves, carving out melodies and runs as if they were soft clay beneath his nimble hands. *This guy,* he thought, *is the guy who should be known all over the world.*

When the set ended, Grady nodded to Julian, laid his trumpet down in the open case on the bandstand, and headed toward the bar. Up close, Grady looked tired, worn. It had only been a couple of days since Julian had last seen him, but he swore he looked older now. Half moons of loose skin bagged beneath his eyes, and the whites were red-veined. His white shirt, though clean and pressed, looked two sizes too big, and gray stubble flecked his gaunt cheeks and chin.

The bar stool next to Julian whined as Grady sat down and leaned against the counter. He caught the waitress's eye, held up a finger and pointed to Julian. "Bring this man another one of whatever he's drinking. His money ain't no good here."

He and Julian shook hands. Grady took a package of cigarettes from his pocket and lit one up. "What's up, Homes? You ready to play?"

The waitress sat another beer in front of Julian and he took a drink. "Naw, I'm just listening. Sounding good, man."

Grady let out a long stream of smoke, then put the cigarette out in a glass ashtray. "Kinda slow tonight, but thanks."

When the waitress turned the volume dial on the flat screen TV above them, both men looked up. The headline news station showed a T-shirted reporter standing in Jackson Square with the spires of the Saint Louis Cathedral glinting in the backdrop, dispensing the latest in a series of reports on the current situation of the flood-ruined city downriver as its residents returned. The state of Louisiana, he said, had just declared the tap water in most of New Orleans drinkable, except in the Ninth Ward and the East. And, he added, the first wave of government trailers had rolled into town to house the thousands displaced by the flood.

Grady waved his hand dismissively. "Like that's gonna fix anything. This whole thing, man. It's bullshit. The whole thing. You know what they called us down here? *Refugees*, man. Like people who ain't got a home. They act like this thing is our fault, like we did something wrong. Act like they don't want us here, man. You hear about the levees? Now they're saying maybe they wasn't built right. Like we didn't know *that*. I been hearing about those damn levees for years."

Grady ordered a brew and a plate of hot wings, and when they arrived, he took a bite out of a drummette and followed it with a long gulp of Bud Light. It didn't take Julian long to figure out what had gotten into Grady's craw: he and his wife had been arguing about where to live. Since Julian had last seen him, Grady's wife had gone back to Dallas to be with her relatives, and had given in to their gentle coaxing to "look at a few apartments, just in case." Now she wanted to move there permanently, while Grady, who'd never considered living anywhere but New Orleans, wasn't having it. But when he tried to find lodging in the unharmed parts of the city, all the rents were sky-high, in some cases double what they'd cost before the flood.

"She told me to call her when I came to my senses," Grady said. "I told her to call me when she came to hers. *Dallas*, man. Can you believe that? Where am I gonna play in Dallas?"

Grady went on to tell Julian about his aunts, elderly uncle, cousins, three sisters and three brother's kids who'd just come back from Atlanta. With their Ninth Ward houses washed away, all thirty-eight had crowded into an aunt's four-bedroom two-story on the edge of Uptown, where the water had only reached the bottom porch step.

"Everybody living on top of each other, man. Crazy. But what are they gonna do?"

Julian listened quietly, taking a swig from his beer now and then.

"So you wouldn't move here, I guess." Julian figured Grady had already considered Baton Rouge, but it was the only solution that came to mind.

Grady took another bite, put his barbecued chicken wing down. "Here? Baton Rouge? Baton Rouge ain't New Orleans, man, you know that. Besides this place is crawling with musicians looking for work. Manager at this club wants to spread the wealth, so my gig is up at the end of next week. So now I gotta figure out how to get a gig, find a place to live, *and* get my wife back."

Julian had an idea for one third of Grady's problems, and this seemed like the perfect time to mention the funeral for Matthew Parmenter. "There's only one thing," he said. "We need the whole band. I don't know where everybody is. And I don't know if anybody wants to play with me, after the way I left."

When Julian told Grady how much the gig paid, he let out a long slow whistle. "For that kinda money? They'll play with Humpty Dumpty. Let me handle it. I know where they are."

Grady turned up the end of his beer. "Who is this cat, man? He must ain't got nothin' *but* money."

His father's best friend, Julian explained.

"Your daddy?"

Julian's gaze lowered to his beer as he took a long, slow drink. When he told Grady what he believed to be true about his father, his old friend clapped a hand solidly on his back.

"Man, I'm real sorry." He lowered his head a moment, pursed his lips, and looked thoughtfully at his mug. Then he lifted it.

"Here's to your daddy, man. Here's to Brother Simon," he said, and they both drank.

They talked on about each other's lives, how Grady had been doing great, playing almost every night of the week until the flood happened. And Julian told him about running into his ex-fiancé, and their excursion to look for his father, and the situation with his father's land. And how, even though he didn't believe his father had survived, he was determined to find out what happened to him, no matter how long it took.

When the thirty-minute break ended, Grady looked at his watch, then signaled to his trio; the pianist was just coming out of the men's room, and the bass player and drummer were at a nearby table talking with two dark-haired women who looked like identical twins.

Grady clapped his hands together. "All right, man, let's go. Go get your horn. I know you got it with you. It'll be like old times."

Julian swallowed hard, took another drink, then put the glass down and stared into it. "Look man, there's something I gotta tell you."

Julian had felt humbled by his friend's soul-baring, and in turn, wanted to hold nothing back. The embarrassment he thought he'd feel simply wasn't there. And when Julian poured out all the details of the accident, the long depressing months of surgery, recovery, canceled gigs, and the Tokyo disaster, Grady nodded in true sympathy. Nobody understood what he was going through like another musician, and as they talked, all the years that had passed since they were young boys melted away. Julian felt like he was talking to a brother.

Grady turned up the last of his beer, set it back on the counter, and frowned thoughtfully.

"How long's it been since Tokyo?"

"Six weeks maybe. Right after the storm."

"You had any pain since then?"

"None to speak of."

Grady got up and slapped his credit card down on the counter for the waitress. He looked at Julian. "If anybody can get through this, you can, man. You know, I always knew you were the best. Between us, I mean."

Julian's eyebrows flew up. *Was he serious?*

"What do you mean?"

Grady put two dollars in the waitress' tip bowl. "Well, you know, you always had mad technique, man. You were the cleanest player I knew. I had to bust my chops to keep up with you."

Julian felt his face flush. "Oh, I think it was the other way around."

"You kidding." Grady laughed sardonically. "Whatever, man. Bottom line, though, you just got to get back up on that horse. Get your juice back. You're a trumpet player, man. You know how we do."

Julian had to laugh. It was a line from their youth. *You know how we do! Fake it 'til you make it.* Even Mr. Martrel had told them that, sometimes teasing and joking with them about the trumpet player's colossal ego, and how sometimes a little BS—bravado, he called it—was just…necessary. *Act like you know what you're doing. Get everybody to believe it, and eventually, you will.*

Grady grabbed Julian's hand and shook it. "Go get your ax, man. I'ma give you five minutes."

Grady went to the bandstand and Julian went to his car. The black asphalt of the parking lot shined like patent leather from the light shower that had just ended, as the semi-dark sky held the pale, gray wash of high, formless clouds. Water hung in the muggy air, the dampness coating his skin like dew. He looked up at the sky and thought about just driving back to his room, but opened the trunk and pulled out the horn instead. He took it out of the case, felt the cool brass in his warm hands. By the time he got back to the bar, Grady was just finishing up "Round Midnight."

Applause and whistles filled the room, and then Grady spotted Julian at the door. "Y'all are in for a treat this evenin'!" Grady told the dozen or so people sitting at the tables and the bar. "Tonight, I want y'all to welcome my homeboy from New Orleans, Blue Note recording artist, Julian Fortier!"

More applause and a few more whistles from the surprised patrons accompanied Julian's slow stride to the bandstand, and as soon as he stepped up, the drummer and the piano player kicked off a lightning quick tempo to "Seven Steps to Heaven." A four bar intro of block chords in syncopated staccato, and it was on.

Julian's nerves tightened as he listened to Grady, an old pro working that rhythm, riffing a rush of sixteenths flying like confetti in a strong wind, so fast Julian could only hold his horn and admire. But when Grady left him a wide opening, Julian jumped in, swimming in the flow. And in a moment it was old times, two friends taking turns, first leading, then supporting, dovetailing, weaving in and out, playing quick hand-off and snatch-and-grab and catch-me-if-you-can.

As the set wore on, a larger crowd of patrons gathered, some dressed in Saints jerseys, clearly from New Orleans and hungry for the music. They yelled out their traditional favorites and the band obliged them—"St. James Infirmary" in a down-tempo groove, "Basin Street Blues" with Grady crooning in a gravelly Satchmo voice, and "Little Liza Jane," with the whole audience, now in full party mode, singing along on the chorus.

His pulse racing, Julian felt high, lightheaded, drunk in the groove. And all the while he felt Grady beneath him, above him, all around him egging him on, holding him up. When he felt himself flagging, there was a solid hand pushing at his back; *go, go.* And he felt he couldn't fail.

When it was over, Julian felt his whole body relax, his face fixed in a smile of relief. *He could have buried me*, Julian thought. *But he didn't.* He didn't know whether his old friend had felt pity, or if everybody's ego-fire burned a little cooler these days. His forehead dripped sweat, but he never once thought about his jaw. Grady's face was wide open in a huge smile as he bumped Julian's fist with his own.

Not his best playing, Julian thought, but he'd more than kept up. He felt good. Damn good. If he wasn't all the way back, he was almost there.

The next morning, lying across the bed with his clothes still on and his horn in his hand (something he hadn't done since he was eleven), Julian woke from murky dreams to a phone screaming like a siren. Kevin calling. He'd just been contacted by a man named David John Wilder, a lawyer for N&L Associates, Nathan Larouchette's company. Kevin had called Wilder earlier and left a message that he was representing Silver Creek owners in a planned suit against the sale of the land.

"Can you get back to Local by noon? The First Bank building?" Kevin asked. "They want to have a meeting with us. They want to talk about a deal."

What kind of a deal?" Julian sat up on the bed and wiped sleep from his eyes.

"He didn't say. Just said he might have figured out a way everybody could walk away happy."

Julian frowned. He couldn't imagine being pleased by any deal that would make Nathan Larouchette happy. But he was curious to hear what the man had to say.

"OK, I'll be there."

Kevin was silent a moment. "Well, this may not be everything we want, but we should at least hear what they got to say. I've studied all the land dispute cases I can find around here, I've gone over the contract four times. It's tight. Nathan's boys have gotten sharper. They didn't leave anything to chance."

He paused a moment, then added, "This might be our best shot."

Julian looked at the clock, then got up from the bed. "OK, I'm leaving now."

But as soon as he hung up, there was another call—Sylvia, her voice sounding tired and strained.

"Good morning, baby."

"Sylvia."

She took a breath, and sighed. "Well, I got some news. Matthew Parmenter. He's gone."

17

The news about Matthew Parmenter managed to stun Julian. A surprising sadness swept over him, and now that the old man was gone, he wished he'd been more forgiving about the business deal with Simon, if only for his father's sake. And even more, he wondered what it was that Parmenter claimed his father "owed" him, and what Parmenter would have given him—the gift he wouldn't have been able to refuse—had both men been able to meet again. But as he steered the Neon under a blue sky to Local to meet Kevin and Larouchette's lawyers, there was little room in his crowded mind for thoughts of his father's friendship with the man who had just died.

Before he left, he'd tried to call Velmyra. He wanted to tell her about Parmenter dying and how he felt about it. And about seeing Grady and how good it was to play with him, and how he'd been practicing a little every day and could feel his chops coming back. And about the dreams he'd had about his father. And about Kevin calling and the meeting, and... He wanted to tell her every single thing that had happened to him and every thought he'd had since the last time he'd been with her. He hadn't realized how much he'd been depending on her for support until the rock he'd been leaning on had slipped from beneath him. Now all he could feel was the soft, shifting ground.

She left him a text message—*Things r crazy, will call u later*—but after waiting a while, then leaving two more messages on her cell phone, he'd decided to pull back. Maybe she was telling him something. *Let things be, for now.* And so he'd told himself, *Give the woman some space.* He reminded himself that she had her own worries. Her parents had lost everything. They surely needed her now.

He told himself that was the reason she hadn't returned his calls. But their history gnawed at him. Maybe whatever it was that caused her to leave him the first time had reared up again in her mind.

If he'd been paying attention back then, he might have seen it coming. The uncertain tone of her voice that one night when he'd talked to her on the phone, when an awkward silence that had never been there before dug into the space between them like a fallen ax. The way she'd complained about leaving her beloved students, and the way she joked about what she could possibly find to do in New York that would occupy her while he was busy becoming famous.

But it was on a spring night, right before his gig at Donna's, that the whole thing had fallen apart.

He'd arrived a little early to pick her up. She wasn't ready. But instead of rushing around like she usually did—slipping on her jacket, finding her comb and makeup mirror and tossing her keys in her purse—she invited him in. Her eyes red, teary, her face flushed.

She pulled at the ends of her hair.

Could he sit down a minute?

She sat opposite him on the ottoman, and all he saw was her hands, busy fingers intertwining and releasing.

A deep breath. It wasn't that she didn't want to move to New York ever, it was just that she wasn't ready, not now. She loved her job. Her students needed her. She hadn't realized what it would mean, leaving New Orleans, leaving everything behind for something totally unknown.

His face grew warm, his voice cool. He'd already made plans for them for the fall, set things up.

They had already discussed this.

Anger flashed in her eyes. Why was it always about him, what he wanted?

He blinked, looked away.

She'd tried, but she just wasn't ready to go. And why did it have to be right now? Wasn't it the most important thing that they were together? Maybe in another year...

No. No way. Another year might become another, and then another. And then they'd be stuck.

Would that be so terrible? To stay here for a while?

He stood up. He couldn't believe what he was hearing. Hadn't she understood he'd always planned to leave? How many times had they talked about it? Didn't she know he belonged on a bigger stage than any this place had to offer?

They settled nothing that night. After the back and forth had worn both of them out, he'd just left.

He'd gone to Donna's alone, then gone home, had a drink with his feet up on his coffee table, thinking. Maybe he'd been a little rough. Maybe she was right. Maybe it was all about him, had always been.

He calmed down. He'd call her tomorrow, set things right. Maybe they could compromise. A few months wouldn't make that much difference.

But when he saw her again, ready with his words, hers were already in the air.

Look. I don't think this is going to work.

What do you mean?

The ring he'd given her was already off her finger. She'd placed it neatly back in the box, and handed it to him.

It felt as though she were handing him his heart in a box too small to hold it.

He shook his head, as if the memory were a web of dust he could shake off. As much as he wanted to think about her, about them, there was no point in going down that path now. This time, he would try something new—patience. So instead, he made a couple of phone calls to Brooklyn, something he'd put off for days. The mortgage was due, and Hector, the bass player in his band, had been offered a two-week gig in Italy in November, and what were Julian's plans? Would he be coming back to New York any time soon, and more importantly, could he play?

Julian had no answers. Playing with Grady Casey had been encouraging, and every day he'd been practicing long tones for hours, but he was still a ways from being able to pick up and resume his career. There was too much going on here, and now—with the fate of Silver Creek still up in the air and no news of Simon—New York and Matthew Parmenter both jockeyed for space in the smallest corner of his mind.

Real life stared him dead in the face. Besides his mortgage, there were other bills to pay. His money was running low, and even though there was a paycheck coming from the Tokyo gig (a very small one, thanks to his early bail-out), he didn't know how long he could live on the little savings he'd stashed away. Not long, probably. He'd have to decide something soon, figure out exactly where his life was heading, and what to do after he got there.

The First Bank building, on the southwest corner of the square in Local, sat like an old granite fortress next to the old courthouse, surrounded by giant magnolias and pines. The see-through elevator creaked as it levitated at a frightfully sluggish pace to the offices of N&L Associates on the second floor. In the windowless reception room, a dreary little fluorescent-lit space, a girl of about eighteen with iPod buds plugged in her ears sat at the one desk next to a large gray credenza. A huge potted plant leaned, thirsty and wilting, in an unlit corner.

The receptionist pointed the way to a conference room across a narrow hall. Inside, Kevin sat at a long, walnut table, dressed for the first time since Julian had met him in a long-sleeved white shirt and a red striped tie, his knuckles nervously tapping against a manila folder. The man sitting opposite him, around seventy years of age and wearing a cream-colored suit, got up to shake Julian's hand.

"Pleased to meet you," the man said. "Nathan Larouchette."

"Uh...pleased to meet you. Julian Fortier." Julian's voice halted in surprise. Kevin had told him only Nathan's lawyer was coming.

Grinning as if he were a dealer about to show him a used car, Nathan said, "I was about to send my attorney over here to meet with y'all, but I thought, what the hell? I'll just drive over myself. Haven't seen my grandson here in a while, and I'm sure we can settle this thing civilly so everybody benefits."

The man seemed unduly jovial, considering the circumstances. Julian sat and looked over at Kevin, his wet, blond hair combed straight back off his face, his complexion pale, clouds of irritation shadowing his eyes. Clearly, he too had been surprised by Nathan's appearance.

Nathan Larouchette was not the ogre Julian had pictured; he was slight of build, like Kevin, but where Kevin's body was arrow straight, Nathan's seemed locked in a 170 degree angle, with a slight bend starting at his back. His nervous smile, almost a grimace, spread thinly beneath the sad eyes of a basset hound. His skin was so lacking in color that his whiteness seemed to glow from within. His hair, receding inches back from his forehead, was feathery and white, and at intervals, Nathan would reach up with a hand and sweep the wispy comb-over back into place.

"I'm glad you could make it here, son," he said, giving Julian a nod, drumming his fingers on the table top, his words rolling out in a broad southern accent. "Let's not beat around the bush. You've got a beautiful spread of land, which my company has just purchased through auction. My grandson here tells me you're not too happy with this deal."

Julian almost laughed. *Not too happy? How about pissed? How about mad as hell?*

"The land has been in my family for over a century, sir. It belonged to my great-great-grandfather."

"Well, now, I know it's hard letting go of family property, but keep in mind you are getting a fair price for the land, almost one hundred and twenty thousand. I've seen much worse deals for families in these situations." Nathan leaned back in his chair and crossed a long leg under the table. "Let me tell you what I have in mind."

And Nathan laid out his plan. The Fortiers could continue to own the house, the storage shed, and the barn, and the land on which the three buildings sat. It amounted to about three and a half of the 240 acres. And the family would still get the $118,000 the land was auctioned for, minus the legal fees, to be divided amongst the heirs.

Nathan glanced at the paper in front of him; there were seven family members who shared ownership in the land, and with all the taxes, legal fees incurred by the auction, and the paperwork, every member of the Fortier clan would get about $11,000 each.

Again, Julian held his astonishment in check. This was the deal? According to Kevin's research, the land was worth at least three times what Nathan paid. And the eleven thousand for each family member was an insult.

"Eleven thousand? That's all?" he said.

"Well, as I say, the legal fees must be paid from the sum. But your auntie could still stay in the house," Nathan said, grinning his nervous grimace more broadly now. "Everything would continue as usual. I'll even throw in an extra $5,000 to sweeten the deal. All I ask is that you drop this ridiculous lawsuit idea or whatever you have in mind, which you will almost certainly lose."

With his last sentence, Nathan's tone, formerly a syrup-covered drawl, hardened into a metallic whine. Julian looked over at Kevin, who gave him a solemn look that did little to hide his disgust. There was surely no love lost between these two. But Kevin had painted an accurate picture of his grandfather; men like Nathan Larouchette cut themselves a slick path in the world while expecting others, without the hubris, gall and money to match them, to just step aside and let them pass.

Kevin had been right; this guy was a piece of work.

"And what about the creek?" Julian asked.

Nathan seemed puzzled. "What do you mean?"

"What if I told you that I wanted the creek to be part of our property?"

Nathan frowned. "Well, no, the creek would be essential to the retirement community we have planned for the..."

"And the cemetery?" Julian asked. "Where my family is buried?"

"Well, that would not be part of the..."

Julian looked at Kevin. "Let's go," he said. He got up and looked at Nathan. "Thank you for your time."

Kevin had been quiet the whole time, his face shaded with what looked to Julian like an old, long-harbored hatred. But he said nothing until he reached the door of the office. With one hand on the doorknob, he turned to Nathan.

"One thing, sir. Tell me you didn't hire some goons to padlock these nice folks out of their house, and that they didn't shoot off rifles to try to scare the hell out of them."

Nathan glowered at him. "Excuse me, but after the auction took place, the whole of Silver Creek became the property of N&L Associates. One certainly has a right to protect one's own property. But as for shooting, I don't know what you're talking about."

Kevin glared back at him. "You don't."

"No. Well, I did secure someone to guard the property after the auction, of course, to protect from trespassers and poachers, but I certainly never authorized anyone..."

"And I guess you didn't have anything to do with what happened to Mr. Parette."

A pause. "Who?"

"The Parette property on the other side of the creek? Mr. Parette? The old man whose car got run off the road."

Nathan stared at him, his lips tight and brows furrowed, then blinked. "I don't know anything about that."

"Right." Kevin smiled wryly, then shook his head. "You know Nathan, I owe you a real debt of gratitude."

Nathan gave him a cautious look. "Why is that?"

"It was because of the likes of you that I decided I wanted to be a lawyer."

As they both turned to walk out Nathan called them back.

"Now, wait a minute, boys. Mr. Fortier." Nathan's bushy eyebrows angled downward. He unbuttoned his jacket and put a hand in his pocket. "From what I understand you live in New York. And from what I also understand, you've enjoyed considerable success there. What could this land possibly mean to you? All you will do is impede the progress of what I'm afraid is inevitable. Now, I have given you a generous offer. But why don't you tell me what would be fair? What would it take to get you to drop this lawsuit? What's your price?"

Price? Julian thought a moment. He'd never given a thought before to what it would take to give up his family's land. Half a million dollars? A million? He smiled to himself, feeling power he didn't realize he had.

What was his price? A few years ago, none of this would have mattered to him. But everything was different now.

"There's no price, sir. The land's not for sale."

Nathan scoffed. "For sale? Have you forgotten? I've already bought the land. Quite legally."

"For now." Julian shrugged. "You may even wind up with it one day. But if I have to keep you in court for the next ten years to—what did you call it? 'Impede the progress of the inevitable'—then that's what I'll do."

Nathan's eyes flamed, and his small mouth began to twitch. "All right. All right. Go ahead. I have tried to offer you some of your land back, through my own generosity"—his voice louder now—"but you will lose everything if you continue." He glared at his grandson. "Both of you will lose."

Julian glanced at Kevin, then back at Nathan, as he reached for the door. "Have a good day, sir."

The creek on the Fortier land snaked along a winding path that went deep into the piney woods, then curved like a long S toward the open clearing at the south end of the property. The recent rains had extended the high water season, and the creek rushed along the deep bed, the water warbling in a trebly gurgle over the rocks and glimmering in the blinking light between the shading trees as if strewn with a million tiny mirrors.

Where Julian and Kevin sat, on a bank beneath the shade of an old live oak while their shoes sunned behind them on a distant, rocky rise, the water was clear enough to see the stones edging the bottom.

After the meeting with Nathan Larouchette, Kevin, turning to Julian in the parking lot, said, "Let's go fishing." Kevin's eyes were glassy, his voice tight and curt, and Julian decided this was not the time to argue. He had a hundred things to do, including driving back to New Orleans to pin down a meeting at Simon's house with the insurance agent, calling Sylvia to check in on the search for Simon, meeting with Parmenter's attorney to get the details of the funeral, and so on. But in Kevin's eyes he'd seen a need that, he guessed, could only be satisfied by fishing, and the idea of trespassing on what Nathan considered his land must have held a certain perverse appeal, too.

Julian knew it had been rough for Kevin in there; at the end of the meeting, his young friend had been visibly shaken by the encounter with his estranged grandfather. He was closemouthed on the way to the creek, but as he reached for a cigarette in his truck's glove compartment and lit up (Julian didn't know he smoked), his thin fingers twitched like a palsied old woman's.

Kevin had pulled two brand-new graphite fishing rods from the bed of his truck and a tackle box full of plastic lures. Within a few minutes they were both sitting on rocks in the breezy shade near the first bend of the creek, Kevin with his shirt off and feet dangling in the water, and Julian, shirt unbuttoned to the breeze, sitting next to him.

They had been there for fifteen minutes, both lines in the water, an occasion zephyr rustling the high grasses, before either one of them mentioned the meeting.

"Well, now, that was something, huh?" Kevin scoffed a little, then looked across the creek as the rippling water lapped against the earthen bank. "Man, I hate him for what he's putting y'all through."

Julian said nothing. He was thinking about the last time his father had brought him here to fish. Or try too. It was his twelfth summer, and he'd come here only to humor Simon. To his surprise and his father's delight, he'd caught a catfish, a huge one big as his arm. "You got Caesar!" Simon beamed, elated, but made him throw it back. "He's as old as this creek, let him live a while longer." But for the next few years, Simon bragged about how Julian had snagged "ol Caesar," his first time out. It was the only fish he'd ever caught in his life.

Kevin stood up, reeled his line in, and cast it further across the water. When he sat back down, he blew out a long puff from his cigarette, his fourth since he'd gotten out of the truck. "You know, my mama's a Creole woman, and her great-granddaddy was as black as the bottom of this creek at midnight, they tell me." He paused, as if waiting for Julian to show surprise at his mixed ancestry. Julian nodded thoughtfully, and Kevin went on. "When my daddy took up with her, ol' Nathan liked to had a fit. Not *his* son, by God. Never said more than two words to her the whole time Daddy and Mama were married. But then Nathan took up with a woman he'd been seeing on the sly, and guess what *she* was."

Julian's eyes widened. "A Creole?"

Kevin smirked, nodded. "*Black* and Creole. Ain't that something? Hypocritical bastard." He reached into his wallet and pulled out a photograph of a woman, black-eyed with long curly black hair and skin the color of cantaloupe rind. "That's my mama. She lives in Montana now. Moved there when she married again after Daddy passed."

"Beautiful lady," Julian said.

Kevin nodded. "I grew up hating Nathan, the way he treated

my daddy and my uncle, and then my mama. The way he'd run off sometimes and leave Daddy and his mama and brother when they were little, then come back the next month like nothin' happened. He and my daddy hardly ever spoke the last few years of his life, before Daddy's stroke. But sometimes whenever Nathan's name came up, I'd see Daddy staring off into space, thinking. I always wanted to ask him what he was thinking about. But I knew." Kevin picked up a smooth stone and skipped it across the water. It hopped four times before disappearing beneath the surface as Julian watched in awe. He had never gotten a stone to hop more than twice.

Kevin looked at Julian, his brows arched up in the middle of his forehead apologetically. "I have to tell you this. So far, we don't have much. The truth is, after Prof died, I haven't had much luck with these cases. I keep tryin'. But when they get this far along..." He let his sentence disappear into the sound of the water.

Julian looked out over the creek. "I know."

"I was thinking about your cousin, Miss Genevieve? Didn't she say your great-great granddaddy won Silver Creek on a bluff in a poker game?"

Julian nodded. "Right. That's what she said."

"And that your great-granddaddy, what was his name—Moses—that he got the land when his brother had to leave the state after almost getting shot?"

"Right."

"Well, I hope that poker-face luck runs in the family, 'cause we're looking at one lousy hand."

"Yeah," Julian said, feigning attention, still lost in thought. He was hot and the air was sticky, but the breeze of the oak that cooled his face and billowed the soft cotton of his shirt away from his skin was as pleasing as fine spring rain. And he realized he hadn't had a headache in two days.

When Julian was in college after his mother died, Simon would take off for Silver Creek after a long week at the restaurant, just for a day or two, to "get his mind right." He'd always return looking a little younger, Julian remembered, with a little more spring in his step. Now he knew why. As much as his father loved New Orleans, it was a city. And this was a place where a man could open his chest to the sweeping air, look across a field unhemmed by buildings and see a landscape of possibility.

Leaning back, his elbow on the rock, his head resting on his fist, he looked straight up through the leaves of the live oak at the gauzy glare of filtered sun. He closed his eyes to it, stared at the warming orangey glow behind his eyelids. For a moment, he had not a care in the world.

Kevin stood up and found a fist-sized rock to balance his rod while he reached in his pocket for another cigarette.

"Gotta quit this smoking thing before little Suzy, that's the baby's name, before she comes."

Julian sat up and took a drink from one of the beers in the six pack of Bud they'd gotten in Local. He tried to imagine a little girl looking like Kevin.

"So what do we do now?"

Kevin shrugged. He'd spent hours poring over the land dispute cases in Pointe Louree Parish. Not one case had been decided in favor of the plaintiff, the original landowners, in the last three years. For decades, families had lost acres and acres of land, gas, oil, and mineral rights, all through the shenanigans of companies like Nathan's.

Even the case with the Parette family had quietly gone away, Kevin said. The accident had been officially determined as just that—an accident, despite the second set of tire tracks near the ditch that would have indicated Parette had swerved to avoid a collision. After he died, the family, who lived out of state, had sold the land to Nathan for a song.

"We can buy a little time maybe, but what we need is some kind of a will. I know you said before y'all don't have one. But it doesn't have to be anything fancy. Just something written down somewhere saying who the land's intended for. Judges can be pretty liberal in these kinds of cases."

He explained that in Louisiana they had something called "olographic" wills. It could be hand written on a napkin for all the judge cared, but if it's written by the decedent who owned the land, and dated, it could be binding in court.

Julian frowned. Nothing like that existed as far as he knew. Even Genevieve said so. His father hadn't yet written a will (with only one son, he hadn't seen the need), and Julian's grandfather Jacob, as far as he knew, hadn't either.

Kevin pulled his line in and recast it in deeper water. "Well, like you said, we'll keep his lawyers busy as long as we can. Maybe something will come up."

"Maybe so." Julian had an odd feeling in his gut. It may have been the comforting sun, his easeful mood, but the fleeting assurance that in time, everything would work out as it should, warmed him like a gentle, steadying hand. He looked across the bank of the creek to the groves of pines and poplars and cypresses in the distance as far as his eyes could see. *This could all be mine*, he thought. Then he corrected himself. *Is mine.* And for a brief moment he felt as if the whole thing with Nathan Larouchette had never happened.

"Hey, look!"

Kevin pointed to Julian's bobber, which bounced in the water while the tug at the line ripped wide shimmying circles across the surface.

"Grab it!"

Julian, who had been leaning back against the rock, jumped up on his feet. He grabbed the rod while the line loosened, the bobber trailed farther out into the water, and the crank of the reel spun. It was a good, solid strike. Not a big fish, but it had an impressive pull.

He let the line go a little slack, then cranked it in tighter to set the hook.

"By God I think you got that sucker!" Kevin stood next to him, grinning. "If I didn't know better, I'd swear you knew what you were doing."

He worked with the catch for minutes, reeling it in, letting it run, then reeling again. Stepping down on the bank closer to the water, bare feet tracking the grit of rock and sand, he repeated it over again as sweat beaded on his forehead and his heart raced.

Kevin's eyes opened wide, gleeful as a child's. "Damn! The little son of a gun wants to give you a fight."

Julian bit his bottom lip as the rod bowed with the tension. *I've got him hooked. If I can just outlast him, he's mine.*

And then he saw his father's eyes light up like the blaze of sun that flashed through the live oak leaves above. "Just hold on," Simon was telling him, as he had before. "He's already yours, you just gotta fight to keep him."

Sometimes that's the hardest thing. Holding on to keep what you've got.

With a splash, something broke the surface of the water. Julian slowly reeled in the catch. The line much shorter now, Julian lifted the rod, smiling the way he had when he was twelve, as a catfish, no bigger than his hand but feisty with life, twitched and danced and dangled in the late summer light.

18

By mid October, the city of New Orleans, like a prizefighter pummeled and pressed to the mat, strained to raise its head from an unconscious, near-death state. Its pulse, though faint, was steady, its prognosis in doubt, and even the struggle back to its knees would be long and arduous. Six weeks after the biggest disaster it had ever seen, a stream of residents, armed with faith, hope, and whatever courage they could muster, still flowed in daily to face an uncertain future in the city that had broken their hearts.

But while the city crawled to life, every hour news stations reported stories of struggle and tragedy as the death tally spilled beyond the flooded city's limits—infirm or elderly citizens, ferried to outposts of safety in distant towns survived the storm and flood, only to die in Houston, or Atlanta, or Dallas or dozens of other places, from lack of critical medicine or some long standing illness worsened by heartbreak. And even some who were healthy when they left perished as their bodies buckled under the shock of tragedy and the load of loss.

But stories of impossible survival and answered prayers softened the hearts of the most hardened cynics: a three-year-old boy, helicoptered out of harm's way and leaving his tearful father behind, reunited with him after weeks alone and lost in a shelter in Colorado; an unlikely pair—a five-year-old black girl and her white, eighty-nine-year-old wheelchair-bound neighbor—braved three harsh nights on an overpass before being transported to safety, a journey that involved three cities and nearly every known mode of transportation.

For days Julian had poured over these happy-ending stories in the online edition of the *Times-Picayune* in the computer room of the Best Western, still holding on to hope. As much as his mind worked to accept Simon's death, his heart could not, and would not until he had proof. Each TV news dispatch, radio story or newspaper photo cut line of a happy reunion bubbled in him like a tonic, so he combed the pages one by one, praying to find a story of a seventy-six-year-old black man, maybe wearing a brown straw hat, with or without a big leather Bible and carrying a hand-carved African cane.

Standing in front of a bar in the Faubourg Marigny section of the city, a rock's throw from the French Quarter, Julian watched the fading light of the October sky and thought about those stories. Anything was possible in this bizarre netherworld that had replaced his hometown on the other side of the nightmare. He looked at Grady standing next to him, lighting up, then taking a long drag on his cigarette. Grady was the only man he knew who could smoke like a fiend and still play the hell out of the trumpet. And though Julian had never smoked a cigarette in his life, he thought of asking him for one. There was something about the comfort it seemed to bring, like a child's pacifier, that looked appealing.

"Don't even think about smoking these things, man," Grady eyed him as if he'd read his mind. "I thought I was done with them but since all this mess happened..."

He let the unfinished sentence dangle in the drift of the breeze from the river. Julian gave him an understanding look, then glanced down at his watch.

"So you told them eight, right?"

"Yep."

"So you sure Little D's coming?"

"Little D. Yeah."

He nodded, looked at his watch again. "Easy Money, too?"

Grady tossed his cigarette on the ground and smashed it with his foot. "Quit worrying, man. They'll be here. Every one of 'em said they would. Don't forget, don't none of the clocks in this town work anymore."

"Besides," he added, "I told 'em what the gig pays."

Julian nodded. They had only been waiting a little while and it was only a little past eight. The autumn sky still held faint traces of blue, the shadows lengthening on the street. Wood and glass-fronted shops on Frenchmen Street—a hookah bar, a tattoo parlor, a coffee house, a tiny café/deli, more than a few night clubs and other small businesses—stood mostly in shadow like hollowed ruins. On a normal weekday night, music would have blasted from every other doorway while college-age kids, musicians, and a few hip locals and tourists streamed from the bars and milled in the streets, their laughter a tickle in the air, pulsing with a rhythm of its own. A brass band might be tuning up to jam. A jazz trio from one of the colleges might be setting up for a late set, or a guitarist might sit crosslegged on the sidewalk, playing some good Texas blues for tips. But on a street that had once been the pulse point of the city's music scene, every noise that resembled the sound of pleasure had been drowned by the flood.

A man in his twenties cruised by on a ten-speed bike, and three girls in shorts and tank tops, no doubt volunteers from some distant city, walked by. One of them, the youngest-looking one, with shoulder-length brown hair and freckles, stopped and asked Grady for a cigarette. He fished in his pocket and offered her his pack.

"Where y'all young ladies from?"

A tall blond girl wearing a red baseball cap smiled. "We came down from St. Louis."

They were members of a United Methodist Church group who had come to help gut houses in St. Bernard Parish.

Grady smiled. "Long way from home."

"We drove all night," she said. "Got a light?" The younger girl held the cigarette up to her lips.

"Oh, here you go." Grady found his matches and lit one.

The girls had come to the city when they read an article in the *Post-Dispatch* about one of their church member's relatives, whose newly built house in St. Bernard had taken on eight feet of water. They'd gotten permission to miss a week of classes to help with the friend's house and others in the neighborhood.

The third member of the group, a brown-skinned girl with a round face, a silver nose ring, and a puffy Afro highlighted with blue dye, joined in the conversation. "I like it down here," she said. "I think I might come back and stay longer, when things get better."

An SUV full of young people who clearly knew the church trio pulled up alongside them. "We're gonna go find some food!" one of the girls in the vehicle yelled out. The three girls said goodbye to Julian and Grady and got in.

Grady and Julian waved as they pulled away. Before they reached the corner Grady yelled to them, "Thank y'all for coming down to help!"

"Well, at least somebody thinks this place is worth bothering with." Grady reached in his pocket for another cigarette. "You wouldn't believe all what I been hearing, man, stuff about the city never coming back, or coming back with none of *us* in it. Crazy." He shook his head.

"Maybe Cindy's right," he said. "Maybe it's not worth trying to make it here."

"Hey, come on, man. Sure it is." Julian's words tumbled out like a reflex, but landed without conviction. He wasn't at all sure he believed them. The truth was, he'd been so consumed with Simon, Silver Creek, Velmyra, and even Parmenter, that he'd thought little lately about the future of this place where he had been born and raised.

"I don't know, man." Grady shifted his weight to one foot and leaned a hand against one of the posts supporting the wrought iron balcony above. "You know what they're saying up in Texas? Dude told my wife he heard the city was dead. All gone." He shrugged. "I ain't gonna lie, I thought the same thing myself, a time or two. It's like one of those disaster flicks, where the dude knows the world is over, like, everybody's done for and he's the last dude on earth, but he still goes around searching for food."

Grady looked at Julian. "But you wanna stop the guy and ask him, 'Why?'"

Julian nodded thoughtfully at the movie analogy, a comparison he'd made himself just a couple of days ago. *Why?* It was a question he'd asked himself every day as he prayed for good news about Simon. Giving up just wasn't in his blood; he'd figured out it felt... unnatural. But keeping on—hoping—that was a natural thing. *Hope.* Maybe it was something that folks were just born with, the real proof that you were alive. It's what his grandfather'd had, for sure, and no doubt his daddy too. And it was the only thing that kept him going now, searching for Simon.

Grady lifted his head back and blew a long, slow stream of smoke up toward the balcony. "What do you think, bruh? You think this place can come back?"

Julian turned up the collar of his shirt as a cool breeze floated by. He looked out toward the outlines of buildings and sky across the street where he'd spent many a summer evening hanging out, playing his horn. He felt a slight chill as he imagined the most dire predictions coming true. *Did he? Really?*

"Guess we gotta believe so."

A silver van pulled up to the front of the building and a stocky white man with a full salt-and-pepper beard got out, his keys jangling. "Sorry guys," he said. "Been waiting long?"

"Hey! Man! You made it!" Grady grabbed the man's hand and shook it. They had only gotten there fifteen minutes ago, Grady told him. "Hey, thanks a lot for letting us use your place."

The man, Charley Graviere, had owned the small bar for seventeen years, and had hired the band often. "Charley's Sweet Spot," like many of the businesses along the street, had not suffered flood damage but was still closed, since few of the employees had returned, and those who had tried couldn't find a place to stay.

Fifteen minutes or so after Charley unlocked the door, the musicians of the Soul Fire Brass Band began to arrive and crowded into the wood-paneled, slightly musty space. Grady was right. Every one of them showed up.

They all had been fairly close when Julian was with the band, but two of the guys, Dereek Bradford, trombonist, and bass drummer Thaddeus "Easy Money" Church, had been among his closest friends during his dues-paying days of marching bands, second-line parades, and jazz funerals. Yet they had given him as much grief as the others had the night he announced his departure, not so much with words but snide grunts and cold, silent stares.

Of all the men, the one he most regretted disappointing was Dereek, the youngest in the group, who'd been in his late teens when Julian had played with them, and had shadowed Julian like a fawning little brother. When he'd phoned Dereek to say goodbye, his young friend had never returned his call. And when he dropped Easy Money a postcard from New York—*Come on up, you always got a place to stay*—he'd never heard back.

But this was no time for holding grudges—they had bigger things on their mind than whatever ax they had to grind with him. Each one had lost his home to flood water, and three had lost their instruments. But Parmenter, generous in death, had provided for the purchase of new instruments for those who needed them. It had taken Grady three days to locate and contact all of them—some had been scattered across the country as far away as California, New Mexico, and even Massachusetts.

They all shook hands with Julian, some grabbing him in a bear hug—*Thanks for the gig, man!*—and the warm reception was a relief. In minutes, cases and instruments—trumpets, trombones, drums, a sax, a slightly tarnished sousaphone—lay strewn about the room, and the men ran through the standard New Orleans funeral and second-line music quickly. The minute they began to play, the music exploded, and Julian remembered: there was nothing like the sound of a New Orleans brass band. Thick, raucous, hot and free, with a life of its own. It pounded the walls of the small room, bursting it at the seams and spilling into the street.

After an hour or so, they adjourned to one of the few reopened bars about a block away. Once inside The Spotted Cat, already high on the music, they ordered a round of beers and shared flood stories.

Casey's tale of being trapped on the balcony of his apartment for forty-eight hours paled next to what they heard from the others. Dereek had watched the rolling sea from his rooftop for five days after sleeping in on the morning of the levee breach and waking to water floating his bed. The snare drummer, Claude Joubert, swam through neck-high currents to rescue his cousins from a burning house, only to bring them back to the dubious safety of his boiling hot rooftop, where they waited two days for the sweet music of U.S. Coast Guard helicopter blades. And Easy Money, the diminutive postal worker, silenced the table with his story of trudging miles through a river of oil, waste, and slime up to his chest and making a makeshift raft out of a mattress to rescue four elderly women from the brackish waters of his drowned neighborhood.

Once away from the flooded city, all had watched the tragedy play out on the TV screens of spare bedrooms, shelters, and church basements around the country. As the men talked, the noise level rose with the alcohol levels in their blood. There was so much anger, so much that needed to be said, as the winds of betrayal had blown powerfully from every direction. The mayor. The governor. The president. The heads of the Federal Emergency Management Agency, who had bungled the aftermath of the flood, and for days had turned a blind eye to the chaos in the city. The Army Corps of Engineers, architects of the poorly built levees that had been ignored for decades by uniformed commanders whose chests bulged with bars and stripes.

All had let them down, then passed the blame from one to the other like a Christmas fruitcake. The blame was so abundant it would have taken the bandsmen days to dispense it fairly, but after a couple of therapeutic hours of drinking and venting, the men breathed easier, their joints loosened, their nerves calmed. Bonded by the music and the memories of growing up in the city, they reminisced and even laughed and joked as the dark closed in, the wood paneling holding the comforting scent of stale beer, a precious sign of normalcy in an abnormal world.

Miraculously, none of the other men had suffered the loss of loved ones, but all fell silent when Grady brought up the subject of "Pops," their nickname for Simon. "I sure will miss him, man." Easy Money looked over at Julian, bowed his head in reverence. Simon had fed them many a late night after gigs; sometimes, after a parade with his buddies in the Elegant Gents, Simon would open his door to find seven or eight pairs of young legs stretched across the furniture in his living room. As if that were his cue, he'd reach deep into a cabinet, grab his best iron pot, and start up the stove, still whistling "When the Saints Go Marching In." When one of the boys, knowing how much Simon loved Louis Armstrong, had called him "Pops," the name stuck—Simon loved nothing more than sharing a namesake with the greatest jazzman the city had ever produced.

When the evening wore on into the next morning, the men got ready to head back to their motels; the funeral was only a few hours away. When Julian headed to his car, Dereek called out to him.

"Hey! Wait a minute."

He caught up with Julian just before he got into his car.

"So sorry, man," he said. "About your daddy."

"Thank you."

"Hey, look. If there's anything I can do."

"Yeah, thanks, man."

He put his hands in his pockets, looked up toward the sky, then leveled his gaze at Julian. "I was pretty pissed at you when you left, you know."

"I know. I don't much blame you."

"I just want to say that, you know, it's OK. I get it now. I get why you left."

Julian's heart sank. He knew what his old friend was saying.

He looked Dereek in the eye. "No, man. I love this place. This is home. I just...at the time, I just had to get away. To try something new."

Dereek nodded, looked across the street at the vacant buildings. "I know. Everybody got to do his own thing, right?"

Julian clapped his friend on the shoulder. "How you making it, man? You dealing with everything OK?"

Dereek told him again about his last day in the Ninth Ward house he'd grown up in, which, having lasted through four previous generations in his family, was swallowed in minutes by the flood. When the helicopter's rescue basket lifted him high above the neighborhood, he had looked down at the horror. As he rose higher, so did the water, it seemed, engulfing the house as it collapsed and floated in the current, disappearing from view. He knew his house and every other house of the block would not survive this. The world he'd known was gone.

He had promised his father years before when he died that he would take good care of the house and pass it down the line. Children, grandchildren, great-grandchildren. Each new generation of Bradfords born with a house waiting for them. He had plans to bump out the kitchen the way his mother, who years before lost a mid-life battle with diabetes, had always wanted. But now, the rumors about the future of the Lower Nine kept him awake at night.

"My granddaddy owned that land, free and clear, and so did his daddy before him," he said shaking his head. "That piece of land is all I got, you know what I'm sayin? It's like family. It's *mine.* They got no right to it."

Julian had heard the rumors, floating mostly from meetings held around town as city officials grappled with the fragile future of New Orleans. To many, it seemed the close-knit black community was as disposable as the land near his father's house in the Treme that had been destroyed forty years ago to make way for the 1-10 overpass. He understood who "they" were: the planners and players, movers and shakers who, now that so much of the city was uninhabitable, talked of reshaping it with a different footprint, one that left out the lower-lying neighborhoods of the working class. The guys in the suits didn't seem to know much about how their ancestors—freed slaves, many of them—had all sweated blood over their own patch of land for the future of their children and children's children, and they didn't much care.

Julian's life in New York was far removed from the thrust and parry, the pull and give of precious family land. His thousand square foot co-op over a Brooklyn Wash-a-teria was free of the ties of ancestral history. But hearing Dereek's words, he thought of Silver Creek. That plot of land had placed him, alongside his old friends, square in the middle of a struggle to preserve the past. His father had tried so many times to tell him—land meant history, and history meant you knew who you were. It was the legend that helped decipher the map of your life.

Even if you were poor and didn't have, as his father used to say, two dimes to rub together, land meant you always had a place in the world. Julian had grown up with folks who owned little more than a ragged patch of dirt, but held their heads up high. At least they had *that*.

With the street lamps not working, the only light on the block was the glimmer of the pale autumn moon. Dereek had always had a youthful face, and usually looked younger than his twentysomething years. But now, washed in hard angles of light and shadow, it glowed with the deep pallor of a man in struggle, the young eyes aged by a reflection of all he had seen. It was a look that had become too familiar in New Orleans lately: lost, despairing, stunned. But somehow, Dereek's large, dark eyes still reflected the faintest trace of hope.

"Hold on, man." Julian said. "Don't let them take your land. Do whatever it takes. It's yours. You fight for it."

Dereek nodded. "Yeah. I will."

"What are you going to do? You OK where you're staying now?"

He told Julian his plans to go back to Austin after the funeral, where he was staying with a cousin who had a spare bedroom in a townhouse close to the university. He'd get a day gig, then check out the music scene and see what freelance work he could get.

"Then I'm gonna come back and rebuild my house," he said.

Julian nodded, smiled. "All right, then." He looked at his watch. "Get some good sleep. I'll see you in the morning. Bright and early."

They shook hands. As Dereek turned to walk away, Julian called after him.

"You keep your head up, Little D!"

Dereek looked back and smiled at the nickname his friend had given him years ago, when they had been as close as brothers.

"Keep my head up? Don't worry. With all that water, I had plenty of practice."

On a cloudless morning beneath a brilliant sun, a shout of brass and a rhythmic rumble of drums split the hot, thick air.

No one knew exactly when the tradition got started—the funereal cadence, the somber march in slow, studied steps, the swell of trumpets and trombones wailing a mournful cry before escorting the departed soul to a jubilant release—but of the music's source there was no doubt. Born on a breeze that swept across the African plains, it winged west to the cotton fields of America and seated itself in the soul of the South. It slumbered through the long night of slavery, stirred in the hopeful air of campground meetings and Sunday-morning-witness prayer circles before finding life and breath in the beating heart of New Orleans. The marriage of jazz and funerals may have been an unlikely pairing, but once done, the love-match was as much a part of life in the city as the river that shouldered its shore.

In singles, in pairs, and in small clusters, the mourners of Matthew Parmenter gather at the St. Louis Cathedral near Jackson Square. When the short service ends, strains of "A Closer Walk With Thee" roll out, elegant and elegiac, as the procession of bandsmen, friends, former employees, a small knot of family from out of town, and the stately black hearse begins from the Cathedral down the cobbled streets of the Vieux Carré. Parmenter's mourners are many, but when the music starts, dozens more who have never heard of the wealthy restaurateur appear, straggling out of the reopened bars and restaurants to join the procession, longing for what has been missing in the city since the flood— the martial roll and snap of snare drums, the blast of trumpets and the gritty growl of trombones, the deep *blaatt* of the sousaphone and the booming *thump* of the bass drum, and later, after the soul's full release, the strut and swagger of second liners, footsteps high and arms waving, shoulders shaking, their flared umbrellas lifted, their white handkerchiefs like linen doves fluttering high above their heads.

Leading the musicians of Soul Fire, Julian lifts his horn in the air to signal a turn at the corner, and the notes and chords of "Just a Closer Walk with Thee" come so easily to mind it is like spelling out his name. He spreads his shoulders as his tone swells in the open blue and the other bandsmen follow his lead, as he is testifying now, blowing clean and pure as if there is no bulk of brass, as if the shiny coil of metal is just a conduit for the song in his soul.

The music filling the air around them, they stroll on for blocks before turning onto Esplanade. When finally the hearse picks up speed, breaks away from the group, and heads toward the highway and Baton Rouge (where Matthew would be buried alongside his wife), the group of mourners, now numbering more than a hundred, circle around to head back to the Square, and the bass drum thumps out a livelier beat.

Now it's time to 'cut the body loose,' as the band breaks into an upbeat "I'll Fly Away," and the second liners—the friends and strangers and family stepping behind the band—start to sing as mournful dirge becomes exultant dance; *Some glad mornin', when my life is over, I'll fly away....* The bells and slides of horns, once low or level, now tilt upward to the trees and balconies of the Quarter and the blazing sun, and the trumpets let out a joyful scream, and the trombones peal in a gritty moan and the snares and bass drum snap and boom in tight two/four time. Horns swinging side to side, the bandsmen declare every man for himself now, each flying high in his own groove, wrapping their notes around each others' in a hot embrace, keys abandoned, harmony and dissonance squabbling like irascible lovers, notes locking horns and bumping heads, and nobody caring.

And for a brief speck on the long arc of time, they have all forgotten—hearts unburdened, minds swept clean. No flood, no broken levees. No death, no drowned city. Only grief drowned by song. Only the triumph of a trumpet lifted to the sky. Defiant against the mad turns of fate, hopeful against all reason, the revelers pick up their heels, their umbrellas, their skirts, and in a rocking sea of rhythm, dance their troubles away.

In the middle of it all, Julian stops playing—eyes wet, throat clogged with unexpected tears. He begins a new tune, the one that he heard over and over on the belted turntable in the living room from the time he was six years old. One by one, each man picks up the tune, the one they'd heard whistled over a boiling pot on a kitchen stove on a Saturday afternoon—and "When the Saints Go Marching In" rolls out, sweet and sassy, in the mid-morning air.

After an hour or so, exhaustion claimed all the revelers and mourners and as they parted company, laughter replaced tears. All the members of Soul Fire hugged each other, rubbed heads, clapped backs, wished each other luck in the coming weeks and months of difficult life-rebuilding, and promised to keep in touch.

Grady grinned at Julian, punched him in the shoulder. "I never heard you play better man. I swear it."

Julian nodded. Yes, he felt it, somewhere in the middle of all that sound. He was a player again. He was back.

He turned when a familiar voice caught his attention. Sylvia, whom he'd spotted earlier, had brought up the rear of the second liners, strutting along with a red satin umbrella trimmed in black fringe.

"Thank you, baby. I needed this," she told him, dabbing at her eyes. She was dressed in a fitted suit of Navy blue, her hair pulled back, makeup impeccably applied. She gave him a hug, and promised to call him later. Their work, finding Simon, was not yet done.

He was heading back towards his car when he spotted Cedric Cole standing next to his black Jaguar parked near the empty stalls of the French Market. He wore a tailored gray suit, dark shades, and a respectful smile.

He clapped his hands as Julian approached him.

"That was awesome," he told Julian. "Mr. Parmenter would have been pleased."

"Thanks," Julian said, shaking the big man's extended hand. "It was a good thing, I think, for everybody."

Cole nodded. "Indeed. By the way, I got your message. That won't be a problem."

"Great. Thanks, man."

Julian had asked if it were possible that the fee for each musician (not including himself) be increased to two thousand. Somehow, he explained, the men had gotten the wrong idea of the pay. But he figured Grady, either thinking wishfully or remembering incorrectly, had relayed a more generous fee to the men than Julian had quoted.

"There's something else I need to tell you," Cole said. "Your presence is requested one more time. Tomorrow at my office over on the West Bank—the address on the card I gave you. Around two, if it's convenient. If not, we can change the time."

Julian didn't have anything pressing. "Sure. But there's no rush. You can just mail those checks to me at the motel."

"Oh, no, it's not that." Cedric Cole took off his jacket and his shades as he opened his car door. "You'll need to be present," he said, stepping in and starting the car, "at the reading of Mr. Parmenter's will."

19

Cedric Cole's office, just across the river in the flood-spared West Bank town of Harvey, was slickly appointed with original oil paintings in bold flashes of color adorning the wheat-colored grasscloth walls, and two pieces of abstract metal sculpture on wood pedestals lit with columns of soft florescence from track lights above. On the wall opposite a huge canvas of a New Mexican sunset in the mountains, bookcases of brown, leather-bound law books reached toward the ceiling.

As soon as Julian arrived, Cole's secretary, a plump and smiling middle-aged woman, escorted him down a long hallway and into the conference room, where seated around the oblong table of dark walnut were four people he'd never seen before: a thirtysomething man with a long, dark ponytail, and dressed in jeans and a black shirt; two suntanned, auburn-haired women, one in her twenties and the other forty-something; and an older man with thin locks of whitish hair, dressed in a well-tailored black suit and staring constantly at his Blackberry.

Shortly after Julian took a seat, the door opened. Cole entered smiling and sat at the head of the table.

He opened his black briefcase, shuffled papers, then looked up. "OK. So. Everybody's here. Has everybody met everybody else?"

They proceeded with the awkward introductions. The two women, Matilda and Brittany Jacklyn, a divorced mother and her daughter who'd flown in for the funeral from Minneapolis, were Parmenter's grand-niece and great-grandniece, descended from his deceased older brother, Mark Abraham Parmenter. The thirty-something man was Freddy Tallent, Parmenter's gardener, driver, and sometime cook for the last eleven years. The older man was Jackson Buckner, Parmenter's wife's nephew by marriage, now living in Chicago.

Julian, Cole explained to all, was the son of Parmenter's best friend, the well-known head chef at Parmenter's restaurant. "And you might recognize him as the leader of the brass band at the services yesterday," he added.

At this, they all smiled and nodded, chattered about how "amazing" the music was, how special the tradition, and how unique to hear such "interesting" music played at a funeral.

"I've never seen anything like that in my life! Uncle Matthew would have been thrilled!" the grand-niece Matilda said.

The others nodded, smiled, making approving noises.

"Well," Cole said, "That's the New Orleans way."

He removed a manila folder from his briefcase. "All right. Here we go."

The reading of the will went quickly. The majority of Parmenter's liquid assets, a little more than $170,000, he left to the endowment fund of the New Orleans Opera and to the medical school of Tulane University. To the two women, Parmenter left the deed to a vacation condominium in Destin, Florida. To the gardener/driver, Parmenter left his automobile, a 2004 Cadillac Escalade, and $15,000 cash from his personal account. Parmenter's wife's nephew received $13,000 and the shares of two major companies' stocks Parmenter owned.

Cole turned to Julian, and every pair of eyes in the room shifted in his direction.

"And to Simon Fortier, the best chef in New Orleans and my best friend in the world, and in the event of the aforesaid's premature death, to his son and heir, Julian Fortier, I leave my New Orleans home on St. Charles Avenue and all the contents therein..."

Julian's choked cough was clearly audible, and around the room there were the sharp intakes of breath, the clearing of throats and shuffling of feet.

"...as well as full ownership of Parmenter's Creole Kitchen Red Beans and Rice Mix."

Again, Cole shuffled papers, removing another sheet from the folder. "And days before his death, Mr. Parmenter added this codicil," he said.

"And to my friend Simon, my heartfelt apologies."

Frowns and puzzled looks traveled around the room.

Cole closed the folder and clasped his hands together on the table.

"This ends the reading of Matthew Parmenter's last will and testament. Are there any questions?"

Silence around the table.

"Good. If there are no questions and no contesting of the will, you'll all be contacted by my office soon to be advised of how Mr. Parmenter's bequests are to be carried out."

Another moment of quiet. Everyone looked at each other with a mixture of curiosity and a measure of satisfaction at their own good fortunes. But eyes lingered on Julian as each one said their goodbyes and left the room.

Moments later, the room was empty except for Cole and Julian.

"Got a minute?" Cole said. "Let me buy you a drink."

Ten minutes later, Cole and Julian, in Cole's black Jaguar, pulled into the parking lot of Sherman's Seafood Grill near Highway 90, less than a mile from Cole's office. The bar area, separate from the dining room, was paneled in dark wood, and the bar itself was empty; a television behind it noiselessly flashed highlights of a major league baseball game. From a bass-heavy stereo system mounted somewhere in the walls, Louis Armstrong's gritty voice belted out "What a Wonderful World."

Cole removed his jacket and draped it across one of the high, tubular chrome bar stools. Julian sat next to him.

"I come here after work a lot," Cole said. "They make the best martini in town, and their shrimp cocktail is primo." He glanced at the bar menu, then looked up at Julian. "So I would imagine you're a little surprised?" He grabbed a fistful of peanuts sitting in a dish on the bar and popped a few in his mouth.

Julian, unsmiling, shook his head. Parmenter. Wow. Did he think, somehow, that this would make up for the injustice to his father? Now, when his father can't enjoy any of it, when his father is probably dead somewhere, *now* is when Parmenter gets religion.

Julian thought those thoughts, but said only, "Yeah, you could say that."

Cole got the waiter's attention and ordered a martini. He looked at Julian, eyebrows lifted.

"I'll just have a beer, whatever's on tap," Julian said.

When the drinks arrived, Cole lifted his glass and took a small sip. "Well, Mr. Parmenter was very concerned about your father, toward the end. At Mr. Parmenter's request, I have been making calls all over town, trying to find out about what might have happened to him."

Julian looked at the nut dish, picked out three almonds, and ate them. "Thank you. I really appreciate what you're doing."

"Well, I'm just following my boss's wishes."

A thoughtful silence passed between them.

Cole held up a finger to the bartender. "Another one of these, please." And to Julian, "How about you?"

"I'm good."

The bartender brought another martini and placed it on the bar in front of Cole.

"But now, with your father missing, things are a little complicated. Legally, I mean. As your father's heir, you, of course, will inherit what Mr. Parmenter indicated—the house and its contents, as well as the profits from the sale of the red beans and rice mix. Oh, by the way, I bought a bag about a week ago. Found it in the airport in Dallas. I cooked it for a couple of friends who came over. Good stuff."

"Anyway. Sorry to put this so bluntly, but the problem is that your father is not dead. Not according to the law, anyway. And for you to inherit the house, et cetera, it has to be legally confirmed. Which means, we really need to find out what happened to him.

"I talked to someone at the U. S. Coast Guard. The lists of names is very sketchy—some people were in pretty bad shape—so they have no way of knowing for sure whether your father was one of the ones airlifted to the Convention Center or the Superdome, or a hospital somewhere. We do know that he was not on any of the buses that left both those places headed for shelters in other states."

Julian nodded his head soberly and took a long swig of the beer in his frosted mug.

"But he may have been picked up by someone else. There were so many other groups—Department of Wildlife and Fisheries, volunteers, private citizens with boats. There are all kinds of possibilities. Anyway, I want you to know I intend to hire an investigator, as Mr. Parmenter provided. We'll find out what happened to him, sooner or later."

"I've got one question."

"What's that?"

"Why, after all this time, did Parmenter finally decide to do right by my father? He knew all along that that whole business deal was wrong. So why now? What happened?"

Cole took the swizzle stick from his martini and ate the large olive at the end. He frowned thoughtfully.

"You know," he said, "Mr. Parmenter wasn't a bad person. I've known him—both him and his wife—for a long time. My father used to work for him, a long time ago."

Cole's father, he explained, was a plumber and small-time contractor who'd met Parmenter through doing some work for the restaurant when the toilets were backed up. He'd ended up working at the house on St. Charles, painting, plumbing, doing small remodeling jobs, and he and the older man had become friends.

It was Parmenter's wife, Clarisse, who had taken a liking to the bright young boy who hung around the house, giving his father a hand.

"It was just the two of us after my folks got divorced when I was six. I guess I was a smart little kid. When I finished high school, I was third in my class. I wanted to be a lawyer. When Mrs. Parmenter—Clarisse—found out I couldn't afford to go to college, let alone law school, she insisted Parmenter pay my way all the way to my last year at Tulane. In return, I agreed to work for him on retainer for two years. I kinda liked the gig, and two years turned into twenty."

Cole looked toward the window as traffic on the busy street raced by. "I'm sure Mr. P.—that's what I called him—he would never have sent me to school, if his wife hadn't insisted on it. He just wouldn't have thought of it. But he would have done anything to please her. He loved your dad like a brother, you know, but he was a businessman to the core. He saw the thing with the red beans and rice mix as a gamble that just worked out better for him in the end than for your father. Simple.

"But when your father came to Mr. Parmenter's house a year or so after the mix took off nationally and saw how he was living, things changed. Oh, your dad was still kind, they were still friends, but things were different. Then, when your mom got sick and your dad was struggling with medical bills, Clarisse came down hard on Mr. P. She knew your father's recipe was the real reason they had so much wealth. She insisted that he do something to help, but your dad, he was a proud, stubborn man, he wouldn't take any money, wouldn't take any 'charity.' Even from a friend.

"Mr. P. told Clarisse that. 'He won't accept any money from me, not now,' he said. But she wouldn't buy it. Before she died she told him, 'Promise me you'll do the right thing.' That's one of the reasons he wanted so much to see your dad before he went. It was her wish. And her wish became his."

Julian remembered the day Clarisse came to their house. How out of place she looked in his neighborhood—ramrod straight spine, pale white skin clothed in white linen, blue eyes luminous against the backdrop of shotgun houses and barbecue grills. A picnic basket on her arm holding a salad of tuna on lettuce leaf, a pot for clove and sassafras tea. The way his mother smiled when she walked into her sickroom.

"Finally, not too long ago, Parmenter got your dad to come over; he'd invited him several times over the years, but your dad kept refusing, always 'too busy.' It was just the two of them. Parmenter brought out a bottle of his special ninety-five dollar port, and he and your dad got pretty plastered."

Parmenter, Cole said, talked him into playing dominoes, for money, nickels and dimes. They were having fun, a couple of old friends, when after about the fifth glass of port for both, Parmenter had an idea.

"Let's play for something big, just for fun. I'll put up my house against your land, your Silver Creek. It'll make the game more exciting."

"Your dad thought it was just a joke, all in good fun, so he said OK. Well, you know your dad, he was a domino player from hell, a demon, and Mr. Parmenter had never played before that night. Of course, your dad won, like he'd been doing all night long. It was just for fun, they both had a good laugh and Mr. P. said, 'Well, take a look around, it's all yours now!' Your dad cracked up, said something like, 'You got two weeks to get outta my place!' and never gave it another thought. But Mr. Parmenter—I think he knew his time was short. This was his way. This was the way he could do 'the right thing' in a way your dad would have to accept."

Julian stared into his beer. You just never know. Never know what's behind people's actions. He had to give it to Parmenter, he had craft, and even a little bit of style. And considering the deathbed promise to his wife, he even showed a little bit of heart.

Something still puzzled Julian. "So what was it that my dad owed Mr. Parmenter? He told me, 'I want to see your dad. He owes me something.'"

Cole thought a moment, taking a sip of his martini. "Oh, that. Well, Mr. Parmenter lived for your dad's red beans and rice. Not the dry mix, because it wasn't nearly as good, but the real thing. Parmenter had never tasted anything like it before he met your dad, or since. He was always raving about it. He'd not had any since the restaurant closed, and he begged your dad to—just once more—cook him a pot. Even offered to pay him like two hundred dollars! Your dad would smile, and say, 'Sure, I'll do that. And you don't have to pay me.' But he never did."

"Hmm," Julian said, nodding, lost in thought, not saying what he was really thinking. For his father, cooking was an act of love—if he didn't feel it, he didn't do it. For Julian, there was sweet irony in the fact that Parmenter, who could afford any indulgence, was to be denied the very thing—the simplest thing—he most desired.

But Julian had his own ideas about what Parmenter believed Simon owed him. Absolution. That's what the old man wanted from him—the chance to die with his heart and mind at peace.

When the two men stepped out into the sunshine of the afternoon, it was after four. Julian had told Sylvia he'd meet her at 4:30. Blessed Redeemer, her church (as well as Simon's), had organized a volunteer group to take homemade boxes of essentials—canned goods, toiletries, soft drinks, bottled water, Tylenol and other first-aid supplies, Kleenex, and even a few Creole-flavored MREs—to deliver to parishioners who'd returned to deal with their flooded houses. Julian had offered to help with the deliveries.

Cole drove Julian back to his car in the parking lot near his office. They shook hands, and Cole said, "Oh, let me give you this." He reached inside the pocket of his jacket and pulled out a stack of white envelopes. "The checks, for you and the band. You guys did a hell of a job."

"Thanks," Julian said, opening the door of the car and putting the checks in the glove box. "The guys—all of 'em—they'll really appreciate this."

"Tell me something, Fortier," Cole said. "You ever think about moving back here?"

This caught Julian off guard. Everyone who knew him knew not to ask this question, mostly because the answer was so obvious. He loved his hometown; it had made him the man and the musician he was. But a musician who wanted a world-class career, like him, had to leave. It seemed it had always been that way. That's what he thought before the storm, and now, with the city's future in dire doubt, returning seemed foolhardy indeed.

He quickly censored his first impulse—*Are you kidding?*—and instead said, "I think New York is where I'm supposed to be right now."

Cole nodded, then looked up and squinted at the sun. "Yeah. Too bad. The city's in for the fight of its life. It could use all the help it can get." He looked at his watch. "Well, gotta run. I'll make some more calls tomorrow about your father. Keep the faith, man. We'll find him."

By now, Julian's hope for finding Simon alive, which had shifted between abundant and minimal all these weeks, had dwindled to almost nothing. Optimism was a fabric easily worn thin by unrewarded use, and his had become so thin it was transparent. Now, he just hoped Simon hadn't suffered too much. And that he could give him his final wish—to be buried on Silver Creek land, next to his wife.

It was the least he could do.

A half-hour later, Julian pulled up to the parking lot of Blessed Redeemer in the Bywater section of the city, a low-slung modern structure of terra cotta brick that looked a little out of place in a neighborhood of century-old shotgun houses and elegantly ornate cottages. Situated close to the river on slightly higher ground than the more damaged neighborhoods of the city, it had been spared the ravages of the floodwaters. A portable marquee on the lawn advertised a sermon never given, the last one planned for the Sunday before the flood: "The Dark Hurricane of the Soul."

The lot was empty except for one car, and it wasn't Sylvia's. He looked at his watch—4:40. She must be running late, too.

He debated about whether to sit outside in the car and wait for her, but then decided to go into the church. He found a glass side door open and followed the wood-paneled hallway to a spartan-looking room with drop-ceiling tiles and about half a dozen steel tables and folding chairs set up on the far side—the room where church teas, dinners, and prayer meetings were held.

Built in the late sixties, this was the church where Julian had grown up, where his mother (and later, Sylvia) had sung in the women's chorus. He hadn't been inside these doors since he was a child. Even the times when Julian had come back to visit his father over the past few years—Christmases, Easters, Thanksgivings—Julian would pass on Simon's invitations to church service, preferring to stay in and practice. He wasn't much of a churchgoer, much to Simon's disappointment. But so much had changed; since the storm and Simon's disappearance, it seemed more than once he'd found himself with a fervent prayer on his lips.

He'd just pulled one of the folding chairs out from the table and was about to sit down where he heard someone from the direction of the back door.

"Anybody here? Can we get some help with these boxes?"

A woman's voice. Sylvia.

Julian walked back out toward the glass doors leading to the parking lot.

"Oh, great. Somebody's in here," he heard her yell to someone behind her.

Loaded down with several corrugated cardboard boxes full of food and supplies, Sylvia came inside as Julian opened the glass door.

"Here, let me get those." Julian took the three boxes from her.

"Julian!" Sylvia said. "I didn't remember what your rental looked like. Sorry we're a little late."

It took him a moment to spot Velmyra, just getting out of her own car. She wore a white sundress, white sandals, and on seeing him, her face lit up in a full smile.

"You're here!" she said. "I didn't even see your car."

Once again, she'd surprised him; she seemed to have a way of just appearing. And this time, it was at the perfect time. The last couple of days had been a whirlwind of mind-bending activity, and not until he saw her did he realize he hadn't really had much reason to smile since he saw a catfish dangling at the end of his line, two days ago.

Before they went back to the car for the remaining twenty or so boxes, she gushed an apology. She was so sorry she hadn't returned his calls: her folks had been so stressed about the house, and the insurance company was giving them grief, one of her parents' neighbors was still missing, and she'd finally gotten a plumber to agree to come to her house, but he'd never shown up.

He held the door open for her as they made another trip to the car.

"You look great," he said, grateful she'd worn that dress, but knowing it wouldn't have mattered what she wore.

She was dead tired, she said, so she decided to dress up a little, hoping it would buoy her spirits. As they brought in more boxes, she went on chatting to him about the events of the last couple of days—her eyes flashing, her hands in motion—while Sylvia busily arranged boxes on the table according to neighborhood streets, writing addresses on each one. Julian listened quietly, his face stuck in a slightly vapid smile. He couldn't remember being so happy to see somebody in a long time.

Velmyra's eyes, he thought, had always been expressive. He could always look at them and tell what she'd been going through. Today, they told a story of sleepless nights, stress, worry, and a fierce defiance in the face of whatever obstacles she'd encountered.

Dealing with her parents, her relatives and neighbors, and watching the news, she had felt herself slipping into depression, she said. And when she saw her mother's prescription bottle of Xanax, she almost reached for one.

"But I decided to pull out my paints instead."

Her eyes brightened as she told Julian about the rush of energy and creativity she'd had; she couldn't get the paint on the canvas fast enough. It was like an elixir. "I mean, I don't know if the stuff I'm doing is any good. But I don't care. It's fun again, you know? And it's keeping me from losing my mind."

She paused, took a long, deep breath. "Anyway, listen to me, going on and on. How are you doing?"

He'd missed her like crazy, not fully realizing it until this moment. Several times in the last couple of days, at the oddest moments (sitting in Nathan Larouchette's office, playing in the funeral procession, listening to the reading of the will) his mind had drifted back to the small cabin at Silver Creek, the narrow brass bed that creaked and groaned beneath their weight. The soft rub of her hair against the side of his face. Her calming voice as her hand stroked the knotted muscles in his back. And a million other little things that added up to a sum that equaled love.

Hurricanes and other acts of God had a way of clarifying things; clearing away the grimy film of uncertainty, they polished everything to shine, wholly reassessed, in new light. This is important, that is not. That has value, this has none. Silver Creek, his father, Velmyra. His career, even. Everything looked different after the waters had been drained away. Everything. So simple now: the things that really mattered were within his easiest reach, the things he could reach out and touch, but hadn't.

So he reached out now, brought her shoulders into his, and hugged her.

How was he doing? "Better." He closed his eyes, smiled. "Now."

20

It was one of those autumn days in New Orleans—the air crisper and dryer with the teasing hint of fall, the vast blue shock of sky broken with cottony puffs of slow-motion clouds—that long sufferers of the city's famously intense summer humidity would have called "beautiful," had there not been a flood that suspended use of that word indefinitely. It seemed nothing was beautiful here now, and nothing would be for a while.

With the Neon piled high with boxes of food and supplies for the returning congregants of Blessed Redeemer, Julian and Vel drove to the relatively mildly flooded Upper Ninth Ward, where the houses had only seen four or so feet of water, to make calls to families on the lists.

As they wheeled through the neighborhoods, they each had so much to share with the other that they almost spoke at once. After Vel covered all the details of her family's trials over the last couple of days, it was Julian's turn. So much had happened, he said, he didn't know where to start. Nathan Larouchette's condescending offer did not surprise her, nor did the death of Matthew Parmenter, which Sylvia had told her about. But Parmenter had actually left his house and ownership of the red beans and rice mix to Simon? She was stunned.

"What are you going to do with it?" she asked.

"With what?"

"The house, of course."

He pondered a moment. "To tell you the truth, I don't have a clue."

And he hadn't. Hearing the words at the reading of the will had been surreal. If Julian was now the owner of a million-dollar mansion and a lucrative food enterprise, he sure didn't feel like it. Everything lately felt like a dream, and this latest development felt no more real than the flood that had destroyed so much of the city.

But at least here in the Upper Ninth, the houses, girdled to their waists with water lines, still stood. Their first stop was the home of the elderly Mr. and Mrs. Tubman Miles. Both born in New Orleans and in their late seventies, the former electrician and hairdresser had had hopes of living out the remainder of their retirement years in close proximity to their grandchildren and a great-grandchild, who lived less than three miles away in a house built by Tubman Miles's father in the Lower Ninth Ward. When the Industrial Canal levee burst, the flooding waters slid the house off its foundation, and it landed in a neighbor's yard. The Miles's daughter, son-in-law, and their four children had all evacuated to Illinois, and didn't plan to return.

Mrs. Miles, a small, angular woman with finely sculpted cheekbones and a short gray Afro, stood in the mud-covered front yard while Tubman, facemask strapped on, came out of the pink, Creole-style one-story with a box of sludge-covered items.

"Julian Fortier! Is that you, baby?" Mrs. Miles's face broke into a wide smile.

She hugged him and asked about his father. He shrugged and told her what he knew: nothing. He left the box with her and she thanked him with a promise: "I'ma keep prayin' for your daddy."

Julian got back in the car quietly. "They seem OK," he said to Velmyra, and then wondered what he had meant by that. If being OK meant they were still standing, then they were. But the deep frowns in their foreheads stuck in his mind, and he could only imagine the huge struggles ahead for the aging couple.

"They'll be all right," Velmyra said. "They look like the kind who don't give up easily." She let out a thoughtful sigh. "The neighborhood'll come back, better than ever. You'll see."

He said nothing. They drove on to the other seven houses on the block to find, here and there, neighbors sitting on their porches, fanning themselves, their faces grim masks of puzzlement, despair, resignation. Occasionally there'd be a commiserating huddle of two or three in a yard before piles of debris, bodies slack in postures of fatigue, or sometimes defiantly erect, hands on their hips or flailing as they shared with their neighbors the day's travails.

They drove on through block after block of emptiness, houses standing but water damaged and clearly vacant since the hurricane. Each yard, it seemed, contained towers of debris so large they often overshadowed the houses themselves. When someone was home, they delivered the boxes in person, accepting the "bless yous" and "thank yous" of the grateful church members. When they were not at home but known to be in town they left the boxes on porches with a note attached: "From your family at Blessed Redeemer—may God bless you and keep you well."

Street after street of houses with their own story inside of lives shaken to the core. An unearthly silence presided where there had been the vital sounds of a neighborhood: kids on bicycles, trash trucks trudging through, and car stereos amped up a little too loud. Julian shook his head, an anger he hadn't felt before rising in him like fever. This place was a ghost town now.

After the first house in the next block, Velmyra said, "I mean, I'm not saying it won't take a lot of work to bring the place back, but it'll happen."

Julian turned to look out his window. "Yeah. Well. If you say so."

Velmyra turned sharply to look at him.

"You don't think the city can come back?"

He took in a deep breath. He didn't really want to get into this, remembering that Velmyra had always been a little blinded by optimism. At least, he'd thought so. But today, seeing all the misery in the neighborhood, he felt like telling the truth, the way he saw it.

"Come back? Back to what? The way it was before?"

And once he started, he couldn't pull back. There was the crime. The corruption. The schools. The way they treated the musicians and the lousy pay. And that was all *before* the storm. How much worse would it be now? And even if the city came back completely, which now looked doubtful, it would only be back to the same inadequate place. It would still be the wrong city for anybody with real ambition.

"I mean, look at Grady Casey. The cat is a freakin' *genius.* What's he doing? Playing at the Embassy Suites…"

"Wait a minute." Ice stiffened Velmyra's tone. "What if everybody felt that way—the way you do? What if everybody with talent, with potential, left? Who would teach the kids art and music, who'd give them the opportunities we had?

"Who'd preserve the culture? The history? This city is what *we* make it, and it can only be as good as the people who are willing to stay. And believe it or not, Julian, a lot of people were pretty damn happy here, and some were even successful." She turned to him. "*I* stayed, OK?"

What had he just walked into? He could feel the heat from her eyes without looking. He held up a hand, partly in apology, partly to stop the torrent of anger coming toward him.

"I didn't mean you…"

As he steered around the corner a little too fast, a stray cat ran from one of the vacant houses and dashed in front of the car; Julian slammed his brakes as the frightened cat scampered away and into another yard across the street. His heart raced. He pulled to the curb and turned off the engine.

He lowered his head, took a deep breath, then turned to her. "Look, there's no reason for us to have an argument. I was just saying…"

She cut him off. "You want to know why we broke up? *This.* This is why."

He fell silent. Closed his eyes, exhaled in a tired huff. "Vel. Come on. Let's not do this…"

She inhaled a short breath. Her eyes quieted, her voice softened. "Remember how we talked about where we would live? You were having a fit to go to New York. I wanted to stay here. You kept saying, 'I want more than I can find here.' And I said, 'Why not stay and help make this city a place where people like you would want to stay?' And you said…"

"I know what I said."

"You said…"

"…I wasn't up to it."

"Right. You weren't up to it."

A moment passed, as both stared through the windshield in front of them.

Looking down, Julian spoke, his voice smaller, his words pointed, emphatic. "I just wanted you to come to New York with me. I wanted us to be together. I thought we could have made a good life there. If you'd really loved me…"

Her hand shot up, a stop sign in his face. "Hold it right there. Why does it have to be about *my* not moving to New York? I asked you to stay—not forever, just a while longer while we sorted things out. If you loved *me* like you said you did…"

"I did love you."

"But not enough to stay." She sighed heavily.

Julian's breathing was tight as he guided the car back to the church, and he ran his hand along the side of his neck where the muscles had bunched together in a spasm. This was not what he wanted. There were more boxes to deliver, but he was exhausted, and he couldn't imagine that Velmyra would want to stay in this car any longer than he did. This little jaunt was over. How did this happen? He backtracked in his head, trying to remember how it had gotten out of hand.

Hard woman. That's what he remembered now about her. Always expecting so damn much of him. Yes, he'd wanted to get away from New Orleans and off to a place where he'd have half a chance to accomplish what he was capable of. So what? He was… what was the word? Entitled. He was entitled to try. Even the guys in the band, they knew it too. They may have cocked their heads, made sarcastic noises when he left, but they'd have done the same thing if they had the guts, the opportunity, the…hell, the talent. Well, most of them would have, anyway.

He kept talking to himself, trying to make the case that he was right. But her words sliced his skin so hard they left scars. The possibility that she had a point—given what was happening in the city now—jabbed at the scars, drawing fresh, red blood.

He wished he could start the conversation again and take it someplace else. But as he pulled into the parking lot of the church, Velmyra unlocked her door. Before he'd even applied the brake, she was getting out of the car.

"You know what, I almost forgot. I was going to try to call that plumber again," she said, her head up, looking away from him. "Tell Sylvia I'll give her a call later."

And without looking back, she walked toward her car.

Julian stared after her a moment, still breathing hard. He'd wanted to call her back, but didn't have a clue what he would say. So he walked into the church.

Sylvia was arranging boxes on the table. "Oh, good, you're back," she said, glancing up at him. "I got some more supplies and I've got about twenty more boxes ready to go." She looked at her watch. "Oh, wow. I didn't realize how late it was getting. Maybe we'll just do these tomorrow. Where's Vel?"

He pulled one of the folding chairs out from the table and sat.

"She's gone."

She looked up. "Oh, really?"

"We, uh, we had a fight."

Sylvia's eyes paled. "Oh." She looked down at the box in front of her and put the bag of dried fruit she was holding inside it, and closed the lid.

"You want to talk about it?"

He got up and walked toward the window facing the parking lot and looked out at the street. He answered her without a sound: he hunched his shoulders up, hands in both pockets.

"To be honest," Sylvia said, "I was a little surprised that you two were spending time together again. But then, when something like this happens—the storm and everything—people do things they wouldn't normally do." Julian sat back at the table again. "I told her I couldn't remember why we broke up. Well"—he shook his head with a small, sardonic laugh—"she reminded me."

Sylvia sat across from him at the table. The church still had no electricity, so the room grew dim as the sunlight from the windows began to wane.

"You know, when your dad proposed to me a few months ago I didn't think anything of it. When I think about it now, I guess I kind of—how do you young folks say it?—blew it off. I thought we had so many years left together, and maybe we'd get married, maybe we wouldn't. It didn't seem so important. But now that—" Her voice shook—"now that Simon is…gone, I wish I'd done it. If for no other reason than that I could have been a part of his family—*your* family. I could have been a part of Simon's—I don't know. His *history*."

She put an elbow up on the table and leaned her cheek against her fist. Her hair, normally meticulously coifed, was straw-dry and curl-less, it's gray roots inching up beneath the Clairol red. "I'm not sure what I'm trying to say to you, baby. I'm…just thinking out loud. But I'll tell you this. One of the hardest things to do is to live your life without regrets. But in the end, it's a whole lot better if you try."

"You know Velmyra, she's strong willed. But that's why we love her, right?" She smiled and patted his arm. "Give her a little time. Give her a little time, then talk to her, and tell her what's in your heart."

He stared at his hands a moment, then folded them.

"Yeah. I will. Thanks."

She picked up her purse and swung it over her shoulder, then reached inside it and pulled out her scarf.

"Lord, I tell you." She put the scarf on and tied it loosely under her chin, smiled. "Used to be a time when I'da never left the house with my hair looking like this," she said. "Everything's changed. Some days I'm doin' good just to get out of the bed."

He nodded. "I know what you mean."

A car rolled by and she looked toward the street. "You know, Vel's not saying much. But she's taking all this pretty hard. Oh, I know, she's trying her best to be positive, but you know how much she loves this place. We all do, of course, but Vel..." She stopped, shook her head. "Yesterday we were watching the news, and they were, you know how they do, showing all that footage of the days right after the flood. And Vel just started crying. Took her a long time to get herself together."

Julian blinked, felt a tug in his stomach. He thought of himself collapsed on Genevieve's bathroom floor, Velmyra kneeling beside him, bringing him back to himself. Listening, waiting while he cried. He thought of all the words he'd said to her and now he wanted them back. What had he been thinking? He wasn't the only one who was dealing with grief.

He got up and hugged Sylvia, told her he would be back the following day. "If you talk to Vel," he began, "would you tell her I'm..." He stopped. He just didn't know the words.

"Never mind. I'll tell her myself."

He was walking back toward his car in the dimming daylight, when he spotted something large, a frame of some sort, leaning against the door of his car. When he got closer he realized what it was. A painting on a large canvas.

It was covered with a sheet of thin, translucent paper taped to the frame, he guessed, to protect it. When he lifted the cover, what he saw brought water to the corners of his eyes.

It was a painting of the cover of his album "Boplicitude," his face large and luminous, looking out over the Left Bank of the River Seine in Paris, his trumpet in his hand. Thick, *impasto* brushstrokes applied in a post-impressionist style covered the canvas, and though a patchwork of odd colors detailed his skin—pinks, purples, blues—when viewed as a whole, it all made perfect artistic sense.

In the lower right hand corner, there was Velmyra's familiar signature—an elaborate 'V' and 'H' with the other letters scribbled in a completely illegible fashion. The likeness was amazing. His eyes opened wide; he'd forgotten what an extraordinarily talented artist she was. But it wasn't the portrait he remembered on the album cover. It had all the details correct—the angle of his head, the proportions of his features, the color of his skin—but somehow she had captured something that wasn't in the photograph.

The album cover photo had shown a young Julian Fortier—cocksure, confident, self-absorbed—a man with the world at his feet. This portrait revealed something more. She'd painted him older, his skin etched with the lessons of life, his eyes lit with equal measures of wisdom and vulnerability. And in his expression she'd captured something even more interesting: a capacity for understanding. A quiet, somber grace.

He ran a hand along the back of his head and exhaled a slow stream of air. What Velmyra had painted was not the man he was then, nor was it the man he was now, he believed. This was a painting of the man she hoped he would become.

He covered the painting with the tissue paper. The air was cooler now, and a southerly breeze stirred the trees. He took a deep breath. Then he opened the trunk of his car and carefully put the portrait inside.

He didn't consciously decide not to go back to the Best Western, but when he thought of spending the rest of the evening in his box of a motel room alone with a TV, a refrigerator stocked with beer, and his thoughts, it depressed him. So he started the car and before he knew it, he was driving the streets of New Orleans.

He ended up on Lavalle Street in front of his father's house, and in the oncoming twilight the house looked almost normal. The street, though, was deathly quiet. He turned off the ignition, drummed his fingers on the steering wheel. Even though Julian probably would not have talked to Simon about his fight with

Velmyra—he had rarely discussed the details of his love life with his father—he would have sought him out for company. His father always knew when something was troubling him, and Julian had always depended on the comfort of their unspoken bond. Searching his son's brooding eyes, Simon would say, "You ate anything yet?" And Julian would sit in the kitchen while a cast iron skillet clanked against the stove and Simon talked about everything and nothing—the Saints, the Hornets, local politics, who he beat at dominoes, who in the neighborhood had gotten married, or divorced, or had a grandbaby. As the shrimp etouffee or the smothered Creole catfish bubbled, Julian would nod, then eat quietly until he felt better. And he always did.

But there was no comfort tonight. He watched the darkness surround the kitchen window where his father would look out onto the street while he talked, and tried to imagine sitting with him as the amber glow of lamplights swelled in the purple dusk. A half hour passed. And finally, Julian started the car.

The Claiborne Avenue Bridge was closed since the flood, and it was just as well. Julian had never trusted that strange, rickety bridge anyway, and there were other ways to get to the Lower Ninth Ward. Seeing the place where so much devastation happened was something Julian might have put off forever—the images on television were horrible enough to see, and he didn't think he needed to witness the horror in person. But tonight, he felt compelled. This was his city, and now he was ready to claim it. The Lower Nine was where his friend Dereek had lived. If he could straddle roof shingles and swim through the muck-and-sludge river that filled his neighborhood and survive it, the least Julian could do was witness where he'd done it.

He'd known this street so well; Dereek's mother was a fine cook, and many a night he'd sat around the family's kitchen table while she dished up her extra hot chili. But when Julian turned down the familiar block, his heart skittered, his face went cold; he couldn't have been more shaken if he'd witnessed a murder.

The once flat, green lawns had bulged into mountains of mud. The majestic oak trees looked as if a giant fist had reached around them and ripped them up through the earth by their trunks, leaving their shredded roots to dangle like the wiry, stray hairs of an unkempt beard. That same fist had crumbled houses, swiped them off their slabs, or pounded them to rubble as if they'd been made of matchsticks. In school, he'd seen pictures of Dresden after the bomb blasts of World War II; it was the only thing he'd ever seen that was remotely similar. It couldn't have left any more destruction than this.

He thought he knew exactly where Dereek's house had been, but drove in circles, veering around piles of wood siding, pieces of rooftops flung into the street, cars upended and sitting on what had been porches, or on other cars. His headlights shined on piles of rubble, but only a few things looked identifiable. A dinner plate, a basketball, a teapot, a lawnmower, a toilet bowl, a boot, a lamp. Random items flung together in some sort of cruel, metaphysical collage. All the jetsam of peoples' lives, reduced to piles of nothing.

How many made it out? How many didn't? Dereek hadn't said and probably didn't know. *Please. Let them all be safe.* But he knew if Dereek had stayed through it, then others had too. Not everybody owned a car, or had enough cash for a motel room miles away. Some had surely stayed, some that weren't as young and strong and capable of survival as Dereek.

He never found Dereek's house. He drove back to Baton Rouge in a fog, his eyes sometimes welling up and burning with the memory of what he'd just seen. By the time he got back to his hotel room in Baton Rouge, he was still breathing hard. He took the portrait Velmyra had painted out of the car, leaned it up against the portable refrigerator, and fell onto the bed. It was late, but a sick feeling churned his gut and it was impossible to sleep. He thought of his father's house, his father's neighbors. Even with water marks five feet high, at least it still looked a little like a neighborhood.

He left the room and paced around the Best Western parking lot to calm down, and when he felt reasonably peaceful, walked over to Waffle City and ate a meatloaf dinner he barely tasted. That night, after two beers, he slept in fits and starts, waking now and then with the images still in his head. Now he knew what helplessness felt like. As much as he wanted to do something, there was nothing he could do.

The next morning a bright sun sliced across his bedspread, pulling him out of sleep, and even lifting his spirits a little. A new day. He thought to call Velmyra, then realized she probably had appointments all day—her folks, their insurance company, her own house and a plumber who might or might not show. She likely wouldn't pick up anyway, and honestly, he wasn't sure what exactly he would say.

But he dialed her number anyway. Her outgoing message—*Hi! This is Vel. Please leave your name and number*—had an upbeat lilt: sweet, perky, optimistic. It was an old message, obviously, recorded by a woman who hadn't yet had her life turned on its head.

When he heard the "beep" to leave his message, his tongue froze, his heart raced. "Hey, Vel. I…sorry to, uh." Sigh. "Look… can we talk sometime? Maybe we could…I, uh, I just want to talk. To you. OK? OK. Later."

Damn. So lame. Normally, he would have been embarrassed, leaving a stuttering message like that, but he didn't care now. He was weary of trying to act like he had it all together. He felt raw, and didn't care if she knew it.

He called New York. There had been a message on his cell phone from his agent in Manhattan, Morris De Camp of Galaxy Artists, Incorporated. Something about a concert coming up in New York.

He answered on the second ring. De Camp asked about Julian's father, and when Julian told him they'd still had no luck in finding him, De Camp quickly offered his condolences. And then he got to the business at hand.

He knew all about what happened in Tokyo, and had one question for Julian.

"Can you play now?"

Apparently the New York City mayor's office was interested in New Yorkers contributing somehow to the recovery of New Orleans. The mayor's personal assistant's mother was born there and though no one in her family still lived there, they had close ties to the neighborhoods destroyed by the flood. A benefit concert somewhere big, maybe the Met or Avery Fisher Hall, featuring a Grammy-winning trumpet player who was from the area, would be a great way to draw attention to the situation and raise money to help out.

"And after that Tokyo thing, this'd be a great way to get you back on track, career-wise," De Camp said. "That is, if you think your chops can handle it."

De Camp, a native of Queens, was a bottom-line businessman who did not mince his rapid-fire words. It had taken a while for Julian, with his sweet-tea-and-cornbread cordiality, to get used to his bluntness. But the man had been a good manager for four years, always with an eye on the big picture of Julian's career.

"I'm not interested in doing a solo concert."

"What? Look, Julian, you've got to start playing sometime. Your doctor said, or at least you told me, you were in good shape. It would just take—"

"I can play," Julian said. "I'm sounding better than ever."

"Then what is it? Look, I can get you some decent money for this. Even though it's a benefit—"

"It's not the money."

An exasperated sigh that Julian had heard plenty of times came through loud and clear.

"Julian, talk to me. What is it?"

Julian paused. "I don't want to play a solo concert. But I've got these friends from home who could use the work. A brass band. Hire them, and you've got me too."

De Camp didn't know what a brass band was—*What? Some kind of military thing?*—and the century-old New Orleans tradition had to be explained to him. But it hadn't taken De Camp long to warm to the idea. He was certain he could find money for all the men—to cover their expenses, and compensate them well for their work. The funds would go to the rebuilding of the areas hit hardest by the flood. As the plan grew, one benefit concert became three—at Avery Fisher Hall, The Apollo Theater in Harlem, and the Brooklyn Academy of Music, where Julian taught a few students—set for the Christmas holidays. Before the year was out, De Camp promised, Manhattan, Harlem, and Brooklyn would vibrate with foot-stomping, jazz-flavored Christmas tunes—New Orleans style. And Julian's friends would have a little something to jumpstart their lives.

Julian didn't know if Grady had ever been to New York, but Dereek, he was almost certain, had never ventured outside of Louisiana before the flood. Easy Money had always fantasized about the city. He pictured the guys diving into the crisp sheets and soft beds of the Empire Hotel on Broadway, and himself taking them around to his favorite haunts—the Village Vanguard, Birdland, and the Blue Note, where all the great musicians played—and a slight smile came to his face.

It felt like spitting in the ocean, for all the difference it would make to the enormity of the disaster in their lives. But it was the best he could do.

He'd started up the drip coffee pot on the bathroom countertop and was brushing his teeth when the phone rang.

"Hello?"

It was Kevin. His voice was a little agitated, but Julian swore he heard in the background the sound of a singing creek. Imagining his friend sitting barefoot on a bank, his fishing line cast in the water, a cigarette or a beer in his hand, Julian halfway wished he could be there with him, away from Baton Rouge and New Orleans and the constant reminders of the flood. He hadn't forgotten about the family home, but the problems with Vel, the drive down to the

Ninth Ward, not to mention the thing with Simon and Parmenter, had certainly taken his mind off it as his thoughts skipped from one brushfire to another.

Kevin explained that he'd been working on the land situation, still with no luck. But he'd gone over to Genevieve's cabin and saw something troubling. Somebody had taped an eviction notice to the screen. And they had put a wooden sign in the yard: *PRIVATE PROPERTY: KEEP OUT.*

Julian swallowed hard.

"Nathan's really pissed, now," Kevin said. He went on to tell Julian that a judge had turned down his petition to review the case.

"Nathan probably found a way to pay off somebody, one of his buddies on the bench, I bet. We're losing ground, man. I'm hating how this is turning out."

Julian looked at his watch. "Have you talked to Cousin G yet?"

"I'm fixin' to call her now."

"Good. I'm on my way. Can you meet me over at the cabin in a couple of hours? Maybe together, we can figure something out."

"OK" Kevin cleared his throat. "It's not looking good right now—I'm sorry."

"I know, man. So am I."

21

Late for work again, she stared at the unforgiving clock as she rushed to the nurse's station on Two West. She had been on time, mostly, the whole week, but today her alarm clock had failed, again, and she was twenty minutes late getting her eight-year-old to school; a car accident clogged the main street of her usual route; and she'd gotten a ticket for speeding when she'd tried to make up the time.

All good reasons (except for the alarm clock, which had accounted for all the others), but the head nurse had been on her case from day one, and being late three times in the month did not help. The only thing keeping her in good standing at Mercy was the fact that she, more than any of the other newer nurses, was the one every patient seemed to love.

She checked on all of her patients: the elderly woman in 244 who had had open heart surgery and was improving daily, the young man in 214 who'd had his appendix removed. For each one she said a special silent prayer, and gave them her broadest smile.

She'd tried not to favor any above the others, they were all equal in God's eyes. But there was one for whom she'd actually dropped to her knees in prayer, when it became doubtful if he would make it.

She opened the door to room 242. Peeking into his room, she found him sitting up in bed, a lunch tray before him, smiling at her.

"Good afternoon, Mr. Fortier! How you feeling today?"

Finally. He'd been waiting all morning for her. First, because she was such a sweet young lady and always made him feel good, and second because now he could tell her, nicely, of course, that the meals here were not fit for a dog you wanted dead.

First of all, the stuff had no flavor. Beyond bland, it was like that mess his wife Ladeena used to feed Julian when he was an infant. Second, it was all overcooked. Green beans no longer green but dull gray, cooked so long you could mash them with the back of a spoon. Mashed potatoes out of a box, and not even a very good box. Did they expect him to actually *eat* this? He was a chef. He knew food, and this was not it.

But she was smiling, so he smiled back. Later. He'd get to the food later.

"How you doing yourself, Miss Lady?"

She reached for the pillows behind his head. He hadn't realized he'd been uncomfortably slumped in the bed; she always knew just what he needed even before he needed it.

She was an attractive young thing, probably about twenty-five or so. Mexican maybe. Or from somewhere down there where they speak Spanish. No wedding ring. He'd wanted to tell her that he had a nice-looking son a little older than her who was single, but worried that she might be offended. So he said nothing. For now.

"Did you bring it?" he looked up at her, eyebrows lifted innocently as she smoothed his lumpy bedspread. She smelled nice. Something with vanilla in it. He'd always been partial to the scent of vanilla.

She looked around, then dug into her pocket. Pulled out a small bottle of Louisiana Gold hot sauce, and placed it on his tray.

"I had to go to three markets before I found one that sold this brand," she said. "I want you to know I would not do that for just *anybody.*" She winked at him.

"Bless you child," he said, giving her his broadest, twinkling smile, and sprinkled the hot sauce on the inedible Salisbury steak. Lord have mercy, it needed the help.

"You're looking good today, sir, much better." She went to the window and opened the blinds to let the afternoon light in.

"You're looking very nice yourself," he told her, his voice a little lighter, lifted by guilt. He'd been a little cantankerous these last couple of days, and had even worried that she would not come back to see him. He had just wanted so badly to get out of there, once he realized he wasn't going to die.

It had been a miserable time. He had been so weak, his throat dry as stone, his head dizzy, and sometimes he had trouble breathing. In and out of sleep, never knowing whether it was day or night. Once he swore he saw Julian standing at the foot of the bed, but realized it was one of those machines with the colored lights, beeping. The stuff they gave him, whatever it was, made him dream strange dreams. Took his mind where he didn't want it to go.

But as he began to feel better, stronger, more hungry, he might have been a little hard to deal with.

Especially after the nurse had turned on the TV, at his insistence. He wanted to see what was going on back home. He saw it all, and it made him weep. They had all said someday it would happen, and it had. It looked, he thought, like Judgment Day. Judgment Day in the city he loved.

He watched, his mouth open, as the camera panned the neighborhoods, the streets beneath the I-10 overpass, St. Claude, South Clairborne Avenue, the Circle Food Store, the sections of eastern New Orleans, the Lower Ninth, all sitting in a vast, dark sea. That was when he *had* to go home. Somehow he had to find out about his house, his neighbors, his friends.

But they told him it was impossible. They had evacuated the whole place, and no one could come back to the city until it was drained and the services were restored. And besides, he wasn't well enough. His blood count was inexplicably low, he was still dehydrated, and there were questions about his prostate. His numbers were not quite right, and he was too weak.

He had another home, he'd argued, nowhere near the flood. The one where he'd been headed when he'd passed out. Not far away. And he had a cousin there who could look after him.

I'll call my son, he said. *I got a son, I know he's looking for me. Or you can call my cousin. Or my lady friend. The numbers are all in my phone.*

Phone? The night nurse had frowned. *We didn't see a phone with your things. Clothes, a Bible, but no phone...*

He sat back, defeated. He hadn't brought the phone with him. All the numbers he would have committed to memory in the old days before cell phones, were now logged in a phone somewhere more than a hundred miles away, probably floating in five feet of water.

We have to get you well first, sir, then we'll worry about your phone. Besides, the last we heard, none of the numbers in the 504 area are working anyway.

We're doing everything we can to find your family. It shouldn't be long, now that we got your name right. As soon as you were able to tell us, we called the Red Cross and put you on the missing persons list, but apparently they got your name wrong. They had you listed as Simon Portier, kind of like that actor, what's his name, Sidney Poitier? Anyway, it's all straightened out now. Your family is surely checking the list daily.

His best smile again, eyes shining. "Darlin.' Now, I appreciate all what you've done, but I need to get out of here. I just need to get over by Silver Creek. That's where I'm from, over in Pointe Louree Parish? It's just a few miles away."

"No, sir, I'm afraid you're not able to travel just yet."

"But I feel fine," he said. He grabbed the rail, lifted himself away from the pillow and attempted to get out of the bed on his own for the first time since he arrived, but his legs didn't seem like they belonged to him; they were weak and wobbly. He fell to his knees three feet away from the bed.

"Sir!" The young lady had grabbed his arm as he descended to the floor, then had to call for help to get him back in the bed.

She was none too happy with him after that; he could tell. He sat back against the pillow, silent, brooding.

"Mr. Fortier, I hope you don't try anything like that again." A hint of steel in her voice. "Doctor will see you this afternoon. He'll tell you when you're well enough to leave."

Smiling pertly, she'd pulled his covers up to his chin and adjusted his pillows. "We just want what's best for you, Mr. Fortier. The important thing is that we get you well."

She turned to leave, then hesitated. "Oh, there's something else. The couple who brought you in. The ones that found you. Oh, you didn't know? A very nice couple found you passed out on a bench near the Chevron station right off the highway. Anyway, they've called every day. Tomorrow they'll come and see you!"

She left the room. He didn't remember any couple bringing him in. In fact, he didn't remember much more than the street full of water. The view from his rooftop, the whirl of helicopter blades. He hadn't been in one of those things since Korea. They'd dropped him off at the Convention Center, said "good luck." Right away he'd known that was not the answer. A mass of people, thousands, standing around in the brutal sun, looking hopeless. Babies crying, hungry, everybody waiting for somebody to come help them. Silly. Wasn't nobody coming to help. He had two strong legs and the word of God. He'd sweet-talked an emergency vehicle driver, a woman wearing a military uniform who looked like she could have been his daughter, to give him a ride to the highway. There, he struck out on foot, his Bible in his hand, his thumb in the air. The sun burrowed into the back of his neck, his shoulders. He walked for hours, days, it seemed.

He'd vaguely remembered the truck driver, a tall, muscular black man in his sixties, balding, with a face like a country preacher's, his big rig as bulky as a train at the truck stop. A firm handshake, a barreling bass voice. Talking as the truck cruised miles of Louisiana highway. And when they parted, only about fifteen miles from the Fortier cabin at Silver Creek, he'd walked from the highway seven miles toward the nearest gas station.

That was the last thing he remembered.

And there was a couple? And they had brought him here in their car? And if they were coming tomorrow…

"That'll be fine," he said, smiling, and doused his steak again in hot sauce.

He took a bite. Wasn't as bad as he thought. If they served it again before he left, he'd ask for some garlic powder and a little butter.

The couple arrived the next morning around 8:30. He was a tall, scholarly looking man with a blond beard flecked with gray, she was olive-toned (fair-skinned black he thought at first, but then decided she was Indian, like the people in India), with hair like blackbirds' wings and the largest eyes he'd ever seen. They were both dressed the way young folks had dressed back in the seventies: sandals, khaki, loose cotton shirts tie-dyed in bright patterns of color.

The woman, soft-spoken, smiled broadly, reached over to peck him on the cheek. *We're so happy you're doing so much better!* And the man, her husband, thin, angular, long-necked with a protruding Adam's apple bobbing as he spoke. Both teachers, they said, she a teacher of math at the high school, he a professor of literature at the community college.

They had watched the news reports of the flood every day, horrified. How awful it must have been. Could they do anything to help him?

It was not long before he asked them, nicely, but with a spark of desperation. *I need to get home, I got a place just up the road a piece, Silver Creek. My son and I planned to meet there in case something like this happened.*

Of course they would take him, as soon as the doctor released him.

No, I need to go now. My son, he's probably worried sick. I've got to see him. I've got to go home.

But if you're not well…

Silence. He tried again. *I lost my house when the levees broke. The whole neighborhood's flooded out. The only house I got now is at Silver Creek. No flood there. My house there is safe.*

I need to go home, you understand. I need to go as soon as I can.

They looked at each other, then looked back at him.

The early morning rain had lifted and thinly parted clouds revealed patches of blue by the time they rounded the last bend of the Creek, and Simon was full.

The fullness began deep inside him, climbed up from his heart to thicken his throat and then the back of his tongue before it climbed higher to spill over, a pool of joy, from his eyes. He was almost home.

Sitting in the back seat of the couple's car, he grabbed the cuff of his sleeve into his fist and rubbed the water from his eyes the way he had done as a boy on the day his father, Jacob, died. It may have been the knowledge that the New Orleans house his father had built was ruined that brought on the flood of emotion. Well, that house may be gone but Silver Creek, his father's true love, was right here before his misting eyes. The sixty years that had passed since he was a boy here, swimming in the creek, plowing the land, cooking in Auntie Maree's kitchen, had done nothing to whittle down his child-wonder at its magic beauty. As they rambled down the packed-dirt road, a shallow breeze stirred the pine needles into a perfume he knew so well; the branches of willows bowed to greet him and the egrets lifted their wings in salute. Sunlight danced on the wave-tips of the creek water as they passed, and the woman in the front seat brushed black hair from her eyes as she turned around to speak.

"This is quite beautiful. Are we near?"

Simon suppressed the giddy joy in his voice. "Be just another mile or so."

When they reached the ruins of the old stone church in the open meadow and the old cemetery that held his wife's remains, and where Jacob, Moses and all the others slept, Simon placed two fingers on his lips, floated a kiss on the breeze.

The road narrowed to a path shaded by majestic pines and the tunneling arms of cypress trees. When they passed the barn, he pointed ahead. "There, right there."

It had taken a while to figure out that the couple would not take him, without a doctor's release, to his home. When they had finally agreed to at least talk to Dr. Singh, Simon's young Indian physician, Simon listened with his heart in his throat. The young doctor insisted, in an accent similar to the young woman's in the front seat: *You're still a little weak, you were out of it a long time. I'm going to prescribe another transfusion—*

Simon had said, a little too loudly. *I told you, I feel fine. I'll feel better if I can just get out of here, get back to my own cooking.*

He regretted saying that. Insulting the hospital's kitchen did nothing to help his case. Besides, he knew the folks down there sweating over those hot gas stoves were probably doing their best, and underpaid to boot.

Still, he had to make his point. *I promise I'll come back. Just let me go and see my home.*

A compromise. The doctor agreed to let him go if he would come back as an outpatient in three days. So after a complicated rigmarole involving Medicare forms, written prescriptions, and future outpatient appointment dates, the Letinskys agreed to drive Simon to Silver Creek.

When they pulled up to the yard of the cabin, Simon wanted to open the door and run. He believed he could, he felt so young now, as young as he did when his father, tall and thick-muscled with arms like steel, had picked him up and tossed him into the creek so he could learn to swim. As young as when he plowed these very fields after his father had taken ill. There was something in this air, he thought, that gave a man back years of his life.

He did not run. Rather, he opened the door gingerly and reached back for his Bible, the white bag containing three plastic bottles of pills, and the cane they had given him at the hospital. He thought about the beautiful, hand-carved cane Julian had brought back from Africa, still in the house, no doubt ruined by water with all the rest of his things. The thought of Julian forced an uneasy feeling; things had not been left well between him and his son. The boy had told him not to stay, to get out of the city, and the disrespect in his tone had bristled like barbed wire against Simon's thin skin. But the boy had been right. No question now, the boy had been right.

Out of the car, Simon arched his back fully to stand upright. When Stanley Letinsky tried to help him to the steps, he shooed him away. *Oh, I'm all right now,* he said, smiling broadly. *Y'all can go on. I'm home now. Thank you. And God bless you.*

He made it to the steps slowly, then looked back as the car pulled back onto the gravelly road. Waved his hand in the air. *Thank you, thank you so much.*

He peered into the screen door of the cabin, too dark to see inside. He pulled one of the rockers away from the window, and sat, his spindly knees popping as he lowered his body into the chair. Put the cane down next to him on the cedar floor, rocked, and smiled.

A cooling breeze swept up and soundlessly stirred the leaves of the closest magnolia tree. Quiet here. So quiet. Sweet air, good to breathe. Genevieve would be so surprised, he thought, and wondered where she was. That old Buick she tooled around in was nowhere in sight. The woman never stayed at home anymore. Church, work, and whatnot, and didn't she say she was seeing somebody? A younger man, ain't that something. He smiled and clicked his tongue. Her husband Jack had been a good twenty years older. And now she had herself a young thing—probably five, six years younger. Maybe even ten, knowing Genevieve. He couldn't wait to tease her when he saw her.

When he gathered himself and felt fairly rested, he got up to go inside. But something stopped his steps. A note pasted to the window. Not a note, a notice of some sort.

He read the yellow slip of paper as best he could. His glasses didn't work so well—got to get a new prescription.

Eviction?

This was some kind of mistake. He'd straighten it out, now that he was here. He opened the door, looked inside. Some of the furniture lay under white sheets, like large stone ghosts. He went back outside onto the porch.

He sat in the rocker, his heart racing, his head a little light. Something was wrong. Genevieve was not staying here. Something had happened. He took off his glasses, rubbed his hand along the back of his head.

Aw, Daddy. No. This can't be.

Tears burned his eyes. Genevieve had tried to warn him what was going on. They had lost Silver Creek. It was somebody else's place now.

When he awoke an hour later from a bone-deep and weary sleep, still sitting in the rocker, the sun was high above the cabin. He looked out over the tall pine trees, behind which lay the meadow and the cemetery. He wondered if he could walk that far. He needed to talk to Ladeena, to Jacob, needed their counsel and the comfort of their company. But he felt weak now. Weaker than before.

The notice was still in his lap. He wondered if there was anything he could do. He hadn't talked to Genevieve since the night of the storm. She'd been talking about the Parettes. Had she known this could happen? She must have suspected something. Something had happened since that night of the storm.

Well, he would just have to fight to get his land back. Hire a lawyer. Genevieve and he would put their heads together. And maybe Julian could…

Julian. He heaved a deep sigh. Julian did not want this land, and had produced no children who, someday, might. And it occurred to Simon that no matter what he did now, eventually his son would let the land go anyway. Of that he was certain. And how many more years would he, Simon, be on this earth? There was no reason to fight.

He got up from the rocker, reeling a little as he stood on his feet.

He was hungry. He had barely picked at that hospital breakfast of hard dry toast, hard dry egg, runny oatmeal, and lukewarm tea. They had to be joking, calling that a breakfast for a grown man. Surely Genevieve would have left some food in her freezer he could heat up and eat. She always did. Whoever this house belonged to now would just have to wait for it until after he'd eaten.

He was about to go back inside the house when the distant sound of a car engine broke the quiet.

He turned to see a small car making the bend from the main road. Genevieve? No, it wasn't big enough, Genevieve always had to have herself a big car. This looked like one of those little rental jobs the tourists in New Orleans would cruise around in.

The car didn't turn at the bend like most cars did, headed down to Local. It seemed to be coming right towards the cabin, but it stopped in the middle of the road. A young man got out. Darn these glasses; they just didn't work the way they ought to. He strained to see better.

The young man stood in the road for a moment looking his way, shading his eyes with his hand, then broke out into a run, legs kicking high, right toward him. And in that moment, Simon recognized the same gangly stretch of his own legs when he was a young man, and the tilt of head that had always reminded him of his own father, and the long, ropey arms that had marked every man in his family, as he walked to the edge of the porch, smiling, heart thumping wildly, to meet his son.

22

He had stopped the car in the middle of the road.

Once he had spotted the figure on the porch, he had to stop, get out, and see without the barrier of the windshield, had to be certain what he was seeing was not just what he wanted to see, had to be sure that it was real. So many times before he'd dreamed of his father in a scene much like this—Simon in the distance, smiling, waving toward him—and then awakened from the dream.

But he had not been sleeping this time. Simon was there, sitting on the porch of the cabin the way he had each summer when Julian was small, calm as you please. As if there had never been a storm.

He'd left the car there in the middle of the rock-strewn path that led either from the woods to the cabin or from the woods to Local, a road not well traveled. It didn't occur to him that he could get back in the car and drive the remaining yards to the house; he'd simply broken out into a fierce run, as fast as his legs could carry him.

He was short of breath when he reached the porch, chest heaving, and at first he just reached out his hand to his father; they had always greeted each other with a handshake. But like a moth pulled into fire, he could not help grabbing his father's thin body, pulling the smaller, older man close into his chest and hugging him with all his might as the tears slicked his face.

"It's all right, son," Simon said, patting his back, his voice quivering. "Everything's all right."

When he pulled away, Julian wiped his eyes, then sat in the rocker while his father sat next to him, his words tumbling out like spilled rocks.

"Daddy, we've been looking, we didn't know...we thought you..."

"Well, I told you I'd be here. I just didn't say when."

Julian leaned forward nearly panting, both forearms on his knees with his hands clasping nervously. "Are you OK? What happened? How'd you get here? Are you OK?"

Simon shook his head, voice nearly in a whisper. "You told me I shoulda left. I don't know why I didn't. I shoulda listened to my son." He smiled, held up his Bible. "But the good Lord brought me through."

Julian was full of questions, his eyes lit with the kind of joy he hadn't known since the Christmas mornings of childhood. But after a few minutes, Simon held up a hand and pointed toward the path a few yards away.

The Neon still sat there, door open, dead in the middle of the road.

Julian laughed. "Wait here. I'll be right back."

When he'd brought the car up into the yard and climbed back up onto the porch, Simon told him everything he could remember: the water swelling and rising in the house, the water in the streets, the sun burning the back of his neck, the helicopter ride over the city, the Convention Center insanity, the long miles walking in the miserable damp heat. The truck driver, waking in the hospital with the nice young nurse, the couple who'd brought him here.

"They tell me I passed out on the road," he said. "I don't know much else."

Julian bowed his head, eyes closed, imagining his father lying on a road somewhere, left to the mercy of strangers. "I'm sorry I said stuff to you that..."

Simon held up his hand. "Son, that's all past now. I shoulda listened. Let's just leave it at that."

The slip of yellow paper on top of the Bible next to Simon's chair caught Julian's eye.

Simon looked down and picked it up. "Something happened, didn't it?"

Julian nodded, speechless, a boulder stuck in his throat.

Again, his eyes filled up. He rubbed his temples. Then, like a floodgate opening, the events of the last several days poured out: meeting Kevin and learning all about the auction and the sale of the property and trying, with no luck, to get the land back.

He stopped talking, unable to push more words out around the tears.

Simon's shoulders flinched, his heart sinking, though Julian only confirmed what he suspected, and even his own instinct told him this day would come. Twice, Genevieve had mentioned to him about trouble brewing, once before the hurricane, once during it. Nothing she'd said had sparked a sense of urgency until Parette's accident—that had sent a shiver up his back. He'd promised himself he'd see about the land as soon as the storm was over. *The storm.* Ladeena had told him so many times, "Simon, you just don't believe fat meat is greasy!" She was right. He'd always been a bit stubborn, and now he was old and stubborn. When it came to the storm warnings, the one for New Orleans as well as the one for Silver Creek, he just hadn't seen the danger in those darkening clouds.

But looking now at Julian, all Simon could think about was his reaction—not at all what he expected. Before, Julian had never seemed to want to hear about Silver Creek; now, the sadness that shadowed his eyes, the tears—his son cared, it seemed, and not just because he, Simon, did. Speaking of Silver Creek, Julian looked as though he had lost his best friend. *My, my. Something in my son's heart has changed.*

Both turned their heads when the engine noise of a truck and the sputter of gravel from the road interrupted the quiet. Kevin parked the Ford in the yard and got out, his eyes curiously fixed on Simon. His mouth opened with a look of stunned surprise, then recognition registered on his face, as if the man he'd never met before were a long lost friend.

Julian got up and introduced him. Kevin looked at Julian, grinned widely, and grabbed Simon's hand to pump it. "Sir, this sure is a pleasure."

They pulled their rockers together and sat, and leaned their heads back and breathed in the sweet breezes from the creek, as if a large piece of the puzzle of each of their lives had just been found and snapped into place. Kevin was as full of questions as Julian had been, and Simon regaled them with stories of his adventure: the fear, the uncertainty of his life, the certainty of his death. The moment in the hospital when the belief that he would not make it gave way to the giddy joy that he would.

After a while, the subject turned again to the eviction notice atop Simon's Bible, and Julian explained the situation: meeting Kevin, the partitioning laws, Larouchette's company, and the auction. And finally, the insulting offer from Nathan himself.

Kevin's voice quieted. "And I should confess to you, sir, the man is my grandfather."

"Your grandfather?" Simon's eyes glazed.

Kevin's head hung, his tone apologetic. "We're not close. In fact, I been working on this a while, trying to help people who are about to lose their land to men like my granddaddy. I'm still trying with your case, sir, but without a will," he paused, shrugging, "it's real hard with these cases."

"Well," Simon said, "We're in trouble, then."

They talked on, rocking in the painted rockers, the tone more serious as they tried to figure out the next steps to take. Things looked grim, but Kevin promised to "keep trying until I see the bulldozers coming."

Julian mentioned he needed to call Genevieve over at Pastor Jackson's, and Sylvia, who'd said she'd be in Baton Rouge today. He pulled out his cell phone and dialed the numbers. Both women's screams of joy could be heard across the whole porch.

"I wondered where Genevieve was. She's staying at Pastor Jackson's?" Simon asked.

"Ah, yes, she is."

He nodded his head. "Well, it's nice of the pastor to give my cousin a place to stay while all this mess is going on."

Julian quietly considered ways to change the subject.

He brought up the house in New Orleans. It had fared better than some of the houses—at least it was still standing, even though the furniture and nearly everything inside was ruined and the walls covered in mold. It would have to be gutted, and the insurance agent had told him they would not cover the damage since it was done by water, not wind, and Simon had no flood insurance. They might be in for a long fight.

"I told them, if there hadn't been any wind, there wouldn't have been any storm, and no flood," Julian said. "But they weren't buying it."

"Now I been paying on that policy for forty years, and they can't pay me?" Simon said, his voice pitched high. He shook his head, sighed deeply.

Julian wasn't sure how to tell Simon about Matthew Parmenter. He decided to wait—he'd already gotten so much bad news. But Simon must have read his thoughts. He'd asked about his friends from church, and from the Elegant Gents Social Aid and Pleasure Club. Sylvia could tell him more, Julian said, but as far as he knew, everyone from the club and from church had evacuated. All were safe.

"And Matthew Parmenter too?" Simon asked.

Julian's eyes paled. His voice dimmed as he broke the disheartening news. Simon's gaze dropped to his lap; he nodded, not surprised.

"He told me a while back his time was short." Simon said quietly. "Did he go peaceful?"

He'd been to see him the day before, Julian said. "He seemed like a man at peace."

Simon pursed his lips and frowned. "Son, I know you didn't much care for Matthew. He wasn't perfect, I know that. We saw a lot of things differently."

Julian leaned forward in his chair, his elbows resting on his knees.

Simon sat back in the rocker and folded his hands in his lap. "He was always the ambitious type, always looking to do better. I just never was that kind of man. Like I say, we were different. But we got along."

"Daddy, you really didn't care at all about the recipe, the money and everything, did you?"

Simon smiled wryly. "To tell you the truth, I never liked the idea of the whole thing from the beginning. Dried herbs? Little pieces of dried vegetables? Shoot. That wasn't my Auntie Maree's recipe. Didn't taste nothing like it. Didn't bother me all that much that the Fortier name wasn't on it."

Simon let out a tired huff of air, leaned his head back against the rocker. "But then, maybe I should have cared, though, for you and your mama, especially when she got sick. I was just never bent on chasin' that dollar. But there's a lot of folks in the world like Matthew Parmenter, minds always set on gettin' ahead, restless, never satisfied. Some folks, you know, just like that. I never held it against him though."

His eyes met Julian's. "Never held that against anybody."

What was he telling him? Julian blinked. He never considered that he, Julian Fortier, would have much in common with Matthew Parmenter. But maybe Simon thought so, and maybe he was right. Ambition. Always looking to get ahead, no matter what. Shelving friendships, even love, in the pursuit of success. Had he been like that?

Julian looked for a sign in his father's eyes, but they gave nothing away. Maybe he wasn't making any such comparison, and it only existed in Julian's mind. But if he'd learned anything through all this, it was to see himself differently. And he couldn't deny the leap from Parmenter's thinking to his own was, at best, a short one.

Julian told Simon about the funeral, the parade, the band, and the second liners in the Square. When he told what happened at the reading of the will, Simon's eyes and mouth opened wide.

"He did *what?*"

"I know. I couldn't believe it either."

For a moment, Simon was speechless. Finally he said, "You know, I wondered what that whole thing was about." He told Julian about the night they got drunk on Parmenter's good port and played dominoes late into the night.

"I didn't think anything of it," Simon said. "We were just having some fun, you know. I didn't think he'd do something like this."

"He owed you, Daddy," Julian said. "He wanted to make it up to you."

"Well." Simon shrugged. "What am I going to do with all that house? I already got a house."

Julian wanted to say, *No, you don't*, but thought better of it.

"You'll think of something."

Twenty minutes later, Genevieve and Pastor Jackson pulled up in his Mustang, the backbeat of Al Green's "Let's Stay Together," thumping from the speakers. Genevieve got out, both hands on her hips, her head cocked to the side. "Well, look what the water done washed up! Simon Fortier, is that you?" Then, laughing like a woman filled up with the Holy Spirit, she clapped her hands together and with the lively steps of young girl, climbed to the porch to grab Simon in a hug.

"God bless you, you old fool," she whispered in his ear.

She introduced him to Pastor Jackson, who Simon remembered from years ago as a young boy growing up near the creek when he'd come back to visit Auntie Maree from New Orleans.

"Sure nice of you to let my cousin stay with you while we get this mess all cleared up," Simon said.

Pastor Jackson gave Genevieve a playful wink. "Ah, it's no problem."

By the time Sylvia arrived with Velmyra, Simon had already gone back into the kitchen in search of something decent to eat.

Sylvia found him rumbling through Genevieve's pots beneath the sink.

"You," she said, shaking her head with a smile that verged on breaking into tears, "you had me worried sick!" She flung both arms around his neck and hugged him. "Don't you ever do anything that stupid again!"

He grinned boyishly, eyes twinkling. "So you missed me, did you?"

"Oh, silly man, how many nights did I pray?" She held his face in both hands. "Thank God for taking care of babies and fools."

Velmyra smiled shyly from the kitchen door, waiting her turn for a hug.

She planted a kiss on his cheek. "Mr. Fortier, I want you to know that your son never gave up on you. He would not stop searching for you."

After a while, Simon, uncomfortable with so much fuss, shooed everyone out of the kitchen and back onto the porch so he could cook.

He wanted to cook because he was hungry and missed his own cooking, and because there were people he loved gathered around, and because when things went crazy, this was the way he calmed his nerves and did his best thinking.

And because he was breathing, and for him the two things went together.

He found two unopened bags of Camellia brand red beans in Genevieve's pantry. Better if they could soak overnight and then have a half a day to cook to get good and seasoned, but as much as he hated a rush job, in a couple of hours, this pot of beans would be better than anything he could find in some store or restaurant nearby. From Genevieve's garden, he brought in thyme, onions, bell peppers, sage, and parsley; from her cupboard, bay leaves; and from her refrigerator—did she have any?—yes, there it was. Fresh garlic in the bin, some chopped celery in a plastic container in the freezer. Genevieve was always prepared for emergencies, because, like Auntie Maree had taught them both, you just never know. He put on a pot of water to boil, then searched through the drawers to find Genevieve's good chopping knife.

He put the beans in the pot, brought them to a quick boil to release the starch, then let them set, and took a deep breath. He shook his head. So much going on, so much happening. Most of his beloved city in ruins. Matthew, his good friend, gone. And now he owned the man's house? Something he never asked for. He kept chopping onions and bell peppers, his busy hands helping his mind to take it all in.

He opened Genevieve's freezer and looked for the special bag, and was worried when he didn't see it. Surely she had put together some of Auntie's special spice mix—the basis for every pot of red beans he'd ever made. If she didn't…

There it was, on the top shelf of the freezer, a cheesecloth bag of secrets, sitting next to the andouille sausage, another key ingredient.

He pulled out the bag and the sausage, and cut the frozen sausage into one-inch pieces. He figured he could fix up the Treme house with a little help, even if that durned insurance company wanted to act a fool. His daddy had built that house himself, and surely, he could make it livable again. But Silver Creek. That news had left a hard bruise on his heart.

That, he could not fix. Silver Creek was gone, and not the victim of a flood, unless you counted the flood of greed. It would have been easy to blame somebody, Genevieve maybe, certainly himself for not paying closer attention to what was happening. The truth was, it was no one's fault. It was just the way of things. But when he remembered Julian's face, clouded in sadness and regret at the loss, well, Simon could have been knocked over with a feather.

He poured the starchy water off the beans, filled the pot again, brought them to a second boil, and plopped the spice bag in, and wondered what was going on between Julian and Velmyra. Something was happening there, and if there was anything good to be found in all this mess, at least the boy had come to his senses and reached out to that sweet young lady again. He poured vegetable oil into a cast iron pot and put the chopped vegetables and garlic in to sear (Auntie Maree would have used bacon grease, but the oil was his one concession to the occasional spike in his blood pressure), then looked up to see Julian standing in the doorway.

Speaking of the devil, or thinking of him, at least. Hands in both pockets, looking lost. Looking the way he did when he was a boy and had something big on his mind.

"Hey, Daddy."

Simon smiled, nodded. Turned the flame down from under the pot.

"You OK?"

Simon looked at him. How many times was the boy going to ask him that? "I'm alive. I'm cooking. I'm as good as gold."

Julian picked up a spoon from the counter and put it back down. "Daddy, I just wanted to say I'm sorry…"

Simon put down his knife as the vegetables cackled over the fire. "Son, look, I don't blame you. Not for any of this."

"I was just thinking. Maybe we, you and me, could buy some property down here. Something small, a few acres. Maybe something with a pond where we could go fishing."

Simon looked crossways at Julian. *Fishing?* Somebody musta kidnapped his son and sent this look-alike stranger in his place.

"Son, don't let it worry you. It's just a piece of land."

Julian looked away toward the open window facing the yard.

Simon sucked at his bottom lip. He probably shouldn't have said something that Julian could see right through. God knows, and Julian did too, it wasn't just a piece of land. More like a piece of his heart, his daddy Jacob's heart and soul. He wanted to reach out to Julian, wipe away the film of sadness that veiled those young eyes, but he was never too good at comforting. That had been Ladeena's job. It was always Ladeena who'd kissed the bruised knee, the wounded elbow, rubbed salve on the congested chest. Made life's bogeymen disappear. He only knew how to do what men like him did best; offer distraction from whatever the problem was.

"Good to see Velmyra again. She sure is a nice young lady."

"She was trying to help us—me and Kevin—get the land back."

"Umm, hmm, well, that sure was nice." Simon looked down at the skillet, stirred at the vegetables with the knife. "Son, as long as you're standing there, reach into that drawer and hand me that mixing spoon."

Julian opened the drawer and found the wooden spoon. But when he pulled it from the drawer, something fell onto the floor. He reached down and picked up a leatherbound journal, frayed and weathered with age.

Simon looked up from the pot. "Oh, that's Auntie Maree's cookbook. She wrote all the recipes down she made up. Said one day she'd publish it, but she never did."

Julian held it in his hands and tried to open it, but the crinkled pages were stuck together.

"It's so old, lots of secrets in that book. It first belonged to Claudinette, then she gave it to Liza, and Liza gave it to Maree. I can't read a word of Claudinette's writing. Some of it's in French—that's what Claudinette spoke. She was your…let me see…"

"My great-great-grandmother. John Michel's wife."

Another shock. He'd not talked to him about Claudinette since he was a child, since he could still get him to listen to the family tales.

When he got the middle pages separated, Julian ran his fingers over the wrinkled sheets of linen, considering the old woman's script—written half in French and half in English, wondering just how many times Claudinette had stood in the very spot where he was standing. Wondering what was on her mind when she wrote the page before him. Thinking about all the generations of Fortiers in this kitchen between that day and this one. He put the book back into the drawer.

"Anything I can do to help?"

Simon looked up. "Yes. You can stop your moping, boy. This ain't the end of the world, and I'ma tell you, things got a way of turning out the way they should. Why don't you go out there and talk to that pretty young lady?" He winked at him. "Awful nice of her to come, but only a fool would think she only came here to see me."

Julian went back to the porch where Genevieve, Pastor Jackson, Sylvia and Kevin sat talking and drinking iced tea spiked with Genevieve's white lightning.

"Join us?" Sylvia pointed to an empty rocker next to her.

"In a little bit. Where's Vel?"

Sylvia pointed around the side of the cabin, and he found her, sitting crosslegged on the grass, sketchbook in her lap, a piece of charcoal in hand, drawing the huge live oaks in the yard.

"Hey."

"Hey."

"Daddy kicked me out of the kitchen. He sent me out here to talk to you."

She smiled, and looked up from the sketch, a teasing light in her eyes. "Anything in particular he tell you to say?"

Julian looked back toward the house. "Uh, let me go and find out. I'll be right back."

She laughed, her eyes catching the play of afternoon light from the sun.

"Listen," he said. "That painting. The album cover? Wow. Thank you."

Her eyes widened. "You like it?"

"Like's the wrong word. More like 'humbled' by it. I'd forgotten how good you were."

She patted the ground next to her.

"Come. Sit."

He sat facing her, his knees bent and his arms around them.

She tilted her head, squinted from the light. "So when did you find out your father was going to be here?"

"When I drove up and saw him sitting on the porch."

"You mean you didn't know, and you just happened to show up on the day he arrived?"

"Exactly. Crazy coincidence."

Velmyra smiled, nodded. "Well, you know I don't believe in coincidence. Synchronicity, maybe. Like twins who know what the other is feeling, or parents who know when one of their children is in trouble."

"Yeah, maybe so."

She looked up as a cloud passed over the sun, fading the shade on the ground and deepening the color of the leaves of the nearby pecans. "It's so amazing, this place. I just wish there was something we could do."

He looked across the road as a red-tailed hawk left its perch on the pine tree and flew toward the creek.

"Sylvia told me something the other day after you left. Something about how hard it is to live your life without regrets. Well, for me, they've been stacking up lately."

"Don't be too hard on yourself."

He looked toward the porch, the rockers moving in disparate rhythms, the air so quiet he could hear the creak of wood and the clink of ice tea glasses from where he sat.

"I regret not seeing this place earlier, for what it is, what it means." He turned to look at her. "And I regret what happened between us. You were right, about a lot of stuff, really. I couldn't see it then. I'm sorry for that."

Velmyra closed her sketchpad and placed it on the ground next to her.

"Julian, I want to tell you something. You wondered why I got married so soon."

He blinked. "You don't have to tell me that."

"No. I want to."

He shrugged, frowned. "OK. Tell me."

She halted, looking away, her eyes searching the sky as if cues were written in the clouds. She leaned over and touched her forehead with her hand. "Something happened, something that would have stopped you in your tracks. After it happened, I think I had to prove to myself that I wouldn't do just anything to make you stay."

He looked puzzled. "What do you mean?"

She let out a deep sigh. "Something happened."

She stared at him narrowing her eyes long and hard, long enough for the tears to form, and for the meaning of her words, spoken and not, to settle into his mind.

And in that moment everything was clear. His eyes grew cool.

"Just tell me. Just say it."

She looked down at her lap, rubbed her hands against her knees. "When you left, I thought my heart would stop. I needed something, somebody, and Michael was right there. I taught with him at school. I knew him before you, we'd gone out a few times. When you and I broke up, he called. Turns out he was just waiting for me. Sort of."

She paused. "You hadn't been gone that long when I found out my...condition. I told Michael. We'd only been going out a few weeks but he wanted to get married right away, raise my son—yes, it was a boy—as his own."

Julian's heart fluttered, his breath quickening as she spoke.

She went on, the tempo of her speech slower, her voice breaking. "But he…didn't make it." She covered her eyes, paused, fighting tears. "He was a little fighter, but he only lasted forty-two days. He never left the hospital. Michael was devastated; I was shaking for a week. We named him Michael Jr., on his last day."

"He was born with a little hole in his heart."

Julian looked at the ground, at his feet, anywhere but at Velmyra.

"Things fell apart between us after that. There just wasn't enough love there, if there was ever any at all. It was as if he'd only wanted to rescue me, be the hero. It seemed like there was no longer a reason for us to be together."

Julian pinched his eyes shut, his brows furrowed, trying to understand. He, Julian Fortier, had been a father for forty-two days. A child of his, a boy, had been born, lived, then died; a whole life flashed by in seconds.

He cleared his throat. "You should have told me. I would have…"

"Done the right thing? Oh, I'm sure you would have, which is why I didn't. It would have been OK for a while. But there would have been a day when you would have looked at me in a way I wouldn't have been able to stand. You had your life mapped out. You had plans, you were headed someplace. I didn't want to be the reason you didn't get there. I just couldn't carry that load with me." She shrugged. "Or at least that's what I thought at the time.

"So. You were talking about regrets," she said, her eyes now glassy. "I've had a few myself. Sometime, a while back, I would lay awake at night and wonder, what if I'd told you? What would our lives have been like?"

Julian held his head between his hands, closed his eyes to the pain between them. She should have told him. *She should have told him.* A flurry of emotions flashed before him like playing cards dealt from quick, nimble hands: sadness, anger, jealousy, resentment, confusion, and most of all, doubt.

What if she had told him? And what if the child had lived? Would he have, as she said, looked at her one day in a way she could not stand? He wanted to think not, but the other possibility blinded him like an inescapable, glaring light, and he wondered if maybe that tiny hole in his heart, the one *he'd* been born with, had ever really closed. Wondered if that small defect might have leaked out some vital stream of selflessness that could have created in him the loving, willing father a child would need. For a fleeting moment, he hated the man who had so eagerly, so willingly stepped up in his place. *If he'd only known…*Maybe never knowing what he might have done was the price he'd paid for the life he chose.

There was no use in thinking about that now. He looked at Vel, whose reddened eyes mirrored the regret he now felt. But these weeks since the storm, and especially these last few days, had been a time of accepting what was, and dealing with it. Doing the next thing, even if that meant starting over. Old lives washed away, new ones begun—like it or not, ready or not.

If there was anything he'd learned since the storm, it was that even though some things could not be undone, they could be survived. They could be accepted. One could lay back and howl at the moon, or one could take whatever came, handle it, and then move on.

Julian was silent a while. Then he got up abruptly, and extended his hand to Velmyra. When she was on her feet, he circled his arms around her waist and drew her into him.

"You know, you've always had my heart," he said. "You know that."

She leaned her head against his shoulder, tears flowing, as he stroked her back.

"God, I wish I'd told you. You had a right to know."

When he pulled away from her, he took her hand.

"Walk with me," he said.

"Where?"

"Down to the creek. I want to see it one more time."

They walked a mile or so along the creek, then took off their shoes and waded in the clear shallows along the bank. They skipped rocks across the water, and stopped to study a heron basking in the sun on a floating branch, and tried to coax a turtle out of its shell with a stick. They wiped sweat from their faces with their sleeves, and, sitting on a rock, turned their faces to the sky to let the warming light of the sun glaze over their closed eyelids.

They did nothing at all for almost an hour. And when they returned from the creek, they inhaled the rich, spicy aroma of red beans that had wafted out to the yard and beyond.

The others were still sitting on the porch, this time their laps holding Genevieve's good china plates nearly running over with beans, rice, and andouille sausage, tumblers of sweet tea sitting on the floorboards next to their chairs. Julian and Velmyra piled their plates, pulled chairs from the kitchen onto the porch, and sat next to them.

The air was still. Except for the chirping of birds, the occasional rustling of the high grasses, and the rare breeze stirring the cypress and pecan trees, there was no sound as they all ate; as usual, eating a meal prepared by Simon Fortier was not to be interrupted with conversation.

But after the last fork was laid down, Pastor Jackson sat back, loosened his belt, and the usually quiet man issued a rare declaration: "When I die, I hope St. Peter meets me at the gate with a plate of red beans as good as these, Simon."

Kevin raised his glass and said, "Hear, hear."

Not looking up from his plate, Simon grunted. "St. Peter don't have my recipe," he said. "And he ain't getting it."

The laughter that followed, only mildly laced with liquor, was light-hearted and free-flowing. All were making an effort to keep the mood light and their spirits high, despite the veil of gloom that surrounded what was likely the end of their time at Silver Creek.

Pastor Jackson asked Simon about his journey through the storm, having missed the telling earlier. Simon decided to tell him the shorter version. He reached down to the floor and held up his Bible.

"This book goes back to my great-granddaddy, more than a hundred and fifty years ago," he said. "My daddy told me everything I would ever need was in this here book, and this is how I got through."

"Yeah, you right," Pastor Jackson said.

Kevin's eyes glinted with curiosity. "You mind if I have a look at it?"

He opened the book, worn and yellow with a century's age. He looked at the first pages, where the family tree, complete with dates of births and deaths, was written.

"An old friend of mine, Professor LeClaire, told me sometimes folks would write down important stuff in Bibles. I was just checking to see if somebody wrote something down we could use. But I don't see anything here."

"Can I have a look?" Julian reached a hand out for the book.

He opened it, fanning the pages. Nothing. Then, he took another look.

Like the cookbook, the first few pages were stuck together. After he separated them, he stared at one of the pages, then looked up. He passed the book back to Kevin who looked at the separated pages and smiled, his blue eyes suddenly full of light.

"Folks," he said, "I think maybe we've got what we need."

Two Years Later

With wings spread wide and arcing low against the trees, an eagle dips, then soars high across the creek as an amber sun breaks the mauve-tinted morning sky. The bayou chorus wakes in full voice: a madrigal of morningbirds, the percussion of woodpeckers, the tremolo of water lapping rock. Magnolia blossoms scent the air, spoonbills nest in leafy beds of ancient oaks, and everywhere at Silver Creek life, willful and unstoppable, begins again.

Louisiana springs always arrive in a storm of color, scent, and sound—a lesson for the observant in the art of renewal—and for the Fortiers, the third spring after the Big One saw most of the hard work of renewal completed. On a spring morning two years after the flood, all the Fortiers gathered again at Silver Creek, their legacy intact, the spread of land handed down from generation to generation just as breathtaking as ever.

My daddy said everything I would ever need was in this book. Simon had held the century-old Bible up high, brandishing it on the porch that October day, and he was right. On the first page, Jacob had scribbled the future of the Fortiers at Silver Creek. And though it was crudely written and barely visible, it was enough to satisfy a judge in Pointe Louree Parish that the land was intended for the Fortier clan, and no one else:

To my son on the day of his berth: My 240 acres of land at Siver Creeke, shall be the property of my son Simon, and my neece Genevieve, and there chilren and there chilren's chilren, anod nobody else, until there are no more Fortiers left.

Jacob Fortier July 8, 1932

An "olographic" will, as Kevin had said, was as good as any in a Louisiana court of law. Nathan Larouchette protested mightily, pouring money and energy into getting the decision overturned, but to no avail. Judge H. Townsend Turner, a seventyish, bespectacled black man who'd grown up in the area and watched the landscape change for forty years, had no sympathy for good old boys with designs on black-owned land, and decided in favor of the Fortiers in fifteen minutes.

Meanwhile, a hundred miles downriver, the struggle for renewal went on. When Julian drove Simon back to New Orleans in late October to see his house, his mouth dropped open, then closed again and set defiantly. (After "Oh, Lord Jesus," his next words were, "We got to get started fixing this.") And as the whole city swarmed with hardworking volunteers from all over the country, Julian, Velmyra, Sylvia, a group of young law students from Penn State, and six Pentecostals from the Church of the Everlasting Light in Chicago gutted Simon's double shotgun. While they dismantled drywalls and sorted, piled, bagged, and hauled Simon's things, he shuttled back and forth between Sylvia's house and his newly inherited mansion, where he discovered, to his great delight, Parmenter's $5,000 restaurant-quality oven. In chef's heaven, he refined a tasty new recipe for crawfish and oyster soufflé, and volunteered daily at Blessed Redeemer, preparing soup kitchen meals for returning New Orleanians working to piece back together their damaged houses and deconstructed lives.

The next two winters in New Orleans were hard. The dead had been buried, but the living struggled with survival and sanity while hospitals, schools, churches, apartment buildings, groceries, nursing homes, convenience stores, daycare centers, hotels, restaurants, and universities stood empty or nearly so. Block upon block of neighborhoods still lay dark and quiet, inhabited only by piles of sludge and debris, towering weeds, and the ghosts of promises unfulfilled. Four months after the flood, most of the city, save the areas barely touched by water, remained every bit as damaged as it had the days after the levees were breached.

But at the end of the year, while make-do government trailers for the enormous houseless population dotted the landscape as abundantly as pecan trees, Christmas lights, holly wreaths, mistletoe, reindeer, plastic Santas, and elves with ironic smiles sprang up throughout the city—on porches, rooftops, in trailer windows, in yards, and, oddly, atop rubble piles in trashed neighborhoods—as the city' sense of celebration (and humor) prevailed in desperate times.

Like so many families wanting to make the most of the season, the Fortiers were determined to have a normal, traditional Christmas, crippled city or not. After the Soul Fire band returned from New York, where they drew huge crowds for their Christmas jams and raised thousands for the Treme and Ninth Ward rebuilding efforts, Julian drove to a tree nursery outside Baton Rouge, strapped a fourteen-foot Scotch pine onto the bed of Simon's Ford truck, and drove it back to town, where he erected it in the great room of the St. Charles mansion. Four of Velmyra's art students whose parents had brought them back to the city decorated it with popcorn garlands and hand-painted papier machê ornaments, and Simon paid them for their work in Christmas cookies and as much chocolate raspberry bread pudding as they could eat.

The old Parmenter mansion became a refuge for the extended Fortier clan—their friends, their friends' friends, and anyone else who needed a place to crash for a night, a week, a month, or two—with a revolving door open to all. So on Christmas Eve night, with eight of the eighteen rooms occupied with some of Julian's musician friends and two of Simon's displaced neighbors still waiting for FEMA trailers, Simon concocted a batch of his creamy, bourbon-spiked egg nog, cooked an eight-gallon pot of gumbo, smoked a twenty-two pound turkey, and turned out five sweet potato pies. The house boomed with the noise of fifty or so friends, old neighbors, church members, and musicians. Julian built a blazing fire in the great room fireplace, and the lights from the tree and the scents of woodsmoke, pine, and gumbo set the holiday mood while everyone drank, ate, laughed, and celebrated being alive. The city might have been on its knees, but damn it, it was still New Orleans. They could still party with the best of them.

"Is it just me, or is it getting a little chilly in here?" Sylvia put down her wine glass and hugged her shoulders, talking loudly to be heard above the raucous laughter at a well-timed joke somebody told in the great room, and the silky stereophonic tenor of Nat King Cole. The fire, which roared and crackled an hour ago, had quieted to a flickering glow.

Grady Casey looked toward the living room. "Yeah. That fire's getting a little low. I'll fix that."

He took a sip of his egg nog, then yelled toward the kitchen, "Hey, Fortier, come and fix this fire!"

Julian came out of the kitchen, checked the dying fire, and stoked the golden embers with an iron poker. "There's some more wood on the porch," he said.

He stepped out onto the gallery into the night air and looked up at the clear sky toward the river. The winter stars pulsed, winking against the velvet black. During the holiday season, with the scarred city trying to look its best, it was only at night that the details of devastation could truly hide in the dark. The houses across the street, like the Parmenter place, were festooned with Christmas lights and rooftop reindeer, and the live oak branches reaching over the streetcar tracks dripped strands of brightly colored beads.

Julian spread his shoulders and sucked in the night air. *It feels good out here.* The air in the house had gone dry with the fire, and the cool, night breeze on the porch felt refreshing, carrying a hint of dampness from the day's early rain.

Things had been going well, or as well as they could. Simon's house was still a few months from livable, but the New York trip had been a huge success, the guys had all had a great time, Julian was playing well, and his father seemed healthy and happy. The insurance company had failed them, insisting that since Simon carried no flood insurance, the years of premiums for wind and storm damage would not cover his house. But the transfer of ownership of Parmenter's Creole Kitchen Red Beans and Rice Mix had come through, and the new flow of checks would finance the renovation.

Julian's stalled career was back up and running; he'd spent most of the past weeks since the storm in New Orleans, but had flown back to New York to complete his second album for Blue Note, *Wading Home*, which he dedicated to Simon and which, he believed, demonstrated his best playing yet.

The thing between him and Vel was still up in the air. There was simply no time to deal with that—too much going on in both their lives. But tonight, he'd brushed past her in the crowded dining room; a whiff of her lavender oil took his breath away and he felt momentarily light-headed. With her hair up a little in the back and curls spiraling near her ears, a blouse of bright red silk and diamond studs in each ear, she'd dazzled him to distraction. In the past few months he'd stepped back to give her breathing room while she helped her parents; they had not been as fortunate as Simon. With no flood insurance and no money, they lived with Velmyra in her tiny two-bedroom off Magazine Street while they waited for a FEMA trailer that should have arrived weeks before, and their own house still sat in ruins.

So, he'd left her mostly alone, except in his persistent dreams. Tonight, it was hard to look at her without his mouth going dry, hard not to think of all that had happened between them, their time together at Silver Creek, the child they'd made years ago. There might be a time for them, someday, but this was not it.

Julian looked down at the floorboards of the porch and pursed his lips. Damned if all that wood he'd just bought and stacked neatly the day before didn't lay strewn recklessly across the whole porch. A dog, probably, the hound he's seen loping up and down the street since his first day back. Dogs had to eat, too. He'd left the gate latch open with a bowl of water and a plate of pork chop bones out for him, and this is how he repaid him.

He sighed, reached down to gather and restack the wood.

"Hey there!"

In the shadows of the giant magnolia he couldn't see who was yelling to him. He put the wood down and walked toward the edge of the steps. Probably a homeless man. He'd seen so many of them lately, walking the streets looking for a dollar or two or a meal. Sad that someone would be out on Christmas Eve looking for a handout, but not uncommon these days. The man was dressed warmly, a black leather jacket, a red plaid scarf, and a leather fisherman's cap. Didn't look homeless, but you never knew. Nowadays the word had taken on a whole new meaning.

The man walked a little closer to the wrought iron gate. "Saw your chimney smoke! Got some good dry firewood for ya! Forty a cord!"

"Got enough already!" Julian yelled back. "But thanks."

He started stacking the wood again.

"Maybe you want to check this out!"

The man came up to the gate, a beautifully designed large wreath of long-needle pine branches and holly berries, woven and wrapped in red velvet ribbon, in his hands.

"You don't have a wreath on your door! Ain't these pretty? Fifty percent off now, since the season's almost over. Five dollars. Made 'em myself. You'll have something nice for New Year's Eve."

The man explained that he'd just come back to town from Cincinnati to learn his job as a waiter in the French Quarter was gone, since the restaurant where he worked was unable to reopen.

"That's OK, though. I'm starting my own business! Firewood for the rest of the winter. And handyman work. I do roof repairs, carpentry, drywalling, insulation, you name it, I do it! I give a you fair price, not like some of these jackasses around here! You can trust me, sure as my name is Jacob."

Julian smiled. Jacob. Fairly common, but it meant something that this man shared his grandfather's name. His eyes looked kind, hopeful, lit as brightly as tree bulbs, and his cheeks were flush, reddish with the night cold. He'd combed the city for supplies, the man explained, found fallen pine trees and cut enough branches and discarded chicken wire to make wreaths. Then he'd found enough dry wood from uprooted oaks in devastated neighborhoods to chop, split, and sell as firewood door to door when the weather had turned cool. He'd found acorns from the dead pines and sprayed them red and gold and green to make tree ornaments, and sold out of them.

He reached in his wallet, pulled out his business card, gave it to Julian. Julian found a five in his pocket and handed it to him. The man thanked him, then went to his truck and came back with an extra wreath.

"A little lagniappe for ya!" His neon smile lit up the night. "Merry Christmas!"

"You too." Julian waved, watched as the man's truck pulled off down the street.

He finished restacking the wood, setting enough aside for the fireplace, then looked at the man's card. *Building the New New Orleans...Jacob W. Boudreaux, Handyman, At Your Service*, it read.

In the last month or so Julian had noticed that the talk of a disappeared, dead New Orleans had, itself, died; no one was saying anymore that the city was finished. They'd completed repairing the Convention Center, and now they were talking about renovating the Superdome. He'd been torn about that; he loved his Saints, but those two places had seen so much heartache. The slow upward climb had begun. People might be carrying their heartaches on their backs, but they were still walking.

He turned Jacob's card over to see a small fleur-de-lis, the new symbol of the reviving city, on the back. He wondered what the man's story was; everybody had one. Wondered who or what he had lost. Wondered where he'd been, what he'd gone through, and what he'd seen when he returned. And he wondered if that light shining in his eyes had always been there. Or if maybe it had dimmed to near darkness, then revived itself like a dying fire stoked with the irons of faith and will.

Julian thought about a conversation he'd had with his father when he was little. He'd come home from school crying when a classmate told him that the city where they lived would eventually be swept away by a hurricane that would wipe it off the face of the earth.

It had been a winter night like this one. His father poured him a glass of hot milk, and told him about an old city where the streets were filled with water, and that for years experts claimed it was sinking, and someday would be gone.

They might be right, Simon told his son.

"But they tell me Venice is still there."

Early May, and all arrive at the hour Julian has set, 9:30, and the day's heat is just beginning. A small gathering of friends and family, they didn't come to celebrate death (even though it was on all their minds), but life itself, since each death affirms the eternality of all things living, each life as eternal as the trees whose roots run deep into seasons past, the sky above, the creek, or the land itself.

Kevin Larouchette and his new bride, Raynelle, a pixie-like brunette with an effusive smile, along with their two-year old, Suzy, and their two Labradors, Jack and Ruby, rambled up the road to Silver Creek in the slightly used Caravan he'd bought his first year at Piaget and Foster, a small law firm in Local. Genevieve and Pastor Jackson, now living together at the Silver Creek cabin (since a fire at Pastor Jackson's near Elam C.M.E. nearly destroyed the house) ate a quiet breakfast, then dressed in their finest for the occasion, the Pastor in his gray Lord & Taylor Sunday suit and Genevieve in a new summer frock of bright blue silk.

Julian and Velmyra, who'd driven from New Orleans, had been living out what Genevieve called "one of those newfangled relationships," traipsing back and forth between New York and New

Orleans and anywhere else they cared to go, "jumping around the country like a couple of rabbits," as she put it. (Who did they think they were—Oprah and Stedman?) Unable to define their place in each other's lives, but unwilling to accept that no such place existed, they carried on like many a modern couple: him flying from New York to New Orleans to visit her, her flying from New Orleans to New York when he wasn't on tour with his band. Spending summer months together at the European jazz festivals while Vel's school was out, spending winter months in New Orleans when the New York cold was too much for either of them.

They had just returned from Europe when Velmyra, sitting across from Julian at one of their favorite coffee shops in SoHo, gave him her news. Julian listened, not believing her words at first, then, dumbstruck, closed his misting eyes and let a wave of joy wash over him. "I hear that twins," she said, reaching for his hand, "are usually easier to raise than people think." Julian felt like he'd been given a second chance. "Thank you," were the only words he could manage. This time, he would be there. The whole world, finally, seemed right again.

Their wedding, a no-fuss New York courthouse affair with Velmyra dressed in white and lavender linen and Julian attired in the same deep blue suit he'd performed in the last night of the North Sea Jazz Festival in Rotterdam (to great reviews), lasted all of nine minutes, with Julian's young drummer, in a blue blazer and slightly baggy jeans, serving as a witness. And after that, they were only somewhat more settled; they set up housekeeping in the St. Charles place after Simon's house was completed, sold half the antiques and other furnishings, and occupied the cavernous, empty rooms for half the year, meanwhile keeping Julian's apartment in New York as an East Coast base. In New Orleans, they gradually converted many of the unused, light-filled rooms of the mansion into a nursery, a music studio, a recording studio, a painting studio, and an activity room for a nonprofit they formed called Living Dreams, a program for teaching art and music classes to the returning but still at-risk children of the struggling city.

Julian stood in the dust-covered yard at the foot of the cabin steps looking at his watch, wondering what is keeping the others, and had begun to regret asking everyone to dress up a little, even though they were only going to the cemetery a few yards away. Their spirits high on this auspicious day, no one would have suspected the somber nature of the occasion, and it had been decided this would not be a typical funeral, no New Orleans style fanfare, no brass band or second line, simply a graveside ceremony with family and friends at Silver Creek.

It had been Julian's idea, this kind of ceremony, and Velmyra and all the others agreed.

That morning, he'd awakened early in their spacious, almost empty bedroom on the second floor of the St. Charles house and watched Velmyra snoring softly, wondering if he should fix her coffee or herbal tea before the drive (she loved both), and wondering what he'd been thinking all those years, choosing a life without her. He'd stroked the side of her face with the backs of his fingers, and decided it would be coffee, if there was any CC's left. She'd slept anxiously the night before, and he wondered if she had been thinking what he was thinking—about the day ahead and what might be in store. Funerals were a tricky business; you never knew how the occasion would affect you until you were there. But this one had a certain rightness to it; they were laying one of their own to rest in a place where he belonged.

It had been early still, not quite light, and oak-lined St. Charles Avenue, visible from the sheer-covered French windows of the bedroom, still wore the glaze of the night's rain. He'd peeked into the bedroom down the hall; satisfied, he scuffed his bare feet across the polished hardwood of the hallway and descended the grand mahogany staircase down to the huge kitchen. He'd fixed a full pot of coffee, and after sipping from his cup, carried another upstairs.

She was waking as he sat on the bed, leaned over, and kissed her temple.

Her eyes opened wide.

"I love you," she'd said reaching up to touch his cheek with one hand, rubbing sleep-heavy eyes with the other. She'd smiled, said, "What time is it?"

"Time to get going, babe. Big day."

"Is that for me?"

He'd handed the cup to her. She'd sat up, sipped.

"Are they awake?"

He'd smiled. "Not yet."

"Good. There's time." She'd lifted the spread for him to climb back in.

He'd held her close. It would be a long day, but they would get through it. They'd survive, just as they had survived everything else—this death (the one that would take them to Silver Creek today), a flood that changed all their lives, a city almost lost and a love all but dead, rekindled from glowing ash. In the coming years of their lives together there would be more times like these. Because when it came down to it, living was just that: walking headlong into the wind and coming out on the other side. Surviving the storms, the trials, the comings and goings, and then doing it all over again.

They had decided to walk the short distance from the cabin to the graveyard, rather than take cars, as the weather was perfect, dry and crisp, with the faint odors of honeysuckle and wisteria sweetening the breeze.

At 9:45 they were to assemble in the yard to begin the walk across the dusty road and through the clearing toward the place where all the family had been buried since Silver Creek began. The children—Kevin and Raynelle's daughter Suzy, and Julian and Velmyra's eighteen-month-old twins, Christina Maree and Jacob Lawrence Fortier (both born with perfect hearts), had been left at the cabin with a sitter, Pastor Jackson's niece, Gloria, a wide-eyed, surprisingly responsible marine biology major at LSU.

But at 10:05 they were still straggling onto the porch, each preening and pulling and straightening their clothes as if the dirt road before them were a red carpet teeming with paparazzi. (It had taken Genevieve two hours to find her new dress for the occasion at a Macy's in a Baton Rouge mall, and Pastor Jackson a half hour to find the right polish for his shoes.) Genevieve came out on the porch first, adjusting her V-neck to allow a tasteful bit of cleavage to show, followed by Pastor Jackson, Velmyra, Raynelle, and Kevin.

More than a few minutes later, Sylvia emerged from the porch onto the yard, her hair perfectly coifed in tight red curls, her lemon-colored linen pantsuit shimmering in the late morning sun.

Julian walked back from the car, new camera in hand.

"Forgot this," he said, checking the battery.

"Morning, baby." Sylvia reached a hand to straighten his tie. "You look just like your daddy," she said, a motherly smile playing around her eyes. "You know, I see why you always made him feel so proud."

He kissed her cheek. "You look beautiful."

She hugged him. "I know this isn't easy for you. I'm proud of you too."

Velmyra walked up behind her husband, touched him gently on the back.

Taking a deep breath, she said, "Everything OK?"

He smiled, leaned down to kiss her cheek. "Yeah. You look great."

He turned to the others, all looking at him. "Everybody ready? OK. Let's go."

Taking Velmyra's arm, he began walking toward the road.

"Wait a minute." Genevieve looked behind her.

"Where's Simon?"

Sylvia looked around, sucked her teeth. "Still in there gettin' pretty. That man will be late to his own funeral."

And finally, Simon came out, his new black suit elegantly framing his slender shoulders, his black Florsheims polished to a fare-thee-well, his hand-carved African cane, rescued from his flooded house, in hand.

"Somebody call my name?"

"We just waiting on you," Genevieve said.

"Well, you coulda started without me. It ain't like I don't know my way over there."

"Now you tell us."

So they walked, Julian and Velmyra in the lead, Velmyra holding tightly to the small brown urn of mottled glass carrying the remains of the couple's first child, Michael (named Davenport, but, in truth, the first in the new generation of Fortiers), to be buried alongside a century of his forebears.

When Julian had suggested the idea to Velmyra, that the cremated remains of baby Michael—stored in a tiny urn in a cool room at a New Orleans mausoleum all these years—be buried in the Fortier cemetery, she had smiled and hugged him.

"Yes," she said. "That's a perfect idea."

And when they had told Simon what they had in mind, a tear sat suspended on the ridge of his eyelid before it fell, unabashed, down his cheek. "My first grandchild," he said. "He was a Fortier, too."

And so they planned it for May, when the pecans and cypresses begin to bud, the egrets and spoonbills begin to nest, when the dying time of winter has finally ended and the cycles of life begin anew.

They took high steps across the weedy grasses and the unpaved road, the women deftly lifting their pump-clad feet over the ruts and divots in the road and between the cattails and dandelions and wildflowers of the clearing, as the creek breeze ruffled their hemlines. When they reached the cemetery near the ruins of the old stone church, they held each other's hands and formed a circle around the small opening already dug into the earth, next to the headstone of Jacob, and just above where Ladeena lay.

The sun, slipping from behind a cloud, splashed golden light across all the headstones, including the newest one, reading: *Michael, Beloved Son, April 1, 1999–June 12, 1999.* Pastor Jackson stepped forward to read from the book of Ecclesiastes about time and purpose and the seasons, and then, eyes closed, prayed a traditional prayer, beseeching God to watch over the couple's first born child, and imploring the ancestors to "hold this infant's spirit gently with both hands."

He knelt to the ground, gathered red dust into his hands, and sprinkled it over the urn, as Julian placed the remains of Michael Davenport Fortier into the ground, and everyone sang the first verse of "Amazing Grace."

Stepping forward to the center of the circle, her hands clasped together beneath her breasts, Sylvia began a soulful "Nearer My God to Thee." Her silvery soprano, unrestrained, effortless, accompanied by the soft strains of the nearby creek, slipped along the air above their heads, and brought mist to every open eye.

When she'd finished there was a resounding 'Aay-*men!*' from everyone, including Kevin and Raynelle, who, though white and Catholic, had spent enough time in black churches to understand the customary response to a thing well done.

When the ceremony ended, Julian took his wife's hand as they began the walk back to the cabin.

"You did well," Julian said, leaning over to her and whispering. "You didn't cry."

"Are you kidding? I cried all last night while you were sleeping," she said with a self-mocking smile. "I didn't have any water left."

The walk back along the creek, through the clearing again, and onto the dust-packed road, was not as somber as the walk over had been, for what could have been a sad occasion had become a joyous one. They had taken one of their own from a cold city vault to the shade of the lives oaks, cooled by the breezes of the nearby stream. There was laughter and light-hearted banter as the notion of the picnic lunch of red beans and rice with homemade andouille sausage, crawfish pie, collard greens, peach cobbler, bread pudding, and sweet mint tea awaiting them filled everyone's minds. And Sylvia, unable to contain the music stirring inside her any longer, broke into the chorus of "I'll Fly Away," and everyone joined in as they walked. And while it wasn't exactly a second line, it was as close as they could get to it, dressed in their finest, stepping along the rutted earth near the piney woods.

In the evening, when fading light deepened the colors of the creek, the earth near the cabin, and the shady spaces between the trees, they all sat on the porch, rockers aligned and creaking in odd meters, digesting Simon's incomparable meal.

"Well, Simon," Pastor Jackson said, "You did it again, brother."

Simon nodded, wiping a crumb of crawfish pie crust from his mouth with a napkin. "Yes, I 'spect I did."

Kevin and Raynelle sat rocking in opposing rhythms in the two larger rockers, while their daughter played in the dirt. The two dogs, Jack and Ruby, frolicked back and forth while Kevin tossed a beat-up tennis ball out on the dirt a hundred times as they took turns catching it and bringing it back for him to throw it again.

Julian sat in the blue rocker, Christina Maree on one knee, Jacob on the other. Christina chatted noisily, her hands in constant motion grabbing her father's nose and ears, while Jacob, the younger of the twins by eighteen minutes, suddenly teared up and began to cry.

"He's sleepy, as usual," Velmyra said, getting up from her rocker on the other side of the porch next to Genevieve and Pastor Jackson.

She leaned over, kissed Julian, and took the crying child from him. "Come on, sweetie," she said. "I'll take him in and put him on the sofa."

Julian started to get up to follow her with their daughter, but she said, "No. Stay. Enjoy."

As the sky drew darker, Kevin and his clan piled into the Caravan to return to their new house in Local. The van kicked up dust and Kevin waved, pointed and yelled to Simon—"Don't forget. Six a.m!"—and made the turn toward the road.

"You going fishing tomorrow?" Sylvia asked Simon.

"Yep. Can't wait." He rubbed his hands together.

Sylvia looked up at the sky, the gathering of stars in the twilight.

"How does it feel, finally having grandkids?" Sylvia asked.

"Makes me think about gettin' old."

She laughed. "Simon, you *been* old."

"Not as old as I used to be," he said.

"What's that supposed to mean? "

"Means I think I got more years left in me than I thought before."

"Yeah? How many?"

"No tellin'. Twenty. Twenty-five." He smiled, looking across the road. "Be a while before I join the rest of 'em over there. Being back home, I feel a little younger. Shoot. I *am* younger."

Sylvia leaned back in her chair, folded her hands across her lap. "Remember that question you asked me a couple years ago?"

"What question was that?"

"You know the one."

"Oh, you mean the one where you shot me down after?"

"That one. Why don't you ask it again?"

"Why should I do that?"

"The answer might be different this time."

"How do I know that?"

"Ask and see."

"Ask so I can get shot down again?"

"Maybe you won't this time."

"How do I know?"

"Ask and see."

"Well, I ain't asking if I don't know the answer." This went on for a while, until Sylvia, realizing she was being teased insufferably by a master, slapped Simon's shoulder and said simply, "Marry me, you silly man." And he laughed and put his arm around her, and said, "When?"

When the bread pudding was all gone, and Genevieve and Pastor Jackson had turned in for the night, and Simon and Sylvia had gone to check in at the bed and breakfast in Local, and Velmyra had laid her son on the sofa to sing him to sleep, waiting for her husband to come to the roll-away bed Genevieve had set up for them in the living room, Julian rocked his daughter against his chest, wondering when she would fall asleep.

Between the two, this child was the liveliest—like her mother, forever alert, looking up and around her, fascinated with everything in view. He'd never be able to get up in time for fishing if this little one kept him up all night. He decided to play the word game with her. It was the best way he knew to bring sleep to those bright, busy eyes.

"Tree? Tree?" he said, taking her tiny finger and pointing to the live oak next to the house.

She said nothing, fascinated with his shirt button.

"Dirt?" he said, pointing to the yard.

Again, nothing.

"Car?" He pointed again, knowing she knew this one, but was being stubborn tonight.

He rocked her again, and finally she opened her mouth wide, her eyes dancing.

"Mine!" she said, gleefully, both arms flung out wide toward the treetops, as if encompassing the whole world around her.

Julian smiled, looked out at the land, the tall pines, the live oaks, the yard toward the road as it disappeared before making its way to the creek.

"That's right, baby girl," he said. "All yours."

Night falls on Silver Creek. Fireflies light the dark, riding the backs of breezes as stars gather, diamond studs on velvet black. The air is heavy, but moves along a creek as eternal as earth, and whispers of timeless evenings when the oldest trees were young.

He looked at his living child and thought of the one who was not. His first child, now safe among family, brought from the shadow of history to sleep in the shade of ancestors. And Julian wished, for the son he had never held, peace. Christina fidgeted on his lap and now, like her sleepy brother, began to cry. Funny, he thought, how they all do that. Out of fear, probably, of surrendering to the closing dark, not yet understanding that another day is coming.

Not understanding that light follows dark, day follows night, and endings become beginnings—always.

He kissed his daughter's tiny head and, believing her days would be many, hoped that when the time came for him to tell her the story of the ones who came before, he would be able to remember all of it. He got up from the rocker as his girl-child lay her sleepy head on his shoulder, patted her back as her eyes closed. Let's see. *There was a Frenchman, and a beautiful African woman, with skin like midnight sky....*

Acknowledgments

For their help, encouragement, and support, without which this book would not have been possible, I thank:

My publisher and editor, Doug Seibold, for his wise editorial eye, for his integrity, and for his unflagging belief in my writing, and also Diana Slickman, Eileen Johnson, and the entire Agate staff for their hard work.

My writing buddies David Haynes and Sanderia Faye Smith for their encouragement throughout this project.

Maxine Clair, Jane Owen, Elisa Durrette, and Jamal Story for reading and providing intelligent insight and guidance with the manuscript in its various stages.

Kalamu Ya Salaam for editorial advice and for his vast knowledge of New Orleans history, geography, and culture.

My favorite artist and good friend Jean Lacy and her son, Nathaniel Lacy, once again, for the cover drawing "High Water Blues."

Lolis Eric Elie and Dawn Logsdon for the inspiration of their masterful film *Faubourg Treme: The Untold Story of Black New Orleans.*

Friends and helpful residents of New Orleans for their support: historian, author and WWOZ DJ Tom Morgan and his wife Hild Creed (for helpful comments on the text), and Ricky Sebastian and Cheryl and Cameron Woods for hosting me on various trips to the city, as well as to the attentive and efficient staff of the Hotel Provincial.

Corky Bruce of the Natural Springs Garden Center in Natchitoches and Beth Perkins of the Banting Nursery in Jefferson Parish for information on the wildflowers of Louisiana.

Alvena Brock-McNeil, for sharing her Katrina photos and stories with me.

My friend and colleague Sterling Procter, for his superb musical graphics (a belated thank you for my first novel!).

Writers Tod Lewan, Delores Barclay, and the Associated Press writing team for their superior investigative reporting on the troubled and sometimes violent history of black landownership in the rural South, detailed in their 2001 series "Torn From the Land." This team deserves far more credit than it ever received for exposing the calculated removal of valuable American land from the hands of its African-American owners in the past 150 years.

The wonderful staff and fellow workers at Habitat for Humanity, New Orleans for inspiration and for their commitment to rebuilding the city.

The great trumpet players of New Orleans who uphold the tradition of Bolden and Armstrong: Marsalis, Blanchard, Mayfield, Payton, Jordan, Scott, Ruffins, Allen, and a seemingly endless list of others for their contributions to the history of a great American art form, and for keeping the music alive.